RUSH WEEK

RUSH WEEK

A NOVEL

Michelle Brandon

An Imprint of HarperCollins*Publishers*

RUSH WEEK. Copyright © 2025 by Michelle Brandon. All rights reserved. Printed in the United States of America. No part of this book may be used or reproduced in any manner whatsoever without written permission except in the case of brief quotations embodied in critical articles and reviews. For information, address HarperCollins Publishers, 195 Broadway, New York, NY 10007.

HarperCollins books may be purchased for educational, business, or sales promotional use. For information, please email the Special Markets Department at SPsales@harpercollins.com.

FIRST EDITION

Designed by Diahann Sturge-Campbell

Part opener photo © Darryl Brooks/Shutterstock

Library of Congress Cataloging-in-Publication Data has been applied for.

ISBN 978-0-06-342443-2

25 26 27 28 29 LBC 5 4 3 2 1

FOR THE REAL ADL—

Cherish your sisterhood the way I cherish you.
You all mean the world to me!
Kisses, M

AUTHOR'S NOTE

Dear Reader,

When my editor approached me about writing a juicy Bama Rush book, I was immediately on board. My mind went wild with the possibilities, and almost instantly Taylor, Brooklyn, Asana, and Annabelle were knocking around in my head, begging to be put on the page.

Rush is a huge trend on TikTok and other socials. Schools from across the US post their dance routines and chants, and people flock to the pages to check out the latest OOTDs (outfits of the day), jewelry trends, how to wear makeup, and let's be honest, to hear the TEA. There's no other school more popular than the University of Alabama, so much so that they ended up having a documentary created about their rushing habits. But there are dozens of other sororities and schools that share their journeys as well.

While I played in this world with Taylor, Brooklyn, Asana, and Annabelle, sharing their OOTDs, social media videos, friendship dramas, and juicy secrets in their "Spill Book," all with fun and wild abandon, I also touched on some of the more serious things that occur during rush, in the Panhellenic lifestyle, as well as college life in general.

I have nothing but respect for Greek Life and the many women who've shared their stories.

This book is in no way to be confused with any one person or place, and all the characters and plotlines were created by me and my editorial team. I did find inspiration, however, in the thousands of TikTok posts, YouTube videos, discussion forums, articles, documentaries, and my own experiences in college, as well as those of my friends and family members. You can get lost on the interwebs with a single search.

I hope you enjoy the wild, juicy ride! Taylor, Brooklyn, Asana, and Annabelle can't wait to invite you into their world. Who's ready for Rush Week?

Kisses,
Michelle

Part I

CONVOCATION

The act of being summoned . . .

CHAPTER ONE

Dear Alpha Delta Lamba Sisters Alumni,

You are cordially invited to attend this year's Rush Week at the University of Alabama!

We especially hope you're present as we open our sisters' time capsule early on Bid Night! The capsule was packed on the centennial Founder's Day of our sorority, five years ago, so this will be a very special night of sisterhood and fellowship.

Alumni are welcome for all nine days. Once a Bama Sis, always a Bama Sis! We hope to see you there!

Kisses,
The Current ADL Execs

Annabelle

Now

The unexpected invitation arrived on thick card stock with gold embossed lettering, crimson and white ribbons that curled, and all the sweetness of youth and sisterhood Annabelle Walker remembered from her days at Bama.

There was also a second, inconspicuous letter, her name written in black-ink block letters on a plain business envelope, which she hadn't opened yet. Envelopes like that were usually junk. But there'd been something about it that caught her curiosity. A subtle hint of perfume.

She slipped both into a drawer and returned to work. The clock was ticking for her to complete this project, and then she could address her mail.

Rainbows danced over Annabelle's wall. She tilted all thirty-five carats of the scaled-down Hope diamond look-alike back and forth, admiring the sparkling design. At its center was a massive grayish-blue diamond pendant, surrounded by smaller colorless diamonds, like the strand itself.

An ultraviolet light shone under the center diamond had glowed red, its phosphorescence proving that it was a real blue diamond.

She held it up to her neck, glancing at the mirror behind her desk, and sighed with regret that she was about to break this baby up and sell it for parts. A shame really, because it could be on display at the Smithsonian in Washington, DC.

Not that she would give it to a museum. Heck no. She wanted to keep it for herself.

In two hours, her husband would be home from work—if that's where he really was. Greg loved young, bubbly blondes—he filled his firm with them like most people stocked office supplies—and often walked through the door smelling like cheap perfume and sex.

She'd have to pretend not to notice the musty tang or smudges of lipstick on his collar while she told him she was staying in a hotel for nine days during Bama Rush Week. Where he'd probably insist she take their son, because why should he have to bother with him, and she'd have to tell him no, that Rush Week wasn't a place for children. And that meant he'd be balls deep in the nanny by midnight in retaliation. Good thing she had a service she could call before she got home to have her replaced.

Not that her husband's infidelities bothered her. Annabelle used to *think* she loved him, but now being married to the most prominent criminal lawyer in Tuscaloosa was more like a liability insurance policy, and his dick rammed inside another woman was the upfront attorney retainer.

A reunion with her sorority sisters was an exciting prospect. Besides the occasional phone call, she hadn't seen Brooklyn since her wedding to Drew, Taylor since an alumni event a few years ago, and Asana since graduation because she'd been too tied up with work in New York City to join them. Bogged down in their own personal dramas and lives, they'd not had a chance to get together the way they'd all promised.

Rush Week, her friends, and the time capsule opening were an unexpected surprise. Everyone was probably very eager to see what was inside.

There was one damper on the upcoming week—she was dreading competing for space with her mother. Annabelle had been on the exec board of her sorority as treasurer, almost following in the footsteps of her mother, who was a legacy president in Alpha Delta Lambda and never let her forget it.

Lily Walker was a legend and still active in Greek Life, encouraging Annabelle to mentor young women who wanted to join the sisterhood. Which she did, to keep up appearances. That part wasn't so bad. She loved to foster those relationships and share the joys of being in a sorority. Sisters for life.

And she donated regularly to the house's philanthropy. Just last year she provided their weekly flower arrangements for all twelve months. This year, she was sponsoring all the chapter meetings. Taylor would love that. Tea parties inspired by Tiffany—and paid for by gems like these. Though rumor had it they weren't calling chapter meetings tea parties anymore.

No one was any the wiser that Annabelle's donations came

with a price. Not much, just a token here or there. A few shining proudly on her private office wall display that she kept hidden behind an Andy Warhol. Some habits were hard to kick, harder if you didn't really want to. And taking things she admired was something Annabelle enjoyed.

Curiosity getting the better of her, Annabelle set down the necklace and returned to the mysterious envelope, carefully slicing the seam with her Hermès letter opener.

I know what you did. Come to Rush Week, or I'll tell everyone else.

Seeing her friends, opening the silly time capsule, competing with her mom, none of those things made her heart race like the anonymous letter, which included a picture of words she'd written in the infamous sorority Spill Book.

The thought that they'd all blindly spilled the tea—their darkest secrets—like good little sorority sisters, during Taylor's tea parties, was bewildering. In the five years since graduation, she'd regretted writing nearly every word. Even the seemingly innocent ones. Because if one of those notes got out to the public, she'd be screwed.

Like maximum-security-prison screwed.

How the heck the anonymous sender got their hands on it, Annabelle didn't know. Probably an elaborate joke. She'd assumed when the Spill Book didn't show up at the last tea party at ADL that Asana had burned it—she burned a lot of secret things.

Taylor never mentioned the book again—and she and Asana had not been on speaking terms at the time. Sister drama.

Was it possible that Taylor hadn't burned the Spill Book? Even crazier, was it possible she put it in the time capsule? No, she wouldn't do that.

Annabelle needed to talk to Taylor. ASAP. Probably some idiot found a stash of Taylor's blackmail material, which she hadn't hesitated to use on any of the sisters. Maybe she'd not brought the Spill Book to the last tea party because she thought someone would try to steal it.

Taylor was hard to read. And not always forthcoming with information.

And really, the particular entry that Annabelle wrote that was called out in the anonymous note wasn't as bad as some. Just a dumb little poem. But that didn't mean they didn't have the rest of the entries she'd made.

And those were worse. Much worse.

The more she thought about it, the more she was sure Asana had something to do with this. She was part of the Machine—a secret society on campus that pretty much ruled everything from campus dining and homecoming queen to the Student Government Association and local political elections—those donkeys tried to dictate everything.

Maybe she thought it was funny.

With a groan at how much the stupid letter was taking up her brain space, Annabelle tugged down her magnifying visor, flipped the switch on the light, and placed the necklace on a white velvet working pad. She didn't have time to be panicking about a stupid prank.

Focus, darn it.

This necklace held its gems in with prongs rather than a bezel setting, which encased the stone with a metal rim. Prongs made her job all the easier. Still, it would take time to remove the stones, because she needed to work slowly so as not to damage the gems.

People always thought that diamonds were indestructible, but it wasn't true. Hit hard enough they could chip or, worse, break apart—like friendships. Annabelle was an expert at deconstructing jewelry, and had never had a casualty on her watch. Unlike some of her past relationships.

Using her pliers, she bent each prong outward, until the stone was free from the platinum fingers that had held it captive. She removed the big stone first, then went to work on the rest of the necklace, taking her time until she had a pile of colorless diamonds on one side of her velvet pad, and the blue diamond sitting alone on the other. In the center were the platinum remnants, which would be melted down, but not here. The smell of that would send her husband and their staff sniffing around her office.

She called her office her sanctuary. A place she could come and do her yoga and meditation. Read novels and be unbothered. And if one were to simply look, that's all they'd see. A retreat inside a massive Alabama mansion.

And if they looked closer, they'd still see nothing beyond the calm neutral tones of a woman's haven.

It had been Annabelle's idea to have their house built—and she'd chosen the design and architect herself. Didn't Greg think he should have the biggest and best? Show his clients he was worth the fortune he charged? Stroking his ego, and then blowing him right after, had sealed the deal. And then she'd paid for her own clandestine safe room, designing it herself.

An innocuous bookshelf, filled with novels her husband would never go near. Hidden within was a tiny latch, which opened to her *real* office.

Once she was inside, the bookshelf went back into place, and it looked like she wasn't in the room, in case anyone came looking.

So, while her son was on his way to school with his nanny on watch, Annabelle was doing her "yoga." And now that her project was complete, and she was done pretending to be downward dogging, she would walk to her favorite coffee shop and be seen in town. The dutiful and devoted wife of big-time lawyer Greg, and the loving, doting mother of Liam.

Appearances were everything. And she'd been keeping up with those for years.

So, she would do the Stepford wife thing today, and she would plan to go to Rush Week.

While the local ladies cooed and oohed, none of them would be any the wiser she'd just spent the last three hours prepping to fence jewels and making more money in that time than they likely would in a decade.

Unless of course they were the housewives she was selling to.

Namaste.

CHAPTER TWO

Well, hello there, nosy little bee.

Are you looking for a gossip flower? You're about to get drunk slurping on more than just our sorority nectar.

This is an Alpha Delta Lambda tea party, and we're about to spill our sticky, not-so-sweet secrets all over this book.

Kisses,
Taylor

Brooklyn

Then

First impressions were everything.

And people were very judgmental. Anyone who said they weren't was probably the worst offender. Sort of like people who said "honestly" a lot—did that mean they were normally lying?

Brooklyn was very good at making first impressions. A hobby really.

A *lucrative* hobby.

Brooklyn clicked the lock on her dorm now that her roommate had scampered off, and adjusted her phone on the tripod, the camera aimed at her sneakered feet. She hit record, then slowly, seductively untied her shoes, tugging on the laces in a playful way, before sliding her shoes completely off. She stroked her tapered fingers over her bare ankle, slid a finger under the fabric of her Bombas sock, and then slowly peeled it off. Sock tossed aside, she stretched and pointed her toes, tipped with pink nail polish.

Her second toe was longer than her big toe. On it she wore a silver ring. Off with the next sock. She stroked her feet together slowly, sensually. Wondering just what kind of weirdos were at home rubbing one out to her foot striptease. With a final sexy arched-foot pose, she clicked off the camera. A few more clicks, and the video was uploaded. All she had to do was watch the dollars roll in for her OnlyFans name: Sporty Spyce.

But calculating how much she'd have to keep up with the sorority drip was going to have to wait.

Right now she needed to get ready for the first event of Bama Rush Week. The first day of the rest of her life, however clichéd that sounded. She'd been planning for this moment for years.

Brooklyn tucked the folder containing her sorority headshots and résumé into her rush bag. Though she'd already sent them out to each of the Greek houses she was rushing, it didn't hurt to be prepared with more. Also in her rush bag was a first aid kit, stain remover, deodorant, a brush, perfume, makeup, an extra shirt, a water bottle, a power bank, a mini-fan (it's hot AF in Bama), a notebook, colored gel pens (black and blue were boring), slides for when her sandals got uncomfortable, sunscreen, a granola bar, a sewing kit, a mirror, breath mints, and hair spray.

She liked to think of her rush bag as an emergency kit for any situation, and it was just as deep as Mary Poppins's carpetbag, only more stylish and not so old. Plus, it'd gain her points, she was sure.

With a tap of her neatly manicured bubble-gum-pink-colored nails on the ring light, she clipped her phone back to the tripod and clicked on the TikTok app, where she was Brooklyn in Bama. Time to make another impression to her hundreds of thousands of fans. By the end of Rush Week, she hoped to top a million. That's when the sponsorships started to roll in.

"Good morning, y'all! Time to Roll Tide. I've just got done with an early soccer practice and now I'm getting ready for the first day of Bama Rush Week," Brooklyn gushed into the video that she'd upload. She liked to come off as lovable and innocent, especially because most people thought gingers were feisty and ready to bang. What if she was? It was all about the impression, and the what-if. "It's Convocation today, where basically we learn about the different sororities and the benefits of being a part of Panhellenic life. I'm so excited."

She posed again, her full body in view, giving her viewers a moment to admire her.

"Are y'all ready for my first outfit of the day?" No Potential New Member—or PNM—would dare leave their dorm without an OOTD post.

Brooklyn swept her long, slightly curled red hair over her shoulder, and then posed, hands beneath her chin and a smile as sweet as buttermilk pie. "My skirt is from Gold Hinge." She pointed to her hips, then moved the rest of the way through her fit check. "My shirt is from Lulu, shoes are from On Cloud, bracelets from David Yurman, necklace from Tiffany, earrings from Altar'd State, and my rush bag is from Chloé." She lifted the large Woody Basket, with the long Chloé logo ribbons, showing off the last of her killer ensemble. The expensive things she wore were mostly gifts from her admirers. Whenever she got something in the mail, she was still excited. How was this her life?

She posted and tagged: #OOTD #BamaRush #GreekLife #RollTide #RushWeek.

Outside her dorm, the sun was in full UV mode, likely a six, which was perfect for tanning, but the humidity made the air look a little wavy. Brooklyn was glad she'd opted for the tank top. Girls were walking from all directions, dressed in their cute skirts or dresses, their hair all done. A sea of blond—or wannabe blondes. She might have been the only redhead. That was all right though, because Brooklyn liked to stand out—in ways that counted.

She was a sexy soccer star, a top-tier PNM—not just a kid at Bama on a partial scholarship ride trying to make ends meet and hoping for social media stardom. At first glance, she had enough money to pay for her place in the sorority, and no one needed to know *how* she afforded it.

"Oh, I love that necklace." A pretty brunette with fresh highlights poked the diamond at the center of Brooklyn's throat. "Tiffany?"

"Yes, how did you know?" Brooklyn was glad the other student hadn't looked closer at her other jewelry, one of which was a knockoff. The necklace at least was real, a gift from her daddy—by definition, a sexy, charismatic older man with money—but that was another story.

"I've got an eye for these things." She put her hand on her hip, her frame tall and athletic. "I'm Annabelle by the way."

"Brooklyn."

Annabelle twirled a long lock around her bejeweled finger. "Like the city?"

Brooklyn wrenched a smile from somewhere, annoyed by the question, and started to walk, not wanting to be late to the assembly. "The one and only."

"You don't sound like you're from New York." Annabelle kept pace.

"I'm not."

"Named after the place your parents hooked up?" Annabelle wiggled her brows.

Brooklyn didn't laugh. It was a joke a thousand people had attempted, and none had ever been able to get a rise.

"Sorry, didn't mean to offend." Annabelle laughed nervously and held up her hands in surrender.

Brooklyn quickly laughed and gave Annabelle's arm a gentle squeeze, realizing she'd let her mask drop for just a second too long. This might be her first friend during Rush Week, and she didn't want to ruin it—or risk Annabelle spreading rumors about her being an uptight bitch. "None taken. Who are you rushing?"

"Only top-tiers for me; Alpha Delta Lambda is my number one. My mom was their president back in the 1900s."

Brooklyn's eyes widened, and then she laughed. "Wow, I bet she just loves to hear you say that."

Annabelle giggled, until she snorted. "She hates it, but a girl's gotta be able to dig in a little when her mom's acting like the stage director of her life."

Brooklyn smiled softly, unsure what to say besides, "oh bless your heart," which didn't seem appropriate in this case. Her own mother didn't care what she did as long as she didn't have to pay for it. Annabelle looked well taken care of with diamonds of her own, highlights in her hair, and acrylics on her fingernails. Just to keep up her look alone must be at least a few hundred a month, and that didn't include attire.

They reached the historic auditorium with its brick facade and imposing stone columns. Girls gushing as they rushed inside took away from the seriousness of the building's history.

Its racist history.

The famous "Stand in the Schoolhouse Door" incident in 1963, that even *Forrest Gump* portrayed.

Brooklyn swallowed, taking note of the lack of diversity. She stood out as a ginger. Black girls stood out because of their skin.

"You all right?" Annabelle was staring at her like Brooklyn had morphed into half the girls in her hometown—run-down and out of place.

If *I* drop *my* mask one more time . . . "Hell yeah! Just like totally overwhelmed. Can you believe we're here?"

Annabelle grabbed her hand and tugged her through the doors. "Come on! Let's go inside."

Brooklyn had been dreaming about being a part of a sorority since she was a tween and had watched *Legally Blonde* about four thousand times. When she found out she could still play soccer, it felt like the stars were aligning. She could kick ass and wear pink? *Sold.*

"Oh my gosh, will you just look at all of us?" Annabelle practically squealed as they entered the auditorium with a couple thousand other girls, dressed, made-up, and jeweled to impress.

Brooklyn was the first in her family to attend college, and nobody understood how important rushing was. Her mom worked her fingers to the bone cleaning houses for rich assholes, and her dad was a security guard who spent most of his working hours drinking beer, and thus was always getting fired.

Brooklyn pinched herself to make sure she wasn't dreaming as she took in the streaming lights, the stage, the crimson stadium seats. This right here would be the most important week of her life.

"Sit up front?" Annabelle pointed to two spots right in the center in front of the stage.

"Of course." Brooklyn grinned. Despite their rocky start, she had an idea that she and Annabelle might get along.

"What's your major?" Annabelle asked as they settled into their chairs, rush bags in front of their crossed legs.

"Broadcasting."

"Oh, you'll be perfect for that, you have a great voice."

"Thank you." Brooklyn knew it but always enjoyed hearing it from someone else. "What about you?"

"Geology. Never saw a stone I didn't like."

"I used to have a rock collection when I was growing up. Never admitted that to anyone before."

Annabelle laughed. "I have a rock collection still, only now it also includes a few gems."

"Okay, so now we have to be friends."

More students filed in, the din echoing in the massively high ceilings.

Brooklyn introduced herself to the PNMs around her, chatting about the different sororities they wanted to visit. The lights flashed, and a collective gasp of excitement sucked the air from the room. She tapped her feet on the floor and squealed, "Here we go, ladies!"

An elegant blonde walked onto the stage and sat down. Other Panhellenic council members did the same. Annabelle stiffened beside her, her face frozen in a smile that looked brittle enough to crack.

"You okay?" Brooklyn wasn't the only one with a mask.

Annabelle offered a fake laugh. "Of course, why wouldn't I be?" But her gaze fell back on the woman who happened to be staring right at them.

CHAPTER THREE

I sold a picture of my feet on OnlyFans for $500.
Who knew that was even a thing?

Kisses,
Brooklyn

Asana

Now

Whoever said money couldn't buy happiness clearly hadn't had
enough.

Asana Duke moaned in pleasure, splayed out on a lounge chair
by the resort's purple-lighted pool, one ankle on some hot-as-fuck
guy's shoulder as he drove into her, and the breasts of whoever
dangled over her face.

It was a hedonistic paradise. A sexy playground for the rich
and richer. A purlieu for those who met on her secret website,
Matinee. The caveat? Married members only. Except for her. She
was the boss. And if there was one thing Asana had sworn never
to do, that was get married.

Stars shone overhead. Only a few dozen feet away, water
crashed on the beach. The resort was lit enough to see the other
moaning, writhing bodies indulging in one another.

After the Ashley Madison scandal more than a decade ago,
people needed someone new to trust, and why not her? She had

her reasons for taking up the mantle as a heartbreaker, and they were nobody's business.

When work became too much—which was basically always—Fantasia was one of Asana's favorite places to escape. No ridiculous PR campaigns to run, no spoiled-rotten executives with reputations that needed saving. Just a sex-positive elite resort that catered to people like her: rich, sexy, and down to fuck. Kind of like the swap parties they'd had on Greek Row back at Bama.

Only if anyone found out about this, she and her entire family's mega corporation would be screwed.

She arched her back, an orgasm just a thrust or two away, when a phone started to buzz. This grotto was no place for calls. Someone hadn't followed the rules. She ignored it, knowing it couldn't be hers.

The buzzing continued.

"It's yours," crooned the woman bent over her.

"Impossible." Asana had turned her phone off. At least she was pretty sure she had. Between the glasses of champagne and the sexy pool relay races, she remembered powering down. Or at least pressing the button. Had she slid the power to off?

Why was she even thinking about that when she was getting laid?

The buzzing turned to dinging.

"Def yours," lover boy said as he pounded away.

"Don't stop," Asana ordered, wrapping her other ankle around jacked dude's hip, and flicking her tongue over the nipple of the curvy blonde. "I don't care."

Buzz. Ding. Buzz. Ding.

She lifted her hips higher, sucked harder, trying to ignore the cell, but no one called her back-to-back unless it was an emergency.

"Fucking A." She pushed the woman away, bucked off the

dude, and stood, yanking down her leather miniskirt, which she wore with no underwear, and tucked her breasts back into her red corset top. "Sorry. You two finish. Whoever is calling me better be fucking dying."

She slipped on her stilettos, which had been kicked off in the heat of the moment, grabbed her purse, and yanked out her phone.

Asana swiped on the first message, and did a double take. A picture she hadn't known existed filled her screen.

A picture she wished had never been taken.

A picture she was certain to get *screwed* over.

Her and Taylor Collins, lips locked, wearing ADL T-shirts with little pink hearts all over that gave the year away.

Taylor Collins. Her onetime BFF. The first sorority friend she'd had. A mouth she hadn't felt on hers in at least five years. Any effects of the encroaching orgasm disappeared, leaving her feeling as though a bucket of ice water had been dumped over her head.

Asana swallowed hard, batting aside the thought that if she could have had Taylor to herself, she wouldn't have needed any trips to Fantasia. Wouldn't have even started a dark website for people to cheat. Wouldn't be so jaded and fearful of a relationship to begin with. But Taylor had made it clear that the two of them being together would never happen.

"What is it?" asked lover boy.

Asana glanced over her shoulder to see that the blonde was kneeling between his legs, a towel tucked under her knees, sucking him off like her life depended on it, while he watched Asana have a near meltdown over her phone.

"Work," she lied.

She returned her attention to the cell, the picture, past memories swarming up from the depths where she'd buried them.

Who the fuck had taken this picture? And why the fuck were they sending it to her now?

Playtime was over. She needed a plan of coordinated attack, and to nip this bullshit in the ass.

Seething, she marched into the resort lobby, jammed her manicured red fingernail onto the elevator button, and took it to her penthouse suite.

The clicking of her red Louboutins on marble was only muffled when she crossed over the plush sheepskin rug toward the window that looked out over the Caribbean Sea.

Being head of PR for Duke Corp was a blessing and a curse.

A blessing because she was rich beyond measure, and a curse because her daddy was Duke.

A curse because she was always solving other people's problems. Making their mistakes look like good decisions. A blessing because she was so damn good at her job that every victory was the best kind of high.

And tonight, the mistake was apparently on her.

She clicked through to the next text, a second picture. This one in New York City at Club X, where she was caught in another compromising position—after all, it *was* a sex club. Asana had a bottle of Cristal at her lips and a brunette's mouth between her thighs.

What consenting adults did behind closed doors shouldn't be anyone else's business. And all of Asana's partners had consented. If it went beyond a one-night stand, they also signed an NDA. She'd learned her lesson the hard way.

And now apparently somebody was making her sex life *their* business.

The biggest problem? This picture had been snapped during a Matinee takeover of the club.

There was only one reason she could think of that someone would be sending her these—money. People were always threatening to extort her. She was one of the wealthiest women her age—a billionaire heiress, listed in *Forbes*.

There was a voicemail, too, from an anonymous number. Gritting her teeth, she clicked play, eyes not seeing the rainbow of lighted colors across the resort grounds.

A robotic voice spoke. "I know who you are. And soon the entire world will too. I imagine a lot of unhappy people. Three million if you want to keep the exposé piece from going live the day after Bid Day. No wire transfers. Cash only. Next week at ADL. Come alone. No police. And by the way, I have the book."

The book? What fucking book?

At first her mind didn't connect what that meant. But like pieces of a puzzle clicking into place, the entire picture became clear. There was only one book she'd ever cared about.

Someone had the Spill Book.

This picture of her and Taylor had clearly been put in there, and now they were threatening to expose her secrets. To spread them out for some rag mag to print and then the world to start talking about. And someone had clearly done a deep dive into her life. The picture taken at Club X could have just been a creepy voyeur, except for the fact that it was on a Matinee night. That meant whoever had taken it knew about her website. Knew about her past at Bama. What other photos might they have—what other information might they have uncovered?

Not that she was embarrassed about any of the pictures they'd sent. She was a sex-positive woman. And they could go to hell. Pictures meant nothing.

But there were secrets attached to those pictures.

Another secret in that book they were edging too close to for comfort.

One that could put her in danger.

One that could ruin her career.

One that would definitely bring Duke Corp back into the spotlight. That was the last place her father wanted to be, especially after her brother's fiasco the year before when he'd beaten a paparazzo with his umbrella.

Exposing Matinee would be catastrophic to Duke Corp's investors. Half of them were members of Matinee, and they certainly didn't want their spouses to know. They would pull their investments out of Duke and her family would go bankrupt. The backlash would not be something she could recover from.

Asana let out a frustrated groan and threw her phone across the room, where it shattered so hard against the marble floor, pieces of glass sprinkled the surface like diamonds.

Well, that wasn't smart. Now she needed a new phone. Her lifeline.

Asana plugged the hotel phone back into the wall since she never left it in, and called down to the front desk.

"I need a new cell phone. Top-of-the-line. Now."

"Yes, Miss Duke."

"Like yesterday fast."

"Our pleasure, Miss Duke."

Who in their right mind would blackmail her into going back to Bama? That was literally the most asinine request of any extortionist yet. Three million she understood. Being forced to return to her sorority house? Was this some kind of joke?

The invitation to the ADL Rush Week had been sitting on her office desk for weeks. She'd ignored it. When she'd been eighteen, belonging to the most popular sorority on the planet had been a dream. Women in her mother's circle talked about Alpha Delta Lambda, and while Asana had an eye for business, she liked the softer side of a sisterhood too. Belonging to something that men couldn't infiltrate had been important to her. To be a powerful woman, she had to befriend powerful women. What better way than to be a part of something bigger than herself?

But by the end . . . well, things had soured some, and she and her "BFF" Taylor hadn't exactly left things on good terms. And it wasn't like she had a habit of ripping her own heart out.

But now she had no choice.

Because it wasn't just her reputation on the line, but Taylor's, her father's company. And if they had the Spill Book, well, then her reputation was the last thing she needed to worry about because it would be her *life* on the line.

It was either go to Rush Week or risk her father's wrath. Worse, a scandal would probably send her mother back to Lenox Hill to recover from "exhaustion," also known in the world of the elite as a mental fucking breakdown.

She kicked off her heels, shed her clothes, and jumped in the shower. A cold shower. Letting the icy water sluice over her skin was always cathartic and helped her to think. To plan. To organize a methodical strategy for how she would handle this both privately and not so privately, if it came to that.

No one messed with a Duke.

Being in control, powerful, was everything.

Dressing in a chic business suit, her hair and makeup done— some habits were good to keep—she tossed her things into her Louis Vuitton weekender and called her private pilot.

"Wheels up in thirty, Bob."

"Yes, ma'am."

"And, Bob, I'm going to need a drink. And a sandwich. Make that a burger." Her stomach growled. "With fries."

Another old habit—binge eating when stressed. Thank God her plane also had a treadmill.

In the lobby, a sleek new top-of-the-line cell phone waited for her. She uploaded her information from the cloud.

A bellman took her bag and held the door for her, indicating the waiting limousine. Disappointedly, Asana slid across the smooth, cool leather seat, regretting that this bullshit was coming first, when all she wanted was a weekend of endless orgasms and a string of beautiful lovers.

Hadn't she earned that?

Dammit.

CHAPTER FOUR

Twinkle, twinkle, little gemstone,
How did you get here all alone?
The only thing that makes me calm,
A sparkling diamond in my palm . . .

Kisses,
Annabelle

Taylor

Then

"Excuse me, oh my gosh, I'm sorry, excuse me." Taylor giggled as she slid down the auditorium's second row of seats, her rush bag bumping into a few girls, maybe on purpose, but maybe not.

Cheer practice had run a few minutes late, which completely threw her off, and if she was going to make captain by next year, she had to stay until the end and be the number one for spirit at all times.

The stage was filling with Panhellenic council members, which meant that at any moment they'd start the Convocation assembly. She needed to have her ass in a seat and full attention on the Greek legends.

She'd recognized a few girls from her cheer team, moving swiftly to sit beside them. But from the other end of the aisle, another PNM was hurrying through, vying for the same spot in the center of the row. *Oh, no you don't!*

Taylor hit a few more faces, stepped on a few more toes, and climbed over a lap in a race for the seat. At the last second, she dropped into the chair, at the same time as the other girl, winning the seat and the other girl on her lap.

"Sorry," Taylor said with a sweet smile. Fighting the urge to curl her fingers around the girl's hips, she sent the other PNM on her way with a little push.

"You're quick. I thought for sure she was going to beat you," one of her cheer team members said.

Taylor smirked. "I don't let anyone beat me."

On her other side, a pretty blonde who looked a lot like Serena van der Woodsen from *Gossip Girl* grinned. "Me either."

Ooh, a challenge. "Then we may have to become best friends."

"We might." The Serena look-alike pulled a tube of pink glossy lip plumper from her Hermès Birkin bag, the same shade of red as Taylor's.

"Love that color and the way it tingles. I'm Taylor."

The blonde laughed. "Asana."

"Nice bag." Taylor held her matching purse. "Another sign we're destined to be BFFs."

Asana squinted as she grinned, the kind of grin that is also skeptical. "Are you one of those?"

"One of what?" Taylor straightened, her spine pressed to the cool red plastic *A* for Alabama on the back of her chair. She was used to people liking her, not being all . . . judgy.

Asana, cool as the air-conditioning blowing down from the ceiling vents, tucked her lip gloss away and answered without even bothering to look at her. "People who see signs."

Maybe they weren't going to be besties. "Of course. The Lord works in mysterious ways."

Asana made a small humming sound, side-eyed her with a tiny smile, then faced the stage. Taylor clamped her lips shut. She knew better than to talk religion during Rush Week. It was part of the forbidden five Bs: Bible, booze, bucks, boys, and ballots.

With her mother being a legacy for her number one choice—Alpha Delta Lambda—she'd had it drilled into her not to mention a single one, and here she was already making a mistake. Well, that wouldn't happen again. Taylor didn't make mistakes. What self-respecting perfectionist did?

And she supposed she didn't actually make a mistake. At no point had she asked Asana what church she went to or, heaven forbid, if she believed in God. No, what she'd said could just be construed as an often used idiom, like "God bless you" when someone sneezed and "Bless your heart," which really meant two things. One good and one condescending.

And technically speaking, the five Bs were forbidden topics when speaking with *active* sorority sisters, which they weren't, yet. Still, she needed to be more careful.

Luckily, she was saved by the tapping of the microphone attached to the podium as a gorgeous blonde about her own mother's age took center stage.

"Good morning, ladies," the woman said, pressing both of her hands to her heart, her head cocked softly to the side as she stared out into the vast audience of enthralled young women. "I'm Lily Walker. Camille couldn't be here today, bless her heart, and as I am past Panhellenic president, she asked me to step in. I'm currently the collegiate relations and recruitment director for Alpha Delta Lambda in this district. And I'm so overjoyed to see all of your fresh faces here today, including my own daughter."

In front of Taylor and Asana, a redhead leaned toward a brunette and whispered, "Is that your mom?"

The brunette didn't turn, eyes on the stage, and nodded.

Taylor and Asana glanced at each other, eyebrows raised—all past judgments gone—and a silent we-need-to-meet-her message passed between them.

Lily Walker continued, telling them about the Panhellenic organization and listing the number of sororities on campus, and reiterated the rules about each PNM choosing twelve chapters they wanted to visit, but everyone knew there were only four top-tier houses on campus and Alpha Delta Lambda was on top, with Zeta Tau Alpha, Phi Mu, and Alpha Delta Phi coming in next.

"Today is Convocation, the first of a life-changing nine days. I can still remember Rush Week my freshman year, and I wish the same endless joy for all of you. Following today, we'll have three days of Philanthropy, three days of Sisterhood, Preference Day, and my personal favorite, Bid Day, where bids will be distributed in person in the stadium, and you'll find out which sorority has chosen you. In nine days, most of you in this room will be celebrating together at the Bryant-Denny Stadium."

Taylor bit the inside of her cheek. There wasn't a running list of how many other girls were going to be rushing ADL, but along with herself and the brunette girl in front of her, she was pretty certain the list would be long. And Lily had said "most." That meant not everyone in this room was going to get a bid. Either they'd drop out of the process or they wouldn't receive an invitation back for a Preference event, meaning they'd been dropped.

"That's my number one," Asana murmured. "The top-tier sorority on campus. It's the whole reason I came south."

"Where are you from?"

"New York."

"You don't have a New York accent."

Asana laughed. "Nobody in my school did."

The redhead twisted around to shush them, then her eyes widened as she took in Asana, recognition flaring. But Asana did not return the look, and the redhead turned back around. Maybe she was from New York too.

A short time later, after meeting with their assigned Sigma Rho Chi group—essentially their recruitment counselors—Lily Walker dismissed the PNMs to go visit their favorite sororities for open house.

"Alpha Delta Lambda first?" Asana asked Taylor.

Taylor tried to quell the excitement that Asana hadn't dismissed her—she was better than that. Usually the most popular girl in the group. But there was something about Asana that made her self-conscious, an unfamiliar and unwelcome feeling. "ADL only."

Asana flashed an approving smile. "My style."

They filed out of the auditorium, only to find the redhead and brunette apparently waiting for them. The two rushed forward to block Taylor and Asana from walking toward Greek Row.

"Asana Duke?" the redhead asked.

Taylor tried to play it cool, pretending she didn't care about this entirely interesting confrontation. Just who was Asana Duke?

Asana cocked her head and drew in an annoyed breath. "Yes. Why?"

"Huge fan," the redhead gushed.

"Of what?" Asana looked as confused as Taylor was.

"Your style!" The redhead laughed and then nudged her friend. "She's practically in every issue of *Teen Vogue*. I'm Brooklyn, by the way."

"Not by choice. Anyways, you clearly know who I am." Asana nodded toward Taylor, who seemed to have lost her voice.

Asana was in *Teen Vogue*? Was she a model? What did she mean "not by choice"? Her rush ensemble looked just like everyone else's. Cute tennis skirt, tank top, sneakers.

When Taylor didn't speak up, Asana gave her a little elbow nudge and said, "This is Taylor."

Taylor drew in a breath and let out a short laugh. "Sorry, I'm so out of it—late night with my boyfriend." She winked, liking the edge it gave her. "I'm Taylor Collins."

"O-M-G, Taylor Collins?" the brunette crooned. "I'm Annabelle Walker. My mom and your mom rushed together. How blessed are we to be doing this together?"

Taylor's mother had mentioned Lily Walker more than once, and that she'd beat her out by one vote for president of ADL. "I hope they left on good terms."

"As far as I know they did." Annabelle shrugged, clearly not that aware of their mothers' rivalry.

"Let's hope," Taylor lied sweetly. "That could be awkward, assuming you're going to ADL?"

"We are. Walk together?" Brooklyn asked.

They made their way across campus to Greek Row. Every house was decorated with massive colorful welcome signs, rainbow balloon archways, gigantic Greek letters made from flowers on the front lawns. And everywhere, excited PNMs and sisters hugging, chatting, TikToking. The atmosphere was electric.

Taylor had been waiting for this moment since she'd been old enough to look through photo albums of her mother pictured with a bunch of other perfectly put-together girls. But it wasn't just how pretty they were, it was how *happy*. How they leaned on one another. How they were all best friends—even her mother still got together once a year for a sorority sister retreat at the beach. Taylor wanted that closeness, the lifelong friendships.

She'd even learned the ADL chant by watching videos on social media. Taylor was determined to be front of the line for that cheer too. Back of the line was for the girls who weren't as coordinated or messed up the choreography. Front was for the perfect ones. Like her.

They walked up the brick front stairs to the massive porch of the ADL mansion and were welcomed inside by sisters and their perfectly white enameled smiles. The marble-floored foyer featured a center console table with a striking display of pink and white roses and a circular staircase that was almost as impressive as the one at her house.

"I'm home," Taylor sighed.

"We all are," Asana agreed.

CHAPTER FIVE

The Machine's motto is: "Little is known and what is known is kept secret." But I'll tell you this little nugget, I did drink from the diamond goblet handed to me.

Kisses,
Asana

Brooklyn

Now

Brooklyn Tolley smiled into the camera as she sliced through the tape on a large cardboard box that had been delivered earlier that morning. This was something she did on her TikTok account daily.

Sponsorship packages arrived sometimes by the hour. She moved Styrofoam aside to reveal a state-of-the-art blender.

"Just what every busy woman needs," she said with a manufactured squeal, and then lifted the blender from deep within the box, along with every attachment ever made, showing it off for her audience. "Smoothies for me and Mr. FixIt."

As if on cue, and maybe it was but she'd never tell, her home-improvement television-star husband, Drew, rounded the corner in their perfect white-marbled and vibrant brushed-modern-brass-fixtured and white-cabineted kitchen and said, "Hey, hey!

I love smoothies." And then Drew gave her a chaste kiss on her temple and she smiled lovingly into the camera.

"What about us?" Twin ginger-headed three-year-olds bounced into view behind her. A boy and a girl. Couldn't get any more perfect than that, now, could she?

"You get a smoothie too." Brooklyn winked into the camera.

"Yay!" They pumped their arms in the air and jumped around in genuine excitement. The kind of excitement about a smoothie that only a young child could have.

The perfect ending for Ginger Mommy—her social media name—to click off the camera. While her kids ran around the room waiting for her to make them breakfast, she added the appropriate caption and hashtags. *Upload complete.*

First video of the day done, she pulled out fruit, then rinsed it.

"You're amazing." Drew snuck up behind her and stole a strawberry. His hand on her waist still gave her the same tingles it did when she'd first met him at a mixer in college. He knew nothing about Sporty Spyce—her sexy OnlyFans name from back in the day—or her time as a sugar baby. When they'd met, he genuinely liked her for her, and she was still mesmerized that with him, she didn't have to perform.

"No, you are," she said, turning around, her ass pressed to the counter and her tongue tasting the remnants of strawberry on his lips.

"I would much rather stay here," he groaned into her kiss. "But the houses won't fix themselves, and my producer will kick my ass. I gotta finish getting ready."

She giggled as he stole a hunk of pineapple and trotted out of the kitchen.

While she cut up fruit, mixing it with yogurt and honey in her own blender for the promised smoothies, her phone played its usual morning music of one ding after another, indicating she had messages, likes, comments, and shares. Most people found that noise annoying. And she might have too, except it had become a habit since she was in college. To enjoy the sound of the dings—each one signaling without a doubt that she was a success.

Smoothies served to the twins and her own protein shake in hand, she scrolled through the comments, hearting them all, and then moved to the messages.

One stood out. Stood out in a stab-you-in-the-eye kind of way that made her hands tremble enough she dropped her protein shake all over the floor. Pink splashed everywhere on the white floor, cabinets, her sneakers.

I love your little nicknames. Ginger Mommy. Sporty Spyce. Hope to see you next week at ADL Rush. Actually, make that: I will see you there.

"Mommy, Mommy, you spilled!" The twins were frantically trying to get her attention, tugging on her arms, their bare feet slipping in the sludge.

"Are you all right, hon?" Drew rushed back into the kitchen, tugging his *Mr. FixIt* T-shirt over his head.

Brooklyn snapped out of it, shoved her phone in her pocket, and grabbed paper towels to clean up the mess all over the marble-tiled floor. Drew lifted each toddler, putting them in the sink and rinsing their feet.

"Yes." Brooklyn giggled. "Just being klutzy today, I guess."

Drew narrowed his eyes, and the question in them burned through her enough that she had to look away. She was never klutzy. Five years post college soccer and one massive pregnancy later, Brooklyn was still athletic, her body honed with regular intervals of HIIT, yoga, Pilates, and weight training, and she was on a recreational soccer team.

But she flashed him an "oops" face and her husband just shrugged, taking her at her word. Because as far as Drew knew, she never lied.

"How about we help Mommy?" The enticing expression on his face didn't do anything for the ginger twins, who balked.

"All right, then let's go brush your teeth for school?" he offered.

"No, we want to help Mommy." Toddler help was really not that helpful, and it took twice as long to wipe down the cabinets and mop the floor.

"Thank you," she said to her family, but her voice was distant, the message replaying over and over in her head.

I love your little nicknames. Ginger Mommy. Sporty Spyce.

No one that she knew of was aware of Sporty Spyce. Not any of her sorority sisters. Not Drew especially. The name, her past lifestyle, the way she'd made money in college, was something she'd kept close to the vest. Closer than that even, erasing it from her own mind. After all, if the wholesome mommy blogger and influencer Ginger Mommy was ever found out to have once been a very highly sought-after sugar baby named Sporty Spyce, or there were literal videos of her stripping online, her entire life would be over.

Sporty Spyce still had thousands of videos, none of her face—thankfully—online. And a string of daddies who had enjoyed her company for a price for several years. That was until she'd accepted a bribe to keep her mouth shut after witnessing something awful.

If Drew found out about any of it, he would take the kids and leave.

Her audience of moms and housewives would be scandalized that they ever took any advice from her.

Her sponsorships would quickly withdraw, and with them all the money they brought in. Which was millions. No longer was she worth five hundred dollars for a foot pic. Or five thousand dollars a month as a sugar baby. But seven figures a year.

"I'm going to go for a run. Can you get the kids off to pre-school?" she asked Drew, feeling guilty because she knew he was already late, and that he would say yes.

"Of course. Are you sure you're all right?" Drew tugged her toward him, his arms looped around her waist, as he stared at her with concern, a look she rarely saw from him, because usually nothing bothered her. Or at least she pretended very well.

Brooklyn used one of the tricks she'd honed in college when she didn't want to talk to her sugar daddy. She pressed her body to Drew's, slid her fingers into the hair at the base of his neck, and then pressed her lips to his for a kiss that would make him forget he'd had a question, let alone a plan for the day other than stripping naked.

Then she let go, winked, and headed for the door. She didn't even take her headphones. No music could drown out the message on repeat in her head. She needed the sun, the wind, the heart thumping, foot pounding of a hard run. To drench her worries in sweat. Eight miles, maybe ten. Full speed.

She didn't even warm up. The buzzing in her veins made her start sprinting the moment she shut the door behind her. Running from the message. Running from the panic. Running from her past. Running from the destruction promised.

But no matter how far she ran, or how much she sweated, this was a problem that wasn't going away. Nor was it easily solved.

There was really only one choice for Brooklyn, and that was to leave the safety net of her home in Florida and go back to Alabama, to Bama Rush Week, and find out what this person wanted. To find out what it would take for them to shut the fuck up, no matter the monetary cost. Whoever this was needed to never let the words Sporty Spyce come out again.

Sporty Spyce wasn't a mistake.

Brooklyn had known full well what she was doing. And it had worked.

But she had a different life now. A perfect life. A rich and full life.

Sporty Spyce had been laid to rest, reincarnated as Ginger Mommy.

And she wasn't going to let someone ruin that. Not ever.

CHAPTER SIX

When I was blindfolded and reached my hand into the toilet, feeling the long, squishy turd, and my Big told me I had to bite it. There was a moment's hesitation. But it was either eat shit and win my bid or drop it back into the bowl and cry all the way back to my dorm. Thank God it was a banana. I was willing to eat shit.

Kisses,
Brooklyn

Annabelle

Then

Walking through the Alpha Delta Lambda house was like stepping into a past life. But not necessarily a life she would have chosen without her mother's insistence. And she was reliving it over and over again.

Annabelle already knew the building's layout like her own home. Alpha Delta Lambda had been such a popular topic of discussion when she was growing up, it might have been the first words she uttered. Even her dollhouse had been a replica of the ADL mansion, her dolls tiny sorority girls who she made have sleepovers, makeovers, and tea parties.

When dressing her up for pageants, her mother would tell her that every win was a step closer to being a part of ADL, as if to be a sorority sister, she had to also be a pageant winner.

Pretty girls win.

Pretty blond girls win even more.

Her mother had gotten her highlights when she was seven. *Seven.* Annabelle wasn't even sure what her real hair color was anymore, though her mother often said it was the same shade as her dad's, an Italian with a full head of salt and pepper.

Working for Panhellenic had been her mother's dream, and she was also one of the highest-paying alumna sponsors. Of course, the money came from Annabelle's dad, who owned a worldwide chain of high-end hotels and would do anything for Lily Walker, including indulging her sister-for-life attitude.

They had more money than half the British royal family, at least that's what her dad bragged when they didn't think she was listening.

At any moment, she expected to see her mother breeze through one of the doorways either to the living room or the dining room and gush about seeing her daughter finally in the place that she loved so much. Loved even more than Annabelle, it felt like.

There was the original sorority house painting on the wall depicting what the mansion looked like a hundred years ago. The bronze sister statue—four young women holding hands and smiling. The window her mother used to sit by to sip her coffee. Every wall, nook, and cranny, Annabelle knew.

Even with her mother's involvement, she'd hardly ever brought Annabelle to the house. She'd insisted that Convocation should be special, and not spoiled by too much familiarity. Well, she was here . . . and the feeling was anticlimactic.

In the living room she discreetly opened a drawer, noted the decks of cards, and closed it again. A cabinet contained board games, some of the cardboard lids looking as old as the house. Had literally nothing changed since her mother had been in college?

An elbow in her ribs had Annabelle frowning, but it was Brooklyn, who was staring toward the front door, where Lily Walker and half a dozen ADL sisters were clapping and chanting. A secret handshake. Then they laughed and her mother hugged the girls, the smile on her face wider than when she hugged Annabelle.

"Your mom knows everyone," Brooklyn said, mesmerized.

"Not everyone." What she meant was "not me."

"Let's go say hi, please?" Brooklyn pleaded, Asana and Taylor making similar beseeching expressions, complete with prayer hands.

Annabelle pasted a smile on her face and said, "Sure," because that was the appropriate thing to do, when really, she wanted to turn around and go the opposite way. For this day to be hers.

What college freshman wanted their mommy with them during Rush Week?

Annabelle led them toward her mom, keeping her smile on and noting how the other PNMs and sisters watched her. Though it was only Convocation and an open house, this was also an audition, and if she failed, there was a real chance her mother would disown her.

"Mom, I wanted to introduce you to some friends."

"Oh, how lovely," her mother said, the pink diamonds at her neck winking in the sunlight filtering in through the Palladian windows of the foyer. "You are all so beautiful." But Lily's eyes homed in on Asana's blond hair and Taylor's platinum locks with approval, grazing over Brooklyn's ginger head the same way she glanced over Annabelle's darker hair. No matter how much she highlighted her hair, it would never be light enough for her mother.

"Welcome to ADL House," said the president of ADL, a perky blonde beside Lily Walker. "You must be Annabelle, I'm Larissa."

"Yes, and thank you so much. We're so excited for Rush Week." She glanced at her new friends, somehow feeling like the connection they'd made today was going to be important. And because she didn't want to be singled out as Lily Walker's daughter.

She wanted to rush like everyone else. To go through the process like everyone else. To be someone else, at least for these nine days before she took up her place in the house and on the exec board. Though she'd already decided she wasn't going to be president. That was Lily Walker's place, and there was a sense of not usurping her mother. Her mother needed that legacy to remain hers forever.

Larissa reached forward, a Cartier bracelet on her wrist and a diamond-and-ruby band on her middle finger, a classic way to show school colors. She gripped Annabelle's hand in hers, and Annabelle felt the gems of the ring against her fingers—an eternity band—and smiled. "I hope we'll be seeing you the rest of this week."

"Of course."

Behind the president's head, Lily Walker smiled and nodded at Annabelle, as if it were already a done deal.

"It was nice to meet you, but we don't want to keep you," Annabelle said.

"Enjoy the open house."

"Do your thing, sweetheart," her mother said with pride, and Annabelle took that as a cue for dismissal, signaling to her friends that they should walk around.

They toured the rest of the house with the other girls, meeting more rushees.

Annabelle took note of who had on designer-brand clothes and jewelry versus knockoffs. Some of them were cleverer than others. It was a skill she'd honed from a young age, when she was admiring a picture in one of her family's hotel lobbies and thought it was real. She'd been embarrassed when her father said he'd never put a real one in the lobby and she should know better.

She never made that mistake again.

She twisted the ring on her right finger. A pink diamond band that matched the necklace her mother wore. A gift for rush since pink and white were the ADL colors.

But her mother's necklace on Annabelle's neck, now that would make the set complete.

Maybe one day—if she was offered a bid.

Annabelle glanced at Taylor, who was wrinkling her nose. She turned in the direction she was looking and saw a couple of girls who'd just entered the sorority house with no makeup on, their hair in messy buns. They wore oversized University of Alabama T-shirts and jean shorts. Barely one of the three required components of hair, makeup, outfit applied.

"Yikes," Annabelle said. "They must not know the rules."

"Never leave your room without at least two of the three done," Asana offered.

"They're on my team," Brooklyn said.

"Team?"

"Soccer."

"Oh. I didn't realize you played." Annabelle kept her jealousy well hidden. "Will playing interfere with your sorority responsibilities?"

"No," Taylor answered for Brooklyn. "I'm on the cheer team. They won't conflict. The more school spirit the better, right?"

"Exactly." Brooklyn and Taylor high-fived.

Annabelle smiled and nodded, but on the inside, she was frowning. At five foot ten, and a heck of a good volleyball player, she'd been recruited to play for the university, but her mother had said no, because it would interfere with her sorority obligations, which was what she really wanted, right? And besides, there was a beach volleyball net set up on sorority row, so she could show off her talents where it mattered.

Where it mattered to Mommy dearest.

Annabelle felt her smile crack, and turned away, hoping no one had noticed.

"Let's do a TikTok," Brooklyn said. "New PNM besties."

Annabelle shoved aside her envy. She needed friends. She needed sisters. This was her chance to have them. With an arm in the air, she crooned, "Heyyyy."

CHAPTER SEVEN

When my Big wasn't looking, I swiped a strawberry from her fruit bowl. It's just a strawberry. But the thrill of taking something from her without her seeing it, of eating the berry she wanted to eat, man, there was power behind that.

Kisses,
Annabelle

TAYLOR

Now

Taylor rarely had regrets.

Regrets were for people who weren't perfect—and Taylor was always perfect.

Regrets were for spelling errors in tattoos. Or having one too many drinks and swiping right instead of left, resulting in a subpar one-night stand. Regrets were for people who weren't calculated in their choices or careful enough to think ahead and realize what could happen on the other end of a bad decision.

Everything Taylor did was premeditated, and it had been that way from the moment she could remember having a cohesive thought as a toddler. The way she'd worn her hair, joined the cheer team, become captain at University of Alabama. She dated the most popular boys, only got As, and went to church every Sunday. Becoming president of Alpha Delta Lambda, the number one top-tier sorority at Bama had been a calculated move in the making for nearly a decade. The first rung on her political-career aspirations ladder.

Even marrying a powerful senator twice her age had been by design.

Perfectionism was everything.

So, before today, the total regrets in Taylor's secret I-hate-myself box that she never looked in were precisely three.

And one of them gaped in glaring pixels from the laptop in front of her on the desk in the second-floor office of her Tuscaloosa mansion.

Remember me? The subject line was enticing enough that she'd clicked on the email, often getting cute little notes from past Panhellenic sisters.

This was not cute.

It was ugly. Horrible. Mean.

There was nothing written in the body. No words could have done a better job than what was translated in the photo splashed on the screen.

Displayed in all its haunting glory was a throwback from five years in the past. A photograph of a little yellow pill with a honeybee emblem stamped on it. She hadn't seen the pills in years. Hadn't touched them. Well, not those anyway.

That little yellow busy bee rested without hesitation on someone's tongue. A girl, judging by the shape of her lips and the pink shine of her lipstick. A girl Taylor didn't recognize, or at least a tongue she didn't. The photo was zoomed in, cutting off the rest of her face. There were a few wisps of dark hair, so it wasn't hers. She'd kept her blond hair highlighted and glazed since she was thirteen.

"Fuck."

Remember me?

Without hesitation, Taylor deleted the email. Out of sight, out of mind.

But reality didn't work that way, did it?

Pushing problems aside only made the pile of complications bigger.

What adult had time for stupid pranks? Not her. She had a husband. She had a job as manager of her husband's campaign. Both of which took precedence over this dumb email.

Taylor closed her laptop. From her oversized and beautifully organized closet, she selected designer black pants and a white blouse. Very demure. But her pink heels, those always made a splash.

She checked her makeup one more time in the Venetian silver mirror made from Murano glass. She always maintained the three necessities of hair, makeup, and outfit, never leaving the house without looking like a complete package. Old sorority habits were hard to lose, especially if they made sense.

A grandfather clock chimed eight times from somewhere in the house. Perfect timing.

Nothing out of place and everything in elegant order, she descended the spiral staircase toward her foyer, her heels echoing on the marble in the empty house. Well, sort of empty. Her housekeeper was around somewhere, and her chef had likely made her a green shake.

Her husband, Elijah, a congressional senator, was already at his campaign office, going hard for the upcoming election. She'd slept alone again last night. Because he'd either stayed at a hotel near his office or snuck into a guest room. Elijah said that waking a woman in a fragile state was a sin.

According to him, she was always in a fragile state. As was every other human with a pair of ovaries.

He hated that she worked and begged her to stay home like his constituents' wives. To show just how wholesome she was, so they would like her more—like *him* more. But she hadn't taken the trouble to get a political science degree, and then her law degree, only to sit on the sidelines, even if it was only to work for him. Of course, that hadn't been how it started. Taylor had political aspirations of her own. Interning at his office, then working as an aide. But her dreams of becoming a real power broker had some-how turned into her being the other half of a power couple.

So instead of running for city council and rising in the ranks of her own merit, she'd agreed to continue working for her husband. Each promise had been a step down the ladder rather than up. And two years ago, she'd promised him that as soon as they saw the pink lines for positive on a pregnancy test, she'd put in her resignation and quit working altogether.

Elijah's wife, the mother of his child, would not work and run a household.

Who even was she? Taylor five years ago would scoff at who she'd become.

So far in two years of marriage, she'd had her period every single month. They'd given it some time, her husband saying if God wanted to bless them, he would. But then she'd started to think of his age—which started with a five—and wondered if maybe it wasn't her husband. In this instance, did God really have much to do with conception? That was a question she would never dare voice aloud.

The viability inquest of her husband's sperm count, however, was solved when he'd jerked off into a cup, revealing plenty of swimmers, which meant the problem lay with her. And Taylor had been too scared to get tested—though she'd set up the appointment and canceled several times. There was Big Regret #1 that was likely to blame, and she didn't want to think about that either. The pile of *not thinking about that* was growing bigger by the second.

The entire ride to work, her phone buzzed in her purse. Even with the radio loud, the little red text message numbers on her car's display screen ticked up.

Taylor didn't want to click on it. Worried the incessant dinging had something to do with the email that was still making her hands tremble. And she needed to get over that. She had a long day of work and a campaign fundraiser tonight for Elijah. It wouldn't do for her to be out of sorts—he hated if she showed any kind of emotion in public, or in private really.

And she wanted him to win. Because his win was also hers in the twisted way her dreams had become entangled in his.

At a stoplight, she popped a bottle from her purse and swallowed a Xanax dry, realizing she'd forgotten her green shake.

The incessant buzzing continued, and in the elevator, she finally took it out, tapping a perfectly manicured nail on her text message app and seeing a name she hadn't read in ages. Brooklyn Tolley—one of her sorority sisters and college best friends. It'd been the four of them glued to one another's sides all four years—her, Brooklyn, Asana, and Annabelle—including ruling the exec board their senior year.

Together, they'd shaped Alpha Delta Lambda into what it was today, taking it from the number one top-tier at Bama to the most talked-about sorority in the nation. Incoming freshmen applied to UA just to get into ADL. The best girls, the best parties, the best charity fundraisers, the best everything.

BROOKLYN: Did you get my email?

Fury latched on, zapping the calming sensation of the Xanax and tossing it into the trash. Was this some kind of joke? What was Brooklyn thinking playing a trick like that? So un-Brooklyn of her.

> **TAYLOR:** You sent me that? What the fuck? Not funny.

> **BROOKLYN:** Um . . . are we talking about the same email?

Taylor's finger hovered over the Outlook app on her phone, but she couldn't bring herself to tap it. Opening her email account would only bring up the other one she didn't want to see. Just because it had been deleted didn't mean she'd deleted it permanently, and it probably still sat smugly at the top of the Trash folder.

> **TAYLOR:** Maybe not. What did you send?

> **BROOKLYN:** Bama alumna events for Rush Week.

Taylor frowned down at her phone, then quickly stopped, not wanting to create wrinkles. Botox was good, but it wasn't a miracle worker. Forced out of the elevator, she walked down the hall with her head high. A woman should never walk with her head down, but neck straight, if she didn't want a hunchback later in life.

Brooklyn had not been one of her "customers" in college, and really, sending a picture of Taylor's signature molly wasn't Brooklyn's style. No, Brooklyn liked pictures of *other* things.

Taylor adjusted her shoulders, hoping to roll some of the angst right off, but it settled back on her spine, like a spider clinging to its web. She hated that the email had rattled her more than it should. It's not like she was a drug dealer or something. What respectable woman didn't have a little stash of uppers and downers? What good friend didn't offer it to another who was in need?

Every time she'd gone to the ladies' room in the country club growing up, she'd witnessed pills and potions. So what? All anyone had to do was claim a little backache and they'd have a script in hand—legally.

Needing this conversation to be over before she started making campaign calls to the elite housewives in Tuscaloosa, Taylor texted one more time.

> **TAYLOR:** Sorry wrong email, lol. I'll look into it later.

> **BROOKLYN:** Hate to be a nag but, you really need to be there.

Taylor frowned down at her phone and started to type: Last time I checked, I was president of ADL when we left. But deleted it and instead clicked on a thumbs-up emoji. The old Taylor would have pressed send. Taylor hardly recognized herself anymore.

She and Brooklyn hadn't spoken in years, maybe even the five years since they'd graduated. None of them really had. Why the fuck was she texting her now and making demands?

Taylor riffled through her purse for a stick of gum, smiling at the receptionist as if nothing at all was bothering her. Perfect, perfect, perfect. Everything was fucking perfect.

But it appeared Brooklyn wasn't done texting, her words coming up on Taylor's watch face.

BROOKLYN: Someone has THE book.

The book. There was only *one book* that Brooklyn would be worried about. The Spill Book Taylor had created during Rush Week, and then brought to every sorority meeting they'd ever had, making the rushes, PNMs, and sisters all confess their darkest secrets. She'd read them all. She'd written her own.

Some were funny.

Some were sad.

Most of them were very, very bad.

That could only mean one thing. Someone had dug up the time capsule she'd buried the Spill Book in. That wasn't supposed to be done for a hundred years, on the bicentennial Founder's Day of ADL. When they were all long dead, and people could just gossip about them rather than accuse them of anything.

She'd never told anyone she put the Spill Book in the time capsule. But Taylor was pretty sure they'd suspected. Now they'd know for sure.

BROOKLYN: Did you read the emails??? They are opening the time capsule early. House Mama Jenny passed away, and her kids want her stuff out of it. Something about a ring. It's all over the news. Did you put THE BOOK in there?

But Taylor hadn't been watching the news. Not during election sweeps. It was too flustering to see people talking shit about her husband on one channel and stroking his ego on another. Her assistant kept her updated on anything important she needed to know.

The time capsule was being opened? *Now?*

Fuck.

Whoever had the book had to be the one who sent the email. Someone must have slipped in a pic of themselves taking E. But the pills weren't the only thing Taylor was hiding. Regret #1 and Regret #2 were also listed in the Spill Book. Double fuck.

BROOKLYN: Taylor? You there?

CHAPTER EIGHT

My Gucci Porter beauty case isn't just good for a makeup makeover—but a spiritual one too. Lift the false bottom and take your pick. I've got blue pills, yellow ones, and powder too. Sniff sniff, ladies.

Kisses,
Taylor

Asana

Then

"Asana Duke? Like Duke Corp?" Three ADL sisters rushed over the lawn toward them.

This was a question Asana heard often. Her dad was basically Rupert Murdoch's replacement and owned the world. Which meant she was heiress to the world.

Born into the Upper East Side of New York, practically American royalty from her first breath, her entire life had been catalogued, photographed, and printed. Even now there was probably a paparazzo asshole hiding in the bushes taking a photo of her as she left the Alpha Delta Lambda open house.

The elation of crushing this rush process and the possibility of joining a highly coveted sorority evaporated with the snap of a picture.

Coming to Alabama had been partly about getting away from

all that. Starting off in a place where she wasn't recognized. As much. The elite circles in New York were small, and most of her friends she'd known since they were pushed out into the world. Here, she could start fresh, be herself, create a whole new persona if she wanted. There was something intoxicating about the unknown. Which is probably why she didn't even tell any of her friends she'd applied or been accepted until it was too late for them to follow.

But once a Duke, always a Duke, and she supposed there was no hiding that.

And because she was a Duke, the other reason for being here was because there was a clandestine organization on campus that her father seemed to think she wouldn't be able to infiltrate. Challenge accepted, Daddy.

"Yes," she said with a cheerful smile, hoping that would mean she was at least going to get an invitation back to ADL on Preference Day.

If she was going to give up her life in New York City for the South, she might as well go big or go back home.

The enamored smiles on the sisters' faces were telling: she was in if she showed up doing all the right things.

"Thanks for coming today. We hope you'll be back."

"I will. Everyone has been so welcoming."

"See you tomorrow, then."

"See you." Asana swept her hair over her shoulder as she turned away from the sisters, realizing she was absolutely going to rule this place one day.

She and her new friends reached the end of the brick walkway leading toward the sidewalk when another girl, dressed in a short white tennis skirt and ADL tank top jogged up to block their path. "Asana, hi."

Asana didn't recognize her, nor was she surprised the ADL sister knew her name. That happened a lot. People thought they knew her because they read about her in the tabloids or watched her on social media. But what they didn't realize was that everything they read or saw was carefully curated. Orchestrated and then implemented.

And one day Asana was going to be the one planting stories, making her family and her daddy's mega company shine.

"Have we met?" This was Asana's typical response—a reminder to whoever the stranger was that, no indeed, they weren't acquainted and they should back off. She realized a beat too late that she shouldn't pull that here. During Rush Week, she wasn't at the top. Not yet, anyway. And she needed to make good impressions only.

The sister cocked her head, eyes squinted as she regarded Asana, the expression acknowledging that Asana had made a faux pas. "I was wondering if I might have a word?"

"Of course." Asana, needing a redo, glanced at her new friends and said, "I'll be right back."

The ADL sister linked arms with her and led her back inside the floral-perfume-scented house and down one of the long hallways to a quiet room that miraculously none of the PNMs crawling all over the building had raided yet.

The sister tugged her toward a small sofa and sat down, Asana sitting beside her.

"Can you keep a secret?" The ADL sister leaned close, her eyes taking on a little bit of a fiery, frenzied look.

Asana wanted to say it depended on the secret, but given this was obviously a test, instead she said, "Always."

The sister smiled, showing her perfect, white, straight teeth. "Are you scared of the dark?"

That was an odd fucking question. "No."

"What do you think about secret societies?"

Asana kept her face neutral. Ordinarily she might have gotten a creepy vibe from a conversation like this, but a secret society was half the reason she'd sent in her application. "Like a sorority?" Asana played coy.

"Kind of." The sister folded her hands primly in her lap, showing off a silver ring with two keys crossed over each other like pirate bones on her middle finger.

Bingo.

Asana narrowed her eyes, not letting it show she was fully aware of who this student represented. "Are you getting all skull and crossbones on me? *Dead Poets Society* is one of my all-time fave classics."

The sister laughed. "Carpe diem."

Asana also laughed, but hers was fake. "I didn't catch your name?"

The sister ignored her. "You're going to be perfect."

Not even a few days on campus and she was already getting what she wanted. "For?" Asana pressed her hands into her knees, ready to leave.

"For everything." The sister's smile was definitely a nine out of ten for strange.

Asana was having a hard time deciding whether to laugh at the absurdity of this conversation or tell whoever this sister was to fuck off.

"I'll take that as a compliment," Asana said tightly, standing up.

The sister stood as well—too close. "We hide in plain sight."

"Are you a pap?" Asana fake groaned, still playacting. "This is just messed up. I can't believe this."

The sister gripped her forearm, her face turning serious. "I'm not paparazzi. Sorry, you're just the perfect recruit."

"For the sorority?" Asana shook the sister's hold loose, her pitch rising slightly in annoyance. Presenting her with the society was one thing, but touching her? Just no.

"Yeah." But the slight tilt of the sister's lips said that there was much more behind that small word. "I'll be in touch."

"Thanks." Asana smiled, intrigued, triumphant, and a little creeped out. She'd thought it was going to be harder to find them, but they'd made a beeline for her. Why?

"You can go now."

For a split second Asana was going to ask why, but decided against it. Let this girl think she had the upper hand.

So instead, Asana nodded and hurried out of the small den, finding her friends outside. The warmth of the sun on her skin took some of the chill that seriously abnormal girl had brought on. By the time she was standing beside Brooklyn, Annabelle, and Taylor, she'd managed to shake off some of the vibe.

"What was that all about?" Brooklyn asked.

"She wanted my autograph." Asana rolled her eyes. "Annoying. I'm not even famous."

"You are though," Brooklyn said. "You're famous for being famous. Like the Kardashians and Paris Hilton."

"I should have listened to my dad and brought a detail." The last thing she'd wanted was for one of those assholes to follow her around.

"Personal security?" Brooklyn asked with a wiggle of her brows. "Are they hot?"

"Sometimes." Asana winked, letting that one gesture play out in their minds.

Taylor wrinkled her brow. "Aren't they old?"

Asana laughed. "Not that old. They have to be in shape and have plenty of stamina."

"Maybe you *should* get a detail," Brooklyn teased. "We won't mind."

"A detail would probably hurt your chances though," Annabelle said. "Panhellenic secrets are meant for sisters only."

Asana blinked, Annabelle's words a stark reminder of the strange conversation she'd just had.

"True. And I wouldn't want to ruin my chances."

"Besides, a detail might put a damper on some of the fun we'll have at the frat parties." Brooklyn did a little twerking move.

"Shh . . . ohmygod, stop," Taylor said, her furtive eyes checking to see who might have heard and seen. "No talking about boys."

"Right, oops." Brooklyn stopped dancing, pinching her lips like she was locking up the word.

All these rules. Asana wasn't used to following rules. But she wanted to be a part of Greek Life. Wanted the sisterhood that came with it. Lifelong companions. The comradery of sharing secrets with friends. Living in the sorority house. It just seemed like icing on a delicious cupcake.

"We're going to make it," she said to the three of them. "Alpha Delta Lambda is going to be ours."

"Can you imagine if one day we're on the exec board? The four of us?" Taylor gushed.

"I can," Annabelle said, and the smile she gave seemed to be the first genuine one Asana had seen today. Funny how she hadn't noticed before.

Annabelle was really good at masking. And Asana was pretty good at picking up on that, especially since her daily life included wearing a mask.

"Let's do another video out here," Asana suggested. "Feed the beast."

Brooklyn gave an excited whoop and pulled out her cell phone. "I got this." They all fixed their hair, added another layer of lip gloss, and then showed off for the camera.

Part II

PHILANTHROPY

Working together to achieve a common goal . . .

CHAPTER NINE

Katy Perry isn't the only one who kissed a girl and liked it . . . I bet you want to know who it was. I'll give you a hint: she tasted like cherry ChapStick, whiskey, and lemonade.

Kisses,
Asana

Annabelle

Now

There's a difference between appearing authentic and true authenticity. Annabelle was an expert at blurring the lines.

With a comforting touch to the trophy diamond at her throat, Annabelle took one exceedingly long last look at herself in her Mercedes rearview mirror, sparkling lip gloss, perfectly straight lightened hair that hid the fact she was a natural brunette. And she hadn't looked herself in her real eyes in at least five years. Her contacts were tinted so she had hazel irises versus brown. Even her eyebrows were bleached to fit in with what people expected. And by people, she meant her mother, and the half of Tuscaloosa who thought she was Greg's arm candy.

In fact, when Liam was born with dark hair, even Greg had questioned his paternity until she reminded him, under her breath, she was actually a brunette. As their son had aged, he looked like the perfect cross between them. Her natural hair and eye color, her olive skin, Greg's nose and brows. Her husband conceded, but she'd thought he'd insist on a DNA test, which was ridiculous, because he was the only one screwing around in their relationship, not to mention she'd been a virgin.

And considering what she'd known about him prior to saying "I do," there was really no surprise. Most women believed they could change a man by locking him down. That they would be the one thing that would turn him from a womanizer. Laughable. Greg was only ever going to do what Greg wanted. There were no consequences for him. Never had been. Never would.

If having secondhand embarrassment at yourself was a thing, Annabelle for sure had it for her naive college-aged self. But knowing what she knew now, would she have changed course?

Probably not. And she didn't expect anyone to understand. Greg was her insurance policy. The best criminal lawyer in town, with a powerful judge as a father. And they had a child—the moment she'd found out had sealed the deal.

Annabelle twirled the emerald on her finger three times for luck, and then, climbing from the car in her priority parking spot, was instantly surrounded by hundreds of young women. Dressed in their Lulu skirts, On Cloud sneakers, and Greek Life T-shirts, with mini-backpacks and rush bags, they swarmed Magnolia Drive the same way fences swarmed a new mark.

Potential New Members.

Potential New Marks.

The innocent and not so innocent.

They reminded her so much of when she'd first walked down sorority row. Staring up at the big brick houses, white columns, massive Greek letters, and balloon arches.

Maybe it was a good thing she'd come back here. A chance to see her friends, reconnect, right the wrongs. What she didn't want to admit was that some part of her needed them, needed to come clean. And that the need to come clean might also mean changing a world she'd grown tremendously accustomed to.

She couldn't help smiling through the anxiety of seeing her mother today. And being found lacking. By now, nearly three decades into life, she should be used to it. But for some reason, Annabelle couldn't stop trying to impress Lily.

Annabelle swung her pink bag over her shoulder. In her pink leather, gold-column-heeled Louboutin sandals, she walked as though she didn't have a mom-sized weight on her shoulders toward the Alpha Delta Lambda house.

"Love your bag," one of the actives gushed as she passed by, flashing her recently whitened teeth.

"Thank you." Annabelle smiled, remembering a time when she was so carefree. Before marriage and motherhood left her feeling less than human.

Lily Walker exited the wide front doors of the house as if she were still president, and it was still 1998. Dressed in white pants, a white blouse, and a pink scarf elegantly tied around her neck, she stood there, ankles pressed together, feet in pink rhinestone kitten heels, no doubt Versace. Lily's designer fashion taste was probably the only thing she'd passed down to Annabelle.

Her mother had the strangest Spidey-sense to Annabelle's presence, and it never ceased to impress and terrify her. She hadn't even bothered trying to sneak out as a teenager, because Lily would almost certainly be waiting on the other side of the door.

"Darling." Lily held out her arms in greeting, her eyes scanning Annabelle from the top of her highlighted hair down to her bubble-gum-pink-painted toenails. "You look lovely."

Annabelle smiled, mumbled a thank-you, and gave her mother a hug that felt more like a stiff bump of two bodies than the warm, motherly hugs she'd always coveted.

"The girls were just sharing with me that you donated the Tiffany tea parties. Why didn't you tell me?"

Annabelle shrugged, because the answer was that she didn't tell her mother a lot of things; to do so was only to invite criticism and to learn how her mother did it better. Being married to Greg was enough of an ego beating; she didn't need to add her mother's opinions on top of that.

"Don't shrug, dear." Lily frowned, the turn of her lip lasting less than a fraction of a second, and her forehead never moving at all. But even just that tiny hint was enough of an admonition.

Annabelle dutifully straightened her shoulders, and wondered why her mother didn't ask about her grandson. Then again, the only interest Lily had ever taken in Liam was to make sure everyone knew he was born "premature." Math and reputations mattered.

She followed her mother over the threshold of ADL, her heels clicking on the marble tiles. Everything still looked the same, even smelled the same. A combination of hair products, candles, and perfume. Despite the fact that the kitchen was in constant cook mode, there wasn't even a little hint of food odors.

Never one to stick around for long, Lily slipped away from Annabelle's side, taking some of the inevitable pressure with her. Annabelle wandered the house, touching the surfaces within reach, pocketing a pencil left on a table.

So far, she hadn't seen Taylor, Asana, or Brooklyn, and it occurred to her that maybe she should have reached out to confirm they'd even be here. Not that it would have changed her RSVP. She needed to find out what happened to the Spill Book.

Meandering back toward the foyer in search of her friends, Annabelle was practically accosted by four incredibly blond, tan young women, all with blinding smiles. The right look. The look she'd been trying to achieve since she'd been old enough to be cognizant of expectations.

"You must be Annabelle Walker."

Annabelle greeted the new executive board, studying each of their faces to see if they might have been the ones to send the anonymous note. But they all seemed more in awe than vindictive.

"Has the time capsule already been dug up?" Annabelle asked.

The sisters glanced back and forth at one another, then one leaned in, conspiratorially whispering, "Well, yes, but don't tell. We had to give back the ring."

"The ring?"

They nodded in unison. "Mama Jenny apparently put a ring in the time capsule and her family wanted it back. They said it was in her will."

Annabelle's belly fluttered. "It was already returned to them?"

Again, they nodded in unison. If they'd had to sift through the time capsule . . . had they found the Spill Book in there?

"So, you all looked through the time capsule already?"

"Oh no!" their president said, shaking her head with exaggerated force, and then fixing her hair when a strand fell against her cheek. "We would never. That's for Bid Day."

Four sets of comically wide eyes stared at her, but Annabelle had been sifting through lies for years—and was herself an excellent prevaricator. They could feign innocence for days if they wanted, it wasn't going to make her believe them. Still, they were giving away no hints about the one question she had—was the Spill Book in the time capsule?

"How was the ring located, then?" Annabelle kept her voice soft, inviting.

All four of them pinkened, as if a makeup artist had come by with Rare Beauty liquid blush and swiped Bliss on their cheeks.

One of them opened their mouth to answer, but before their lies could reach Annabelle's ears, the words were drowned out by the classic ADL door stack chant, whirling Annabelle back in time.

CHAPTER TEN

When I tell people a gift is from my daddy, they definitely take it the wrong way. My daddy is definitely not my father, and this sugar is definitely not his baby.

Kisses,
Brooklyn

Taylor

Then

Taylor's phone chimed with several texts from her friends. She didn't like to be summoned, not even by her boyfriend Brad, who had abs that could cut glass. However, in this instance with her new friends, she decided to give them a pass. After all, it was for a good cause. And, let's face it, she was the hottest.

Brad's dick came out of her mouth with an audible pop. "Sorry, baby," she said, holding up her phone. "I've got to go."

"What? Were you on your phone just now while you sucked—"

Taylor stood, leaning over his almost naked body, her breasts brushing his chest as she gave him a deep, wet kiss. "Just a little taste of what's to come later—me."

Brad groaned and grabbed her ass, trying to keep her right where she was.

"Later, baby," she crooned. "I already showered. And I have to go. Get dressed."

Ignoring his protests, she left her dorm room to find her girls in the hallway outside.

"Everybody crowd in, we're doing an OOTD together this morning." Brooklyn held open her door and waved them inside.

Taylor made sure she was first—a precedent she'd set. If she was going to be president of ADL—because of course she'd get a bid—then she needed them to know she was their leader. There was no other alternative. Go big or go home.

Brooklyn's sleepy roommate rolled over in bed and pulled the covers up over her head—she wasn't into Greek Life and, according to Brooklyn, had let her know it. As soon as Taylor had found that out, she never bothered to learn the loser's name.

Annabelle and Asana whispered "good morning" as they watched Brooklyn set up her phone on a ring light tripod, but Taylor gave her "good morning" the full force of her cheer voice, eliciting a groan from the bed rotter.

"Okay, I'm going to hit record, and we'll say 'good morning,' then line up one behind the other and say our outfits," Brooklyn instructed. "I'll go first so you can see how it's done."

They nodded, and Taylor resisted the urge to let Brooklyn know she should go first. Another concession for a good cause.

"Good morning! Brooklyn in Bama here. It's our first day of Philanthropy for Bama Rush, and me and my new rush sisters are going to do a little OOTD for you! Today my skirt is from Revolve. My T-shirt is for Philanthropy, which we received at Convocation." Brooklyn turned sideways and did a little look over her shoulder as she lifted her foot behind her and grabbed her heel. "Wedges from Steve Madden. Jewelry from my daddy, enewton, Amazon, and Target."

Brooklyn stepped out of the way for Taylor to go next. Taylor gave a sunshine wave and smiled into the camera. "Heyyy, good morning, y'all! I'm Taylor." She did a little curtsy. "My skirt is from Altar'd State, my shirt is for Philanthropy." She did the same pose as Brooklyn, and then kicked up her heel, but added a peace sign and a wink. "Sandals from Kate Spade. My Love bracelet is from Cartier." She continued to point everything out, then blew a kiss to the camera before giving up the limelight to Asana, who appeared almost bored.

With Asana and Annabelle finishing up their outfits of the day, Brooklyn waved them all back to the camera, and they all told the world to wish them luck.

"And uploaded to TikTok. You guys ready?" Brooklyn picked up her rush bag.

"I was born for this," Annabelle said, and something about her tone implied the seriousness of that statement.

Taylor marched to the door, leading them outside.

The sun was barely peeking over the horizon as they joined the other rushees out on the road, all of them trekking toward Magnolia. Her stomach fluttered with excitement, and nerves. ADL was going to be hers. She hadn't told her friends yet about her future as their president, and it almost burst out of her right then and there. Only because of the current thrill of the row did she manage to rein it in.

Greek Row was alive with cheer when they arrived. All the Potential New Members were crowding around, waiting for the moment when the sorority house doors would open and invite them in.

"I'm nervous, are you nervous?" Brooklyn asked.

"No," Asana said, looking almost annoyed to be standing there.

"We've got this," Annabelle said. "We're already sisters."

Taylor smirked. "Fake it until you make it."

"That's what she said," Asana teased.

All of a sudden the door to Alpha Delta Lambda opened to reveal the actives stacked in the entryway. Some kneeled, some bent over, some stood, and the rows of waving of young women dressed in cute skirts with matching shirts with their Greek letters printed on the front—A Δ Λ—extended into the recesses of the house. The ADL sisters started to clap and sing, and the crowd of PNMs went silent, taking it all in.

"A-L-P-H-A, D-E-L-T-and-A, L-A-M-B-and-D-and-A, we're Alpha Delta Lambda, sisters forever happily, come on in and join us, for Philanthropy. Alpha Delta Lambda! Alpha Delta Lambda! ADL for life!"

Taylor started to clap and chant, "ADL for life," along with the other PNMs, adding in a few cheer moves for good measure. All of the PNMs rushed the door, eager to go inside and learn more about the philanthropic endeavors of the sorority.

"I'm so excited to learn more about their philanthropy," Taylor said. "I love dogs so much."

"Is that what they do? The Humane Society?" Asana asked.

"They do more than one," Annabelle answered.

"I love dogs." Brooklyn pressed her hands to her heart. "Do you think we get to play with any?"

"I hear we get to do yoga with puppies," Taylor squealed.

"It's true, they've been doing philanthropy for animals since my mom was in ADL," Annabelle said with the type of authority Taylor found dismissive, and too much like she might compete with her for president.

"My mom said the same thing," Taylor said with a smile, reminding Annabelle that she wasn't the only one who was a legacy.

Annabelle flashed her a genuine smile that Taylor found unnerving. "We need to find a pic of them and re-create it. How
funny would that be?"

Taylor smiled. "Very."

"The past and the present colliding." Asana's tone held a
measure of dry sarcasm to it that seemed to be her signature.

"Darling."

All four of them turned to see Lily Walker sauntering toward
them, dressed to the nines. Was she always here? Taylor glanced
at Annabelle, wondering if she felt as awkward with having her
mother there as Taylor did. This was a time for actives and PNMs,
not alumni. She refrained from rolling her eyes, and was glad she
did or else she would have missed the judgmental way Annabelle's mother examined her, and the subtle shift in Annabelle's
demeanor. Lily Walker appeared to have the ability to sap her
daughter's joy. Damn, if her mother looked at her like that . . .
Nobody messed with her sisters like that. Not even their flesh and
blood.

"I love that blouse, Mrs. Walker." Taylor's smile was innocent
as she scanned the white silk. "My mom wore one like that on our
trip to Italy last year."

Lily Walker's plastic smile faltered. "I'm sure she didn't. This is
from the Valentino exhibit that happened in spring."

"Then it's definitely the same. My mom gets a preview." She
smiled so sweetly, she hoped Lily Walker puked on the sugar.
"Will you take a pic of us? This is the second best day of the rest
of our lives."

Taylor held out her phone.

"Wait, use mine," Brooklyn said. "I can use my photo app."

Lily Walker took Brooklyn's phone and Taylor smiled not just
for the camera but for putting Annabelle's mom back in her place.

CHAPTER ELEVEN

A tisket, a tasket.
This lipstick wasn't in my basket.
Blah blah blah blah blah blah
I dropped it, I dropped it,
And then I put it in my pocket.
But let's be honest, shoplifting isn't nearly as much
fun as taking from someone else.

Kisses,
Annabelle

Brooklyn

Now

Brooklyn stepped out of her Uber and back in time.

She heard only the last lines of the door stack chant, but it hadn't changed in the nine years since she was a freshman at Bama. Hair freshly blown out, pink mani-pedi done, and a new romper purchased, she made her way toward her old house, with the white **A Δ Λ** Greek letters freshly washed on the brick-and-column facade, and pink balloons in various shades creating an arch over the door.

A woman walked past who from the back looked an awful lot like Annabelle, only her hair was nearly blond.

"Brooklyn."

She'd recognize that cool voice anywhere. Brooklyn rounded to find Asana strutting toward her. Managing to add her signature catwalk hip swish while still being New York executive fast, Asana reached her in seconds.

"You look fantastic." Brooklyn leaned in to kiss Asana on her cool cheek, in stark contrast to how hot she felt.

Florida was hot, but Alabama managed to make even Tampa feel like its temperatures were moderate.

"Ginger Mommy is looking hot AF." Asana grinned and kissed her cheek back.

"Don't say that too loud—I'm trying to blend in." Brooklyn gave an exaggerated side-eye.

"Honey, with that flaming red hair, you'll fail every time."

"I didn't think I'd be back here so soon." Brooklyn glanced up at the house, and then around at all the PNMs. There weren't too many alumni present, and she couldn't help but wonder if the four of them had been the only ones invited to attend.

"I didn't think I'd be back here ever."

Asana's confession surprised Brooklyn. "Really? But you loved ADL."

"I did." Asana squinted toward the house. "But the things we love the most should always be set free, right?"

Brooklyn smirked. "Why do I have the feeling you're talking about something else?"

"Because I'm always talking about something else." Asana flashed her signature publicity smile, then grabbed Brooklyn's hand. "Come on. I'm pretty sure I saw Annabelle already go inside, and you know Taylor will make a late entrance for full effect."

"You're mean." But Brooklyn laughed as she said it, because it was absolutely true. Taylor loved to make an entrance and have every eye on her.

"I love her, we all do, but you know it's true."

"It's absolutely true."

They paused outside the door for a selfie for Brooklyn to use on her Ginger Mommy page. In less than thirty seconds she'd posted and hashtagged it #sistersforlife #gingermommy #brooklyninbama #adlalumni.

Inside the house, the actives and execs were lined up greeting everyone.

"Asana and Brooklyn. I'm Larissa, president of ADL." Larissa stepped forward, perfectly platinum, pink, and pretty. She wore a paisley scarf as a headband that struck a memory. "It is so good to meet y'all. We still watch you all's TikToks from back in the day."

Brooklyn pretended not to be offended by that—they weren't that old.

"I can't believe they are still viewable," Asana said.

"Ginger Mommy reposts," Brooklyn said.

"Such an honor, really. Annabelle just walked through there." The president pointed toward their old living room, where Brooklyn saw the same statuesque blond she'd thought was Annabelle earlier.

"Where did you get that scarf?" Brooklyn asked. She had definitely seen it before, she just couldn't put her finger on it.

"Oh?" Larissa tapped the silk bow on top of her head and laughed. "This old thing? Found it in a local thrift shop. Why? Do you like it?"

Brooklyn nodded, smiling though it didn't reach her eyes. Where had she seen that before?

"Thank you," Asana said, and tugged Brooklyn away. "Why are you being so weird about the scarf?"

"I don't know. It just looks familiar."

"Looked like something Lily Walker would wear, that's probably why. Anyways, speaking of Lily, Annabelle's full-on blond now? Her transformation into Lily Walker is complete."

Brooklyn could only shake her head. Annabelle had been struggling to push herself out of Lily's shadow her whole life, and from the looks of things, she'd sunk right in instead.

CHAPTER TWELVE

I don't know why they call it hazing. It's just a few challenges to test for spirit, merit, and loyalty. If you can't handle a little initiation test, get the fuck out of here.

Kisses,
Taylor

Asana

Then

"What are you looking for in a sisterhood?"

Asana blinked away the exhaustion of the last several days. She'd never say it aloud, but rushing was harder than any of the modeling she'd ever done, including for Versace in Rome. Both of them incorporated a level of performance, measurements, and judging. But with modeling, as soon as she tossed off the latest designer fashion, she went back to her hotel room and ate for the first time in weeks.

Rushing meant practically starving and being dehydrated and judged for days on end. The correlations didn't go unnoticed.

But still, in the end, Asana believed rushing, belonging to a sisterhood, was going to be worth it. Besides, ADL would be the perfect cover for the other society she hoped to join.

And this question about sisterhood, she'd answered it at six different parties already, six different ways. ADL had been last on her invite list, and that was good, because it was the one she'd been practicing for. Every other house up to this point had been a rehearsal.

Keeping her voice soft but not monotone, assertive but not overbearing, Asana answered the question. "I'm really looking for a tight-knit group of girls. In the high school I went to, friendships were more like playing competitive sports. There was a lot of backstabbing, and not a lot of support. I want to be a part of a sisterhood that cares about each other, and has each other's backs." Asana offered a rare smile. "In the past few days, the sisters of ADL have really become women I look up to. I want to be involved not only in the house philanthropy but also in all of the events, get-togethers, sisterhood bonding activities. Dinner in the dining hall. Roommates. Makeover nights. All of it."

The rigid and skeptical way the sister stood in front of her reminded Asana of the head mistress at her school, just waiting for the perfect misstep to pounce. "Where did you go to school?"

"Starling Prep on the Upper East Side of Manhattan."

"New York?"

Asana cocked her head to the side, wondering if there was a Manhattan somewhere else. "Yes."

"I have to ask, with all the Ivies, why did you come south?" The active gave a saccharine smile that Asana wanted to wipe off her face.

"For the same reasons I want to be a sister of ADL. The atmosphere is different here. Softer, kinder. I know it sounds cliché, but I love the Southern charm." Asana laughed and shrugged, then she leaned in like she was going to reveal a secret. "To be honest, between all the modeling shoots and boring board meetings my dad made me sit in on, I'm ready to live my life the way I want."

The sister's eyes widened just like every other active who'd interviewed her prior. Mention of her rich life sans the forbidden bad word "bucks," and she had an in. People liked power. Flaunting it without saying it worked like a charm.

Bonus—she stopped asking why Asana came south.

Asana worked the rest of the room, feeling confident in all her answers. She hadn't trained at the knee of one of the most impressive communications moguls for nothing. She'd been groomed for this. Making people like her and see things her way.

And what she said wasn't a lie, that was the beauty of being a chameleon. She was everything they wanted and loved all at once.

"What is she wearing?" Annabelle shifted next to her. "I'm having secondhand embarrassment."

"She's on my team," Brooklyn said.

A young woman entered the house dressed in jean-short overalls and cowboy boots. She wore the Philanthropy T-shirt, but she'd cut a V at the chest. The look was casual and fun, and Asana would have loved to rock it. But she knew instantly it wasn't rush-worthy. Asana grimaced. Trained in public relations and communications, she knew this was a nightmare for the PNM. "I have to go talk to her."

Annabelle held her arm. "You can't. If they see you talking to her, that's going to be points against you. There's a reason all of us look the same." She pointed around the room to all the cute skirts and uncut shirts. "Appearance matters."

"True. But I'd want someone to tell me." Because knowledge mattered too. Asana hurried forward. "Hey, I'm Asana."

The girl looked nervous, eyeing Asana's skirt and shoes, and then her own outfit. "It's a lot dressier than I thought."

Asana nodded. "Yeah, that's what I was coming to tell you. There's still like thirty minutes left of this party if you live close enough by to change. Which I would advise."

A sheen of tears glimmered in her eyes. "I'm already late."

Asana narrowed her eyes. She knew manufactured tears when she saw them. "That's not good."

"I couldn't help it. I had a flat tire." There was a tinge of whininess to her voice that screamed fake.

The bullshit radar that had been developed over years of dealing with not only the press but her father's colleagues went off inside Asana's head.

"But it's not a big deal." The young woman smiled and whipped out a notebook. "I don't need to dress like you."

"No, no," Asana said, still not one hundred percent on her hunch. "Put that away. You have to memorize your answers, not read them from your notes."

The girl laughed, drawing the attention of others. "Oh, you think I'm here as a recruit. That's sweet."

Asana frowned. Fuck. This was why her father always said to listen to her gut. "If you're going to act like you belong here, then you should know, it's Potential New Member. But I suggest you leave before people figure out what your intentions are."

"Whatever." The girl gave a dismissive wave that made Asana want to snatch her notebook and start shredding it into a million pieces. "I'm here for *The Crimson White*, and I have no problem saying that."

Asana glanced sideways at Annabelle, wishing she'd followed her friend's advice. She never had a bleeding heart. Dammit. "No comment." When in doubt, fall back. She turned her back on the student reporter and returned to Annabelle and Brooklyn's side. "Is she even allowed in here?"

"I don't think so."

Even as the words were coming out of Annabelle's mouth, Riley, the president of the sorority, was escorting the young woman out of the house. But not before she tossed Asana a scathing look.

After shutting the reporter firmly out, Riley marched over to where Asana was. Hand on her popped hip, she appraised Asana the same way Annabelle's mother had judged her.

"Why were you talking to that trash?" she practically snarled. Several actives appeared behind her, lining up like guards.

That was a bit harsh. Asana calculated her answers, slotting them in one by one. Keeping her expression apologetic, her stand straight, she said, "I thought she was a PNM and I was trying to tell her she wasn't dressed appropriately. As soon as I found out who she actually was I excused myself." Asana smiled and shook her head, self-deprecating. "Sisters are supposed to help each other. I can't believe she tried to take advantage."

Riley's pursed lips fell back into their natural formation. "I can't believe the nerve either. They've been trying to get intel on what happens during rush forever. But it's against the rules to come inside."

"Maybe if she dressed better, none of us would have known," a second active member said.

"I might have." Asana cocked her head, staring toward the closed door. "It's sort of a knack of mine. Seeing through people."

"It's true," Annabelle offered. "I've seen her in action."

Riley assessed Asana with renewed interest. "Is that so? Show me."

Asana grinned, eager to wipe the slate clean of her faux pas. "Who?"

The mischievous grin on Riley's face made her uncomfortable. "Her."

She pointed at Taylor. Asana regretted instantly her cockiness. It was either take Taylor down in order to put herself ahead or risk being cut from the sorority for saying no.

Back at Starling Prep, the answer would have been simple. But here, in this environment, where so much of what she wanted was on the line, including Taylor, Asana couldn't do it.

"I'm so sorry." She pressed her hand over her heart. "I just wouldn't feel right about doing that to a potential sister and new friend."

Riley's smile widened, as if she'd just been given the keys to a very large and overly full designer closet. "You passed the test."

Asana smiled, though her mouth tasted bitter. A prickle on the back of her neck had her turning slightly to see an active staring at her from across the room—the same one who'd pulled her into the small den on Convocation Day. The way she was smiling now was more than a little unnerving.

When was she going to invite her to be a recruit for the society?

CHAPTER THIRTEEN

I hate the chants. It's prob why I cheer the loudest, so no one will notice how utterly ridiculous I think we all look. But at least it's better than the black cloaks and hoods I wear in my not-so-secret secret society. ADL for life!

Kisses,
Asana

Taylor

Now

Timing the perfect entrance was an art. If you were too early, then no one would notice. A blip on society's radar. Unnoticed. If you were too late, the potential for notice dropped exponentially as people already had plenty of time to engage with others.

The perfect entrance involved arriving at the precise moment prior to their attention being fully engaged, but just after the initial excitement of their own arrival dimmed. Because of this, she insisted to be the one to cue her husband before every political event to time his entrance. And she was damned good at it.

The green manicured lawn of Alpha Delta Lambda was clear, as were the overly watered lawns of every other house on Magnolia.

"Perfect," Taylor murmured as she sauntered up the brick walk-way to the impressive front stairs she'd climbed thousands of times before. Her stairs.

She drew in a deep breath at the door and was about to reach for the handle when it creaked open and Lily Walker of all people ushered her in with a wave and an exacting smile.

"You're late," she said under her breath, with more than a hint of disgust. For the entire four years Taylor had spent at Bama, Lily had not been a fan. Seemed like things hadn't changed.

"You haven't aged a bit," Taylor said, pressing a fake kiss to Lily's collagen-pumped cheek. Of course, she had aged, just no one could tell underneath all the filler and Botox.

"Can't say the same for you, dear." Lily's voice was as syrupy sweet as Taylor's.

"Oops, careful." Taylor brushed at an imaginary speck on Lily's shoulder. "Your envy was showing."

The two of them stared at each other for half a breath before Taylor turned her back on the old bitch and made her way toward the dining hall of ADL, where she could hear a mesmerizing chant going on.

Taylor lingered in the doorway, watching for half a second be-fore the chant ended, and the room of a hundred pairs of eyes turned toward her. A feeling close to euphoria curled over her limbs. She got high on attention. Forgot how good it felt to be the one in the spotlight. For several years now, it had been all about Elijah, and Taylor had gotten lost in the frenzy of his power and ambition.

As she tried to soften the bitter smile that took hold, her aware-ness settled toward the rear of the room.

Leaning against the back wall were the three women she'd once claimed were her sisters for life. A lot had changed, and yet, so much had stayed the same. Despite what had happened, she still yearned to run toward them. Hug them. Brooklyn grinned, clapping and waving. Annabelle was a bit more stoic, but still smiled. Asana wore her typical resting bitch face. To be fair, she looked like a bitch even when she smiled. Even when she came.

Asana's eyes met hers, and for the briefest of moments, she could have sworn that stoic and stony expression flickered with remembered heat. Taylor drew in a shaky breath, plastered a smile on her face, and focused on Annabelle and Brooklyn, who were waving her over.

Taylor hurried around the room, the click of her heels fading into the chant onstage about the animal shelters they would support this semester.

"Dr. Collins," Brooklyn teased out as she pulled her in for a hug.

Taylor snickered. "I'm not really a doctor."

"You have a law degree, right? Isn't that what JD stands for— juris *doctor*?" Brooklyn lifted a shoulder. "Own it."

Taylor rolled her eyes.

Annabelle tucked her arms around Taylor's shoulders, surrounding her with the same Versace perfume she wore in college. Though her body was warm, there was a distance in that closely held hug that felt cold.

"You look stunning." Annabelle tapped Taylor's earrings, two-carat pink diamonds that she'd worn especially for today. "Nice choice."

"I thought you'd appreciate them." Taylor turned to Asana, who was staring at her in a way that was indecipherable. "Hey."

"Hey." Asana leaned forward, and Taylor kissed her cheek, pulling her in for a tentative hug. Memory flooded her of sultry nights, days spent caring for animals in a shelter, quiet study hours where they'd make eyes over their textbooks. Drunken hours of playing Heads Up! with their phones until they fell over laugh-crying.

They'd not seen each other since college, but there'd been more than one day since then that she'd thought about her. Regret filled Taylor for how Asana had hurt her and never even tried to make amends. And now here they were, acting like nothing had happened. Maybe, sometimes, forgiving and forgetting helped people move forward. But did she want to?

"Campaign manager for a senator." Asana smirked, the first grin since Taylor had entered the house. "I'm surprised you haven't surpassed your husband yet. Or at least changed your mind about becoming the first female president to become a pharmacist instead."

Taylor grinned, a snarky reply about never seeing a pill she didn't like on the tip of her tongue, until she remembered why she was here. There was a reason she'd been nicknamed the Pharmacist in college.

She sank into the line with her friends, each of them pretending to listen to the presentation on ADL's philanthropy on the makeshift stage, each of them really thinking about the reasons. Taylor scanned the room of actives, PNMs, and a few other alumni, recognizing some and not others.

"Anyone seen the time capsule?" Taylor whispered.

"Not yet. But the president was acting super weird about it. I know they opened it to take out Jenny's ring, and I think they may have already sifted through the contents. I know I would," Annabelle said. "Tell me you didn't . . ."

"Obvi, I did. Think that's how whoever it is got"—Taylor swallowed, realizing that this entire thing was her fault—"the book?"

"I don't know." Annabelle shrugged, her eyes shifting away.

A few minutes went by with Taylor feeling more antsy than the pill she'd taken before arriving could handle. The only way she was going to calm down was to find the capsule and see for herself.

She excused herself to use the restroom, catching a glare from Lily on her way out. A glance behind her showed she wasn't being followed, so she bypassed the ladies' room and went out to the rear garden.

Stepping through the door felt like stepping through time. Nothing had changed. The same wrought iron tables on the paver patio. The same pink and white roses spilling from pots along the brick-walled patio, and the garden itself was alive with color and fragrance.

They'd buried the capsule back here in the center of the garden, just in front of the fountain, a baby elephant that spewed water from his trunk, a symbol of their sorority. Sure enough, the exact spot was cordoned off with pink and white twisted rope. In the center of the ground was a gaping hole. But when she peered down the deep cavernous hole, the time capsule she'd purchased on Etsy wasn't there, just more dirt. Where would they have put the capsule? And what had she actually planned to do, ruin her manicure by digging in the dirt?

"Looking for something?"

Taylor whirled around at the sound of the familiar, controlled voice. Asana stood behind her, arms crossed over her chest. There'd been no sound of her approach, meaning she could have been on Taylor's heels or only just arrived.

"Did I scare you?" Asana asked with a confident smirk.

"What makes you think that?" Taylor tried for the same control, the same poise, that always made Asana seem untouchable.

Asana moved forward to look into the void. "Wouldn't be the first time."

Taylor's mouth went dry at all the secrets and memories they held. Years' worth scribbled onto paper, and etched in ink from a photo.

"How is Mr. Power?" Asana asked.

Taylor bristled at the nickname Asana had given her husband—and the connotation behind it, that Taylor was Mrs. Powerless. "That's not his name."

Asana shrugged as if she didn't really care, and the truth was, she probably didn't. Did Asana care about anything?

"He's fine." Taylor bit her lip. "Where do you think they are keeping it?"

Asana glanced around the empty garden. "My guess is in the basement vault."

"And only the president and house mother have a key." Which meant right now, there were only two people that had the key—Larissa, who was looking guiltier by the day, and the new house mother.

Asana ran a hand through her short-cropped blond hair. "Who is the new house mother?"

Taylor had been waiting to share what she'd overheard. "You'll never guess. I don't think Annabelle knows."

Asana's eyes widened. "Oh shit, are you serious? It's her mother?"

Taylor laughed in that throaty way that had always turned heads. "Yup."

"Damn. That's so strange." Lily Walker—house mother? The position didn't suit her. But Taylor assumed she'd take the opportunity to rule over ADL any way she could. "You'd think she had better things to do."

"Actually, I wouldn't." Taylor laughed. "She's been so obsessed with ADL. I mean, I loved being in ADL, and I still love every-thing about it. Except for . . ." She waved her hand toward the capsule. Putting together this idiotic blast from the past had been a mistake, she knew that now. How many times over the last five years had she thought about digging the damn thing up?

She waited for the accusation. The question about why she'd put the Spill Book in a place anyone could find. But the answer was stupid. They would have all been dead when it was supposed to be opened. What made sense to her five years ago made zero sense now.

"Any ideas who might have taken it?" Asana asked.

"None. You?"

Asana shook her head.

"That book will ruin me. It will ruin Elijah's career." She fisted her hands beside her, imagining the beautifully perfect life she'd built crumbling out from under her. And ignored the small voice that said: *Would that be so bad?* "I need to get the book back before it's too late."

"It will ruin all of us, Taylor." This time it wasn't Asana who answered but Brooklyn, and Annabelle was standing right beside her.

"That book was so fucked-up," Asana said.

A lump formed in Taylor's throat. She wished she could take back so much, but without a time machine, the Spill Book, her tea parties, and everything else was out there now waiting for whoever had stolen it to expose them all.

"We need to find out who took it, and we need to get it back." Taylor stared at each of her friends, the words "I'm sorry" itching to burst out. The reason she'd come here in the first place was to say she was sorry. To make amends and fix the very problem she'd created. To bury the past and keep it in the deep, dark dirt where it belonged. To figure out just what she was going to do with her life. "You're going to hate this, but we need to have another Spill the Tea Party."

CHAPTER FOURTEEN

I don't normally give it up for a daddy, but he paid for the entire semester at Bama. A girl's gotta do what a girl's gotta do. It doesn't make me a whore if I didn't mind, right? He was pretty good at it.

Kisses,
Brooklyn

Annabelle

Then

There's an art to shoplifting that people don't normally think about. Annabelle mastered it when she was in elementary school, starting with "accidentally" spilling her teacher's cup of deliciously scented markers and pocketing her favorite smell—cherry—as she "helped" gather them up.

Play it cool. Nothing to see here.

It helped that her parents were richer than anyone had a right to be and that her clothes cost more than some people's salary.

No one expected the little rich girl to steal.

But that's what made it so exciting.

She started off small with markers, pencils, hair clips. And she prayed for forgiveness every night. No punishments came raining down on her, so she figured God was cool with it. Soon, her small swipes graduated to bracelets, rings. It was amazing what people didn't feel. Sometimes she took lipstick from the kiosks at Ulta and other stupid little things. The only problem was, the thrill wasn't there if no one was going to look for it.

Sure, whenever the manager took inventory they'd notice a discrepancy, but there was no personal attachment there. Just a write-off. Annabelle liked to take things that held emotional value for people. The need to take was a physical itch that would literally make her start to tremble if she didn't scratch. It's why she didn't mind taking a pencil or some other silly thing that belonged to someone. But if she were being honest, it was the sparkly things that really drew her attention.

Like right now.

The #OOTD for Pref Day was done, and the four of them were filing out of Brooklyn's room to make their way to ADL. Thank God all four of them had decided to pledge and stick with it. She really liked having a set of friends, of people she *actually* liked.

But right now, sitting on the edge of Brooklyn's dresser was a silver ring. She recognized it as the one Brooklyn wore on her middle toe. There wasn't much to the ring, a simply silver band, but it had been polished enough to catch the light.

Would Brooklyn notice if Annabelle took it? She wasn't wearing it today. Had she forgotten? Or maybe she just didn't care about it.

Annabelle had always wanted a toe ring, but the opportunity to try one on had never come. Until now. Would she look good with a toe ring? She couldn't wear it around her friends.

Only one way to find out.

Annabelle walked past the dresser, never stopping, not looking in the direction of her prize, as she swiped it and tucked it in her purse as if nothing had happened. That was the art. To keep moving. Not to look. To act as if her arms weren't even a part of her body.

To give the appearance of nonchalance. Nothing to see here.

The ring burned in her purse, pulsing as it bounced against her hip.

The crowd of women walking toward Magnolia was slightly thinner today. Preference Day was when a PNM selected two of her favorite houses, and those sororities had to invite you to come on Pref Day. Some didn't get any invites back. Some only one. Annabelle had gotten both back, as had Asana, Brooklyn, and Taylor, but they'd all decided who they really wanted was ADL.

Wearing formal dresses in ADL's signature light pink, with styles that ranged from sleek to flirty to classic to match their personalities, they walked with confidence down the road.

"It's reel time." Brooklyn held up her phone and pressed record for her socials. "Pref Day for Bama Rush, y'all! We're dressed up all pretty and headed to Greek Row." She winked and whirled in a circle while the three of them broke out in a short dance. "It's a long day, friends. Catch ya tonight!"

When Brooklyn was done, Annabelle pulled out her own phone, posing for a short selfie and then a video of her shoes walking down Magnolia. She hashtagged her post: #theseshoeswere madeforrushing #blessed #sisterhood #mamasgirl. The latter of which made her want to crush her phone beneath the heel of her shoes.

The sisters greeted the PNMs with a new chant that made Annabelle smile. She'd heard her mom sing it before, and as much as she often felt annoyed at being her mother's legacy, it was also like coming back to a second home.

"A-L-P-H-A, D-E-L-T-and-A, L-A-M-B-and-D-and-A! Boom, boom, we want you to boom, boom, go ADL. HEY—choose ADL! YOU—choose ADL—and we choose you! Alpha Delta Lambda! Alpha Delta Lambda! ADL for life!"

Without thinking about it, Annabelle started to chant the reply she'd always cheer to her mom. "Boom, boom, I choose you, boom, boom, I'm ADL. A-L-P-H-A, D-E-L-T-and-A, L-A-M-B-and-D-and-A, you won't catch any other Greek on me!"

"Yes, girl!" Taylor called out, and then repeated the chant with a few extra cheer moves thrown in, with the other PNMs waiting to go inside, answering the call.

The actives cheered louder, parting in two lines on either side of the entrances for the PNMs to enter, clapping and smiling. Annabelle felt a thrill rush through her that wasn't unlike the thrills she got when she took things. The familiar warmth in her belly spreading in tingles through her limbs.

After another presentation about the sorority and Panhellenic life, the girls were free to mingle, each of them being unofficially assigned an active member to talk to about the sorority and gain a deeper understanding of what ADL represented and what being an active member would be like.

"Annabelle." The president of ADL waved her over. "I've been dying to talk to you all week."

"I'm excited to chat with you too."

"How are you liking it so far? The rushing, I mean?"

"It's been . . . a rush." Annabelle laughed. "Exactly as I dreamed, and maybe a little more."

"Your mom's legacy is impressive."

"It is. But I do hope to make my own legacy."

"With that song, I have no doubt you will." She stared across the room. "What about her?" She nodded at Brooklyn. "Think she's got what it takes?"

"Brooklyn's a star," Annabelle said without hesitation. "She's not only great at social media, which could help with Panhellenic messaging, but she's a soccer player and, from what I hear, really good at it. I think going to the games all dressed up could be fun."

"Our first sports star. I like it."

"Has there never been a player before?"

"Not the sporty kind. I mean, we have cheerleaders." Riley laughed. "I'm not supposed to tell you this. But you're in. And not just because of your mother's generous donations or the fact that she's past president of the National Panhellenic Conference. Though it helps."

Annabelle smiled, feeling a bit sad that she hadn't gotten in on her own merit.

"Also, you didn't hear this from me, but when it comes time to vote for homecoming queen and king, we vote the same."

"The same?"

Riley nodded. "Yup. We'll get the nod for who and I'll let everyone know."

"The nod?"

Riley leaned in close, whispering, "You know, the Machine. Don't play coy. I know you know, being Lily's daughter and all."

The Machine? Annabelle grinned as if she knew what Riley was talking about when in reality she felt completely clueless. Why hadn't her mother told her the queen and king were rigged?

"Oh, I need to talk to her." Riley hurried off toward another sister without a backward glance, and Annabelle took that as permission to sneak upstairs. She found Riley's room and slipped inside, touching the various trinkets. Trying on her jewelry, her lipstick. There was a tiny fake red camellia, the Alabama flower, tucked into a vase on Riley's desk. Annabelle plucked it from the vase and slipped it behind her ear, taking a selfie in the mirror.

A rush zinged its way through her limbs.

If she'd ever wondered about not being in a sorority, this feeling was confirmation she was in the right place.

ANNABELLE SLIPPED EXHAUSTED into her single dorm room. She unbuckled her wedges, kicked them into her closet, stripped off her dress, tossed it over a chair, and flopped onto her bed.

The beauty of not having a roommate was she could sleep naked if she wanted to.

She could also pull her goodies out and examine them. Annabelle hopped out of bed to find Brooklyn's toe ring in her bag. She slipped it onto her second toe, past the first knuckle, and wiggled. It was incredible how a little thing like a ring could make her foot look completely different. Hands on her hips, she viewed herself in the mirror, dressed only in her lace underwear and the ring. She felt sexier somehow. More confident.

Did girls with toe rings have more confidence?

Maybe she'd wear it on Bid Day. Bid Day they were allowed to wear sneakers. No one would see it, but she'd feel the thrill of its weight as she ran from the stadium down Magnolia toward Alpha Delta Lambda.

CHAPTER FIFTEEN

I took our house mother's ring. I gave it back because I felt guilty. I don't usually feel like that.

Kisses,
Annabelle

Asana

Now

Asana stood near the door in Taylor's suite, sipping red wine out of a cheap hotel glass, wishing she was back at Fantasia having a vodka soda with her pick for the night.

Gathering in Taylor's suite for the second night of Rush Week was a little more than a dozen Alpha Delta Lambda alumna sisters and board members who'd come for Rush Week and the opening of the time capsule. According to Taylor, the ones she'd invited had the juiciest confessions in the book. Everyone else who'd come for the event hadn't been titillating enough to warrant a blackmail.

The question was, had the women here tonight also received blackmail letters? Only the four of them had discussed it at this point. And of the four of them, right now Asana was the only one who was being extorted for money.

Given it was her job to read people, Asana didn't let a single person enter without her saying hello first. The other sisters cheerfully greeted her, not a single line of worry on their brows, not that they should be showing at their age anyway, and if they were, Botox could be their friend. But there were other tells, and from what she could see, no one was on edge. No shifty eyes, no finger wiggling or sidestepping.

They poured wine, ate cheese and grapes from the hastily thrown-together charcuterie board, and caught up.

"I can't believe we're doing this." Brooklyn folded her still sculpted arms over her chest. "Tea parties are what put us in this position."

Asana nodded. Tea parties *had* put them in this situation, but they weren't innocent. Everything in that book was true. One thing she hadn't heard mentioned from her friends, however, was if they were being targeted for their current secrets, not just the ones from the past.

"We put ourselves in this position," Brooklyn groaned, putting voice to Asana's thoughts. "And you know what pisses me off?"

Asana cocked her head, listening.

"I don't feel guilty about what I put in there. It was all true. All my own decisions and choices. But I left that world behind when I graduated, and now someone is trying to take that decision from me."

"Normally I don't mind if someone else wants to play a little dirty." Asana swirled her wine, watching the legs drip down the side. "In fact, I kind of like that." She grinned. "But I agree, it's only fun if we consent."

Brooklyn eyed her. "What did you write in there?"

Asana laughed softly. "Wouldn't you like to know."

"Yes." Brooklyn's tone was serious, as was her expression.

Asana sighed, lowered her voice. "I wrote about a few dalliances. My time with the Machine."

"Dalliances." Brooklyn chuckled. "Frat boys you hooked up with?"

"Something like that." She wasn't about to give Taylor away to Brooklyn, not without her consent. Even if whoever was blackmailing them was preparing to blast it to the world, it wasn't going to be Asana who spilled. At least not for a second time.

"The stuff about the Machine . . ." Brooklyn hesitated.

"Yeah. That has me worried the most." Asana scanned the room again. Mostly everyone looked the same. Five years wasn't a long time, and aging from twenty-two to twenty-seven, the biggest changes were their styles, maybe their hair. Like Annabelle's being at least seven shades lighter.

Asana's phone buzzed in her pocket. Retrieving it, she saw her assistant's name flashing on the screen with: UPDATE! Calling you! "I have to take this."

The hallway in the hotel had a hideous art deco carpet that caught at the backs of her heels as she moved away from Taylor's door in case anyone tried to listen in.

"Asana," she answered.

"I pulled backgrounds on the names you gave me."

"And?"

"Nothing, all clean records. And no one linked to Matinee."

Asana groaned and closed her eyes, trying to think. She'd given her assistant the names of everyone that had lived at ADL with her. Everyone who'd put something in the time capsule. Everyone who had something to lose.

"Keep digging." She hung up, opened her eyes, and caught a flash of someone rounding the corner toward the elevators.

No one had left the party. Asana hurried down the hallway toward the elevator vestibule, but by the time she turned the corner, the doors were closing, and all she could see was a blond head and a flash of a mostly obscured profile before the doors closed.

Who the hell was that?

Had they been spying on her, or was her paranoia getting the better of her?

Asana jammed her finger onto the elevator buttons and tapped her foot impatiently. The second elevator opened and she rode it down. But whoever had ridden down on the other one had already come off. She hurried toward the carousel doors, heels clicking in rhythmic echoes. A whoosh of warm air hit her as she pushed through to the Tuscaloosa streets, but she didn't see anyone who looked remotely like the woman on the elevator.

To the bellman she said, "Did you recognize the woman who left before me? Is she a guest at the hotel?"

He shook his head. "No, ma'am."

Maybe it was someone who'd left the party and she just hadn't noticed. Except that Asana noticed everything.

With a disgusted groan, she marched back into the hotel and went up to the top floor.

By the time she'd returned to the suite, everyone was sufficiently drenched with wine to loosen their lips. Taylor stood in the center of the room, clinking her glass with the underside of a diamond ring.

"Ladies, sisters." *Clink clink.* "I call this ADL alumna party to order. I hope you brought your juicy stories because it's time to spill the tea."

"Do you have the book?" one of the sister's asked. Her eyes were bright, and she held up a pink pen with a fluffy poof ball at the end. "I brought the pen."

"*The* pen?" Annabelle asked.

"Yes, *the* pen."

How the hell had she gotten *the* pen?

Asana watched Taylor, who didn't even falter. She wasn't going to let it be known even now that someone had obviously taken the book? Ever the politician's wife. And still so fucking hot. "That ratty old notebook?" She laughed, her head tossed back, exposing the length of her neck. A neck Asana had loved to lick. "The pen has held up much better. I brought a new notebook." Taylor flashed a glittering pink journal. "Time to spill on fresh pages. Who wants to go first?"

CHAPTER SIXTEEN

One, two, three, four. I declare a jiggle war. Body shaming is def frowned upon, but let's be honest, there's a reason why only the prettiest and fittest girls are allowed in ADL. No outliers allowed.

Kisses,
Taylor

Brooklyn

Then

"Tell me how much you want it, baby."

Brooklyn stared up into the heavy-lidded brown eyes of her sugar daddy while he rode her. She refused to call him by his name. That was too intimate. Even more intimate than sex. *He* was her job. *His* happiness her goal. And being a sugar baby was a means to an end. While she didn't have to sleep with every man who paid her for companionship, her bank account grew when she did.

"I want it, harder." And she wasn't lying.

Daddy number three was good to her. *Really* good. She moaned, tossing a leg up on his shoulder to take him deeper, her pert breasts bouncing with every thrust. He might have been three or four times her age—she wasn't going to ask—but he still had the moves that could make her come. A body that was pretty impressive for a guy with gray on his temples, and a cock that got and stayed hard on its own.

"Harder, Daddy," she groaned.

"Oh God," he murmured, his head falling to her forehead as his hands gripped firmly on her hips, lifting her ass off the bed while he plunged with the energy of a dude half his age.

"Yes, yes, yes," she cried out, the same way she did on the field when she was about to score. Goals and orgasms were all the same. They both meant winning a game.

Thirty minutes later, Brooklyn stepped out of the fancy marble shower, then thought better of it and grabbed her cell phone. She filmed her feet under the rain shower, and then stepping onto the luxuriously lush bath mat, curling her toes into the pile, then snapped off the video.

One for the fans. She uploaded under Sporty Spyce, then dried off and got dressed.

The opulence of her daddy's bathroom made her feel a hell of a lot better for what had just happened and the money she was taking for it.

She glanced at the time. Only an hour until practice, and if she was late, there was a real chance she'd be kicked off the team. Already the coaches had been lenient with her rushing and needing to get to and from sorority events. But that'd only last so long.

Dressed, she left the privacy of the bathroom in the guest bedroom and walked through the quiet Alabama manse.

He'd already gone to work, his family out of town. He'd been hesitant to let her stay behind and use the bathroom, but a shower after he'd been inside her was one of her stipulations. And she could be convincing if she wanted to. On the dresser, in a gilded frame, she spied a picture of him with his family. His wife was pretty. In fact, she looked like an older version of Brooklyn. Red hair, fit body.

"Creepy," she muttered, then slipped outside, where a driver waited for her, courtesy of her new sugar.

She slipped into the back of the sedan, her sunglasses on despite the fact it was so early the sun had barely risen, and let the driver take her back to school. They didn't speak. They never did. She didn't know if it was a direction from *him*, or if it was because she'd been too nervous at first and now it was just a thing.

The driver pulled over in a place not near her dorm or the soccer field, so she could get out and walk the rest of the way without anyone noticing. Getting questioned about climbing out of what was obviously not her car was the last thing she needed.

Except when she stepped onto the sidewalk, shutting the door behind her, she did see someone. A PNM, but she couldn't place her. The other girl waved, and Brooklyn thought about not waving back, ignoring her, pretending she had no idea who she was, but thought that might make things a little awkward later if they ended up getting accepted to the same sorority.

Which was—OMG—*today*.

Brooklyn waved awkwardly then hurried toward the soccer women's locker room. Already dressed in her practice gear, she stowed her bag and ran onto the field. Thank God she wasn't the last one to arrive. They'd just started to warm up.

Throughout practice, all she could think of were two things on repeat: Did the other PNM think it was weird she'd gotten out of the tinted sedan? And would she make it into ADL?

At the end of practice, she ran the entire way back to her dorm, rushed inside to shower, and then did a Brooklyn in Bama #Get ReadyWithMe video in record time. She wouldn't even need to speed it up she did it so fast. For Bid Day, PNMs only had to wear shorts and tanks with sneakers. She'd braided her hair after her morning shower, which left it in soft waves down her back.

"Wish me luck! Brooklyn in Bama is about to find out if she's a sister or not!"

A series of knocks landed on her door, and she opened it to find Annabelle, Taylor, and Asana in the hallway, looking as gorgeous as they always did. Each of them had on their white Lulu shorts and light pink tank tops the same shade as the ADL colors, in hopes that when they opened up their envelopes it was Alpha Delta Lambda they saw in bold.

"You ready for this?" Asana asked.

"I was born ready," Brooklyn teased.

"There is only one outcome today, ladies," Taylor said. "And it's the four of us in ADL."

"I really hope and pray that's the case," Annabelle said. "It will be so hard to be in ADL without you."

Brooklyn kept her smile in place, even though inside she faltered. Annabelle's reply was just a reminder that she had a place in ADL as her mother's legacy no matter what.

"I agree." Taylor directed her reply to Annabelle. "It would be so hard to be president without you on my board."

The two of them stared at each other long enough that Brooklyn felt uncomfortable, but then they finally burst into laughter, diffusing whatever tension had been created.

Bryant-Denny Stadium was full of PNMs shouting and laughing, the cacophony of joy making Brooklyn's ears vibrate, and she couldn't stop smiling herself.

Manila envelopes in hand, their names printed inconspicuously in black on a white label, they waited for the countdown. Nervous sweat made her hands clammy, leaving tiny wet fingerprints.

Out of the three of them, getting accepted into ADL was going to change Brooklyn's life the most—though her friends didn't realize that. Growing up, college had been a dream that seemed so far away. Joining a sorority one impossible step further.

But she'd made things happen for herself. And if she could just have this happen too, everything she ever wanted was going to fall perfectly into place. She set up her phone in her lap at the angle she'd practiced to capture the moment for TikTok.

"All right, ladies." Lily Walker's voice boomed from a bullhorn. "Are you ready to count down?"

"Yes!" The affirmation was thunderous.

A nervous thrill shot up Brooklyn's spine, not unlike the buzz of barreling down a field and realizing she had the perfect open shot to kick a ball into the goal.

"Five. Four. Three. Two. One!"

Brooklyn's hands trembled as she tore into the manila packet, her pink nails slipping under the tab, and then she pulled out a light pink envelope with her name written in cursive on the front. On the back was a sticker in pink and white Greek Letters: A Δ Λ.

"Ohmygod!" she shrieked, and tore into the envelope, pulling out the invitation to be a sister in Alpha Delta Lambda.

Without warning, she started to cry with genuine joy, and showed the letter to her TikTok fans. Tears of happiness streamed down her face as she laughed and shook and screeched with the rest of the PNMs—now pledges. She picked up her phone, bringing it closer to her face. "You guys, Brooklyn in Bama is now ADL Brooklyn in Bama! I am so freaking excited. I just can't believe it. I'm so blessed." She turned to her friends, who were all shrieking and holding up the same letters. "My girls," Brooklyn shouted, and held out the phone for the four of them to show their letters. "Time to run!"

They stood up, their invites in hand, and rushed to the exit of the stadium. They ran down Judy Bonner, turning right onto Magnolia with Brooklyn at the head. The great brick Panhellenic houses with their white columns loomed up in front of them, and when they reached ADL, Brooklyn pulled out her phone again.

"I'm home, you guys. I'm home!"

CHAPTER SEVENTEEN

Life is a game, and there are only two outcomes: winners and losers. I refuse to be a loser, and yet, to be a winner, I have to betray myself. I came here to get away from NYC politics and backstabbing. Guess the grass isn't always greener on the other side, and we're all just following orders.

Kisses,
Asana

Taylor

Now

Not looking at Asana was turning out to be harder than Elijah's Viagrasaurus dick on a mission to impregnate her.

Not just because Asana looked completely disturbed after coming back from her phone call, but because of all they'd left unsaid. All that was left buried between them. Secrets that Taylor didn't want getting out and, at the same time, secrets she couldn't *not* think about when the object of them stood less than fifteen feet away.

Taylor snatched the notebook from one of the sisters, who was giggling as she wrote, and clearly not the asshole who'd filched the real Spill Book from the time capsule.

"Hey, I wasn't done—"

"You were." Taylor gave her a look that said not to argue, and just like when they were in college, the once active sis nodded and relinquished the pen too. Taylor marched over to Asana and held out the book. "Want to spill the tea?"

"Are you actually asking, or is this like in college where I didn't have a choice?" Asana hissed. Her eyes burned with unspent words, and Taylor's stomach tightened.

Keeping her voice low so people couldn't hear, even if they strained, Taylor said, "There might have been things we didn't have a choice about in college, but that's not the case now." They were clearly *not* talking about the book. "Bathroom."

"Really?" Asana raised a skeptical brow and scoffed, but she did walk toward the bathroom. When the door was closed, she said, "Who makes the rules?"

Taylor's spine tingled. "I'm not president anymore. Did you take it out?"

Asana took the book, her fingernails lightly grazing Taylor's hand.

Asana didn't make a move to write. "This is stupid, Taylor. And since we're adults I'll pretend not to be offended you asked, but mostly because I thought *you* took it. Writing in the book is what got us in this mess in the first place. Why don't we just ask if anyone here wants to come clean?"

Asana wasn't wrong. Taylor bit the tip of her tongue to hold back the automatic retort, the part of herself that always went on offense without thinking. She needed more Elle Woods than Regina George right now.

"You're right." Taylor drew in a breath, finding it hard to be so vulnerable. "Maybe I'm just afraid we'll find out that no one in here knows a damn thing."

"It's highly likely they don't." Asana let out a big sigh. "Why'd you come back?"

"For the same reason as you. Blackmail." Taylor shifted her gaze toward the mirror, pretending to care about her hair.

"No other reason?"

Asana was always good at seeing through her, and Taylor was always weak when it came to Asana. She quit fiddling with her hair, leaning her butt against the bathroom vanity, arms crossed. It'd been years since they'd seen each other, and yet it felt like only a few days. Time wiped away by all they'd shared. And yet, so much had happened. And not happened.

"I guess I came back because I missed everyone. I missed Bama and ADL." That was close enough of a confession as she was willing to give.

"Me too." Asana cocked her head, eyes squinting a little as she studied her. "Are you happy, Taylor?"

Taylor actually laughed. "Happy?"

"Yeah. Are you?"

Her answer was immediate in her mind, but she held back. No, she wasn't. But that wasn't anyone's business but her own. "Happy enough." She shrugged.

"The Taylor I used to know wouldn't have settled for happy enough. Taylor Collins dominates."

And Taylor, Elijah's wife, did the opposite. "I dominate in a different way now."

Asana grunted, but seeing she wasn't going to get anything else out of Taylor for the moment, she switched topics back to the sisters outside the door. "I think we're barking up the wrong tree."

Taylor crossed her arms over her chest. "In other words, someone's about to piss on our legs?"

"God, I hope not, that's disgusting."

Taylor laughed, the tension broken, thank God. She hated how quickly and easily Asana had disarmed her. How she'd almost admitted to being as miserable and stuck as she felt. They left the bathroom and were joined by Brooklyn and Annabelle, the former staring from the corner of each room and back again, as if she were measuring the distance.

"No one is talking about Mama Jenny," Annabelle pointed out. "Isn't that odd? She just died."

Taylor groaned. "I should have started out the meeting with a prayer."

Asana smirked. "I didn't know you were the praying type."

Taylor grinned. She'd done plenty of praying in her life, but mostly it was in the hopes she didn't get caught. "Maybe we should leave that up to Annabelle."

Annabelle nodded. "I can do it. I did it at the meeting Taylor was late to."

"How did she die?" Brooklyn's brow was wrinkled.

"Good question. All we heard was she passed and her family wanted their jewelry back."

"Greedy. She put it in there for a reason." Taylor rolled her eyes. "Let's see if one of these bitches knows."

Taylor clinked her diamond wedding ring on her wineglass, drawing the attention of the other women in the room. "This tea party is being momentarily interrupted, ladies. I know we did this earlier today, but we felt the need to do it again. We wanted to have a moment of silence for our House Mama, Miss Jenny, and then open the floor for discussion." She winked at Brooklyn.

They all bowed their heads as Annabelle said a standard prayer, and then they were quiet, staring at the darkness behind their closed lids.

"May she rest in peace," Taylor said after the seconds had ticked by far enough that she was starting to itch in the silence.

The chatter picked up again, as if they'd not all just been having a moment of silence.

"I have a question." Brooklyn's voice was soft, her face humble, hand pressed over her heart, not a look she wore often, and it reminded Taylor that Brooklyn was a very good actress. One hundred percent sweet mommy blogger. Hell, they'd all thought in college she had money. Only Taylor knew about her poor family, her penchant for older men with deep pockets, and the dirty fuckers who bought videos and images of her feet. Gross. "I know this is terribly uncouth, but how did Mama Jenny pass? I hope she didn't suffer."

The smiles and laughter faded as all eyes fell on Brooklyn. A wet blanket on a fire. Brooklyn's question had taken all the fun out of the party. But it was a question they all wanted an answer to.

"I have no idea," Taylor offered, and glanced from face to face, waiting for someone to speak up who might know the truth.

"The invitation didn't say," Ally, the social chair for their board in college mentioned. "And I didn't have the heart to ask after I saw the snippet in the alumni paper."

The snippet, a single-sentence notification of death. None of them had even thought to find out. Just accepted her passing. Everyone wondered, but no one asked. Why? Were they all that much inside their own heads?

Jenny wasn't that old. Maybe in her sixties? Her children had been students at Bama, and a daughter had been in ADL. After her kids grew up, no longer married, Jenny had taken the position of house mother. A job she'd appeared to love. But to be honest, Taylor spent more of her time shooing the older woman from their business than anything else.

It wouldn't do for Mama Jenny to realize what Taylor had been making them write in the Spill Book as she delivered their herbal tea. And it definitely would have been bad if she found out what was inside.

Taylor cleared her throat, suddenly feeling like fingers were tightening around her larynx.

A woman stepped out from behind two other sisters. It took

Taylor a few blinks to recognize her as Jacquelyn something. She'd been recruited their last year of undergrad.

"Her son told me it was sudden. Heart attack."

"Really?" Taylor remembered Jenny being healthy. Always making sure they ate right, took their vitamins, and kept up with their workouts. Jenny herself was a runner and yoga guru.

Jacquelyn shrugged. "I wasn't going to question what he said." Her comment was a little rude, and she rolled her eyes, looking around for support in her derision. But Jacquelyn must have forgotten who she was talking to, because no one was going to dare say anything against Taylor. Not when she kept their secrets in her vault of a brain. Spill Book stolen or not, they still needed to tread carefully. A fact Jackie clearly forgot.

"Did you end up going to law school?" Taylor asked.

Jacquelyn's face turned instantly beet red, and the way her eyes twitched, she had to be remembering exactly what tea she'd spilled—Dear Jackie had cheated on her LSAT.

"As I recall, you had an amazing score on your LSAT." Taylor cocked her head, sweet, encouraging, but there was a definite threat in her tone. She remembered because she'd been pissed it was higher than hers.

"Yes. I just made junior partner," Jacquelyn said softly, then sat down heavily on the couch, practically on top of another sister.

Junior partner. Jealousy whipped through Taylor like egg whites in a meringue. Even Jacquelyn the cheat had surpassed her career-wise.

"How wonderful," Taylor said bitterly. "Your bosses must think you're a real ass . . . et."

CHAPTER EIGHTEEN

His wife came home when I was giving him a blowie. I had to hide in the closet for two hours while they fucked in the shower. When they finally left to go out to dinner—I snuck out. But his kid saw me. I told him I was just one of their housekeepers. He told me I didn't look like a housekeeper. When I asked what I looked like, he said, one of the girls from TikTok. I'm fucked.

Kisses,
Brooklyn

Annabelle

Then

Swaps. *Swaps. Swaaaapppss.* The tiny little word has so many con-notations.

Swapping numbers.

Swapping outfits.

Swapping places.

Swapping spit.

Swapping digits.

Swapping boys.

Annabelle could go on forever. Because she'd been thinking of swaps since August of last year. In Greek Life, a swap party was supposed to be a sober event between a sorority house and a fraternity house, so that they could all get to know each other in a different environment. At a swap, a brother chose a sister for his date. It was all supposed to be sweet, but that wasn't always the case.

For a wholesome, God-fearing girl like her, the idea of swapping anything was terrifying and exhilarating all at once. The latter, wicked sensation was what made her discreetly cross herself when no one was looking.

Besides, any scenario she tagged onto the end of pretty much every rendition of swaps her mind conjured was exactly what was going to happen tonight anyway.

Tonight might be the night that her life changed forever.

Nervous energy made her lick off an entire layer of her lip gloss. Again. This was the third time she'd reapplied. But a hot girl never let her nerves show on the outside. And Annabelle was good at looking good. Prada good.

The hot-pink designer dress she'd bought was sinfully short: if she so much as curved her back, her ass cheeks were popping from the tight hem. If her father saw her, he'd order her to church.

She'd go too, because Southern good girls listened to their daddies and repented for their sins.

And if she was going to go bad or stay home, she might as well go all the way. Annabelle tucked a hand into the cleavage of her dress and plumped one breast, then repeated the action on the other side, wriggling them into the best position to draw the eye of the hottest frat boy on campus. It was just a shame that he also happened to be the one her mother had pointed out, a boy whose mom she played pickleball with on Thursdays.

Apparently, running every aspect of Annabelle's life also included who she dated. Annabelle had been completely demented to think her mom would stop when she went to college. Oh well, at least he was hot.

And icing on the swap cake—her mother was not here tonight.

A knock pulled her away from where Annabelle had been examining her body in the mirror. She walked steadily on her six-inch heels and opened the door to find Brooklyn in the dorm hallway looking panicked.

"I need your help." Normally the epitome of cool, seeing Brooklyn so cracked was . . . unsettling.

Annabelle motioned her in and shut the door. Brooklyn glanced around to make sure that the room was empty, then faced her, eyes owl-like. "My dress broke."

That was it? Annabelle immediately calmed down. "How? The strap? Zipper? I have repair kits for everything."

"Zipper." Brooklyn turned around to show where the zipper remained stubbornly stuck at the bottom when she tried to move it.

Annabelle tested the stuck zipper. "Sugar cookies. Zipper trying to mess up your swap. Easy fix. Strip."

Brooklyn shimmied out of her dress while Annabelle rummaged in her emergency dress fix kit that she'd had since the pageant world. A teen queen never went anywhere without one. She was surprised Brooklyn didn't have one in her big-ass Mary Poppins bag.

"Pliers?" Standing in her bra and panties, Brooklyn wrinkled her perfectly plucked eyebrows at the needle-nose in Annabelle's hand.

Annabelle was glad Brooklyn was comfortable enough to stand there, her toned, tanned body—albeit with an obvious tank and shorts tan—on display. In the pageant world, they'd never had a choice, and Annabelle had always been embarrassed about how different she looked. How the hair on her arms and stomach had been bleached and, when she'd gotten older, waxed off completely, before electrolysis made her body totally hairless. And if she'd had the obvious sports tan package that Brooklyn modeled, she'd have been laughed out of the pageant dressing rooms.

"Yeah. Watch." With the pliers she plucked out the bottom three zipper teeth, which looked jacked up, where the pull wouldn't go past. Then she manhandled the zipper pull back into place and zipped up the dress.

"Wow! You did it!" Brooklyn clapped, jumping up and down, the same victory dance she did when she scored on the field.

"Almost." Annabelle threaded a needle with the same shade of pink as Brooklyn's dress, then tied the knot and sewed a quick whipstitch to create the new zipper stopper. "Voilà."

Brooklyn touched the fixed and indiscernible zipper. "How did you learn to do that?"

"Pageant life." Annabelle shrugged, then immediately regretted it as her perfectly placed boobs fell out of place.

Brooklyn cocked her head like a puppy. "Didn't you have a person to do that?"

Annabelle snorted as she smooshed her cleavage back into place. "I mean, I could have, and sometimes I did, but my mom thought it better if I knew how to do it myself, especially after Sherry got a flat tire, and one of my zippers broke and Mom had to improvise with safety pins. So ugly."

Brooklyn slipped back into her knockoff dress. Annabelle had noticed the fake tag, the subpar fabric, and wondered if Brooklyn knew it was a knockoff or had been duped. The toe ring she'd taken had looked silver, but after Annabelle slept in it, she'd woken up with a green ring around her toe.

Everyone had ideas of where their money should be spent, and Annabelle wasn't one to judge, that was a sin, but it did make her wonder how Brooklyn was paying for things. Greek Life was expensive, but Brooklyn seemed to be hanging in there, even with her knockoffs. The Tiffany necklace she wore was definitely real, which only made Annabelle more curious.

Brooklyn whirled in a circle, beaming at Annabelle as she popped it and locked it, and the zipper stayed in place.

Annabelle wiggled her arms in classic tutting dance move. "All right, Brooklyn in Bama, you look hot."

Brooklyn grinned, looking in the full-length mirror at the zipper work in the back. "You can't even tell." She met Annabelle's eyes in the mirror. "I owe you one."

"Consider it a favor." Besides, she'd technically already paid her back with the cheap toe ring she'd filched.

"I'd hug you, but I don't want to wrinkle our dresses."

Annabelle laughed. "Air hug."

When they opened the door to head out, Taylor and Asana were teetering down the hallway in their impossibly high heels.

Annabelle slipped out of her own and held up flip-flops. "Ladies, we can walk in these and change into our heels right before the house. Lily Walker special."

"Oh, thank God." Asana leaned against the wall as she slipped off her six-inchers.

"Wow, Brooklyn, you look really pretty." Taylor eyed the pink dress with the same skeptical eye Annabelle had. There was no way she wouldn't notice the ripped-off style.

Brooklyn glanced down at her dress, her palms smoothing over her thighs. "Thank you."

Annabelle waited for Taylor to say something that would embarrass Brooklyn, but instead she just smiled, a knowing curve to her lip that had Brooklyn's face pinkening before she ducked into her own room to get a pair of slides.

"I got us a pledge gift." Annabelle reached into her bag and pulled out the tiny packets. Her mother had mentioned in passing once that she'd gotten her rush besties a present, and Annabelle loved the idea. She handed out the wrapped boxes.

"Oh, I love presents." Taylor plucked off the ribbon and dropped it on the floor, as they all opened to reveal white-gold toe rings.

"Wow!" Brooklyn looked the most excited. "This looks just like one I lost."

"White gold, don't lose it." Annabelle gave a little laugh to hide the guilt in her tone at being the cause of that "loss."

"Thank you." Brooklyn looked like she was going to cry, so Annabelle glanced away, picking up the trash they'd discarded on the hallway floor.

"Should we put them on?" Asana asked.

"Yes!" Annabelle wiggled her toe to show that she already wore hers.

"I didn't get you a gift." Taylor pouted, and for a second Annabelle wondered if she was going to refuse to put it on.

"There's no need to reciprocate. Lily Walker special." It was becoming her new phrase.

Annabelle wondered if at any point this year she would be able to have a conversation and not bring up her own mother. Even she was getting tired of hearing "Lily" over and over again.

"Oh, guys, by the way, I hear we're supposed to vote for Ashlyn and Kyle for homecoming queen and king," Asana said casually. "Let's do it together."

Annabelle nodded, eyeing Asana sideways. Was she part of the Machine?

CHAPTER NINETEEN

At confessional on Sunday, I finally spilled the tea to Father Brown. I took the lion from ADPhi. The cute little one on their porch. My penance for taking something that doesn't belong to me was a Hail Mary for every item taken, and a donation to the church. Writing the check was easy. I'm still saying Hail Marys.

Kisses,
Annabelle

Brooklyn

Now

Brooklyn was pretty sure she was breaking the law.

But it was only illegal if she got caught. Or at least, that was how she was going to play it. So, while she stared sympathetically around the room, nodding, commenting, she was also scanning the three places she'd set up hidden cameras to capture this tea party.

Even though she'd been besties with her girls back in the day, things had changed. Right now all their asses were on the line, and she was going to nail the dipshit who'd decided to escort them to the literal ground. But more like liquid nails versus steel, because it seemed less damaging to the skin, and she did have a reputation to maintain after all.

Everyone would thank her later.

Brooklyn snuck a glance toward where Taylor held court near the center of the room. Some things never changed, just like how Taylor had been annoyed when Brooklyn showed up early to the tea party, until Brooklyn told her to go put her makeup on while she set up. Four years in the sorority together, two of which they'd been under Taylor's reign, and Brooklyn knew how to work the system, knew how to work Taylor.

And since filming was her life, Brooklyn was quick to set up the stage, in perfect triangular formation so she could catch the whole room and each past member of the ADL board at all their angles.

Drink up, lying bitches.

Someone in here was fucking with her. Fucking with all of them. And they could play all innocent, but Brooklyn didn't believe a single batted lash or pouted lip. In nearly three decades of life, she'd known plenty of liars—herself included.

Jacquelyn was fidgety, giving Taylor the evil eye every time she looked away. But Jackie wasn't hiding her hatred, which would have been stupid if she was guilty, so Brooklyn was tempted to cross her off the list of blackmailers she'd started to form. As clever as their liar was, they wouldn't be so dumb as to call themselves out. Which left no one—unless Brooklyn were to add Asana and Annabelle to the list. But they were equally as worried about the truth coming out.

Yep, zero suspects.

Hopefully the videos would show someone acting off, or catch a whisper of conversation. She couldn't be everywhere all at once.

"I know this was supposed to be a secret." Annabelle's sweet Southern rich-girl drawl was over the top, even for her, and cut through the few conversations, drawing attention to where she stood near the television. Center stage. "But I'm just dying to know. What did y'all put in the capsule?" She wiggled her brows. "I'll tell if you do."

Everyone started talking at once, excitement whipping through the room as they offered up their secrets in a way that blended every syllable into a word smoothie.

Annabelle clinked on her glass with her massive pink diamond. "You all remember the rules, we didn't graduate that long ago. OhmyChanel, can you believe it's been five years though?" She touched the corner of her eye, stretching the skin as if she actually had wrinkles to hide. "Worried about lines already."

A bleached and bronzed Jane laughed from where she perched on the arm of a couch in faux leather pants so tight they melted into her toned legs. "You haven't aged a day."

She wasn't lying. Annabelle looked twenty years old still.

"Thank you. Haven't even started on the Tox yet." Annabelle winked, her gaze sliding toward Brooklyn.

Brooklyn lipped the side of her wineglass, suppressing a smile. They used to call Botox "the Tox" together, thinking maybe it had poisoned Lily Walker's brain with all its toxins.

"Well, I put in a pair of panties, but not just any pair." Annabelle waved her hands at her cheeks, blowing out a breath like she'd just made the confession of a lifetime. "*The* pair."

"The pair?" Brooklyn wasn't sure why she asked, because she didn't really want to know the answer.

"The pair I lost it to Greg in. I can't believe I just confessed that." She let out a squeal that rivaled sorority girls at the stadium on Bid Day—only Brooklyn knew just how fake that excitement was.

"Are you saying Greg is the only man you've slept with?" Asana, hip popped, wine teetering on the edge of her fingertips, looked as incredulous as Brooklyn felt.

Annabelle's head fell back, a throaty, almost practiced laugh escaping. But just as quickly she snapped her attention back to the group. "I didn't say that. What did you add, Brooklyn?"

Brooklyn flushed, not expecting to be chosen as the next in line to confess when it had been Asana who'd last spoken. Remembering what she put in wasn't funny or silly or sexy. It was fucking sad recalling her coach's treatment. "My jersey."

Annabelle's smile tumbled hard and fast, but only for a second before she turned with counterfeit cheerfulness and asked Asana to take the heat off Brooklyn. Annabelle had a particular talent for sweeping unappetizing things under the rug and diverting people's attention.

Asana was rubbing her bare middle finger. "A ring."

Brooklyn remembered her wearing a ring. Kind of Gothic looking. Two keys crossed. She'd assumed it was a New York private school thing.

"Oh, wonder if it was as fancy as Miss Jenny's?" Taylor asked.

"I doubt it." Asana's laugh was bitter.

Brooklyn watched as Annabelle's expression flashed fury for a second before the sweet Southern girl popped back into place. Brooklyn used to think she was the only one who'd ever worn a mask, but the more time went by, she realized that the whole fucking world hid behind their own secrets, sins, sadness.

"Taylor, what about you?" Annabelle's grin was challenging, brittle almost.

Taylor didn't flinch. Didn't need to straighten her shoulders, because she'd never slouched a day in her life. With the casualness she used to employ when telling sisters they needed a wardrobe overhaul or that she'd made them all her special cupcakes, she said smoothly, "I put a book in the capsule."

"I never saw you read a book," Annabelle teased, a knowing

intensity behind her brown eyes that she was trying to hide with colored contacts. "Which one?"

Taylor took the opportunity to stare at each sister, the silence dragging on. Her smile growing cruel, the way Brooklyn had seen her look right before she would obliterate someone and call it a favor. "Oh, just a really special one. The kind that is priceless with information. The kind someone would probably steal. Maybe even kill for."

CHAPTER TWENTY

I got called in front of the Panhellenic board for the dryer incident. I still cannot believe they are calling it hazing. Whatever bitch it was who snitched better watch out because this means war. Of course, I talked my way out of it. I'm a legacy, and I'm rich. It also helped that I had my entire sisterhood there on my behalf. I bet it was a girl who got cut. Now just to find out who she is and make her life a living hell—Heathers-style.

Kisses,
Taylor

Asana

Then

When the lights were dimmed and music thumped with such volume that it pulsed through every inch of her body, Asana came alive. A mix of pleasure and energy that she couldn't quite name. Almost as good as sex.

Sigma Chi frat house's lights were dimmed and music pumped through the room in time with colored lights, reminding Asana of one of the clubs in New York City that she'd snuck into with her friends.

With a mischievous smirk she turned to Taylor and asked, "Have you ever sat on a speaker?"

"No, but I'm guessing a lot of these frat bunnies have." Taylor's face wrinkled in disgust. "It smells like budussy in here."

Asana practically choked on her laugh, holding her hand to her mouth as if that might keep her lungs inside her body. "Accurate. But don't all the frat houses?"

Annabelle pursed her lips, confused. She studied the room as if trying to ascertain if the smell was indeed precise. "What's budussy?"

Brooklyn keeled over on a laugh, snorting through her nose.

Annabelle looked ready to practically cry, she could be so sensitive. But it wasn't her fault she was naive.

Taking pity on her, Asana explained, "It's a swampy butt, dick, pussy smell. Budussy."

"Ew." Annabelle's face crumpled as she took a whiff. "It does."

Cardi B's "WAP" pumped from the speakers set up in the corners. Asana grabbed Taylor's hand, and Brooklyn and Annabelle followed to the middle of the crowded dance floor. She danced between her friends as they twerked and grinded with their other sisters—and the frat boys, who were already getting handsy.

"I can't eat mac and cheese anymore." Brooklyn stuck out her tongue as Cardi B compared pussy sounds to macaroni in a pot.

"What? I could really go for some Kraft right now." Asana spread two fingers in front of her mouth and flicked her tongue through it, which only made her friends squeal with laughter.

"I'm starved too." Taylor eyed Asana in a way that made her think she was hungry for more than just old-school mac and cheese.

Behind her ribs, her heart did a hiccup, which made her entire body tense.

"Drinks?" Asana needed to put some distance between herself and Taylor. She was getting all sorts of vibes and it was hard to figure them out. Some girls liked to kiss other girls at parties because it was fun. Other girls liked to kiss girls at parties because they liked to kiss girls. Which one was Taylor?

Asana knew which one she was.

Taylor's boyfriend Brad showed up then, grabbing her breasts from behind, before she turned around to give him a teasing smack. Was it Asana's imagination or was there real venom in that playful hit? Douchebag Brad lifted Taylor into the air, her skirt riding up until her ass was bared, her legs wrapped around his waist, and pretended to air fuck her.

Gross.

Annabelle grabbed hold of Taylor's skirt and tugged to hide the fact that she was wearing a bright pink thong.

"I'll get the drinks," Asana volunteered, unable to watch any longer.

She bounced her way through the crowd toward the keg and held up four fingers for the pledge brother in charge of pours. So far, she hadn't spied the weird sister who'd propositioned her about the secret society. Knowing every person in the secret society also had ties to Greek Life upped her interest in being a part of this crowd. She had a mission after all.

Keg bro eyed her up and down, his eyes on her breasts, which she pushed out hoping for a heavier serve, with not too much head—though she didn't say the last part, already knowing he would tell her all about his "head."

Tits out worked.

"You're hot," he said with a grin that was mostly drunk and sloppy, beer sloshing over the sides of the red Solo cup.

Asana grabbed the beers, liquid dripping down her own fingers as she tried to balance the four cups in her hands. She looked him in the eyes as she licked the foam from the top. "Thanks." For an added reward, she put an extra twitch in her ass on the way back to her friends.

They weren't allowed to have alcohol at the ADL house, but the frats practically had drinks melting from the walls. The whole house smelled like stale beer and a tinge of weed. Red Solo cups and low-carb cans were in every hand, as people danced to the club music.

Doja Cat came on, and Asana's hands shot up into the air as she gyrated to the beat. "I'm a bitch, I'm a boss," she sang. A party like this, dancing, being one with the music was so much more fun than the swaps earlier tonight—which had been a total bore fest.

As if women weren't already hard enough on themselves, the frat boys had judged them as they walked down the stairs, choosing them like they were dogs at a fucking show. They were arrogant, beyond arrogant. So cocky, the chips on their shoulders leaving piles of sawdust behind her.

Asana had been paired up with another freshman, Toby, and within thirty seconds of passing her a flower like they were on an episode of *The Bachelor*, he'd grabbed her ass. She'd pretended to like it while she plotted his demise. Wouldn't do to make a bad impression on the first night, and Toby, bless his heart, was definitely not ready for her real reaction, which might have scarred him for life. Then again, maybe he needed a little scarring.

Besides, what she'd really wanted was the ability to come to this after-party for the purposes of getting closer to the society, and if it meant letting Toby Grabbyfingers touch her ass so she could get in, then fine. But if he thought he was getting laid tonight, he was in for a world of disappointment. And maybe a black eye.

"Bathroom!" Taylor shouted over the music, and the four of

them made a train, dancing toward the line to the no-doubt disgusting bathroom. "I need to give y'all something."

They danced in line, joked about their swaps. Taylor had practically been fingered in the ass by her date when he picked her up and swung her around. That definitely wasn't an accident. How do you accidentally grab someone's ass so hard your finger ends up in their crack?

Brooklyn had already made out with her date, and Annabelle had to decline giving hers a blow job in the bathroom when he'd told her he deserved it for picking her. Annabelle had almost agreed until the three of them had told her BJs needed to be earned.

"You know what I heard?" Asana smirked. "'Swaps' stands for Sex With a Penis, Sis."

Everyone burst out laughing. "Who says 'penis'? So clinical." Taylor was laughing so hard tears were dripping from her eyes.

"Penis!" Asana shouted, her fist in the air.

A chorus of "penis" shouts ricocheted from around the room. The girls crammed into the tiny and disgusting bathroom, locking the door behind them to the catcalls.

"Okay, ladies. I have something . . ." Taylor pulled a tiny bag with purple pills from her bra. "It's like anti–date rape."

"What?" Asana stared at the baggie. She'd been to enough clubs that she should have heard of anti-date-rape pills.

Taylor wiggled the bag in front of their faces. "If a guy is coming on too strong, slip this into his drink. It will knock him out."

Asana raised an eyebrow and flicked the bag. "So, it *is* a date-rape drug?"

Taylor laughed. "Let's call it anti–date rape. Some of these guys are super handsy. And while I'm not a prude, I want to choose myself, not have what and who I do it with chosen for me.

And obvs I chose Brad." She said the last part fast, almost like a hurried afterthought.

"Same." Brooklyn let out a long sigh that made Asana think they might need to unpack that later. "Not about Brad, though." She giggled.

"One tiny pill can make that happen." Taylor looked supremely confident. "Promise."

Asana plucked at Taylor's top, feeling a little thrill as the tip of her finger scraped over the top of Taylor's breast. "What else have you got in there, Miss Pharmacist?"

Taylor grinned. "Wouldn't you like to know?"

Actually, yes, she would.

Someone banged on the door, shouting for them to hurry up. They went about their business with the grungy toilet, then each of them tucked a purple pill into her bra, armed against the frat boys who wanted to accidentally slip it in.

By the end of the night, Asana had been groped more times than she could count, but she'd also groped plenty herself. The one thing she hadn't been successful at, however, was ferreting out the members of the secret society in order to get an invitation.

Back at her dorm, she peeled off her sweaty clothes, the purple pill melted and stuck to her breast. What even was it? She plucked it off and put it in her jewelry box to save for later.

If it really did what Taylor said, then she was all for safety. With what she had planned, she was going to need it.

CHAPTER TWENTY-ONE

Taylor won homecoming queen. It wasn't an accident, and I know that because I'm the one who was "inspired" to sway the votes. Of course, she was surprised, because it wasn't her behind it. Just like she didn't have a choice in the king—Greg Hamm, president of Sigma Chi. God, he's such a dick.

Kisses,
Asana

Annabelle

Now

That escalated quickly.

Annabelle kept her gaze focused on the gathered ADL alumni sisters, because if she were to glance at Taylor, the horror she felt at the situation had a good chance of breaking through the carefully constructed vault she'd built up around herself.

Annabelle never flinched.

It was a skill she'd been honing since the first time her mother told her she looked "foreign." As if looking anything other than bleached and blond was a crime.

Lily Walker was such a bitch sometimes.

The horror she felt inside at Taylor suggesting someone might kill over a stupid book filled with secrets was reflected in the "WTF" expressions of the women in the room.

Time for her to pick up the debris of a Taylor bomb like she'd done so many times in college.

"Oh my goodness, y'all, Taylor's kidding." Annabelle let out a Lily Walker laugh, a peal so fake and so shrill it was like diamonds scraping on glass, if only she had the plastic look to match.

Nervous laughter shuddered out of several of the women, but it was Jacqueline who spoke with a tone bordering on hysteria. "What book, Taylor?"

What secrets had Jacqueline put in the book?

Taylor pursed her lips, the truculent expression on her face familiar to everyone in attendance. And for once, Annabelle wasn't going to shy away from confrontation. Not if they were actually going to get answers. If her secret was found out, it meant jail time. And the last thing she wanted to do was grovel to man-whore Greg.

But before she could say something, Taylor spoke. "*The* book, Jacqueline. The only book that ever mattered to us all."

If Annabelle had interpreted horror on her sisters' faces before, then it had only been a tease, because now their mouths dropped open in silent slasher-film screams. Okay, perhaps that was an exaggeration to go along with the screeching in Annabelle's head.

"Why the hell would you put that in there?" Jacqueline asked the question that Annabelle had been too much of coward to ask herself.

Taylor's Spill Book had been her shield, her weapon, her dynamite when she needed to get something out of someone. And Annabelle, Asana, and Brooklyn had all been complacent to it, even being so stupid as to mark down their own dark secrets.

To think now that they'd all willingly implicated themselves was mind-boggling.

Taylor crossed her sculpted arms over her designer shirt. "That capsule wasn't supposed to be opened for a hundred years. If we were all dead, who cares? And besides, it's not like anyone can prove anything. It could have just been a joke."

"Then that's what they will think now." Ally nodded, her head bobbling like an old doll whose skull had been ripped off too many times, her lips peeled into a smile so brittle it might crack.

"They won't." This time it was Asana that spoke up. "Maybe some of the things, but someone will be curious enough to dig. And when people start digging, they will find answers to their questions. And my guess is, they will find a lot."

Annabelle's stomach twisted. She shouldn't have had any wine. Or any cheese, but she'd been nibbling on one chunk of gruyere after another since she'd missed . . . hmmm . . . every meal today. Acid climbed her throat, and she swallowed it down with another sip of wine.

"Ladies, need I remind you I have an eidetic memory." Though her face remained placid, there was a crocodile smile to Taylor's words as she pointed out that the book didn't matter, because she could recall words without looking.

"Eidetic?" Jacqueline screwed up her face the same way Liam used to before a massive baby fart. "More like selective."

Taylor's eyes flashed murder, and she looked ready to pounce, but Annabelle jumped in. "Oh, Jackie, let's not quarrel. We're all adults here. And Taylor, I'm sure, is just . . ."

"Just what? Threatening us like she did all through college?" Jaqueline stood, her hands fisted at her sides. But even standing at her full height she was half a foot shorter than Taylor.

"Oh please, you'd screw things up yourself if it weren't for me."

Taylor rolled her eyes, as if Jaqueline were nothing more than an annoying gnat.

"Not helping, Taylor."

"I don't need to sit here and take this." Jacqueline huffed and turned around, making eyes with her friends, likely trying to rally the troops.

When no one moved, Jacqueline hissed something under her breath and turned back to face Taylor.

But it was Brooklyn who stepped between them this time. "Y'all! We're supposed to be sisters. Yes, there were a few things we'd all like to wipe from our brains, but let's not forget the fun moments. The moments of us all working together for a common cause. The movie nights, the makeovers, the puppy yoga. Come on now, we loved each other once. Dig deep here."

"Really deep," Jacqueline muttered.

"Fine, dig as deep as you need, darlin'," Annabelle said. "Just as long as you find it in your heart to stay until we hash this out."

"Why should we?" Ally stood from where she'd perched on a chair, which only reignited Jacqueline's crusade against Taylor.

Annabelle closed her eyes for a second. Pictured herself in her safe room. Namaste. One prong at a time. Mentally she bent the metal, until the diamond was free, holding it up in her mind the way she often did to calm herself.

"No one is leaving this room until we find out who took the book." It was Asana who said it this time, and when they all looked toward the exit, she had two gigantic men standing on either side of her. "My dudes will be right outside this door to make sure. Cut the crap, ladies. Some of us have a life to get back to."

Annabelle's hand clutched the diamond at her throat. Her skin prickled as she stared at the bodyguards.

"Now, as Taylor was saying"—Annabelle cleared her suddenly dry throat—"or I'm sure she *meant* to say, which one of you was it?"

CHAPTER TWENTY-TWO

I'm thinking about upgrading from just feet videos and pics to something else, hands maybe. Being a sugar baby is great for the money, but I'm not sure it's worth the cost to my own self-respect. At first it was fun fucking a man who was rich, formidable, older. I felt powerful, sexy. But the whole run-in with the kid was pretty gross, and it made my mind go down a dark path, like what if they got divorced because of me? And I am definitely not stepmom material. Maybe I'll just find a new daddy. One who doesn't have kids.

Kisses,
Brooklyn

Taylor

Then

On the outside, Taylor was outgoing, a sweet blond-haired, blue-eyed Southern belle. In high school, not only was she captain of her cheer team, but she was homecoming queen, prom queen, and voted most likely to charm her way into the presidency.

Nobody knew she had an interest in politics, that was her least favorite part of the taboo five Bs—ballots were an off-limits topic.

And a Panhellenic presidency? Yes, please. Four years from now, as a senior, she was going to rule Alpha Delta Lambda and all these little bitches. And a few years after that, she was going to run for city council, then state senate, then the US Senate, until she had Madam President on her résumé.

What she kept tucked inside was that she was also way more into science than she cared to admit—hence her chem minor—and that she had a bit of a bad-girl streak that no one knew about.

And just like with any good politician, campaigning had to start early. Sneak into the hearts of every constituent before they even realized her name was on the ballot.

And part of that plan fed the inner bad girl.

So, while her chemistry TA thought she was staying after to work on a lab and she pretended to ask really in-depth and serious questions, questions that turned into an after-class make-out session (sorry-not-sorry, Brad), she was really sneaking his master set of keys to make a copy for herself.

Poor guy probably lost his shit when he noticed they were missing, but she'd returned them the next morning, innocent and sweet as cherry pie, saying they must have fallen into her bag while they were . . . you know . . . and then she'd shown him her boobs to get him to forget all about it.

Boys could be so predictable.

Well past midnight, dressed in an outfit she wouldn't be caught dead wearing in daylight—black sweatpants, black hoodie, and Chucks—she used her shiny new key to let herself into the chem building on campus through the service entrance. If anyone saw her, or a camera happened to catch her, with her head down and surrounded by darkness it would be hard to tell who she was. Besides, no one would ever suspect Taylor Collins of wearing Chucks. Ew.

Taylor was conscious of every door she passed. Being the middle of the night, she didn't expect anyone to be in the building, but then again, she was here, and on a campus of more than thirty thousand students, she might not be the only one with bad intentions.

The beat of Billie Eilish's "Bad Guy" thumped in her mind as she slinked down the hallways until she got to the lab. Not the lab she took class in, of course, but one down the hall. Her dad always said not to shit where she ate, and it had never made more sense to her than now.

Taylor put the key in the lock, holding her breath until the bolt clicked and she pushed inside, sighing with relief that it was empty. She locked the door behind her, a tingle racing up her arms as she put on her lab coat.

"I'm the bad guy," she whispered with a laugh as she set up her supplies, which included night-vision goggles because she wasn't going to risk having a light, other than the Bunsen burner flame, and what closet nerd didn't enjoy their gadgets?

Using the same recipe she'd honed in high school, she whipped up a batch of the Taylor Special.

So far, a month into the fall semester, she'd eased the girls into accepting pills from her when she'd given them all her anti-date-rape drug. Which was literally a date-rape drug. Rohypnol worked just as well on college boys with forceful dicks as it did on unsuspecting girls. All she'd done was add a little purple dye.

And right now she was making her MDMA, aka Ecstasy, the yellow bumblebee, the Taylor Special.

She'd gotten the cute little molds on Etsy. And the ingredients? Well, let's just say she was rich and could get whatever she wanted, whenever she wanted. And it's not like it was meth. MDMA had a different chemical component, a different effect, and it wasn't going to rot anyone's teeth or make them scratch those hideous marks into their skin.

Taylor was all about self-care, and if a drug was going to mess you up, then she wasn't going to make it. She had a duty to society. A duty to make people feel good. A little fun never hurt anyone, but an addiction? That was hands down out of the question.

As she waited for her little yellow bees to cure, she did in fact finish her lab work and clean up her mess. She had an A in this class. And all of her other classes. Taylor could never allow herself to get anything less than an A, that would just be embarrassing.

When the timer dinged, she popped the bees into a resealable bag she'd had custom made to look like SweeTarts Chewy candy, and then turned off everything she'd been using, making sure it looked exactly the same as it had when she arrived, and then headed out.

But as she exited from the service entrance, a flash of light caught her attention. Campus security. *Shit.*

Rodgers Library for Science was open until two a.m. She glanced at her watch, it was 2:10. She could just say she was there and was taking a shortcut. What other reason would she have to be out so late? Also, she was an adult, and they couldn't tell her she couldn't walk on campus.

Still, Taylor was careful as she eased along the building, avoiding the sweep of the flashlight.

This was not something she was going to be able to do every week. Maybe not even every month. Thankfully she'd made enough pills to tide her clients over for a little while. The rest of the pills she offered up—Xanies and Adderall—were a lot easier to get.

Taylor slipped past the campus security officer and into the night, feeling high on adrenaline alone.

As she ran back to her dorm, she passed by at least a dozen kids dressed in black hooded robes, gliding across the lawn as if they'd stepped out of some skull-and-crossbones cult. Weirdos.

But one face shining in the moonlight caught her attention. Asana?

CHAPTER TWENTY-THREE

What if me taking things is like a sign that I need to do something for the greater good? Like what if I'm the female version of Robin Hood? Although I think Robin Hood also might have stolen from the church. But he stole from corrupt churches, didn't he? Not really sure. Maybe that's a bad analogy. Lord forgive me. But the point is, maybe I take and give and then it's not really a crime or something I need to confess about. Because then it's philanthropy, and a good sister is always willing to help others and make the world a better place.

Kisses,
Annabelle

Asana

Now

The likelihood of the Spill Book being taken by one of the ninnies in this room was slim to none. But the chances of the women creaming their pants right then and there was looking pretty high.

Jesus.

Asana knew hungry looks well, even if most of them were trying to hide it. If the room had been otherwise empty, and her bodyguard unzipped his pants, hands down half a dozen women would drop to their knees.

Even wholesome Annabelle was biting her lip. Being married to Greg must be such a torment for getting her rocks off.

Maybe Asana should offer up one of her guards later? They were always down to fuck. Asana had tried each one of them when she had an itch that needed scratching, and they were both pretty fucking good. Pun intended.

The dudes stepped outside, and Asana locked the door to exaggerate her point of not letting any of these bunnies go. She came to stand beside Annabelle and Taylor, who surprisingly didn't have this meeting under control. In college, they'd played good cop, bad cop, and Asana and Brooklyn had been more like the silent assassins. But they were falling apart right before their eyes.

Too much pressure.

Asana wasn't sure which secrets each of them had divulged, but considering one of her secrets had been about Taylor, it meant there was a lot more hiding beneath her tight ass.

After Annabelle's accusation, and maybe her own threat with the dudes, the sisters were less than happy to spill the tea. In fact, they were all shouting, mostly at Taylor, and then at one another.

Fucking ridiculous.

Asana tried calling out "Hey!" but no one heard her over the cacophony of shrieks and whines. Brooklyn glanced at her with an expression that said, "Let's bail," and she wanted to. There was nothing Asana hated more than shrill twats.

She put two fingers in her mouth and blew, the ear-piercing whistle one that she would throat punch someone else for making, but it got them all to shut the hell up.

"You all are literally so embarrassing," she drawled. "Can you imagine what the actives and PNMs that are here this week would think if they saw us right now? None of them would believe we were sisters, let alone ADL. This arguing, this hair pulling and name-calling, you look like animals." Asana rolled her eyes. "And as adults, or at least little bitches in adult bodies, you know this will solve nothing."

"None of us took the book." Jaqueline crossed her arms over her manufactured C-cups.

Asana stared right at her. "That's obvious from the basic-bitch brawl you all just had."

"Fine, if no one here is willing to admit to taking the book," Taylor said, "then maybe you have an idea who did. All of us put our secrets in that book. And all of us were invited to the time capsule opening. Whoever stole the book is fucking with us. So, who isn't here that would want to hurt you?"

Asana glanced at her Apple Watch. "I don't really want this to take all night. We've got Philanthropy tomorrow, and I for one loved that part."

Brooklyn held up the new Spill Book. "If you don't want to say the names aloud of whoever might hate you, put it in here." She passed the notebook and pen to Jaqueline, who glared at Taylor like she might just bite her, before cracking open the notebook and scribbling down three names.

By the time the notebook made its way back around, Asana still couldn't put a name to the woman she'd seen running down the hall. Or if she'd just been a paranoid figment of her imagination. So instead, she wrote: *woman in the hallway.*

Taylor looked at her strangely, and Asana mouthed, "Later."

"Why would someone want to hurt us?" Ally pointedly stared at Taylor. "*You*, I can understand."

Asana kept her face neutral. With millions of clientele on the Matinee website, there were a lot of angry spouses that would want to hurt her. And with what she'd done to the Machine in college, well, double that number.

Until now she hadn't cared about that. In the deepest, darkest recesses of her heart, she was willing to admit the biggest reason she'd started the heartbreak site was that she'd hoped to catch Taylor's husband in an affair. Proof he wasn't good enough for Taylor. With nearly half the US senators as members, the odds Elijah's interest would be piqued weren't too shabby.

"Ohmygod, Ally, enough. We get it, Taylor was 'so mean,' blah blah, but seriously, the little jabs aren't going to help." Asana, perhaps a little more irritated than the situation warranted, snapped the notebook closed.

"Sorry." Ally pouted, looking down at her perfectly manicured nails.

"Listen, we need to keep this quiet," Asana said, the media-relations exec coming out with her cover-your-ass big guns. "If anyone finds out the book is missing and what it contains, it's going to send people on a wild-goose chase. The rumor mill will make it like the nineties Girls Gone Wild videos that all the frat boys used to yank it to. So please, keep this between us."

"If you think of anything, even just the silliest thing, please call us. I'm going to make a group chat." Brooklyn tapped on her cell phone, and everyone's devices started to ding. "Just AirDropped an invite."

"I don't have an Apple phone." Jacqueline's voice was starting to grate heavily on Asana's nerves. "Or any cell phone. I don't believe in being attached to a device."

Asana narrowed her eyes. *Good Lord.* If there was one person in the room who'd drive Asana over the edge, it was Jacqueline.

Brooklyn glanced up, pity in her eyes as she asked, "What's the best way to get in touch with you?"

"My home number."

Who had a home number still? "Like a landline?" Asana asked, incredulous.

Brooklyn's carefully curated expression was slipping into annoyance. "Fine. Do you check your voicemail?"

"It's recorded."

"And what? You're going to just sit at home by the phone and play a tape? What is this, 1980?" Taylor rolled her eyes.

"What about email?" Brooklyn asked.

"I have email."

"But do you have a laptop? It's a device." Taylor was gritting her teeth.

Jacqueline's chin notched up ninety degrees. "I do. For work."

"Will you commit to checking it?" Brooklyn asked.

"Yes."

Asana glanced at Brooklyn. "Can you add an email to the string?"

"I'll figure it out." Brooklyn tapped on her phone.

"Dismissed." Asana waved her hand, then unlocked the door. Her guards stepped aside to let everyone out.

When the room was emptied and it was just the four of them left, Taylor held up a small baggie. "Gummies anyone?"

"Are those bumblebees?" Brooklyn squinted toward the bag of bumblebee-shaped gummies.

"Maybe." Taylor shrugged. "I need to take the edge off this fucked-up night. And I have an even better recipe."

"I have a confession." Brooklyn bit her lip, looking proud as hell. "I recorded this entire meeting."

Asana started to laugh. "Of course you did, you little evil genius."

CHAPTER TWENTY-FOUR

I may be a poli-sci major, but I love chemistry. I love the processes of combining elements and creating. I have a new project I'm working on. A lucrative one, but also a fun one. I don't know if it's going to work out, but they might soon be calling me the Pharmacist, and not just because I plan to get my PharmD after graduation.

Kisses,
Taylor

Brooklyn

Then

An alarm at three o'clock in the morning wasn't exactly the glamorous lifestyle Brooklyn imagined for herself when she was making money as a content creator. Unfortunately, the women's soccer team locker room, which she was using as a film set today, would be jam-packed at five a.m. So a girl had to do what a girl had to do.

Her roommate made an annoyed grumble at the incessant alarm, and Brooklyn bounced out of bed, silencing it. She'd been planning this video for days, and had gotten up at three a.m. yesterday too just to make sure that the locker room *was* empty at three thirty. Dressing in the dark, she slipped on her new toe ring from Annabelle and then into her sneakers, grabbed her gym bag, which also contained her tripod, and then headed out into the shadowy campus night.

How ironic that she was passing people on campus who were wandering home after a night of partying or studying, while she was waking up for the day.

A familiar gait loomed ahead, but she didn't recognize who it might be, with the black hoodie concealing their features. The swing of the hips was all Taylor, but Taylor would never be caught dead wearing a sweatsuit. And also, what would Taylor be doing out alone on campus in the middle of the night? Brooklyn actually laughed at the thought, which drew the attention of said hoodie.

Just a quick flash of face in the moonlight. But the sardonic expression was all too familiar.

"Ohmygod, Taylor?"

Taylor rushed toward her, stopping short of running her over. "Shh." She pressed a hand to Brooklyn's mouth and furtively glanced around. Appeased by the lack of any audience, she stepped away.

Brooklyn frowned. "What are you doing out here? Dressed like that? And so paranoid."

"You didn't see me." Taylor kept her voice low, tucking the hood more closely around her face, reminding Brooklyn of how when she'd been a kid, she'd grab the hoodie laces and pull so hard only her nose showed.

Brooklyn blinked. "Okay."

"Seriously, B. I'm not here."

Brooklyn shook her head. "Not at all. Figment of my imagination."

"You have no imagination." Taylor's tone was as flat as paved concrete.

"Not exactly true." But it wasn't like she was going to confess to Taylor what she was about to go do.

"I mean about right now, not your content." This time, Taylor's voice held the slightest hint of apology.

Brooklyn tilted her chin up. "Thank you for clarifying."

Taylor's eyes shifted and she looked ready to bolt. Brooklyn wanted to ask her what she was doing out here like this, but considering how weird she was being, Taylor wasn't likely to share.

"I gotta go." Brooklyn moved around Taylor, walking backward. "Deadlines."

"Right."

That bizarre encounter wasted five precious minutes. Brooklyn hugged her gym bag and took off at a sprint. Being sweaty wasn't exactly part of the script, but it couldn't hurt either. By the time she made it across campus to the women's soccer complex, she was coated in a sheen of perspiration, and it was 3:25.

She scanned into the building with her team card and dipped into the dark and empty room. A flip of the switch illuminated the lockers, benches. There was still plenty of time to film.

Brooklyn had several videos and photos sketched out. With her tripod and lighting set up, she filmed herself walking into the locker room in her practice uniform—her face was always hidden from view. Being recognized would ruin everything for her.

The new toe ring blinked in the glow of her ring light as she stripped down to nothing and then tiptoed to the shower. Shower scenes always got a zillion clicks. This one was bound to get her enough money to pay her dues for ADL for the next few semesters.

After the shower scene, she followed up with her foot fetish fans, by taking pics of her feet with water sluicing down the metatarsal bones to between her toes. A foot up on the locker bench as she dried. Her naked foot curled over a soccer ball, toes pointed.

"Hello? Who's in here?"

Brooklyn froze for a fraction of a second before she was a flurry of naked parts, turning off the ring light camera and trying to shove all her things under the bench and out of immediate sight of the person entering. The person who sounded a lot like her coach.

As silently as she could, she ran back to the showers, wrapped a towel around herself, and answered, "Coach Tamson?"

"Tolley?" The coach rounded the corner and spied her in her towel, hair still damp enough she could claim to have just gotten out. "What are you doing here so early?"

Tamson narrowed her eyes, hands on her hips as she stared around the shower room.

Brooklyn's phone was clutched in her armpit, where she hoped it was hidden from view.

"Wanted to get in an early workout and shower. Couldn't sleep." She laughed to play it off, hoping her coach bought her easy lie.

Tamson grunted, a sound that didn't come off as trusting. "That all you're doing in here?"

Brooklyn perfected the innocent tilt of her head, pulling on a sweet smile à la Annabelle. She used the same saccharine tone Annabelle used too when she said, "What else could I be doing?"

Tamson looked her up and down. "Don't know. Never seen an athlete in here an hour before practice."

"I'm glad to be your first." Brooklyn giggled, hating every second of this interaction. "Well, I'd better get dressed."

Tamson grunted once more, giving the area another thorough sweep with the same observation she used in practice to point out their flaws. Brooklyn thanked God she'd left her equipment out by the lockers. Now all she had to do was pray Tamson didn't follow her while she got dressed.

"No funny business." Tamson's tone was harsh but also dismissive.

"I would never." Brooklyn let out a long, slow breath she hoped her coach didn't hear. She was off the hook.

Tamson made a noise that definitely sounded like she didn't believe her, but she did turn around and walk toward her office. As soon as she was out of sight, Brooklyn rushed to the lockers, jamming the legs of her tripod down where it lay under the bench, shrinking her ring light, and shoving them into her bag so hard she heard a crack.

"Fuck," she groaned, then hurried to dress.

That was a close call. *Too* close.

If she didn't want to lose her scholarship, that had to be the last time she did something so incredibly reckless and stupid.

Part III

SISTERHOOD
Accepting each other unconditionally . . .

CHAPTER TWENTY-FIVE

I think some of these Machine people might drink the blood of their young. They really shouldn't procreate. I bought a giant box of morning-after pills. It wasn't easy, the pharmacy tech prob thinks I'm a hoe, but all I had to do was slip her two bennies to smile and hand them over. I'm going to distribute them at the next meeting.

Kisses,
Asana

Annabelle

Now

Was it possible to hate and love something so entirely that the two sentiments mingled into one glob of a mess that would be hard even for the best trained therapist to untangle?

That was how Annabelle felt every time she pulled up in front of the Alpha Delta Lamba house. She'd arrived early this morning on Magnolia and was staring up at the great house that had been so fundamental in her youth, and even now, as a woman approaching her thirties. If she could go back in time, she'd tell her eighteen-year-old self that some of the things she thought mattered so much really didn't.

And things she didn't care about back then mattered a *whole* lot right now.

Last night hadn't been fruitful. If anything, they were left with more questions. But after the sorority brunch today, they were going to go back to Brooklyn's to rewatch the footage she captured from the tea party. Nothing had stuck out at them before and they blamed the wine and exhaustion. Annabelle hoped they'd be able to find something so she could put this whole thing to bed.

They were no closer to figuring out who had stolen the Spill Book, but Annabelle's skin had started to itch with the need to confess her secrets to her friends. The last thing she wanted was for them to find out about her little habit-turned-career as a fence from some stranger bent on an *I Know What You Did Last Summer* revenge scheme.

Just as she was approaching the door her phone buzzed. A FaceTime call from the nanny. Great, here it was, the call she'd been waiting for. Annabelle groaned, rolling her eyes, then fixed her face into a smile she didn't feel as she pressed the green answer button.

"Concetta, hi," Annabelle said, sweet as sugar.

Concetta did not return the smile, and her voice was full of angry vinegar as she spat, "I thought you should know that I quit. Liam is at school."

Annabelle nodded, letting out a resigned sigh. She'd known this was coming. Had prepared for it too.

"Thank you for letting me know. I'll have the service send over someone right away to be there for Liam."

"Your husband is—"

"Concetta, if you want a recommendation from me, which you'll need, I'd prefer you not say it aloud, at least to me."

Concetta's mouth fell open. "You *know*?"

"Unfortunately. Thank you for all you've done for Liam." Annabelle ended the call. The door to ADL started to open, and she scurried around to the side of the house, out of sight, while the phone rang for the nanny service.

As she explained the situation, not to the full extent, of course, the coordinator of the service sounded exasperated. "Mrs. Hamm, *again?*"

Not Annabelle's surname, she'd never agreed to be a Hamm—she hated pork—and the tart tone from the service agent wasn't appreciated by Annabelle. It was bad enough she'd saddled Liam with the surname, not to mention the father, but she hadn't had a choice in that. And divorce was out of the question.

"We need someone right away," she said, ignoring the judgmental agent. "My son will need to be picked up after school today."

"We don't—"

"Offer time and a half."

"Mrs.—"

"Fine, offer double, but only for the first two weeks."

By then she'd probably have to hire someone else anyway.

"Done."

Around the front of the house, Annabelle could hear the girls setting up for what was probably going to be a song. She didn't want to miss it, but she didn't want Greg to get away with this either.

She watched the way her ring sparkled in the sun as she listened to the ring tone, and then finally his lackadaisical "Greg Hamm," as if he didn't know it was his wife calling.

"What the . . . fuck, Greg?" She rarely used the F-word, but in this case, it seemed warranted.

"Whoaaaaa, Anna, I don't care for your tone."

The nerve! Annabelle laughed. "And I don't care to hire another nanny because you couldn't keep your dick in your pants. At
least have the decency to not shit where you eat."

Greg was silent. She didn't normally talk to him like this. Or
anyone. He was her insurance policy for a reason.

"Won't happen again." His words were clipped, but at least he
showed her enough respect not to deny what she already knew.

"Good. Because if it does, I'll make your life a living fucking
hell." A rush of adrenaline pumped itself into her chest, making
Annabelle feel a little off balance.

"Noted."

"Give Liam a kiss for me."

"You should be here and give him a kiss yourself."

"Appreciate it. Bye, love." She used that same Southern sweet
charm she'd learned from her own mother.

Poor Lily Walker had probably been dealing with a wandering
dick herself.

Annabelle tucked the phone into her purse and marched
around the side of the house with a wide nothing-to-see-here
smile on her face.

The ADL actives were all lined up in adorable blue-and-white-
and-silver Dallas Cowboys Cheerleader outfits, complete with
sparkling poms, the opening chords of AC/DC's "Thunder-
struck" playing on a speaker.

"Song time." Asana grinned where she stood on the sidewalk,
dressed to kill in stilettos and skintight white pants. "I fucking
loved song time."

"Still got the moves?" Annabelle asked.

"Practice a few nights a week at whatever club I want." Asana
lifted her arms into the air before dragging them down the length
of her body, lingering over her breasts, as her hips swayed to the
beat.

"You were the queen of twerk."

"Don't tell Taylor."

Annabelle chuckled. "She knew. My favorites were the dance-offs."

"So much fucking fun."

Brooklyn hurried toward them, dark sunglasses hiding her eyes. "Where's Taylor?"

"Up here, bitches!" Taylor called from the second-floor balcony of the house, where she stood in the center, surveying her domain.

"I think if you could be ADL president for life, Taylor absolutely would have done so," Asana said, watching her.

"Hundred percent," Brooklyn agreed.

"Come up, we'll watch from here," Taylor called.

The three of them weaved through the practicing sisters and inside, up the stairs to the balcony. As they followed Taylor's beckoning, Annabelle couldn't help but think how little things had changed.

ADL looked so much like it did five years ago, nine years ago when she was a freshman, and even twenty years ago when she'd been in third grade and came with her mom to help do some philanthropy thing.

A nearly blond sea of white girls. All thin. All bouncy. All pink and glossy. But in between the white and pink, she caught glimpses of rushes who didn't look the way she'd been told to look her whole life. A few girls of color. And she hoped this year, they'd change things. Accept sisters for who they were, to make friends unconditionally.

Standing on the balcony, surveying the lawn with the women who'd been a huge part of her life, Annabelle had the overwhelming urge to confess. Before she could stop herself, the words were tumbling from her mouth.

"Greg fucked the nanny."

CHAPTER TWENTY-SIX

There's a rumor going around that one of the girls on the soccer team filmed a naked shower scene for OnlyFans. Fuck. I didn't realize I had fans at Bama. Fuck me.

Kisses,
Brooklyn

Taylor

Then

Clink. Clink. Clink.

Taylor tapped the side of her teacup with a spoon, gathering the attention of the fifty pledge sisters in attendance.

"Welcome, ladies, to our very first Spill the Tea Party."

Not a single look of apprehension passed between her ADL sisters as they cheered. All were oblivious to what she was going to ask of them.

"I have a very special surprise." Taylor winked at her friends—even though they didn't know what was going on, she wanted to give the appearance of a united front.

Claps echoed in the chapter meeting room in the basement of their sorority house. Taylor patted the bedazzled lockbox on the table in front of her, then took the key from a chain around her neck and turned the lock. The room was whisper silent. She pulled from the box a large, pink, leather-bound notebook, on the front of which she'd used sparkly gems in various shades of pink to spell out "Spill Book."

"This, my dearest sisters, is our Spill Book." Taylor wiggled her brows and grinned. "I'm honored to have been voted your pledge class president, and to help ease the way into this next chapter of our lives as ADL sisters."

The squealing pitch could have broken the windows had there been any, and Taylor loved their enthusiasm for the unknown.

"Every meeting is going to be henceforth called a tea party, and at every meeting, we're going to do a trust exercise that will help us to, well, trust each other, to bond and grow in our sisterhood." Taylor wiggled the book and picked up a pen with a fluffy pink ball on the end. She did a little fun dance with the book, which only seemed to enhance their excitement. "Our official Spill Book will be kept in this locked box, in my personal possession at all times. So you'll never have to worry about your secrets getting out. They are safe with me until the grave."

Girls were tittering now, some looking a little nervous and a few others gleeful. Secrets were always hard to resist—listening and sharing.

"To start our first Spill the Tea session, Annabelle has passed out to each of you a pink bandanna. Tie the bandanna around your head to hide your eyes."

Taylor waited as her sisters followed the instructions, even Annabelle. In a room full of pledges, Taylor was the only one not blindfolded. There was a sense of power in knowing they were blind while she could look wherever she liked. And she grinned as she scanned the shifting bodies to see who would be the first person to write in the special Spill Book. Well, technically the second; she'd already done the first entry herself.

Silent as a sister sneaking in past curfew, Taylor moved toward

Brooklyn, kneeled in front of where she sat on the floor, and placed the Spill Book in her lap. A shudder passed through Brooklyn that she hoped was excitement as she took her hand and placed the pen between her fingers.

"You're first," she whispered. "Share a secret no one knows about."

Brooklyn bit her lip, her whitened teeth scraping over her peach-colored lip gloss. "No one is going to see this?"

"No one. Make it juicy. The juicier the better. Remember this is a trust exercise, so we all trust each other. We trust ourselves to share, and we trust our sisters won't violate us by reading our entries."

"Even you?"

"Even me. I swear." Taylor kept her voice soft and even, calming. If this was going to work, everyone had to write their shit in the book. Their deepest, darkest secrets. Their most embarrassing moments. And they had to believe no one was ever going to see it, even though she planned on reading every fucking word.

The Spill Book originated as an idea she had for hazing when she became president. To use people's secrets against them. She needed all the insurance she could get with her line of business. But rather than wait until her junior year, when she hoped to run, she'd decided to bring it out now. Pledge class president was still in charge, and this way, she'd have secrets for four years.

If there was one thing her father had taught her in life, it was that insurance policies were of the utmost importance. And not just the legal kind.

"You can lift your blindfold to start, so you don't mess up the lines."

Brooklyn nodded, gripped the pen, and started to write.

Taylor walked around, wondering who she was going to pick next. "Not everyone will get a chance to write in the Spill Book every meeting. There's too many of us. But I'll keep a list. So don't worry, you'll get your turn. Oh, and I almost forgot, sign your entries with 'Kisses,' and your name. What can I say, I love *Gossip Girl*."

"Done!" Brooklyn pulled her blindfold back into place and held up the Spill Book.

"Oh no," Taylor said, retrieving the book and pen. "You don't have to be blindfolded anymore since you wrote in the book."

A prize for confessing, the gift of sight. Taylor giggled to herself as Brooklyn whipped off the blindfold with obvious relief.

Like a hawk circling its prey, Taylor circumnavigated the room. The silence of held breaths broke into panicked little gasps as each sister felt the air move as she passed them. When she thought they couldn't take the torment anymore, she stopped. "Jacqueline, right?"

"You remember my name?" There was a tone of desperation to Jacqueline's voice that Taylor found annoying.

"I'm trying to remember everyone." Taylor rolled her eyes. No one could see her do it, but even if they could, she wouldn't care. Jacqueline was acting pathetic. Enough that Taylor almost said "never mind," but for a girl like that, Taylor couldn't wait to see what she confessed.

Taylor pressed the pen into her hand and flipped the Spill Book open for her to write, covering up Brooklyn's confession with an index card paper clipped to the page. There had to be a way to build trust and to not waste space on the paper.

"Okay, lift your blindfold and be sure to share your darkest secret. Just one—leave room for next time."

Jacqueline stared at the blank space, her pen hovering over the paper. Taylor watched her hesitate. Watched her touch the index card, and wondered if she was going to lift it to peek, but she didn't. She started to scribble, and Taylor walked away to give her the impression she had privacy.

"Done!" Jacqueline glanced up, her face pale behind her makeup.

"Good job." Taylor took the book, clipping another index card in place to hide the confession, but not before she caught a glimpse.

Last year I played seven minutes in heaven and accidentally gave my brother's best friend a BJ in the closet.

How does one accidentally give a BJ? Oops my mouth was open and it fell inside?

Every BJ Taylor gave was always with a purpose. It wasn't like she actually enjoyed stuffing meat in her mouth. She was a vegetarian sometimes. But the fact was, the only way to get a guy to shut up was to unzip his pants. Like last night with Brad. When someone told him she had Xanies for sale and he started asking questions, she blew off his questions while she blew him off.

No more questions.

CHAPTER TWENTY-SEVEN

I think I got roofied last night. I'm not sure. Because I don't remember. So, either I just blacked out or I got freaking roofied.

Kisses,
Annabelle

Brooklyn

Now

So, they were confessing now—in the very house where all these secrets had begun.

Ironic, much?

Brooklyn swallowed hard, unable to look at Annabelle or the rest of her friends as she too decided to word vomit. "I used to fuck daddies."

Without missing a beat Taylor smirked a reply. "Assuming you and your husband still get it on, you're fucking a daddy now."

Brooklyn cocked her head toward Taylor. She of all people knew the truth. Because it had been confessed in the Spill Book over and over again. And Brooklyn might seem stupid, but she wasn't naive. There was no way in hell that Taylor hadn't slobbered all over every juicy bite of that damned book.

"What are you saying?" Asana looked amused, bemused almost.

Brooklyn lifted a shoulder. "For money. I was a sugar baby."

"No shit." Asana's expression was surprisingly impressed. Not shocked.

Brooklyn was amazed that she wasn't getting more shit for her confession. The only one who hadn't said anything was Annabelle. Probably because Brooklyn had basically said she was one of the girls fucking her husband—even if not actually. Oddly enough, Annabelle didn't look exactly crushed though. More contemplative.

"I needed the money." Brooklyn licked her lips, deciding it was now or never to come out with the whole truth. "My parents were poor. I went to Bama on a soccer scholarship, but that didn't pay for Greek Life—and then I lost it." She shrugged. "OnlyFans got me enough to buy the clothes and whatnot, but to keep it up, especially after I lost my scholarship, daddies were the way to go."

"Were they gross?" Taylor wrinkled her nose.

"Is your husband?" Brooklyn retorted. "They were about his age. Graying around the temples and popping blues before we got naked."

"Elijah doesn't need blues." Taylor pouted and rolled her eyes, before grumbling, "Most of the time."

"He will. And you'll be glad he's hitting your V with his V-amped dick." Asana chuckled. "What is he, twice your age?"

"Age is just a number. Don't knock it until you've tried it." Brooklyn popped a hip and blew on her nails.

Asana grinned. "You've got a good point. I have a few friends who love their zaddies."

Brooklyn rolled her eyes at Asana's term for a hot older man.

"Why are we talking about me? Annabelle needs our support." Taylor had the audacity to look at them like they were the monsters. "Poor thing. Did you just find out?"

Annabelle shrugged. "Greg likes strange." She flicked her gaze toward Taylor, and Brooklyn swallowed the sudden sharp, sour rise of bile in her throat.

"Strange? Like furry strange?" Taylor laughed.

"Strange as in lots of different vag. Which are probably furry."

"'Vag' is so gross-sounding," Taylor quipped.

"What would you rather me say? That Greg likes to fuck any cunt he can?"

"Whoa, not the C-word." Brooklyn grimaced.

"People may be buying your bad-girl-gone-good-mommy-blogger bullshit, but you just admitted to blowing old dicks for money," Taylor reminded her. "Saying 'cunt' is probably the prudest thing in this entire conversation."

"I'm not a whore," Brooklyn said. And why the hell weren't her friends saying what she'd had to do was justifiable? Walk a mile in her ratty-ass shoes in high school and they'd have jumped at the chance when a few dollar bills were thrown their way too.

Taylor raised her eyebrows. "I think being paid for sex is the definition of 'prostitution.'"

"It's not the same. Mistresses aren't whores," Brooklyn said. "And I didn't have to sleep with them. I chose to. I'm not ashamed of it."

"Does Mr. FixIt know?" Taylor taunted.

Brooklyn pretended the question didn't ruffle her. "Yes," she lied, immediately feeling guilty. Before Taylor could open her mouth to say anything else that made Brooklyn want to stuff her Jimmy Choo into it, she cut her off.

"You know, we've all got secrets we confessed in that book, Taylor, and you're the only one who knows ours." Brooklyn was happy to redirect the conversation from herself to Taylor.

Everything was always about Taylor.

Queen T.

Total Bitch, she'd heard some of the sisters call her behind her back, but then she'd be all sweet and bake them the best red velvet cupcakes Brooklyn had ever had. They were like crack. So much so, she sometimes wondered if Taylor had slipped something in them.

Music thumped from out on the lawn beneath the balcony. The Dallas Cowboys Cheerleaders were replaced by a sea of pink. Three active ADL sisters started to film with their phones, while the PNMs watched them perform "Dance the Night" by Dua Lipa. The girls converged in a row and started to do the line dance from the Barbie movie, their new president taking the part of Margot Robbie.

"I love this song." Annabelle swayed to the beat.

"I loved this movie." Brooklyn grinned. "This was a good choice."

"I love that every night is girls' night," Asana said in her typical serious tone, her eyes sliding to Taylor, who flicked her gaze away and said nothing.

Was Taylor still mad that Brooklyn had called her out? For fuck's sake, she was saved by fifty Barbies downstairs.

"Hey." Taylor touched Brooklyn's hand. "I'm sorry. You're not a whore. I didn't mean it like that."

Brooklyn swallowed the swell of emotion in her throat, working to get it down enough to speak. She nodded. "Thank you."

"And, Annabelle . . ." Taylor's lips tightened. Her head fell back as she looked up at the sky and let out a dramatic sigh. "I'm really sorry that you married such a fucked-up asshole. And I wish I'd been able to stop you."

Annabelle's lower lip trembled, a sheen coming to her eyes. "Thank you."

Asana put her arm around Brooklyn's and Annabelle's shoulders, waving Taylor in. The four of them hugged one another, leaning on each other the way they had in college. Words said, words left unsaid. None of that mattered in this moment anymore. Just that they were back together again.

As they watched the dancers shake and sing, then do a retake until it was perfect for their TikTok streams, Brooklyn couldn't help but be brought back in time to when they'd choreographed their own sorority dance to "Crazy in Love" by Beyoncé. And this dark mood needed to be lightened.

"When they finish, let's show them ours?" Brooklyn said.

"Oh, no." Taylor shook her head and indicated her outfit. "I don't dance in Dior."

"If you can't dance in Dior, you shouldn't dance at all," Asana challenged.

"You're going to do it?" Taylor asked.

"Of course. You know most of those girls are wondering what a bunch of old hags are doing here anyway. Might as well show them we're still cool. Maybe even cooler than they are."

"Who are you calling a hag?" Brooklyn swept her silky red locks over her shoulder—she didn't pay nearly five hundred a month to keep her hair looking gorgeous for nothing. "We're not thirty yet. Besides, I know I've still got it." She bent over and twerked, her booty bouncing just as good as it had when she was in college.

Asana laughed, smacking Brooklyn's ass.

"See?" Asana turned her eyes back to Taylor. "For old times' sake?"

Taylor's lips were pinched, and for just a moment, Brooklyn thought she was going to tell them to fuck off, but after making them squirm for several moments, she rolled her eyes. "Fine, whatever, but I get center."

"Wouldn't have it any other way," Brooklyn conceded. "Let's go make an impression these sisters won't forget."

Sliding her hand along the balcony rail, Brooklyn glanced back down at the dancing girls, and then across the street to see several non-Panhellenic people watching. No matter the year, the sisters were always good for putting on a show, and nobody wanted to miss out.

Brooklyn paused, because there was one familiar face in the crowd. Notable because she was scribbling on a pad of paper.

"Is that a reporter?" Brooklyn frowned.

"Ohmygod." Asana slapped the railing and then tore off into the house.

CHAPTER TWENTY-EIGHT

It's no secret. Behind every queen stands her guards, and before her kneel her loyal subjects. I'm no different. Just call me Queen T—and either get fucking behind me or kneel, bitch.

Kisses,
Taylor

Asana

Then

Something electric happened when Taylor handed Asana the Spill Book. A little tiny spark that sent a shock up both their arms. Like when she'd been a kid and she and her friends had rubbed balloons on their heads and then touched fingers, sending a jolt of current through them.

She laughed and yanked her hand away from the spark, but Taylor didn't laugh, and for a minute, Asana thought she might say something mean. Taylor was hot and cold and hard as fuck to read.

She might have been Asana's favorite person.

"Spill," Taylor said instead, a grin widening her full red lips.

Asana gripped the pen. There'd been several tea parties since Taylor took office as their pledge president. But this was the first time Asana was taking the pen. Annabelle and Brooklyn had both already written in the Spill Book, secrets none of them had divulged even during late-night hangouts in their rooms where they unpacked everything that had happened that day, including Taylor thinking about breaking up with her boyfriend, and that Brooklyn was dating a nerdy frat boy.

As pledges, they weren't yet initiated into the sorority. A sister but not all the way. A sister in limbo. No one wanted to mess up and get kicked out. And no one wanted to go against Taylor, who reported to the ADL president.

But Taylor wasn't always a total bitch. And to be honest, even when she was, Asana liked and respected her. Taylor was out for Taylor, and Asana believed that it was important to always look out for number one.

Besides, she'd met chicks way crazier than Taylor at her high school in Manhattan.

Asana pinched the pen with her fingers, rubbed the soft fluffy ball on her chin as she tried to decide what secret she was about to spatter on the page. She'd had days to prepare. Wanted to make it juicy. Because of course they assumed Taylor read every line. And she wanted Taylor to trust her. Especially the latter.

She pressed the pen into the paper, making a tiny dot, then glanced up to see Taylor watching her intently. Asana gave her a shoo-go look, but Taylor didn't move away, didn't stop watching. Asana raised a brow, a silent push to give her the privacy she needed to write. Taylor smirked. But she did look away, and then she walked over to the opposite wall and leaned against it in a way that made her breasts push against her tiny tank top.

Asana forced her gaze on the Spill Book page, but she could feel Taylor's penetrating stare. Could feel the way she bored into her soul with those big blue eyes. There was something about Taylor's strength that Asana found both captivating and unnerving at the same time.

Asana had a lot of secrets. Her own secrets. Campus secrets. World secrets.

But perhaps the one that might matter most right here and now, in this sorority house, was that she'd finally been recruited into a secret chapter, one that people called the Machine.

Her gaze slid toward the crossed keys ring on her middle finger. The ring they'd given her after kidnapping her in her dorm room and taking her to some undisclosed location that smelled like bleach and old food, so likely the cafeteria in some building. They'd taken the bag off her head, and she'd stood in a circle with two dozen other bleary-eyed students, and behind them in a cloaked ring were another two dozen at least.

Those in the outer circle started to chant, until a single male student came to stand in the center of the new recruits of the coed secret society.

Asana shuddered thinking about how creepy it had been, but also at the excitement of being part of something so clandestine. That she was *that* much closer to infiltrating the powerful society. She'd always loved the idea of belonging to a secret society, and the fact that they thought she was cool enough to partake was epic.

From the outside, Asana's life was documented in teen magazines and online rag websites. TikToks and reels were filled with her image by friends and stalkers. Strange, because seriously, she wasn't famous or a celebrity. But they still wanted to capture her, post about her. Make a spectacle of her.

But privately, the life of Asana Duke was another story, and belonging to the machine that worked underground not only at the university but across the nation, even the globe, well, that was pretty freaking amazing. They had the power to change situations on campus, but also politically around the world. She'd heard of them before. Seen the nods of men in power in Manhattan. There was a reason they'd chosen her. There was a reason she'd chosen them.

She knew something of secrets. Had stood on the other side of enough closed doors to know what happened behind the scenes in the lives of the upper crust, the elite, the people who thought themselves royal without a drop of noble blood. And it wasn't all diamonds and champagne. There was ugliness there. Scandal. Backstabbing. But there was glory and victory too.

And Asana wanted to own it all. To not just be on both sides of the fence but to be the one who kicked it down and went back and forth whenever the fuck she wanted.

Glancing up, she could see Taylor still watching her through hooded eyes, a small grin on her lips, as if to say she already knew all of Asana's secrets, tempting her to share something completely forbidden. Well, this was one Taylor had no idea about.

Taylor mouthed, "Spill," in Asana's direction, and she couldn't help but notice the way her tongue touched her teeth.

Asana grinned, the little electric shock she'd felt earlier resurfacing as she wrote in neat curving letters, *Little is known and what is known is kept secret.*

CHAPTER TWENTY-NINE

I'm good enough to kiss, to touch when the lights are out, when the door is locked. But not good enough to be seen with in public. Well, seen holding hands. Actually, fuck that, we all hold hands, twerk on each other. Hmm. I'm just not good enough?

Kisses,
Asana

Taylor

Now

If the eyes were the window to the soul, owning a pair of extra-tinted sunglasses was the best armor for someone who wanted to hide.

Taylor marched in front of Annabelle and Brooklyn. Not because she wanted to lead them, although she was technically their leader, but because she didn't want to look at them. She pretended to be in a hurry, rushing after Asana, who'd gone running through the house like fucking Jason Voorhees was coming after her.

In truth, Taylor's mind was still reeling with the fact that Brooklyn had called her out, and she was saved by a damn sister song.

The secrets she'd kept, the ones she marked down in the book, they went so much further than just being the Pharmacist on campus. There were darker ones. And the biggest one of all was now affecting her life, her marriage.

I have a hostile uterine environment. Even my fucking womb is a bitch.

There was only one reason for that, and she was grateful it wasn't revealed in the doctor's exam or else Elijah would have already served her with divorce papers. Further testing, however, would show it. Hence her hesitation to continue.

Throughout her life, Taylor had always found it much easier to focus on other people's problems. To point out their faults and how they could fix themselves. To dissect the human psyche in a way to persuade them to her cause, to believe what she believed. To follow her into the unknown.

Working as Elijah's campaign manager was drowning her own political aspirations, and not to mention bored her to literal tears. But Elijah didn't like the idea of her running her own election when he was trying to win. He thought it too vulgar for a woman to be in politics—a fact she hadn't known until she'd said "I do." And since he was a homegrown Alabama politician with a campaign run on God-fearing family values, well, it didn't do to have wife mucking up all that God had intended. Even if it was the twenty-first century.

Of course, none of that had been evident before they'd married. He'd supported her decision to get a law degree, talking to her ad nauseam about campaigning and politics. Made her believe that together, they'd rise to the political top. But all that had changed when she'd added the Mrs. to her name. What her husband really wanted was for her to be at home in her kitchen, a message that a certain female politician he was running against was promoting by giving speeches at her kitchen table.

And somehow she had . . . settled, asking only to be a part of his world rather than creating her own. *The Taylor I used to know*

wouldn't have settled for happy enough. Taylor Collins dominates.
Asana's words came back to pour salt on her wounds.

Taylor frowned as she stepped into the foyer, the music from the front and the cheers from the actives and PNMs growing louder. A sound that she used to get high off of. A sound that brought back so many memories.

Not all of them wanted.

A sound that brought light to secrets that should have remained buried.

By the time Taylor reached the foyer, Asana had disappeared outside, and Dua Lipa's notes were on repeat. Elijah would cringe. He hated the film. Thought it undermined a woman's true value and place in society. That it gave a woman *ideas.* That it would bring about too much change.

Of course, he'd never seen the movie. And Taylor had driven an hour and a half to Mississippi to watch alone while she munched on popcorn dripping in bad-for-her chemical butter. The snack tasted like sin, and went perfectly with how much she liked that fucking movie.

Taylor scanned the Barbies, looking for Asana, and spotted her across the street speaking with a woman who had a pen and pad of paper.

"Who is she talking to?" Brooklyn asked, squinting into the sun, a hand over her eyes.

"Don't squint, you'll get lines early," Taylor muttered, and Brooklyn pulled down the Prada sunglasses from on top of her head.

"Wouldn't want to ruin my mommy blogger image with a few lines."

Though her shades covered them from view, Taylor could *hear* Brooklyn's eyes rolling.

"I don't know her," Annabelle said with a frown.

"I think she was at the party last night." Brooklyn pursed her lips and Taylor refrained from pointing out the lines she was creating around her mouth. Did becoming a mommy blogger make her forget all about her image?

"If she was at the tea party then she must be a sister—let's go say hi." Taylor started to walk, but Annabelle gripped her arm.

"They don't appear to be having a good conversation." Annabelle's voice was strained.

"Agreed," Brooklyn said. "Maybe we should go watch the videos before dinner instead of after."

Taylor cocked her head, watching Asana and the reporter. "I've never been the nonconfrontational type." *Except with Elijah.*

"We know," Brooklyn and Annabelle said at the same time Taylor stepped into the street and walked with purpose to where Asana was speaking with the other woman.

But the closer Taylor drew, the more the attention of the note taker appeared to be on her, eyes shifting over Asana's shoulder. The woman grew skittish, shuffling her feet, and when Taylor was only half a dozen paces away, the woman turned and marched off.

"Didn't want to stay to say hello?" Taylor asked.

"I told her to leave, that reporters weren't welcome to be filming and taking notes about Greek Life." Asana stared after the retreating figure, something deeper hidden in the words she didn't say.

Technically, being outside, anyone could film if they wanted to, but it was frowned upon.

"Who does she report for?"

Asana's expression was completely flat, bored almost. "Herself."

"Who is she?"

Asana shifted her gaze, avoiding eye contact and the question. "It was like pulling teeth to get her to take a breath."

"Looked heated."

"I've had more heat with nicoise salad." Asana eyed her, and Taylor felt like she could see right through the tint.

Taylor glanced to the house to see Brooklyn and Annabelle approaching, happy for the distraction.

"I think I saw her last night," Brooklyn said to Asana. "Do you know her?"

"I saw her too," Asana said. "But she ran off when I tried to approach her, a lot like she did just now."

Annabelle stared down the street, the woman no longer visible. "Who was she?"

"Someone I used to know," Asana said finally. "Maybe you used to know her too."

"Was she ADL? Another house?"

Asana shook her head. "Well, she pretended to want to be."

"And now she wants to watch? God, get a life," Taylor said. "Is she obsessed with us or what?"

Asana's features twitched for half a second before shuttering back into the face she used on camera at press conferences that Taylor secretly watched.

"I don't know, but I'm glad she's on our list of suspects. I couldn't get her to divulge a damn thing."

Taylor had known Asana long enough to tell when she was lying, and right now, Asana was spitting lines.

CHAPTER THIRTY

Coach Tamson pulled me into her office and slid a picture of my foot across her desk. The only place she could have gotten that pic was from my OnlyFans page. There was no denying it. She'd caught me red-handed. Lost my scholarship. But at least I still get to be on the team—which, to be honest, I'm surprised she allowed. But damn . . . I needed that money. I can't afford college tuition on my own. Guess I need a new daddy. A girl's gotta do what a girl's gotta do. And I do 'em real good.

Kisses,
Brooklyn

Annabelle

Then

The floorboard made the slightest creak as Annabelle slipped out of Riley's room and closed the door with the blinged-out placard proclaiming her ADL president. The inside of President Riley's room had been full of typical pink frills and froths, but nothing juicy. From all outward appearances Riley took her position as president of her sorority very seriously, even down to the weekly tanning sessions and nail appointments.

With a sigh, she patted her pocket. Though the trinket's actual weight was a fraction of a pound, her pocket felt deliciously heavy with the metaphorical weight of it.

She grinned, and then stopped dead in her tracks.

"What were you doing in there?" Taylor stood in the hallway, leaning casually against the wall as if she'd come with Annabelle and was keeping watch.

Annabelle high-kicked a smile onto her face. "Seeing how a president lives."

"Your mom isn't enough of an example?" If Taylor meant for the retort to sting, she didn't know Annabelle very well—because she'd never let it show.

She gave the slightest shrug of her shoulder. "Whose mom is?"

"Good point." Taylor eyed her up and down, staring at her empty hands as if she expected to see a basket full of stolen goods held there. "Find anything interesting?"

Using the same breathing techniques she employed in yoga to remain calm, Annabelle pretended nonchalance. "She's basic." Even the little keychain Annabelle had swiped was your typical I-had-spring-break-in-Cancún-and-all-I-brought-back-was-this-dumb-keychain *and maybe an STD*.

"Figures. We won't be as basic when it's our sorority to rule."

Annabelle grinned at Taylor's use of "we."

"We won't."

"Everyone's in the chapter room. You ready? Or need to maybe take a look around anyone else's room?" There was a challenge in Taylor's words, as if she knew exactly what Annabelle was doing.

Why hide it? "I'll save them for later."

Taylor smirked. "Better keep my room out of it."

"I'd never dare. Besides, I've already been in your room."

"Basic?"

"As basic as they come." Annabelle laughed.

The chapter room was filled with pledges, and Riley, who'd said she wanted to come and observe how they handled their meetings. When Taylor had found out, she'd immediately texted Annabelle, Brooklyn, and Asana to tell them she thought someone might have ratted her out about the Spill Book.

The meeting started without a hitch, and continued on as boring as they could be as they ticked off tasks and news and took a vote on what ice cream flavors to have at the next social. And as Taylor had asked, Annabelle, Asana, and Brooklyn kept subtle watch to see who was paying really close attention to Riley, who was fidgeting, who might be guilty of sharing the Spill Book's existence.

So, while they talked about the upcoming charity fundraiser for Paws for Claws and the yoga class that Brooklyn was going to teach with puppies, Annabelle scanned the crowd. Jacqueline had on a new necklace. But even from here the dull sheen of the diamond pendant looked fake. Beside her, another pledge had little pink rhinestones in her hair. Cute. Out of all the girls, Annabelle would have guessed it was Jaqueline causing problems, but she didn't seem the least bit bothered by Riley's presence; if anything she looked a little nervous.

When Taylor asked at the end of the meeting if anyone had any questions or new business, the questions were lame about outfits and double-checking times.

No one said anything about the Spill Book, as if having Riley in the room automatically silenced them. When the meeting was adjourned, Riley told Taylor she'd done a great job and that she was excited to welcome the pledge class as active members soon. Riley waved goodbye and ran to a class seminar she was late for.

They all listened, still as Tuska's bronze nineteen-foot elephant body in front of Bryant-Denny Stadium, as Riley's footsteps tapped up the stairs, still as they heard her walk across the house. Still as the door thudded shut.

No one else moved, including Annabelle, though she did put her hand in her pocket, wrapping her fingers around the Cancún keychain.

They all wanted to have the official tea party. Taylor's tea. To spill into the book their deepest secrets. How funny. She would have thought at least a few would try to escape. But somehow, Taylor had grabbed hold of them, and no one wanted to move.

"What are y'all still doing here?" Taylor cocked her head, a secret smile playing over her lips, the very picture of aggressive innocence. "You can go."

They still didn't move, looking confused. Glancing from side to side at one another, behind them. Waiting for an answer to the silent question on everyone's mind. *Where's the book?* With President Riley gone, why weren't they getting down to the true heart of their daily meetings?

"I think they want the book," Brooklyn whispered.

Annabelle smiled, nodded. Asana touched her tongue to her eyetooth, her eyes dancing with some sarcastic reply that she kept inside.

Taylor flashed Brooklyn a look, a reminder that the whole reason Riley had been there was because of the Spill Book, or at least they assumed.

One of the pledges stood, a freshman named Ally, and Annabelle fully expected to see her walk out the door. But she didn't. Instead, she walked up to the door, shut it, and flicked the lock. If ever there'd been a more positive sign, then Annabelle wasn't sure how much more blatant it could be.

"We came for a tea party, didn't we?" Ally said.

"You're right, Ally, we did." Taylor looked like she'd just gobbled up the soul of yet another admirer.

Asana dimmed the lights, and Annabelle opened the drawer they'd stashed the blindfolds in, while Taylor pulled the locked box from her large over-the-shoulder bag.

"I don't know how you carry that thing around," Annabelle said.

"I consider it a workout." Taylor grinned and plucked the key from around her neck to unlock the box.

She pulled out the sparkling pink Spill Book and stared at Annabelle. "You're up first today."

Annabelle swallowed, knowing exactly what kind of confession Taylor would want. The one that said why she was in Riley's room, and if she'd taken anything. Not that she'd ever confessed to Taylor about her little habit. But she might have suspected. Annabelle smiled brightly, the same smile she gave her mom that was so false she might have been made of plastic.

"Can't wait to spill," Annabelle said.

She took the notebook and fluffy pen while the rest of the pledges tied their bandannas around their eyes.

Even without looking, Annabelle could feel Taylor's gaze boring into her. She had an intensity about her that made an entire room spark with agitated electricity. But Annabelle wasn't going to give her the satisfaction of seeing her squirm. And she wasn't going to give her the satisfaction of reading her confession either. No one actually believed that Taylor wasn't reading the book when her door was shut.

The thing was, they also knew Taylor had their backs.

If a sister was seen without two of the three done—makeup, hair, clothes—Taylor always had a quick fix in her bag. And when one of the sisters needed a pick-me-up, Taylor was the first to bake them cupcakes in the ADL kitchen. She was also the one who arranged movie nights, trivia nights, all the bonding things they loved.

And that made hating Taylor hard, because as much as she was a bitch, she was also the first one to reach out a helping hand.

Annabelle tinkered on the page, and decided to write a little poem. *Twinkle, twinkle, little gemstone* . . .

CHAPTER THIRTY-ONE

At home, in the back of my closet, if you pull out one of the floorboards, you'll find my stash. But here, in the dorms, no such thing. I got one of those lockboxes that looks like a book, and Jane Eyre protects my prizes. And unlike the key Taylor keeps around her neck, the combination code to my safe is kept in the dark recesses of my brain.

Kisses,
Annabelle

Asana

Now

Maggie Rosenthal.

The name was one Asana remembered as soon as she'd gotten close to the woman. Of course, she wasn't exactly lying when she said she couldn't get Maggie to divulge anything, because the former PNM and Machine minion had tried her damnedest.

But as soon as she'd seen the flash of anger in her eyes, Asana remembered her from the meetings. Remembered her from that last night when Asana had put her revenge plan in place. The way she'd glared at her from across the underground room. The way she'd snatched a cup or paper or whatever it was they were being handed before Asana could take hers. Always needing to be first, to prove she was better.

Asana believed wholeheartedly that anyone who needed to be first that badly lacked both the self-esteem and the talent to be first naturally. So, she let her, because letting Maggie be first actually showed her own superiority. And it made her laugh on the inside.

It had been freshman year that she'd met her for the first time. The reporter during Rush Week who'd posed as a PNM—at first. Apparently, she'd decided after that odd interaction that she actually wanted to take part, and took Rush Week seriously. But Asana never forgot the way she'd shunned their lifestyle on day one. Almost ruined her own chances.

Maggie had been the PNM who'd stood on an elevated surface.

That was against the rules. All potential sisters had to remain flat on the ground, but Maggie had been standing on a makeshift stage in the quad, spouting off whatever cause she was supporting.

And it wasn't like Asana disagreed with Maggie's cause—not that she remembered what it was, because it hadn't been about anything major—but she did believe in sorority rules. They were in place for a reason. If a PNM stood on an elevated surface, which would raise her above all the other rushing young women, then she wasn't about the sisterhood. She was trying to elevate herself.

Maggie could have shouted into her bullhorn from the grass. But she didn't. The moment she stepped up onto that platform was the moment she'd sealed her fate with the sisterhood. And maybe that was Maggie's plan all along—to join a sorority for her stupid article, and then get herself kicked out.

Asana wasn't the only one who'd seen her do it; there'd been a bunch of them, and they'd been with two of the exec board, including Riley, their president. A move like that had to be on purpose.

"Do you think you can find out her name?" Taylor interrupted her thoughts.

Asana nodded. The way Taylor was looking at her, she could tell she knew more. Taylor probably knew Asana better than anyone else in ADL. In more ways than one.

She'd barely opened her mouth before Maggie told her "no comment." Close-lipped and just as stubborn as she'd been in college. But there'd been such animosity in her eyes. Was Maggie smart enough to have stolen the Spill Book, to have done a deep dive into Asana's background and orchestrated a string of blackmail letters? She wasn't sure. But Maggie was definitely bitter enough to have motivation.

"Good. Because that bitch needs to stop lurking. It's creeping me out."

The music paused, and cheers went up among the sisters. They'd gotten their moves down pat and were calling it in.

"Heyyyy," Asana called, tearing her gaze off Maggie's back. "We want to show you ours. Dance-off?"

A resounding cheer went up on the lawn from the actives and PNMs. Several other alumni members from their class rushed to the center.

"Ready for it, ladies?" Brooklyn clapped after whispering the song to the girl in charge of the music.

They all fell in line, each of them having done the dance so many times they could run through the choreography in their sleep. Didn't matter that they'd graduated five years ago, that it had been at least six since they practiced.

The first few seconds were a little rusty, but as soon as Beyoncé sang, "You ready?" they were.

They gyrated to the music, chests popping out, hips rocking, hands above their heads before drifting down their bodies. Moving in sync as each of them swayed around one another like they could do this dance in their sleep. The sisters cheered, and the alumni hugged at the end, each of them a bit sweatier than they were a moment ago.

"I forgot how much I enjoyed that," Annabelle said with a laugh. "Taylor, if Elijah saw you just now with your booty in the air."

Taylor laughed, clearly finding it absurd. Then she must have realized, he actually might see it, there were so many phones up right now filming, and her smile faltered.

"Shit." Taylor paled

"Taylor, if your husband can't handle you having wholesome fun with your sisters . . ." Asana started, and trailed off at the flash of anger in Taylor's eyes.

"You of all people wouldn't understand."

Ouch. Asana felt that statement like a punch. She crossed her arms over her chest. "What's that supposed to mean? And I mean exactly."

Taylor cleared her throat as if that might clear the air, but the tension was so thick Asana couldn't have cut it even if she'd borrowed a chain saw.

"Nothing." Taylor swept back her hair as if the move might wipe away the tension. But it didn't and her next words only made it worse. "It's just, you're not . . . married."

"Oh, right, and being married would have somehow changed who I am. Got it." Asana rolled her eyes. Taylor was lucky Elijah wasn't a Matinee member, Asana had checked. "You know, Taylor, bitter isn't a good color on you."

Asana turned her back on her friends. She'd had enough of this bullshit. Only Taylor could turn a really fun moment into one someone would regret. Why had Asana put up with it? Why had she liked her so much? Why had she . . .

"Wait, Asana." Taylor's call after her was issued in a tone that sounded like she was being strangled.

Not good enough.

Asana rounded the corner onto Paul Bryant Drive and walked straight into the Starbucks. What she wanted was a shot of Patrón, but what she was getting was a triple espresso shot instead.

Maybe the rush of caffeine would help her think more clearly. But she doubted it would calm her down.

She sat in the corner where an air vent blasted cold air on her hot skin. Asana needed to remember why she'd come here in the first place. It wasn't to reconcile friendships, though seeing her old friends had been a part of it. Seeing Taylor, trying to get over her. But the true reason had been because of her part in taking down the Machine—and she couldn't let that information get loose. Couldn't let whoever was behind this expose information about Matinee. To take down whoever was blackmailing her for three million. And if she didn't figure out who was behind this, there were some very real chances her father's company would suffer. That her mother might end up back at Lenox Hill. The Machine had deep pockets and ever deeper lines of allies.

An exposé on Asana Duke was going to destroy lives. And there was only one person who kept showing up with a notepad: Maggie Rosenthal. But would Maggie be so asinine as to stick out like a sore thumb? Maybe, if that was the conclusion she wanted Asana to draw. Hide in plain sight.

Of course, she would do whatever she could to make sure it didn't get to that point.

But even her reach could go only so far.

"Asana?"

She glanced up from where she was nearly crushing her espresso to see Jacqueline.

"Hey."

"Mind if I join you?"

"Of course not." It wasn't like her to agree. What she should have said was, "Actually, I do mind, now kindly fuck off," but Jaqueline was on their list of suspects. This was the perfect opportunity to grill her.

"That was fun back there." She set her Strawberry Refresher on the table and sat down. "Forgot how much I liked to dance. You?"

"I still dance."

Jacqueline cocked her head to the side. "I guess I have seen pictures of you coming out of clubs."

Asana narrowed her eyes at Jacqueline. What an interesting choice of words.

"My life has always been fascinating to others." Asana grinned tightly. The paps had been following her around for more than two decades, and it was not something she'd ever gotten used to.

"Must be hard, always being in the spotlight." Jaqueline sucked on the straw, a piece of dehydrated fruit coming back to life and getting stuck in the center as she sucked harder and harder.

"No, it isn't," Asana lied. "I was born for it, and I'm good at it." Now *that* part was true.

Jacqueline's smile faltered, as she finally clued in to the fact that Asana had not actually wanted her to sit down. She wriggled her straw and sucked some more. "I saw you talking to Maggie."

Asana sipped her espresso, pretending Jacqueline's statement hadn't rattled her one bit.

"And?"

"She had it out for ADL."

"Did she?"

Jacqueline nodded. "We were in a journalism class together. She kept trying to bring up sorority life as possible topics for our projects."

"That doesn't mean she had it out for ADL."

Jacqueline shrugged. "They weren't favorable topics."

"How so?"

"She wanted to expose the rules."

"Most people know the rules. All you have to do is watch a few YouTube videos or TikTok."

"The deeper rules."

Asana didn't comment. Jacqueline had not been a member of the Machine, and she probably didn't know that Maggie was. If Maggie had tried to take down Greek Life, that would have included the Machine. And there was only one person who'd done that, and she looked at herself in the mirror every morning.

And Maggie knew that.

"What are you getting at?" Asana asked. She found in both business and personal life, it was always better to just get to the heart of the matter. Dancing around should be saved for the clubs.

"Maybe she took the Spill Book?"

Asana drank down the last dregs of her espresso. "Maybe. See you back at the house?" She stood without waiting for Jacqueline to acknowledge.

What she needed right now was to release tension. And the best way to do that was to be fucked hard.

Outside the Starbucks her two guards waited. She pointed to Guard One. "You."

His eyes lit up with the knowledge of what she was demanding.

"And you too," she said to Guard Two.

The three of them climbed into the waiting tinted limo. Without needing to be asked, her driver rolled up the partition window, while Asana rolled down her tight pants.

"Who's hungry?" She spread her legs like a feast and fell back with a moan as Guard One knelt between her thighs, giving a ravenous lick.

CHAPTER THIRTY-TWO

*During study hours, I pass out my "special"
cupcakes. These bitches think it's laced with something
that helps them focus. It's just a little $C_{12}H_{22}O_{11}$ . . .
also known as sugar, bitches. And highly addictive,
I might add. But since we all have to maintain a
certain body type, they aren't used to the sugar rush,
and they actually feel high ingesting it. Whatever,
it keeps the illusion of my powers, so I'll continue to
bake the shit out of them.*

*Kisses,
Taylor*

Brooklyn

Then

Brooklyn tapped on the TikTok app, her pink acrylic fingernail hovering over the record button, but only for a split second.

Freshly showered, her long red hair in curls and her makeup on point, she set her phone on the tripod and curtsied into the camera.

"Morning, y'all! Brooklyn in Bama here. The last week of rush for ADL has been so incredible. I can't tell you how much I love being a part of such a tight sisterhood." She pressed her hands together over her heart and looked endearingly into the camera,

#sweetaspie. "Being a soccer player, I've always loved the close-ness of a team. Now I've got my team and my sisters. These four years at Bama are going to be the best four years of my life. I can just tell y'all, I've already made the best of friends. You've seen them here before, and now I want you to get a chance to say good morning to them too."

Brooklyn paused the TikTok video and hurried out of her dorm to knock on Annabelle's door.

Annabelle, already made-up, flung open the door just as Brooklyn pressed record. "Morning, y'all, from Annabelle."

Again, Brooklyn paused the TikTok and rushed to Asana's room. Just as she tapped and held up the phone, Asana answered the door with Taylor beside her, in matching pink gloss. At the same time, they grinned and said, "Morning, y'all, from Asana."

"And Taylor."

Brooklyn turned the camera back on herself for the last ten seconds of the video, her friends gathering around her and leaning into the video with freshly whitened smiles. Together they said, "Besties in Bama," their new catchphrase.

Brooklyn posted the video, tagging her friends and adding all her usual hashtags, which now included #BESTIESINBAMA #BATA (for Brooklyn, Asana, Taylor, Annabelle).

"BATA out." Brooklyn stuffed her phone in her back pocket.

They all grabbed their backpacks and headed out of the build-ing to pick up the coffee order they'd plugged in using their dining hall app. "Ugh, I have a quiz today and I'm so not prepared for it," Taylor groaned. "Why am I taking chemistry again?"

Brooklyn laughed. "Because you're a chemical compound fan."

"Or freak," Taylor said.

"You're the only poli-sci major who is minoring in chem," Asana said thoughtfully. "Why do I feel like you have aspirations to take over the world?"

"Maybe I do." Taylor grinned mischievously, making Brooklyn wonder not for the first time what the hell Taylor had been doing wandering around campus in the middle of the night in all black.

Asana snickered. "You do make one hell of a cupcake."

"Among other things."

Four lattes waited on the counter, and a blueberry muffin for Brooklyn, who appeared to be the only one who ever ate breakfast in the group. Taylor said chewing would ruin her teeth, and so she preferred to drink her meals. Asana claimed to only eat her dates, and Annabelle was a closet Cheetos fan—literally, she had a massive box of snack bag Cheetos in her closet.

"I have a paper due tomorrow and I haven't started on it. They want six pages on the role of public service broadcasting in a democracy." Brooklyn took a sip of her latte, loving the burn on her throat. For some reason, it was always calming. When she'd decided to go into broadcasting, she hadn't realized how hard they were going to make it for her to get her degree. For one thing, she didn't really care about public service. She wasn't planning to be on the news. She wanted to be a host on a fun show, like *Love Island* or *The Bachelor.*

"Six pages, ew." Annabelle made a barfing face. "Sounds boring."

"I don't know, could be interesting." Asana nodded as if she was thinking on the topic. "I can read it when you're done if you want. I have a lot of experience with public service and broadcasting."

"Oh, right." Brooklyn always forgot that Asana's family owned one of the biggest media conglomerates in the country, maybe even the world. "Sure, thanks."

"What do you have going on today?" Taylor asked Asana.

"I'm giving a persuasive speech in class on why our profs should start adding hashtags to our assignments."

"Okay, I want to hear that," Brooklyn said with a laugh.

Asana cleared her throat and effected a straight-and-narrow

stance. "Given hashtags send a clear message of topic and inter-
ests, it would be beneficial for students to correlate the hashtags
with assignments to better decipher the syllabus and expectations."

"Hundred percent," Brooklyn said. "Maybe we should actually
lobby that with the SGA."

Asana choked on her coffee, sputtering as she coughed. "Sorry,"
she croaked.

"See you at the tea party after class?" Taylor asked them.

"Wouldn't miss it."

By the time Brooklyn arrived to the tea party, she wished
she had missed it. Normally she loved getting together with the
other pledges and the secrecy of the blindfolds, but today she
was exhausted from cramming six pages of barely readable words
onto a Word document she'd typed on her phone, and a hard
practice this afternoon in the Alabama heat. She'd barely had
time to rinse the sweat from her body, which didn't really matter,
because she was so hot she was still sweating. And washing her
hair wasn't an option or she would have been late. Thank God for
dry shampoo.

But without swiping on the Veo app to rent an electric bike,
she'd have never made it by Taylor's lock-the-door-you're-out
policy. Even BATA was subject to Taylor's rules. Twirling her
hair up in a clip, she mounted the bike and took off. Even at the
minuscule rental cost for the bike, it was still money she could
have used for food.

Brooklyn arrived at ADL just in time for President Riley to
open the door, arms crossed over her chest and a pouty frown on
her lips.

"Pledges can't ride electric bikes, Brooklyn."

Brooklyn's heart fell into her stomach, and she kicked the kick-
stand a little too hard. "What?" she gasped both in shock and
pain. This had to be a joke. It was just a bike, for Bama's sake.

"It's considered an elevated surface." Riley's tone was full of derision.

Brooklyn's mouth went dry, and her knees felt weak. There'd been no choice. If she was late, she would have gotten her walking card, and showing up on time on the bike apparently was going to give her the same. She stood in place next to the bike, unable to move, to think. Her mind a whirl of disappointment. Up to this point she'd done everything right. *Everything.*

"I'm . . . I . . ." Brooklyn swallowed, trying to force out the voice she'd been practicing for years for broadcasting. "I would have been late to the meeting. I had practice. I didn't realize a bike was considered an elevated surface or I never would have ridden it."

Riley cocked her head, studying Brooklyn, her lips pursing in a way that would have had Taylor crying out at the wrinkles she was about to cause herself.

"You're doing too much, Brooklyn. Soccer and sisters?" Riley shook her head. "If you weren't playing soccer we wouldn't have to worry about the e-bike, now would we?"

If she thought her stomach hurt before, now it was really pulsing. Give up soccer?

"I'm going to fine you for the bike, but I'll give you a second chance."

"A fine?" Brooklyn's being late was turning into a costly tab.

Riley nodded. "Fifty dollars. Into the pot." She held out her hand, and Brooklyn shook her head.

"I don't have cash. I can Venmo."

"Fine. @RileyRulesADL. Send it now or I'm not letting you in the house."

Brooklyn took out her phone, her hands shaking. She clicked on the cash app, typed in Riley's handle, and then sent her fifty bucks. Being late to this meeting just cost her like three days' worth of meals.

"Thank you, Riley." Thanking her sorority president didn't make her feel very grateful, just resentful. And hungry.

Frat boys had been asking her out on dates but she'd been too busy to say yes. And also, maybe a little nervous about going on an actual real date. Maybe this was a sign she should say yes, and get a free meal out of one.

"Don't thank me. Just don't embarrass us again." Riley marched off into the house, and Brooklyn hurried inside, before the sorority president had a chance to change her mind.

When the Spill Book was passed to her, the only thing that was on Brooklyn's mind was that she was down about sixty dollars from the fine and the bike rental. Since she'd lost her scholarship, and already had to pay for room and board plus sorority dues, money was tight. Everything she needed was paid for by working.

And feet pics.

Growing up, Brooklyn had gone hungry enough. She'd be damned if she was going to do it as an adult. Not when she knew ways to make money that kept her belly from growling, and kept her body at peak performance.

OnlyFans and dating sugar daddies, a girl had to do what a girl had to do.

CHAPTER THIRTY-THREE

They all know he's a bad guy. But no one wants to run against him, talk behind his back, or disagree with him in meetings. And yet, we all know. I keep getting this sick feeling in my stomach. Something bad is going to happen, and it's going to be his fault. G.H. is to Bama as Epstein is to Palm Beach.

Kisses,
Asana

Taylor

Now

On the other side of the door, muffled voices filtered through. Taylor had been hoping she'd be the first one to arrive at Brooklyn's suite to rewatch the video, but she'd not been fast enough.

She knocked twice, and waited not so patiently. Ginger Mommy opened the door with a bright smile and a surprised "You're here early."

Taylor nodded and walked past her into the empty suite. She was also first apparently. Four days and nothing to show for it yet. Didn't they all want to figure out who was blackmailing them? "I could have sworn I heard voices."

"Voices?" The way Brooklyn looked at her with concern and

confusion made Taylor want to shake her by the shoulders. But understanding seemed to dawn and Brooklyn laughed. "Oh, it was the video. I was just getting it set up."

Taylor nodded and held up the wine bag. "I brought materials." Taylor wiggled her brows, calling the bottles of wine by the same moniker they'd used in college because alcohol in the sorority house was forbidden, but no one had to know what materials were.

"I love materials." Brooklyn laughed and opened a cabinet in the tiny kitchenette to pull out four wineglasses.

"Have you talked to Asana?" Taylor mused as if it weren't a big deal that she'd rushed off after the dance-off, and by the time Asana made it back to the house for the rest of the rush activities, she'd been agitated and cagey.

"About?" Brooklyn rummaged through a drawer, producing a wine opener like she'd discovered a prize.

"The woman she was talking to." Taylor set the wine bag on the counter and pulled out the various bottles.

"No, but I def want to when she gets here." Brooklyn twirled the bottles, reading the labels and making yum sounds.

But Taylor couldn't just let it go until Asana arrived. "Who do you think she was? The notepad woman."

Brooklyn shrugged. "Sounds like she was either a PNM or pledge that didn't make it all the way through." She chose a bottle and attempted to open it with the shitty hotel wine opener—which promptly fucked up the cork. "Dang it."

"Yeah, I was thinking the same thing." Taylor pulled out the wine opener she always kept in her handbag. It wasn't that she was an alcoholic, though she knew plenty of wives in her circles who were. The conservative ones always seemed to be closet drinkers. The reason she had it in her bag dated back to her sorority days. If you weren't prepared, you were screwed, and she'd opened a wine bottle with tweezers on the road once and was never caught without an opener again. "But it also seemed a little deeper than that. Asana was pretty rattled by her."

Brooklyn glanced up. "I noticed that too."

In a few deft twists, Taylor had the cork popped.

Brooklyn drummed her nails on the counter, her brow wrinkling as she thought hard.

Taylor was about to remind her about wrinkles, but a tappety-tap-tap on the door caught them both off guard. Brooklyn let Annabelle inside.

Annabelle looked tired and, unusual for her, her shirt was a little wrinkled, her makeup not on point. Like she'd taken a nap without washing her face first and then hadn't touched herself up at all. What the fuck? Appearance was high on Annabelle's priority list. Something was definitely wrong.

Taylor glanced at herself in the mirrored wall, noting gladly that she was not as wrinkled and harried looking. Perfect as always. She smiled at herself, though it looked brittle. Perfect on the outside, cracked on the inside.

"Wine?" Taylor offered Annabelle.

Annabelle marched with purpose to where Taylor was pouring and picked up a glass, gulping down a sip that was also not like her.

"Everything okay?" Taylor asked. "You seem . . ." She waggled her fingers up and down in front of Annabelle. "Out of sorts."

Annabelle let out a bitter laugh. "We can talk about it when Asana gets here."

A sharp rap on the door completed their foursome with Asana breezing in, her pace as NYC as ever. She scooped up the last wineglass on the counter and took it to the table where Brooklyn had set up the laptop for their viewing party.

"Shall we get this meeting started, ladies?" Asana took control, like usual.

Taylor had gotten used to Asana's need to be in charge, but in this instance, she was definitely using it to sweep something under the rug.

"What happened with that woman?" Taylor asked, not one to beat around the bush.

Asana flicked her gaze toward her, the corner of her eye twitching. "Maggie. I don't know. She was here at the party, the person that ran off when she saw me in the hallway. I've spent the last couple of hours racking my brain and having my team pull up every bit of information on her that they can."

"Any luck?"

Asana took a lengthy sip of her wine, nearly draining the glass. "She was definitely a pledge before getting kicked out and joining another sorority. Although to be honest, I don't even know how she was accepted into ADL after her little reporter stunt at Convocation."

"So could have been at a pledge tea party, then?"

"Yeah, I think so. She wasn't a pledge long, but there was enough time for her to have attended one or two. Too bad we don't have the Spill Book to see if she wrote in it."

Taylor rolled her eyes and swirled the contents of her glass. "I'm not sure she did. I would have remembered her."

"You can't remember everyone who wrote in the book. There were hundreds. Our pledge class, and then every class after that while we were there." Annabelle got up and poured herself a second glass.

"You don't steal a gossip diary that doesn't have something juicy, and I remember the juicy ones." Taylor winked at Brooklyn, whose face flamed red, but she didn't look away.

"That's right, but you never told us your secrets," Brooklyn replied.

And she hadn't, but neither had Asana or, really, Annabelle: it wasn't her secret that her husband fucked around. And one of Taylor's biggest secrets had a lot to do with Greg Hamm. She uncrossed and recrossed her legs.

"We're not here tonight to divulge our own secrets. We know that none of us stole that book." She looked pointedly at Asana. "What aren't you telling us?"

Asana, who was usually a stone wall when it came to any sort of confrontation, wavered just the tiniest bit.

"Fine." Asana tucked a short strand of her hair behind her ear, not even a tremble in her hand. "I know Maggie from something else."

"What?"

"The Machine."

Taylor watched as Annabelle and Brooklyn flinched. She'd known, even asked her about it one night when they'd had too much to drink. Asana had denied it of course, but Taylor had read it in the Spill Book, and seen her lurking around campus covered in a tacky black robe.

"The Machine? You were a part of the Machine?" Annabelle's mouth popped open in shock, and she quickly filled it with wine. "Like the people who rigged homecoming queen, and even the SGA elections? I knew it."

"Yes." Asana sounded annoyed that she had to admit it. "I was a part of them. And a part of what took them down the year we graduated."

"Oh shit." Brooklyn sat back in the chair. "And this Maggie, she was too?"

Asana shrugged. "She was at meetings. I don't know how much she knows, and she's such a runner she's not fucking talking. But I did have my people pull some stuff on her." Asana scrolled through her phone before looking up at them. "She is a freelance reporter. Her stories have been published in various newspapers, online outlets, and a few television stations for broadcast reporting."

"What would be her motivation for covering this week?" Brooklyn asked.

"The only thing I can come up with is me or us," Asana said. "And there must be a reason why."

Brooklyn nodded. "We need to talk to her."

"I have her cell." Asana flipped her phone around to show a series of typed notes in an email. "We could ask to meet."

"You guys, she's not just going to admit to stealing the Spill Book and blackmailing us. Those are criminal offenses." Annabelle laughed. "That's not how criminals work. My husband is a criminal lawyer—I would know." She added the latter in such a rush of breath she practically wheezed.

Taylor narrowed her eyes, keeping herself from saying she was also a lawyer, because then it would mean having to answer why she was her husband's lackey rather than a badass in her own right.

Besides, Greg had nothing to do with Annabelle's knowledge of crime, but Asana and Brooklyn didn't know that, and it wasn't Taylor who was willing to divulge all their secrets. "Is she really a criminal though, or just someone bent on some sort of revenge?"

"And also, why would she care? What did we ever do to her?" Annabelle pointed out.

"We won't know until we ask her." Asana tapped the table so gently, it made Taylor think she actually wanted to pound it to dust. That maybe Asana did know.

"She's not going to admit it." Taylor shook her head. "Why do you think it's her?"

Asana stared at them each in the eye. "She might know something about what I did to the Machine."

Annabelle shrugged, her cardigan slipping off her shoulder, and she didn't even bother to put it back. "She might. But wouldn't she go to the other members of that society? There has to be a reason, and this seems like such a crime of passion. Why go to the trouble to invite us all here, blackmail us all into coming, if she didn't want the attention, the moment to shine and tell us all off?"

Taylor reached over and put Annabelle's cardigan back in place. "Good point. Let's call her." Asana lifted her cell.

CHAPTER THIRTY-FOUR

I told my friends I was going home for the weekend. But I wasn't. My new daddy wanted me to fly with him to Cincinnati for a business trip. We started with the PPM route (pay per meet), but now I'm going to get an allowance. Also, Cincinnati was meh, and a little awkward. He wanted me to try choking . . . not a fan fave here.

Kisses,
Brooklyn

Asana

Then

The invitations to mock meetings always arrived on a note slipped beneath her dorm door addressed in scrolling calligraphy to make it look more important.

By sophomore year, Asana had started calling the Machine meetings "mock meetings" and these stupid envelopes "Mach summonses." "Mock" for so many reasons—but mostly because they made a mockery of the appearance of democracy. The things she'd learned in the past year . . .

The upside of sophomore year was that she'd been able to move onto Magnolia Drive. Rooming with Taylor in the ADL house meant that she had to wake up first and snatch up her summons, or else Taylor would absolutely open it. Love her, but she had no boundaries.

Anything else, Asana wouldn't have cared if she opened it. But not the Machine. She wouldn't know how to explain her connection to the clandestine society. People knew it existed, but no one talked about it. Bad things happened when they did. And somehow, Taylor always seemed to know everything about everything. Well, maybe that wasn't such a mystery. The Spill Book was basically a treasure trove for every juicy thing that ever happened to a sorority sister.

Plus, Asana was no good at lying to Taylor. Anyone else, she was the very definition of a liar But Taylor? She'd sunk her teeth in, and held on. And really, that was okay, because Asana kind of liked vampires.

Asana glanced back toward Taylor's side of the room, where the white silky curtain she'd put up for privacy to her bed was closed. Behind that curtain she was going to have a silk eye mask, tiny white shorts and top as she slept soundlessly. Her own matching curtain was slid back to reveal her perfectly made bed.

At home in New York, their housekeeper made her bed every day. But here, not so much. At first she'd thought that was part of their house mother's duties, but Mama Jenny had set her straight on that count. And Asana hated the look of a messy bed.

Asana liked order. Everything in its place. Tiny, neat lines. Maintaining control of one's environment was the best way to maintain control of one's self. She was a lesson in contradictions, at least that's what Taylor said. Because Asana liked an orderly neat life, but she had a wild side that craved spontaneity, a little bit of danger, and a whole lot of mess.

If only Taylor knew. One half of Asana was a sorority sister, and the other was a secret society member. Two halves of one coin.

That was probably what had drawn her to agree to become a Machine lackey. Because she definitely felt like one of the help where the crossed keys were concerned. Rigging SGA elections. Rigging real elections too. And there was really only two options: rise in the ranks and take it over, or tear the whole thing apart. To be honest, the latter sounded like a lot more fun.

Going to the meetings was the least sisterly thing that Asana could do. At the meetings she received her orders. Orders that she had no choice but to carry out. And every order went against the bonds of sisterhood. Asana's reasons for joining a sorority might not have been completely altruistic, but now that she was a part of ADL, had made such good friends, every followed order from the Machine made her feel guilty.

The Machine orders made her coerce her ADL sisters into voting the way the Machine wanted, supporting people the Machine supported. She convinced her sisters not to do what they believed in, but instead what the Machine wanted, which for Asana, went against everything *she* believed in. And yet she'd not said no.

Which made her a traitor.

Even now her stomach burned with guilt.

She'd done it all through her freshman year, knowing they were grooming her for something bigger. The whole point of her being here. Always ready to catch the bigger fish. Responsibilities kept piling up, and this year, as a sophomore, the Mach had put her in charge of Student Government Association election persuasion.

She stuffed the envelope into her backpack, finished her hair, makeup, and OOTD—a habit she'd gotten into thanks to Brooklyn—and tried not to think about the fact that she would have to rush from one end of campus to the next to make it in time for the meeting at noon. As a result, she was going to miss lunch, and today was Greek bowls at the house, her favorite.

Asana scribbled a note on a pink sticky and stuck it to Taylor's mirror, asking her to save her a Greek bowl, then slipped from the room. She chose the earliest classes because if she was going to rise to the top in the corporate game, the true winners started before the rest of the world.

Steaming coffee in hand, she hurried to class as the sun rose, knowing she'd arrive first and have time to go over her notes before their quiz.

Two classes later, she was rushing across campus, stomach growling, and then slipping inside the imposing building addressed on this morning's summons. The low murmur of voices hummed along the darkened stairwell. As if someone wouldn't notice people were down in the basement, even if the lights were off.

But then again, they were never interrupted, so maybe they didn't.

Asana showed her ring, gave the password written on today's invitation to the same person who saw her every time, mirroring the rituals of ADL meetings.

She joined the rest of the group that made up the Machine. Mostly male. Mostly white. Mostly privileged.

At the center was the Machine president, Greg Hamm. The biggest jerk Asana had ever met in her life. He was grinning with so much cheese, he practically had orange goo melting down his chin. No way was she going to classify his level of tackiness with a rich and flavorful fancy cheese. Not even a slice of Velveeta was good enough for G.H.

Taking her seat, Asana said hello to the few other girls, one from each sorority on campus, and a few other people. Asana also made it a point to talk to the "men"; they really were boys dressed up in big-boy suits.

"Welcome, welcome," Greg said, his hands raised a little, and she couldn't decide if he was trying to emulate a politician or an evangelical priest. Either way, he clearly had a God complex. "I'm going to let my vice president run today's meeting."

Asana crossed her arms and narrowed her eyes as Jared, essentially Greg's left testicle, took the podium. That wasn't normal. But the reason why became very evident a second later.

This was a private campaign meeting. Greg was running for SGA president and his deputy was singing his praises, which were straight out of Aesop's fables.

Asana had to squint to keep her eyes from rolling. She gritted her teeth to keep from laughing at the absurdity. Greg Hamm, the biggest lunatic at every frat party. The very sight of him gave Asana the chills. He was dangerous. Not that she'd witnessed him doing anything bad—yet. But there were rumors that if you were a female, and you were alone with him, chances were you'd wake up the next day with a headache and no memory of what actually happened.

"Your task, if you choose to accept it," Greg said after his deputy stopped having verbal diarrhea all over them, "is to inspire your respective circles to vote for me."

"Inspire" was just another word for coerce. They never directly said anything; it was all indirect. Whispered in pulled-aside conversations. Insinuated in language that could be untangled to pull out multiple lines, but when put together with the body language and tone meant something completely different.

Greg Hamm wanted to be SGA president—ruling the student body on campus. Not just the fraternities and sororities. Everyone. He'd have control of student leadership, laws and regulations for the SGA, and campus activities and the budgets to fund them. Greg Hamm's hooves would leave an imprint wherever he wanted. And there was nothing anyone could do to stand in his way.

And people thought New York was corrupt.

CHAPTER THIRTY-FIVE

I met a guy. He's a total frat-head, but only on the outside. On the inside, he's so sweet and caring. I feel so good when I'm around him. The other day, I woke up to find my fave latte outside my door with a rose. Dude had to sneak in here to drop it. Only problem is, my friends hate him. Especially Taylor. I think she's jealous.

Kisses,
Annabelle

Brooklyn

Now

"Wait." Brooklyn held up one hand and tapped her laptop. "Let's watch the feed first. We may want to call more than one person to the table, and perhaps it should be another tea party of suspects."

Taylor rolled her eyes. "Why is this starting to feel like a hokey crime show?"

"No negative vibes." Annabelle gave her a tiny elbow jab—very unlike her. "We want to get this figured out, and soon."

"Roll the tape, then." Asana waved a hand and put her cell not so gently back on the table.

Having hooked up her laptop to the hotel television screen,

Brooklyn turned on the video feed and ratcheted up the volume. They watched ADL alumni sisters arrive, all the chatting, the cheese eating and wine consuming. Then on-screen Asana left. On-screen Asana came back.

Jacqueline's ornery ass bitching about literally everything from the scent of laundry detergent to campus landscaping to her bikini wax. Her mouth never stopped moving. Ally's equally shady ass had a lot to say, mostly gossip about which professors were fucking, and that she happened to know the cousin of a friend of the family of their house mother, blah blah, boring.

There wasn't much to the video that they hadn't seen or heard before. Everyone looked the same. They all were shocked. They all were happy. As if their emotions were all linked and synced like a rowing team. Mouths opened in uniform. Eyes widened. Arms moved. Row, row, row. Once an ADL sister, always an ADL sister. But who was the coxswain now?

Normally, Brooklyn would have said Taylor, but she was just standing in the middle of the room letting the chaos unleash around her.

Someone did stand out to Brooklyn, though, a woman in the back. She looked familiar, but it wasn't someone she'd chatted with too often. She'd joined the sorority later, maybe junior year as an alumni relations chair?

Brooklyn paused on her face. The woman was glaring hard, and when Brooklyn followed the line of the sis's vision, it landed on herself. She leaned closer, zoomed.

"Whoa, that's some bitterness right there. What was her name again? She didn't really stand out too much in a crowd, and I remember thinking she was a pity pick." Taylor tapped her nails on the table in a rhythmic pattern.

"I can't remember. . . . Shayna or Cheyenne? Shania? Something like that."

"She is hating on you hard," Asana pointed out.

"She looks like you just stole her Birkin bag." Taylor smirked.

"Or that I had it in the same shade," Brooklyn joked. "I have this vague memory of her. I think she was a year or two behind us. I kind of remember her having an attitude problem, but she was so nice to everyone else, I figured she just didn't like redheads."

"Redheads?" Taylor raised a brow. "Who doesn't like redheads?"

"Lots of people."

"Ginger Mommy would know."

"So would Brooklyn in Bama." *And Sporty Spyce.*

"Hmm," Taylor said. "Keep playing—let's see if she gives you more shade."

And sure enough, there were several more instances, some close up, and some from far away. Even a few whispered and pointed conversations.

"She's talking shit about you," Asana said. "Wow, that's ballsy."

"I wish we could hear better what she's saying." Brooklyn jabbed the volume button several times.

But it was impossible. The room was too loud, and everyone's words jumbled together.

"What did you do to her?" Taylor laughed. "God, it's like you stole her boyfriend."

Or her dad.

The blood drained from Brooklyn's face as a memory, a confusing one, came flooding back. This sorority sister pointing at the necklace Brooklyn was wearing and saying her mom had one just like it. The odd way she'd looked at her. Almost accusing. Brooklyn had ignored it back then, thinking she was just trying to make conversation and was awkward, but that necklace . . . Anytime she saw her, the girl pointed it out.

Fuck. It all came flooding back.

"Shayna is definitely her name, I remember now." Brooklyn swallowed hard. "I fucked her dad."

"Oh . . . fuck . . ." Asana breathed out the breath that had been stolen from Brooklyn's lungs.

"I think they got a divorce too," Brooklyn added. "I used to go on his business trips with him, and one time I answered the phone in the hotel because he told me he'd call me when he was going to pick me up, but he didn't want to call my cell because his wife was monitoring his line or something."

"And it wasn't him, was it?"

Brooklyn shook her head. "Nope. And I was wearing a T-shirt from Austin at school the next day, and she definitely pointed out how odd it was her dad had just been in Austin."

"Damn. That makes sense why she'd hate on you. But the rest of us?" Taylor shook her head.

"Yeah, I have no idea about that." Brooklyn instinctively touched the pearls at her neck. They weren't from Shayna's dad, but Drew. Drew, who was completely in the dark about her past. "Unless she literally just doesn't care. Collateral damage."

"But exposing you means exposing herself." Asana leaned closer to look at the paused image on the screen.

"Her secrets weren't that great." Taylor said it with an authority that none of them questioned, and she pressed play to keep the video going.

"Then she wouldn't care about them getting out," Asana added. "Not like the rest of us."

"If we're all about to get exposed in a few days, then maybe we should actually know what kind of secrets each of us are hiding," Brooklyn said. "I've told you mine. I was a sugar baby, and I posted pics and vids on OnlyFans. Lost my scholarship because of it." Brooklyn narrowed her eyes. "Actually, Asana and I are the only ones who've actually confessed. Taylor? Annabelle? Who wants to go first. It's time for a real tea party. No more Spill Book, just open your mouths and tell us."

Taylor looked nervously at Asana and then at Annabelle. Did they already know? Or was what she was about to confess going to impact them somehow?

Taylor licked her lips and straightened her shoulders, the same way she had when she was president of their sorority before she was able to go into battle.

"I have a hostile uterus." Taylor let out a breath as if this confession meant something.

"What?" Brooklyn narrowed her eyes.

Asana laughed. "This isn't the time for jokes."

"It's true. I do. And the reason is—"

"Holy shit, wait." Brooklyn rewound the video that they'd stopped playing, to see Jacqueline sneak her hand into Taylor's purse and pull out the new Spill Book. She opened it up, ripped out a few pages, and shoved them in the pocket of her slacks.

"Did she just steal the new confessions?" Annabelle guzzled more wine.

"Ohmygod, it's Jacqueline. That thief." Asana slapped the table, her wineglass wobbling until she caught it.

"Is she staying in this hotel?" Taylor shoved away from the table so hard, her chair teetered.

"I'm not sure," Asana said.

Taylor marched to the phone, picked up the receiver, and then in a sweet tone asked to be transferred to Jacqueline's room.

"She's not going to get away with this. I bet she has the original in her room." Taylor let out a groan and slammed down the receiver. "Went to the answering service."

"I'm curious about your hostile uterus," Asana said, sipping her wine and staring at Taylor over the rim of her glass. "Care to explain?"

But their phones lit up at the same time, a text from President Larissa that tomorrow night's theme party at Sigma Chi was "Then and Now," a mingling of the current Panhellenic community and the alumni.

"Are we really going?" Brooklyn wrinkled her nose. Attending a frat party wasn't really on brand for her anymore.

"Of course we are." Asana stood, pressed her hands to her breasts, and wiggled them. "They might be in college, but those hotties are still adults. Did you bring your anti-roofie roofies, Taylor?"

Taylor's smile looked forced. "Never leave home without them."

At least this party would be a lot tamer than the ones they'd attended in college with the alumni there. One could hope . . .

CHAPTER THIRTY-SIX

A few of the girls tried to start a coup. Guess what? Spill Book to the rescue. Now they are blackballed from all Greek Life. Let that be a lesson to anyone who tries to go against me. Also, to the ones who didn't? I bought them all a makeover sesh. It pays to be my friend. And, well, I guess you pay if you're not.

Kisses,
Taylor

Annabelle

Then

Ever since freshman year, Annabelle couldn't think of a swap party as anything other than "Sex With a Penis," except for the fact that she'd managed to go unscathed all through freshman year, and even now.

Nobody knew she was still a virgin though. That was one thing she'd not confessed in the Spill Book, so even Taylor had no clue that there'd yet to be any formal insertion.

That wasn't to say she wasn't willing to do other things . . .

Of course, the Panhellenic governing body did not condone the swapping of bodily fluids. Swaps was supposed to be a mixer with the sorority getting to know members of the fraternity. A way to make friends and be social. But it always turned into more than that. Hosted once a week, it was a chance for the sorority sisters to dress up in a theme, to flirt, to let go on a Thursday night. Normally they were for the freshmen only, but the upperclassmen got to have full house swaps occasionally too, like tonight. The theme was "Librarians and Barbarians."

Greg Hamm, the hottest frat-daddy she'd been paired with yet, knelt before her with a rose in one hand, covered in a torn sheet made into a toga, baring the gym-rat sculpted muscles of his arms and chest. The sheet came to just above his knees, and with a gust of wind, she'd know whether he went full commando or had tied on a Conan the Barbarian loincloth. Out of all her sisters in ADL, he'd chosen her. She felt like she was on an episode of *The Bachelor*. He smiled up at her with a look of promise that made her almost consider going all the way, but it was going to take a lot more than a smile and an offered flower to get her between the sheets. *Maybe.*

"Hey, gorgeous, I think I'm *overdue* . . . for a date with you," he said, eyes scanning over her black miniskirt, blouse unbuttoned to her cleavage, and pink cardigan buttoned just below it. She wore matching pink stilettos and fake "librarian" glasses.

And apparently those words were the hottest syllables she'd ever heard, because she was pressing her hand to her chest and cooing thank you, as if he'd just paid her the biggest compliment. "You can turn my pages anytime."

Ohmygoodness, she couldn't believe she just said that. Annabelle wasn't normally such a sap, but Greg . . . there was something so charismatic about him.

With the tiniest bend to her pressed-together knees, she placed her hand holding the rose over her heart. "Aren't you a sweetheart?"

An impossibly adorable dimple in his cheek winked at her.

Greg stood and offered his arm. She slipped her hand around his elbow and stared at her friends, who were being gifted roses by other brothers. The party was at the Sigma Chi house tonight, and even now librarians and barbarians mingled on the lawn while others trickled inside to where the music was thumping hard.

The inside of the frat house had been transformed into a massive cave with thick brown paper on the walls, ropes that were supposed to simulate vines, and fake lines of ivy strung from one room to the next.

One of the barbarians grabbed hold of a rope and swung from one side to the other, causing screeches of laughter from the librarians. One of whom reached up to squeeze his ass under his toga.

"Can I get you a drink?" Greg asked against her ear, his hand sliding into hers, warm and firm.

"I think we're supposed to remain sober." She blinked up at him, still trying to figure out how she'd gotten so lucky.

"What do you like?" He ignored her, sweeping a lock of hair off his forehead, but it bounced right back, giving him a naughty look.

"I'll have what you're having." If he was insisting, was she allowed to say no?

He grinned at her as if she'd answered the question correctly, and then he headed toward their bar, which had been wrapped in paper painted gray like a big rock.

When he returned, he carried a name tag that he stuck to her chest, his hand lingering a little too long just over her breast. Annabelle's heart quickened, and she smiled, trying to wipe away the nervous feeling.

She glanced down at the sticker. Instead of her name, it said: *Greg's—Don't Touch.*

"There," he said. "I've checked you out. No one else can borrow you."

That was definitely on theme with the barbarian claiming her. Across the room the same brother who'd swung across on a fake vine lifted his date—Ally—over his shoulder and slapped her ass as he carried her deeper into the house.

"Cheers," Greg said, tapping his red Solo cup to hers.

Annabelle glanced into the cup, taking in the foamy beer. Since the very first party she'd gone to, they'd been told not to drink out of a red Solo handed to them if they hadn't seen it poured. But Greg, he was sweet. She could trust him. Besides other freshmen appeared to be drinking too.

The scent of cheap beer wafted up, and she tried not to sniff. She really hated beer, but she wasn't one to complain. Her mama had taught her that. And she didn't want to be rude. So she sipped lightly, the taste bitter, and she let it drop back out of her mouth into the cup, backwashing like a champ without him seeing. Also what her mama had taught her.

Greg might be a charmer, but she didn't like to get too drunk at swaps. Or at all. Made her nervous. She hadn't kept her V-card this long just to have it swiped by a barbarian, even if he was the hottest date she'd had in a year. When the time was right, she wanted it to be special.

"Dance with me," he said, placing a hand on her hip and grinding the general area of his loincloth against her crotch.

Annabelle put a hand on his warm shoulder, the muscles flexing beneath her fingers, and let him dry hump her in lieu of dancing. She'd taken dance lessons for years—as a pageant queen, she had to know every dance medium to perform—and this was definitely not anything close.

A burst of laughter caught her attention, and she looked over to see Taylor bent over, looking mischievous as her date slapped her ass and called her a naughty bookworm. Taylor covered her mouth in a mocking "Oh my" expression. Annabelle laughed and danced over to slap her ass too, the both of them giggling. She started to bend over for Taylor to return the favor only to have Greg haul her back against him. Something hard ramming against her buttocks. There was a flicker of something on his face that might have been construed as anger and desire all in one, but he quickly covered it with a charming grin.

"Two naughty librarians," he said, his grip easing on her hips.

Annabelle nodded and nervously sipped her beer, swallowing before she remembered her own rule.

CHAPTER THIRTY-SEVEN

Wow, somebody doesn't give a shit about girl code. Yeah, I'm talking to you. I know you're reading this late at night like some sick voyeur. The only reason I haven't said anything is because of this fucking book.

Kisses,
Brooklyn

Asana

Now

One leather skirt. One red corset. One pair of fuck-me stilettos.

Prior to coming to Alabama, Asana had not planned to bring any of her club clothes, but she was also practical, and knew she might need to sneak off to an elite adults-only. If that happened to be a "Then and Now" party at Sigma Chi, fine, not that she was likely to get the kind of action she craved.

Frat boys weren't as talented with their cocks as they liked to believe they were. Besides, she wasn't into man-boys.

But the grinding and music and drinks, they might serve to scratch the itch she'd not been able to finish at Fantasia, one that hadn't been assuaged by her guards either, no matter how many times she'd fucked them this week already.

Guard One opened the back door of the limo, and Asana was out first, giving him a we'll-fuck-later grin, followed by her three friends. Annabelle was still acting jumpy; not even the half bottle of wine she'd drunk had seemed to calm her down. Brooklyn kept glancing around like she expected the mommy brigade to leap out from behind bushes with their pitchforks and kitchen knives. Only Taylor looked like she was ready to have some fun.

They walked to the front path of the fraternity house, the music thumping so loud the windows vibrated, tickling their ears.

"I swear I can smell the keg from here." Asana laughed. "Actually, I think it smells like budus—"

Brooklyn groaned. "Don't say it."

There were two types of people at every party. Those who derived a natural high from the excitement, and those who hated it but went anyway. Brooklyn used to be the former, but it seemed now she'd hopped the fence. In another life, Brooklyn would have been a perfect addition to Matinee.

"Let's show these children how it's done," Asana said.

"They are adults," Brooklyn murmured.

"Coddled adults, aka children," Asana said.

"So glad you could make it." President Larissa ran outside the house like she'd been waiting at the window for them, dressed in a tie-dye minidress, hair teased eighties-style, then winked at them. "Cougars, looking for some cubs."

Asana couldn't help the way her lip curled in disgust. Larissa had no idea what she was even saying, that much was evident.

"We're just here to support our sisters," Brooklyn said, going for a sweet vibe that didn't quite fit the girl who used to fuck her sister's father. God, that was a fucked-up situation.

"Aren't you sweet?" Larissa rolled her eyes as she turned. Thankfully Brooklyn didn't see it, but Asana did, and so did Taylor from the way she met Asana's gaze.

They followed the other sisters into the house, the frat boys catcalling that older women had arrived.

"Oh, no thank you, I'm married," Brooklyn said to one.

"I don't want to take you home, sugar, I just want to dance." He grabbed her hips and started to grind.

Brooklyn glanced over her shoulder, and Asana smiled. "I'll go get us some drinks."

"I'll come with you," Taylor said, leaving Annabelle to dance beside Brooklyn, who was being currently pawed, and though she pretended not to like it, there was a spark in her eyes that Asana hadn't seen since they'd arrived back on campus.

As much as Brooklyn wanted to put out the wholesome-mommy vibe, she was a naughty girl just waiting to be let out of her cage.

Taylor grabbed Asana's hand, surprising her enough she almost yanked away, but Taylor gave her a piercing look and tugged her out of the back of the frat and around the corner into the shadows. She pushed Asana against the side of the house, and then stepped so close, she could feel the heat of her scantily clad body against hers.

"Are you going to tell?" Even in the dark, she could see the way Taylor's gaze roved toward her mouth and she remembered the taste of lemonade and whiskey, the swipe of cherry ChapStick, all too well.

"Tell what?" Asana tried to remain still when every inch of her demanded she pull Taylor closer. To feel her against her one last time. To kiss that mouth.

"Not that it matters." Taylor laughed. "Someone already knows."

If only Taylor knew the extent of the threats. The looming exposé on a life Asana had worked hard to hide. "Probably. Is it so bad?"

The lie sounded absurd, even to her.

Taylor flopped her body beside Asana's, leaning against the cool brick. "Elijah wouldn't understand."

Asana wanted to ask why she was with him, then, if he was going to hold her past against her. Better yet, why was she with him to begin with?

"But he's not going to understand why I can't have babies either."

"Is it because of . . ." Asana rotated to the side, staring at Taylor's profile.

"Yeah."

Asana slid her palm against Taylor's, threading their fingers together. "Maybe he would."

Taylor rolled her head toward her. "He wouldn't. His entire campaign is wholesome family values. It's a miracle he lets me even have a job."

Asana practically choked on that. What had Taylor gotten herself mixed into? "You're kidding."

"No, I'm not."

Now she couldn't help but ask. "Why are you with him, then?"

"I love him." She shrugged as if that simple reasoning explained everything when it did the exact opposite.

Loved him like a lover or like a protector?

"Do you miss this . . . us?" Asana asked, her heart pouring out of her mouth when she should have kept it shut.

Taylor didn't answer, but Asana watched the line of her throat bob as she swallowed. Asana reached for that line, the silkiness of Taylor's skin beneath her finger as she slid her hand from the dip in her throat up to her chin, running a thumb over her mouth.

"Do you miss me?"

Taylor let out a sigh that tingled over Asana's hand, but she said nothing, as if the truth was too hard to confess. As if saying it would change her entire circumstance. The same way she remained silent in college, but had no problem sneaking into her room at night, and then when they'd lived in the house, shared a room, their limbs entangled night after night behind a white curtain, and no one the wiser.

Growing bold, and likely to regret it, Asana leaned over Taylor and pressed her mouth to hers. The same sweet taste, mint on her tongue. God, she'd missed this. Taylor whimpered in her throat and, where she'd been frozen before, seemed to finally find the strength in her limbs to move. She ran her hands over Asana's back, tugging her closer, their breasts pushed together, their hips touching. Asana slid a thigh between Taylor's, the heat of her scorching.

This was what she'd been wanting, needing. This was the itch that could never be scratched enough. The ache that was never quite fulfilled, no matter how many people she fucked, no matter how many times she came. It was always Taylor she wanted, needed, and couldn't have.

And then Taylor burst the bubble, like she had when they were seniors. Hands on Asana's shoulders, she gently pushed.

"We need to stop. We can't do this here. . . . Someone might see." Taylor glanced around them in the dark.

Asana backed up, hurt and disappointment trying their damnedest to crush her. She smiled instead, because what good would it do to show Taylor she'd devastated her again? Nothing.

"You're right. And our friends are waiting for their beers."

Taylor nodded, but she didn't move. Her nipples were hard beneath the tiny sequined shirt. Asana looked away, back toward the way they'd come. Voices sounded from the back, but the thought of discovery didn't dampen the need she felt. It only seemed to electrify every nerve in her body.

"Come on," she said, and started to turn.

"Wait." Taylor grabbed her hand and tugged her back. "One more won't hurt."

Asana blinked, but didn't need time to think, not that Taylor gave it to her as she cupped the back of her neck and pulled her in for another kiss, as her hands found the curve of Asana's hip, while her tongue found the curve of her mouth.

God, some things never changed, and she didn't know whether to fucking love that or hate the shit out of it.

CHAPTER THIRTY-EIGHT

Frat parties are so dumb. It's just a bunch of testosterone-laden animals trying to hump everything with tits. I mean, if I want that I'll just go to a sex club in NYC. Okay, confession, I actually love those clubs. Maybe I should just look at frat parties like that?

Kisses,
Asana

Brooklyn

Then

Brooklyn held her phone at a ninety-degree angle, her arm steady despite the drinks she'd already consumed. She whirled in a slow circle, taking in the atmosphere of the party, her smiling face in the bottom of the picture.

"Librarian Brooklyn in Barbarian Bama!" she called out.

But something in the top portion of the video image gave her pause, and her smile faltered for the briefest of seconds before she said, "See you in the morning, y'all! Don't wait up!"

She clicked off the live video on Instagram and then whirled around to stare toward the Sigma Chi house steps that led upstairs to the bedrooms. Greg—Annabelle's date—was hand in hand with Taylor, weaving his way up the stairs with her. When Taylor stumbled—probably because she insisted on those like eight-inch stilettos—Greg picked her up and tossed her over his shoulder, slapping her ass with a smack that Brooklyn felt, as he let out a caveman roar.

A bunch of other barbarians chimed in, chugging their beers.

"What the fuck?" Brooklyn murmured. Where was Annabelle? And where was Brad?

She glanced around the room, but didn't see either of them, though to be fair the frat house was packed, and the lights were strobing like usual. She pushed through the crowd. It went so against sister etiquette to go off with another sister's date.

Taylor had done some pretty heinous things, but this went above and beyond. Stealing Annabelle's date for a fuck?

Brooklyn frowned hard as she tried to meander through the throng of throbbing and gyrating bodies. But she wasn't exactly tall enough to see over everyone's heads, even with her heels.

And she was being blocked in by a table. Fuck it. She kicked off her heels and climbed onto the table, pretending to dance to cheers—thank goodness that, as a sophomore, she could finally be on an elevated surface. She danced in a circle until Annabelle came into view. Passed out on a—no doubt cum-stained—couch with Asana beside her, trying to shake her awake. Brooklyn hopped down and hurried over to the couch, plopping down on Annabelle's other side, grateful tonight's strobe vibe didn't involve black lights.

"What happened?"

Asana frowned. "Roofied, I think. She won't wake up."

"Damn. . . . Here?"

"I don't know. She doesn't normally drink, but that cup is drained. Maybe she just can't handle her alcohol?"

That explained why Greg ditched her for the livelier Taylor.

Brooklyn sighed in disgust. Unless Greg had been the one to drug her.

"We should take her back to the house."

"Yeah. Where's Taylor?" Asana stood on tiptoe, craning her neck to get a look into the crowd.

"She's not down here." Brooklyn didn't want to say what she'd seen, but the judgment came out in her voice.

"But we can't leave without her and Brad isn't here."

They never left a frat party without all four of them. It had been a pledge they'd made to one another freshman year. Brooklyn glanced back toward the stairs. She should go get her. Before she made a mistake. Taylor could be a bitch, but was she really a backstabber? Brooklyn bit her lip. She supposed that depended on who was on the other end of Taylor's knife. And Annabelle had definitely not done anything to offend her, at least not that Brooklyn knew of.

"Is she upstairs?" Asana asked.

Brooklyn nodded, as she was jostled aside, a very drunk barbarian crashing onto the couch, his toga loose as he tossed a leg over Annabelle's lap, his balls falling naked onto the couch. Gross.

"Wake up, lib, I wanna see if my bookworm fits between your pages."

Ohmygod. Fucking disgusting.

Brooklyn rolled her eyes and shifted his leg off Annabelle, tossing the heaviness aside and hiding his nasty balls. "Fuck off."

He grumbled something about her being a bitch and then sauntered away.

"I'll get Taylor," Asana said. "You take Annabelle back to the house."

For the first time, they were breaking up the foursome, but it seemed necessary tonight. Annabelle was three minutes away from being accosted by a barbarian if Brooklyn didn't get her out of here.

"Wake up." Brooklyn tapped her friend's cheek.

Annabelle's eyelids fluttered, and she murmured something.

"Let's go." She tried tugging on Annabelle's arm, but every inch forward she moved her, Annabelle just fell back to the crusty couch.

"Can I help?"

Brooklyn glanced up to see the most sober frat guy she'd ever encountered. His eyes were clear, and he had real concern on his face.

"No, we're fine."

He held up his hands. "Promise, I just want to help."

It was then that Brooklyn noticed his outfit, and the lack of sheet. "Why are you dressed like a turkey?"

"Considered a DD tonight." He laughed. "They made us dress up like farm animals so girls would know the difference."

"Is it working?"

"Not really." His eyes flicked toward where a guy in a cow costume had his tongue deep in one of her sisters' mouths. "But I promise, I'm not that guy. Or any of the other ones. I'm Drew." He held out his hand for her to shake, and Brooklyn found the absurdity of that too funny not to laugh.

She shook his hand. "Brooklyn."

"All right, Brooklyn. Let me help you get your friend home. That's my job. And I take my job very seriously."

"Thank you."

Drew lifted Annabelle into his arms with a gentleness Brooklyn found endearing, and then he headed for the door.

"We live at ADL," she said.

He grinned at her. "I figured."

"Oh, right, it's just us tonight." She laughed nervously, taken aback by the sweet way he was looking at her. "Short commute."

Ohmygod, could she be any more of a dork?

"Easiest one of the night." He walked across the street carrying Annabelle with an ease that made Brooklyn wonder about his workout routine.

"Do you play sports?" she asked.

"Yeah, I'm on the men's soccer team."

Brooklyn grinned. "Cool. I'm on the women's."

"Roll Tide."

"Yeah." She snickered. "Maybe I'll see you on the track sometime."

"I'd like that."

Mama Jenny must have been waiting by the door because she'd opened it by the time they reached the top of the front steps.

"Oh no, not Annabelle," she said sadly. "I'll bring up some tea." She turned and disappeared into the darkened hallway leading to the kitchen.

Brooklyn wanted to ask if she had an antidote for roofies, because tea wasn't likely to do the job. Actually, if there was such a thing as an antidote, Taylor would have it. Brooklyn would have to go raid her stash.

"No boys allowed upstairs," Brooklyn said as Drew put his foot on the first step to carry Annabelle up.

They both stared down at Annabelle's completely unconscious face.

"Be quick. If our house mother or Riley sees us, we'll be fined. Maybe even kicked out."

He wrinkled his nose. "Are you sure? How do they expect her to get upstairs? She's passed out cold."

Brooklyn rolled her eyes. "Yeah, I know. It's dumb. If you have to climb out the window, think you can do it?"

He grinned. "I've definitely climbed *into* a window before. Climbing out shouldn't be hard."

Brooklyn laughed. "I want to hear about that sometime."

They rushed up the stairs before anyone could see them and into Annabelle's room. Then Brooklyn led him toward the back stairs, where they were least likely to be seen, so he wouldn't be forced out a window.

"Thank you, Drew," she said at the bottom of the stairs. "I really appreciate your help."

"Anytime. I mean, I hope we never have to do it again, but you know what I mean."

"I do."

Drew started to open the door, and she wished she had the guts to ask him when he ran on the track.

Then he stopped, turned around. "Can I get your Snap?"

Brooklyn tried not to smile too wide. *Play it cool.* "Yeah. Brooklyn in Bama."

He grinned, pulled out his phone, and added her. "Stay safe, Brooklyn in Bama."

And then he was walking away across the darkened lawn, or more like waddling in his turkey costume.

Brooklyn couldn't help smiling as she shut and locked the back door. Not once since she'd been on campus had she actually allowed herself to flirt for real with another student. A few dates for a free meal, a couple of make-out sessions, sure, but all of her attention and energy went into soccer, classes, ADL, and her entrepreneurial endeavors. The idea of opening herself up for a broken heart was terrifying and exhilarating all at once.

She stared after the retreating turkey, feeling a bit like a dumb bird herself, then hurried upstairs to make sure Annabelle was okay.

CHAPTER THIRTY-NINE

*My anti-roofie roofie doesn't always work.
I would know.*

Kisses,
Taylor

Annabelle

Now

Where the hell were they?

Asana and Taylor had left too long ago to simply be getting beers. Brooklyn was teaching the other ADL sisters how to perfect a selfie angle, and so it was up to Annabelle to figure out what had happened to their friends.

They were not on the first floor, and each of the bedrooms she'd stormed upstairs had other people lip-locked, including one girl she rescued from a hookup she clearly didn't want.

The only alternative was to go outside. Maybe they needed some air—she certainly could use some. She'd forgotten how much frat houses stank.

Outside, some young men were playing a game of what looked like blindfolded Frisbee, and she watched as one of them got hit square in the forehead and was so drunk, he simply just fell backward. Well, that was sad. She was about to go back inside when she heard soft voices coming around the side of the building.

Five years may have passed since graduation, but Annabelle recognized the cadence of their voices, even if whisper soft. Sneaking around the sorority house to swipe things made her keenly aware of even the smallest sound.

Annabelle rounded the corner to see Asana and Taylor. She was about to call out, but then Taylor jerked forward, grabbed hold of Asana, and . . . *kissed* her.

Annabelle's eyes widened, mouth dropped, and she was momentarily frozen in place. For a second, she'd thought that Taylor was going to attack Asana. Punch her, strangle her, claw her, whatever. And she supposed, in a way, she was, but not with violence, but rather, passion. Like *The Notebook*–style passion.

Well, hot cross buns.

Annabelle whirled around and hurried back inside, the vision of what she'd seen playing and replaying in her mind. Two of her best friends were hooking up. Clearly not for the first time. For how long? Since college? Since after? Were they in love? OhmyChanel, was Elijah a ruse?

Questions tumbled over and again as Annabelle weaved her way through the house, grabbed a couple cans of beers, and handed one to Brooklyn, who held it up with a scrunched-up nose.

"Natty, classic."

Annabelle laughed. "So classic."

"Couldn't find them?"

Pulling on her fence front, she answered casually, "They were playing a game with some of the boys; they'll be back in a minute."

"Do you ever miss this?" Brooklyn asked, nodding toward the chaos.

Annabelle nearly choked on her watery beer. "Not this cheap beer and sweaty boys trying to find a home for their dicks, but you guys, yes."

Brooklyn laughed. "Me too. Why didn't we make an effort to see each other?"

"Everyone's been so busy."

"We can't be too busy to not have friends."

"I have friends." Annabelle thought about all the Stepford wives she got together with for yoga, playdates, coffee dates, and book club. "Sort of."

Brooklyn tapped her beer to Annabelle's. "I've got some sort-of friends too. But you guys . . . maybe the Spill Book was fucked-up, but it made us all close. And so did the sisterhood."

"We need a face-mask-and-popcorn night."

"Let's do it tonight. We're not going to be here that long. I hope."

Annabelle thought back to what she'd just seen. The passion expressed between Asana and Taylor . . . Not even in his most romantic moments had Annabelle ever felt that kind of hunger, drive from Greg. Sugar but she was jealous.

She'd always thought it was her, because Greg had been messing around on her for years. Probably always. But she wanted passion. Wanted to feel that kind of desire, to experience someone needing her so badly they'd risk everything.

The most passion she ever felt was for taking things. Collecting had replaced intimacy. Selling fenced jewels to the desperate housewives of Tuscaloosa was nearly as good as an orgasm.

But why couldn't she have both? She certainly wasn't going to find it with Greg. But then she reminded herself of why she'd married Greg in the first place. Not only because she was a good Christian girl but because he was her insurance policy. And to keep herself out of jail, she supposed she had to be willing to give up something. Maybe a passionate, fulfilling relationship was that thing she had forgone.

Brooklyn raised her brow. "So? No pampering night, then?"

Annabelle smiled. "Of course, I'd love that. But first let's play the next round of pong. I haven't picked up a Ping-Pong ball since college, and as I recall, you were hard to beat. But I did beat you."

Brooklyn laughed. "You're on. Putting balls in holes is my fave."

"That's what she said," Annabelle teased.

They squeezed their way over to the table where the current ADL president was dominating.

"Make room for the cougars, boys," Larissa said with a wink, and Annabelle tried hard not to bristle.

The little witch. Annabelle was only five or six years older. Could have been her sister, and she was acting like she was as old as her mother.

"We need to show that little tart the door," Annabelle muttered under her breath.

"Doubles?" Brooklyn grinned mischievously.

"We're going to crush her."

"You know it."

Brooklyn tapped the table with her manicured nail. "Doubles?"

Larissa looked over from where she was poised to toss her final pong. "Wanna put some money on it?" On her side of the table every red cup still remained.

"Only if it goes to Paws for Claws. Sisters are all about philanthropy, aren't they?" Annabelle said.

Larissa's lips split and she kept her gaze on them as she tossed the pong, landing with a delicate splash in the last red Solo cup. She whipped her head back toward her opponent, who was already a little wobbly. "Drink."

"Should we warm up first?" Annabelle tried to sound calm. Of course, five years ago, she would have wiped the floor with Larissa and anyone else in the room, but the closest she'd come to playing pong in the last half decade was tossing diapers into the trash from across the room, and even that had been years ago.

"You feeling rusty?" Brooklyn asked. "Shake out your shoulders and wrists. It's like riding a bicycle."

Annabelle followed Brooklyn's moves as they shook themselves out.

"Have you played recently?" Annabelle asked.

Brooklyn grinned. "Drew and I play water pong all the time with our neighbors. Still all the fun without the hangover in the morning."

"Oh." Water pong, why hadn't Annabelle thought of that?

"Besides, I think we do best two out of three, and kick her ass twice over after losing the first round." Brooklyn glanced behind her to where Larissa was doing eenie-meenie-miney-mo to pick her partner.

"Ah, let her think she's got a leg up."

"Exactly. Then we take her down not once but twice. It will be more fun that way."

"Love it."

Annabelle rubbed her hands together, crossed herself, blew on a pong ball, and took her place at the table beside Brooklyn. One of the frat boys had refilled the dirty Solo cups with beer in the four, three, two, one cup triangle, and a crowd had started to gather. Across from them, Larissa was smirking.

"I'll let you guys go first," she said.

"Aw, gee, thanks." Brooklyn's tone was all sarcasm. She took aim and tossed, hitting the rim of a cup and bouncing off.

"Let's consider that a warm-up?" Larissa asked with a raised brow. "Start over."

Brooklyn tossed again, hitting the rim of the cup. But what Larissa and the rest of the crowd missed was that she hit the exact same spot—because she aimed.

Larissa of course plopped her first ball in a cup and Brooklyn had to drink. Annabelle aimed, and missed for real, but on her second try, even though she was several sips in, she hit the mark. It was like riding a bicycle, and once she had the hang of it, she had to do like Brooklyn and purposefully miss.

"I thought y'all said you were good?" Larissa laughed with her friends, glancing at them and making a can-you-believe-these-old-bitches face. Then she sank them, and they sipped the last of the beer cups.

"Nice win. How about two out of three," Brooklyn said. "See if we can save a little face?"

Larissa tilted her head back, conducting a laugh that shook her hair out behind her in an obviously practiced move. When she finally looked at them, she was wiping away pretend tears. "It's your money."

"And for charity, remember?" *And respect.* Annabelle pressed her hand to her heart.

"Right," Larissa said. "For charity. Fine, two out of three, but we're doubling the stakes."

"Why don't we triple it and make it interesting?" Brooklyn countered.

"You must really love Paws for Claws." Larissa tapped her nails on the table indicating the cups to be refilled.

"It's our favorite," Annabelle answered.

"Whatever." Larissa rolled her eyes like they were taking up too much of her time. "Losers can go first."

Brooklyn grinned. "Bless your heart." She took aim and popped her ball in the center of the far-left cup. "Oh, lucky shot!"

Larissa squinted, then sipped her beer.

"My turn!" Annabelle tossed her ball, landing in the far right.

This time Larissa bristled, and shoved the cleared cup at her partner, who quickly drained the beer.

"Y'all get to go again unless you forgot the rules," she said, tossing the red Solo cup behind her.

"Oh, that's right." Brooklyn played into their act of forgetting how to play.

But Brooklyn surprised Larissa, by bouncing the ball off the table into the center cup. "Drink, you two," Brooklyn said.

Larissa bared her teeth and chugged, ignoring the offer of a cheers from her partner, who also had to drink.

"Oh, me, I get to go again too, right?" Annabelle clapped her hands, blew on the ball, and let her ball bounce off the table toward a cup too.

But before it could land in the beer, Larissa smacked it out of the way—where it bounced off a frat boy's forehead. "Nice try. My turn."

They could have let Larissa and her friend have a go, and maybe they would have, but they tried bouncing balls and Brooklyn and Annabelle had a heck of a good time smacking them away. On their next round, they both aimed for the same cup, clearing three cups from Team Larissa, and since they won that round, got to go again, repeating the move and clearing the last three cups.

"Rebuttal," Larissa declared, and landed a ball in a cup. But her partner wasn't so lucky, missing, and ending the game.

"OhmyChanel, we won, who would have ever thought?" Annabelle and Brooklyn high-fived.

"You said two out of three," Larissa said, then she shoved her partner out of the way and pulled in a new one.

"We did, you're right."

And then they proceeded to kick their asses all over again.

CHAPTER FORTY

I'm a virgin.

Kisses,
Annabelle

Taylor

Then

The world was spinning in a haze.

Taylor blinked, trying to keep her eyes open, but they were so heavy, and someone kept forcing them closed. Tiny little demon fingers tugging her lids down and holding them there.

Open: a flash of a face, the light on a ceiling.

Closed. Tugging on her body. Garbled words.

Open: A face on hers. A wet, hard mouth. Then the ceiling light again.

Closed.

Something wasn't right. She didn't *feel* right. Nothing was working. When she tried to lift her arms, they just stayed at her sides like two downed tree limbs. Cut off.

A heavy weight sat on her chest, stealing her breath.

"Stop," she mumbled, but it just came out a moan. "Stop," she tried again, but it didn't sound like her voice, and it didn't sound like the word she wanted to say. What she *needed* to say.

"You like this, don't you, bitch. Yeah, baby, moan for me again."

What?

Then she was falling, her body rolling, face crashing against sheets that smelled old. Dirty. Used.

There was a smacking sound. A sting on her ass. Another sting between her thighs.

"Stop. Get off me," she said again, but that moaning noise in the back of her throat was all she heard, and her face was pressed against the pillow.

Hard fingers dug into her hips. Pain. More pain. Skin slapping. Hot tears slid from her eyes, her throat closed.

What was happening? Why was this happening?

The sounds of his grunts were dulled, her head underwater. Eyes closed. She wished her body was as numb as her head.

There was a slam. A crash. A few shouts.

The pain behind her stopped. She fell over. Another face. A familiar face.

"Come on, Tay." Asana's voice. Soothing but frantic. "Hurry."

But nothing worked. Eyes closed.

She was floating.

Open: she stared at the night sky, wind on her face, worried voices.

Closed.

Open: Her room. Asana. Brooklyn.

Closed.

"Tay, what happened?" Asana's voice tried to push through the fog.

Taylor pointed toward her jewelry box, but her finger wouldn't move, her arm barely lifted. "Flumazenil." She tried to say the name of the medication that would help fight against what she now understood had happened. She'd been roofied. She'd been raped.

"What is it?" Brooklyn loomed over her. "Say it again."

"Flumazenil."

"Flu something," Brooklyn said to Asana, then bounded toward the jewelry box.

How did she know that's where Taylor kept her stash?

"This says flumazenil."

A moment later, a bitter sharp sting and a squirt up her nose. She gasped, sucked, as the medicine was administered. She snorted, choked, but instinctively knew not to blow it out.

Open: Her friends staring down at her. A tiny nose spray in their hands.

Closed. Safe.

Part IV

PREFERENCE DAY
Who will you choose?

CHAPTER FORTY-ONE

G.H. is going down, and I don't mean on me.

Kisses,
Asana

Brooklyn

Now

Why, oh why, had she drunk so much?

Brooklyn pressed her palms to her eyes, but the pressure inside her skull pulsed with a not-so-dull ache.

There was a stark difference between waking up in your early twenties after a night of drinking, and waking up in your later twenties. Even more so when you were used to drinking better-quality beverages than the Natty Lights Brooklyn had downed the night before—not to mention the shots.

And my God, had she downed them. But—they'd won that pong game, and Larissa was forced to suck their dust. Brooklyn was also acutely aware of how good, and immature, it felt to be gloating that she'd beaten a college student. But she also didn't care. Larissa had needed to be put in her place.

Brooklyn groaned as she rolled over in her hotel bed, feeling like she'd been hit by a truck. Sitting up was an effort. The last time she'd been this drunk had been her bachelorette party, and she'd sworn to never ever, ever, *ever* imbibe that much again.

Rules are made to be broken.

Asana's words tickled in her ear from some distant memory.

Brooklyn heaved herself out of bed, catching herself on the wall when she wobbled, then trudged her cinder block feet to the bathroom. The light was glaring, and when she was able to blink away the dots that danced in her eyes, she caught sight of her face. Dark makeup was smeared from the corners of her eyes and down her cheeks. She looked like an emo chick gone wrong. *Shit.* How had she not washed off her makeup before bed?

She splashed water on her face, which only made her make-up smear more, and also kicked her bladder into overdrive. The stumble over to the toilet was not her finest moment. A knock sounded on the bathroom door that startled her into nearly falling off the seat. Who the hell was in her hotel room? How drunk *was* she last night?

"Hello?"

"Brookie, I need to pee." Annabelle's voice sounded as messed up as she felt.

"One sec." Brooklyn finished and washed her hands, took her toothbrush and toothpaste, and opened the door. "She's all yours."

Annabelle's face was also smeared with makeup—badly combined colors and too much of it. The night before came flooding back. After drinking their faces off at the party, they'd returned to Brooklyn's suite and done bad makeovers, which they never washed off.

"You look gorgeous," Annabelle muttered with a smirk.

"You are a stunner." Brooklyn laughed, then winced when the sound made her head throb.

Annabelle leaned over the sink, her face a few inches from the mirror, and groaned. "My head."

"I'll order room service."

"Coffee. Bread."

Brooklyn nodded and went to brush her teeth in the kitchenette sink; the dry pasty taste in her mouth was enough to make her want to hurl.

Makeup washed off their faces—which took a long minute—they collapsed on the couch to wait for room service.

"Did you get the number of views you wanted?" Annabelle asked.

"Views?" Brooklyn wrinkled her brow and grabbed her phone. Which was lit up with thousands of notifications. Too many to even scroll through. "Ohmygod, what did we do?"

She clicked on her Ginger Mommy TikTok profile to see that she and Annabelle had made a drunk makeover video.

Half the comments she could see said it was hilarious and fun, and made the other mommies nostalgic for moments like that. The other half were not so good.

Fuck.

She'd have to do an apology post to appease the wholesome-mommy set who didn't drink and definitely didn't share drunk videos.

What had she been thinking making a video like that? Her entire reputation and career was on the line. At least half her endorsements would likely drop her after seeing it.

The phone rang, Drew's face popping up.

"Hey," she answered.

"Saw you had a good time last night." He grinned into the FaceTime app, and she covered her face with her hand.

"Too good," she groaned.

"I hope not that good," he teased.

"You saw the video?" Brooklyn peeked through her fingers at his smiling face.

"Yeah, hilarious. You and Annabelle might need to make a few more. It's gone viral, babe."

"I'm getting harassed from some of the more conservative moms."

Drew shrugged. "You're allowed to let loose. It's not like it's the norm for you, and you put out good, wholesome content 99.9 percent of the rest of the time. If they complain, it's prob out of jealousy."

"Thank you." She missed Drew, and how supportive he was. Talking to him helped to ground her.

Room service called from the other side of the door and Annabelle went to answer it, then followed behind the server who wheeled in the mountain of food she'd ordered.

"Hangover brekkie?" Drew said.

"So not my usual smoothie."

He laughed. "Whatever it takes to feel better."

"For real. How are the kids?"

"They miss you, especially when I make them brush their teeth."

Brooklyn laughed. "They do realize I would also make them?"

"Doesn't matter. When you're three years old, nothing is logical."

"True that."

"All right, love, I just wanted to make sure you weren't curled around a toilet bowl."

"I might feel better if I was."

"Eat a piece of bacon for me." In the background she could hear the beginnings of an argument over a toy starting with the kids.

"I will."

Brooklyn hung up, turning around to find Annabelle biting into a croissant. "I haven't had bread in so long."

"Me either." Brooklyn joined her at the makeshift table, the two of them just standing there as they munched. "We're heathens."

"Totally."

"Hope Asana and Taylor got back okay. What happened to them last night? I don't remember seeing them after we played pong." Brooklyn picked up a piece of cantaloupe, juice dribbling over her chin as she bit down.

"Me either. I'm sure they're fine." Annabelle glanced out the window, looking thoughtful.

"What?"

Annabelle jerked her head back toward Brooklyn, her eyes wide and a little frazzled. "Nothing." She laughed. "Zoned out. Hangover brain."

"We need coffee." Brooklyn set down her piece of bacon and poured two steaming black cups. "Cream and sugar?"

"Black."

"Same."

She passed Annabelle a cup, taking her own steaming sip, the burn on her tongue a delightful sting. Each sip made her feel a little more alive and subdued the pounding in her head somewhat.

Rapid taps on the door, and coos from the other side, announced the arrival of their friends.

"We smelled bacon from under the door," Taylor said.

The both of them looked bright and happy, and not like they'd had even a sip of beer, or a regretted shot or four, the night before.

"How do you manage to look so amazing after a night of drinking?" Brooklyn asked. "What's your secret?"

Asana's face shuttered, and Taylor blinked, her smile frozen in place like she'd been standing too long for a photo shoot. Brooklyn wasn't sure if it was just her foggy too-much-beer brain or if her friends were hiding something from her.

"We didn't play beer pong and then do drunk makeovers," Asana said with a laugh.

"Why not? You were killer at beer pong," Annabelle said, biting into a strawberry, the look on her face almost challenging.

"Last night brought up a lot of memories," Taylor drawled out, flicking a glance at Asana, whose reactions seemed forced.

Annabelle looked up sharply, and Brooklyn's heart dropped. Of course, being at a frat party would bring up a lot of memories. And not all of them good. Suddenly unable to stand upright, she sat in a chair, guilt ridden.

This whole week had been about confessions, and Brooklyn had another one she needed to make.

"I'm sorry, Taylor," Brooklyn said softly. "If I'd known what he was going to do, I'd have tried to stop him." She rubbed her face with her hands. "I just thought . . ."

"What are you talking about?" Taylor's voice was wobbly, her brows drawn together in confusion.

Brooklyn glanced up to see her three friends staring at her, each of them puzzled, though the way Taylor's lips were pinched, Brooklyn thought she might be starting to understand.

"Greg."

Annabelle narrowed her eyes. "What does Greg have to do with this or anything?"

"The nannies aren't the only ones he's taken advantage of." Brooklyn practically choked on the words.

"He was here last night?" Annabelle's voice rose to shrill and she squished the strawberry between her fingers, the red pulp dripping onto the table.

"No, no." Brooklyn waved her hand. "I meant sophomore year, when Taylor and you were roofied."

"*Greg* roofied us?" All the veins in Annabelle's long, slender neck popped out.

Brooklyn stared at Taylor, waiting for her to say something. *Anything.* But she remained silent, staring.

Annabelle had never known the extent of what Taylor went through. Even Brooklyn wasn't supposed to know beyond the part where she'd been drugged, but she'd overheard her and Asana talking and put two and two together. If she'd stopped Greg walking up those stairs, Taylor wouldn't have had to go through any of it.

"I'm sorry," Brooklyn said again, tears streaming down her face in a hot torrent.

"It's not your fault," Taylor said, her voice filled with bitterness. "If not that night, another, right?" The bitterness leached into her smile.

"God." Brooklyn sat back in her chair. "I'm sure there were."

Annabelle's face had gone white as a sheet, the flat of her palm pressed so hard to her stomach the skin around her knuckles was stretched. "Another?"

CHAPTER FORTY-TWO

The one pill I need, I can't get.

Kisses,
Taylor

Asana

Then

Pref Day in the Panhellenic world is one of the most stressful. And though she'd been through it now for the third time as a junior at Bama, the intensity of it never waned. Asana stood in the foyer, greeting girls as the newly elected vice president of the sorority, a position that she was fairly certain she would have gotten without the help of the Machine, but they'd claimed all the victory for her success given they'd coerced the sisters into voting for her. Allegedly.

Lately, her lips kept pursing, giving her a pinched look, and she had to keep reminding herself to stop looking like she'd just taken a shot of Jäger. The pressure from the Machine was starting to get to her. Had her looking over her shoulder. At least they weren't burning crosses like they had years ago, that was some serious racist bullshit. But . . . Asana thought that maybe, if the SGA hadn't been shut down in the past for bad behavior, and Greg and his cronies weren't scared of a repeat, they might just pull that kind of crap again. And that made her hate them all the more.

What had her father said the last time she'd spoken to him? *The last thing our machine needs is another machine competing.* He'd been trying to talk in riddles, comparing Duke Corp to a machine, but Duke Corp wasn't a machine. Duke Corp was the engineer that designed the machine, the solid steel that held it together. The machine was but the mechanism. And she was a Duke with her finger poised over the power button.

Over the past year she'd been planning. Plotting. And she was so close to coming up with the perfect scheme to get away with shutting them down forever and no one knowing her part. Greg Hamm and the entire secret society he stood for shouldn't be allowed to rule things around here anymore. People should be able to make their own decisions. Vote the way they wanted.

True power wasn't forced; true power was earned.

Asana greeted each Potential New Member, welcoming them to their last rush party at ADL. Annabelle, Brooklyn, and Taylor were right there with her, the formidable board. They'd worked their way up to this, and now it was all coming together. Annabelle was treasurer, Taylor was president, and Brooklyn was the secretary.

From the corner of her eye, she glanced at Taylor, knowing they shared a secret—more than one secret really.

Summer had been long, and Asana had been in New York City when Taylor had called, wanting to come visit.

But it hadn't been a visit just for funsies.

Taylor still looked haunted. The edges of her eyes shadowed. But she kept up a good pretense, the woman in charge. No one messed with her, or else they regretted it.

The tea parties this rush season had been off the hook. The dares deeper, and several sisters who made mistakes and ended up on the shit list, instead of being fined, were made to read their secrets from the Spill Book aloud.

And Asana couldn't really blame Taylor for her sudden spike in the bitch factor.

Ever since the incident last semester, Taylor had been frosty to Annabelle, who seemed completely oblivious to the fact that she was dating the devil himself. Though Asana wondered if Annabelle knew more than she let on, if there was some deeper secret locked in her chest for why she was with Greg. At least Asana wanted to believe that. Otherwise, it meant Annabelle was an idiot.

But it wasn't Asana's place to tell. Or tell her off.

Annabelle in so many ways seemed like an innocent, wholesome girl. Church on Sundays, prayer before meals. She was still a virgin, for fuck's sake. But in other ways, she too held dark secrets. Like the girls at Starling Prep who let their boyfriends stick it up the butt and still claimed to be virgins.

"Welcome," Asana said to one of the PNMs, who got on her nerves more than the rest. Of course, she was friends with Jacqueline, who'd been a flip-flop of an active, and mostly just annoying. They were like two peas in a pod. Overly excited to the point of being fake one minute, and then a little argumentative the next. But like in a subtle way that Southern women sometimes had. Where you were pretty sure they were being rude, but they did it with such charm and sweetness to take all the sting out of it.

Asana had been working the last three years to hone that in a New York way so she could use it when she eventually took over as president of communications for Duke Corp. Her dream job. One year left in this hella hot state and then she was north forever.

"Will you see how many more are coming in?" Taylor asked.

Asana nodded, even though it wasn't her job. She had a soft spot for Taylor after this summer. Or maybe she was being taken advantage of. It was hard to tell because she was normally the one taking advantage of people and not used to being on the receiving end.

The line was dwindling, thank God; the house was so full of satin, pink, and fluff that Asana was ready to burn it down.

Across the street, one of the former PNMs she recognized as Maggie was standing there just staring at the house. What the fuck was up with her?

She'd been standing on an elevated surface their freshman year. Preaching about something stupid in the quad. Literally everyone had seen her. But Asana had taken it upon herself to report her after overhearing—from her Mach recruiter, of course, so probably BS—that the ADL board had been trying to decide between her and Maggie. The whole thing had probably been a test, and oh well, Maggie had been dropped because of it. Among other things. Maggie had gone off to join Zeta instead, and had been semi-stalking Asana ever since. What was her deal?

Maggie stared at her, unflinching, and Asana felt a moment's guilt for having gotten her removed. But rules were rules, and if they didn't have any, where would they be? Besides, if it hadn't been Asana to tell, someone else would have.

It wasn't her fault that Maggie hadn't been up to snuff. But it *was* her fault that she seemed completely obsessed with her. A lot of people were.

Asana made a shooing motion with her hand. "Move along, Mags."

"See you at the *meeting*." Maggie smiled as if she knew a secret Asana didn't, but it was an empty threat.

All of her threats were. *Idiot.*

Asana hadn't spent all of freshman and sophomore year learning the ins and outs and secrets of every Machine member just for fun. She had a plan. Especially after the incident with Greg and Taylor.

She was going to personally see to it that Greg Hamm and his stupid boys' club went down.

Asana hurried the line of girls inside with a cheerful smile, and then shut the doors. She nodded to Taylor, who rang a tiny pink ADL bell.

"Welcome to Pref Day, and your first tea party."

Brooklyn handed Taylor the new Spill Book they'd crafted the night before, deciding they needed one for this day. It was a test to see who was willing to participate. Who they'd pick to join them in earnest as a new sister of ADL. It was hard to cut PNMs. Asana was a bit more ruthless than the other sorority execs about it having grown up in the cutthroat world of Duke Corp. And Starling Prep.

But this helped.

"This is an Alpha Delta Lambda tea party," Taylor said. "Consider it a test. Whatever you spill in this book will be kept secret forever. And every entry you make is for your eyes only."

Lies.

The PNMs' eyes were riveted on the pink sequined notebook. Shining with excitement about being let in on something supersecret and special.

"Everyone take a seat," Taylor continued. "We're going to hand you a blindfold. Everyone will get a chance to spill, but we only have forty-five minutes, so don't be a pen hog." Taylor laughed sweetly as if this weren't a hazing exercise. "You're going to write down one reason why we should pick you, and one reason why we shouldn't pick the person to your right. Take a look at the person to your right. Even if they are your bestie, don't hold back. If you don't know them, use your initial impressions."

The PNMs looked nervously back and forth at each other. The supersecret special Spill Book suddenly not so chic anymore.

"Don't look so scared," Asana said, with an inviting it's-all-going-to-be-worth-it smile. "We've all done it. This is just for fun."

The biggest lie of all.

CHAPTER FORTY-THREE

I am going to hell, and not because I accept money from randoms. I made a huge misjudgment of a friend.

Kisses,
Brooklyn

Annabelle

Now

The room was starting to spin, and it wasn't because Annabelle had four too many Natty Lights last night. She'd purged those around one in the morning. No, the room was spinning because whatever her friends were discussing was bringing back a fuzzy memory from sophomore year. Little strings tugging at the back of her brain that were trying to unravel buried truths.

No matter how hard she tried to yank against the memory strings to reveal the truth, they only became more jumbled. Like vengeful kittens mucking up the yarn of her brain.

"What are you talking about?" Annabelle asked, even though she was starting to think she knew exactly what they were discussing.

The horror of the idea that she wasn't the only one . . . How could she have been so naive?

Taylor swung her gaze toward Annabelle, and a flash of emotions switched over her face like the strobe lights at the party the night before. Surprise, anger, sadness. Seeing the rush of various emotions fighting for purchase on Taylor "The Rock" Collins's face was probably more disturbing than the memories she couldn't seem to make reveal themselves.

Asana, usually so stony-faced, also looked conflicted.

Annabelle turned her gaze toward Brooklyn, hoping she would be the one to actually tell her what the Prada was going on. "All of you know whatever it is you're talking about. Does someone want to tell me? Or should I just leave?"

Brooklyn nodded, rubbing her hands over her already blotchy face. "Remember the night you were roofied?"

"Sophomore year? Yeah." Annabelle nodded, glancing between all her friends. "What about it?"

"You weren't the only one that night."

Annabelle felt her stomach start to turn and regretted eating any of the room service as acid tap-danced its way up her throat. "Who?"

"Me." Taylor's lips were pressed thin. The genuine smile she'd had on her face when they'd first entered the hotel room this morning completely wiped away. "I was raped that night."

"OhmyChanel." All the air whooshed out of Annabelle's lungs. "I didn't know." She rushed toward Taylor, taking her stiff body in her arms in an attempt to hug her, even though Taylor didn't seem to want it. Never seemed to want anything from her.

"I tried to tell you." Despite Taylor's stiffness, her voice was loose and wobbly.

Annabelle stepped back. She stared at Taylor, then shook her head. "When?"

"When you started dating Greg. When you decided to lose your V-card to him."

"What does Greg have to do with this?" The blood drained from Annabelle's face, as if her body knew the truth before she did. And truly, she should have known. Should have put two and two together, but to do so would have been to fully realize the horror of her own situation. And facing that had been too much to bear.

"I think you know," Brooklyn said softly. "Some people don't really change."

Annabelle's legs trembled, and her skin felt funny. She sat down quickly in a chair before she collapsed. Greg, her husband, the philandering Neanderthal, wasn't just a cheater. He was a rapist. She knew what a manipulative bastard he was, how he could coerce an apple into giving him a blow job.

But rapist . . .

She remembered her first time with him. She'd been drunk. Didn't really remember consenting, but didn't say no either. He'd caught her red-handed that night sneaking out of one of the brothers' rooms with a little prize tucked in her pocket. Fudge her habit. Greg had promised no one would know. That his father, a powerful judge, would make sure she wasn't prosecuted, or he would make sure she got maximum security, if she didn't pay up. And Greg's currency was what she'd prized the most— her virginity.

Rapist.

Had she been lying to herself all these years? Pretending that she was using him for an insurance policy, when really, she was stuck? Forced to have sex with him so she didn't get in trouble. Knocked up her senior year because he'd decided not to use a condom and told her that she shouldn't worry. Married him to keep up pretenses of protection for her crimes and to not have a child out of wedlock. A powerful judge and powerful lawyer in her back pocket. A wedding ring to legitimize her son and keep her family's reputation intact.

The reprisal rained down by Lily, the accusations of betraying

God and the church with her sin of sleeping with a man before marriage. All of it was absolved by saying "I do."

No one had asked questions, assuming that like most wealthy, rich families, an alliance had been formed. They'd had a destination wedding, with plenty of pictures in the society pages. And when Liam was born a month early, well, that was explained away too.

The delusion she'd set up for herself, that she was in control, was the biggest fairy tale of all. A safe room that wasn't really safe, a clientele of women seeking desperately for something beautiful, and she was still a Stepford wife, married to a monster.

Annabelle bolted from the table, rushing to the bathroom, where she dropped to her knees in front of the toilet and puked up not just her guts but everything, the secrets, the shame, the fear.

A soft hand pulled her hair away from her neck as her body continued to purge every cell.

When she looked up, it was Taylor standing there, her expression still a mix of emotions that ping-ponged off her own.

"I thought you knew," Taylor whispered, pity in every syllable.

"I . . . should have. I should have guessed. I'm a freaking idiot." Annabelle dropped her forehead to the toilet seat and wretched again.

Taylor handed her a warm, wet washcloth. "I thought you just didn't care. That you wanted him so badly . . ."

Annabelle wiped her face, angry tears spilling. "I didn't. I wouldn't. I . . . I married a monster. I made my friend watch me marry *her* monster. I'm a terrible person." She sobbed, trying desperately to suck in a lungful of air, but never actually feeling the oxygen hit.

Taylor dropped to her knees beside her and pulled her into her arms. The most unlikely Taylor thing to do. There was no stiffness there, but something akin to warmth, stability. "To be fair, I didn't actually watch you get married."

"How do you not hate me?" Annabelle asked through hiccups.

"I did. For a long time. I tried to fake it the last two years of school because of the sisterhood, but once we graduated . . . I didn't have to do that anymore. It's one of the reasons I don't call."

Annabelle clung to her friend. "We have to take him down. I'm going to take him down." Even if it meant she was going to go down with him. "I have a confession to make."

Taylor laughed. "Is it something you haven't already confessed in the book?"

Annabelle laughed too. "No."

"Then chances are pretty good I already know."

"The elephant?"

Taylor nodded.

"What elephant?" Asana asked, her eyes narrowing in a way that suggested she knew what elephant Annabelle was talking about.

Brooklyn's eyes widened. "Wait, *that* elephant?"

"Yeah. I'm the one who stole Big Al." Annabelle touched the diamond at her neck. The one she'd been wearing ever since. A small smile touched her lips. A fence never forgot their first big heist, and the moment her hands had touched those diamonds, she'd felt a power race through her that had been better than any high, any buzz, she'd ever experienced.

Taylor Swift was right. In that moment, knowing that she was doing something "bad" had never felt so freaking good. And all regrets she might have had evaporated as quickly as raindrops on a hot Alabama road.

"Holy shit," Brooklyn said. "I can't believe you're the one who stole Big Al. How did I not know this?"

"Our Anna girl is a regular thief," Taylor said with a smirk. "Took that diamond-encrusted elephant right from the display case at the football stadium. Stole the prized Sugar Bowl trophy."

"Greg's and my parents donated the elephant," Annabelle said. She thought she'd feel a rush of shame confessing this to her friends. But instead, telling them the truth was oddly freeing.

The collective gasp in the room was a sharpened hiss, echoed in the marble bathroom.

"Did you know that when you stole it?" Asana asked.

"I sure did." That had been one of the reasons she'd decided to plan the heist. Because she hated Greg for what he'd taken from her. And Lily Walker had been over the moon about her marrying into the Hamm family. It was a way to hit them all at once. "I need to tell our sisters."

Three heads shook no at the same time.

Annabelle let out long sigh, guilt filling her chest. "I'm the one who was taking things from them. Remember all those missing trinkets? I . . . should turn myself in."

"You'll do no such thing," Asana said. "No one will press charges. I can promise you that."

Annabelle met each pair of eyes watching her. Raw emotion filled her chest, mirrored in the gazes of the women she'd bonded with what felt like a lifetime ago. "Promises can be broken. I'm proof of that."

Asana shook her head. "Sisters don't snitch."

"I'm not exactly the type that's going to cause any stitches."

"But I might be," Taylor said with a wink.

Annabelle sucked in a breath and let it out in a long, weary wobble. "I'm so sorry, you guys. Taylor . . . I . . ."

For the longest time she'd been hiding who she was. Keeping the deepest, darkest part of herself secret. The only time she'd ever confessed was in the Spill Book. Something about that pink, sparkly temptation had been intoxicating. Lured her into sharing her truth, even if only one person was going to read it.

Now that the truth was out there, with the potential for the world to see it, she needed to own her mistakes and the hurts she'd caused people.

She had to confess.

CHAPTER FORTY-FOUR

The one thing that makes me feel in control of my life is when I take things. And I'm spiraling right now. Which means I need to take something big. Bigger than anything I've taken before. And I don't mean grand theft auto. Leave that to the tweenagers and lonely forty-somethings.

Kisses,
Annabelle

Taylor

Then
Last summer

For Taylor, the world had never been as scary as it felt right now.

She was a perfectionist, and made sure that everything happened according to her own plans, with checks and balances in place.

But when you were drugged and raped by an asshole, all of your agency and power and control and perfectly laid-out plans were shattered.

For a hot second she'd thought about going to the hospital. Or reporting him to the police. But it was all about that he said/she said, and the reputation of "she" would be dragged through the mud while the "he" was touted as being a football star and frat president. Not to mention it was rumored he was a member of the Machine. Everyone thought that dumb society was a secret. The biggest known secret on campus. And they would grease the pockets of anyone willing to take up her case.

Why would she put herself through that?

Besides, her family would never forgive her for putting herself in that situation. Of course, victim blaming was ripe in all areas.

To make matters worse—as if being drugged and raped and forced to keep quiet out of self-preservation wasn't the worst already—the little white stick she peed on pulled up two lines: pregnant.

Abortion was illegal in Alabama—and since her daddy was a senator, everyone knew who she was. Which meant, she couldn't just go to her doctor and say, "Hey, I was raped. I need an abortion." Everyone would find out. Everyone would judge. And she didn't meet the requirements to get one anyway. Rape didn't count. And the smuggled little pill didn't work.

And the perfect life she'd built for herself would be torn apart one layer at a time. The first of which she'd shed last week when she broke up with Brad. She just couldn't look him in the eyes after what happened with Greg.

But New York City could be different. There was something about the massiveness of the city, the height of the buildings, the whizz of traffic, the bustle of commuters that made her feel like she could disappear.

So Taylor booked a flight and called Asana, telling her she was coming for a visit. Abortion was legal there.

Only now, as she stood outside the imposing brownstone on Park Avenue where Asana lived, did Taylor realize how very real this moment was.

A man opened the door, dressed in a tux. He barely looked at her as the chauffeur that Asana had sent to the airport took her small bag out of the trunk and brought it inside while she followed.

"Miss Duke will be with you momentarily. In the meantime, our housekeeper will show you to your room."

"Thank you, sir."

She followed a woman dressed in a skirt suit up a curving staircase. The inside of the house was massive. A mansion in New York City. So very different from the sprawling house Taylor lived in down South.

Barely thirty seconds passed that she was in her guest room when Asana appeared, wrapping her in a hug.

"I'm so glad you're here!"

"I do love New York."

"What do you want to do first?" Asana looked excited as she started to rattle off which shows were playing on Broadway and then gave her a mischievous wink as she named several clubs that would serve them underage. But her face faltered when she took a good look at Taylor.

The puffiness of her eyes, her face. What an embarrassment she was.

"What's wrong?"

"I need your help." Taylor didn't ask anyone for help. Not even her parents, and doing so now felt foreign.

Asana was the only one of their friend group who she knew wouldn't judge. She was as cold as ice, something that matched the insides of Taylor.

"Anything," Asana said.

"Plan B didn't work."

Asana's eyes widened. The morning she'd woken up after being assaulted by Greg, she'd gotten Asana to get the Plan B pill from a friend. The cramping had been awful. The period heavy. But Greg's vile sperm had not gotten the message to vacate, and instead set up camp like a squatter until one of her unsuspecting eggs could be assaulted all over again inside her uterus.

"You're . . ." Asana glanced down at Taylor's belly.

She'd assumed Plan B had worked. That had been three months ago. When her period hadn't come, she assumed it was because of the heavy period after taking that pill. She ignored the fact that she missed it another time. But when the third period didn't come, she'd pulled an Annabelle at the pharmacy and swiped a test.

Positive.

"Yes. And I need to get rid of it. I couldn't do it at home. Everyone knows my dad." She rolled her eyes, trying to play it off like this was no big deal and more of an annoyance than something that could completely derail her entire life.

"Of course. I know someone here." Asana didn't even hesitate. "All the girls at Starling Prep used him."

"All?"

Asana shrugged. "When your parents are famous, you need to have a secret guy."

Taylor felt comforted despite the awfulness of what she was asking. But she had to keep reminding herself, the creature that was growing inside her was not her choice. The bundle of cells was a result of a violent act against her. And every moment that she remained in this state was another moment that she was violated. Over and over again, by Greg.

"I'll call right now." Asana pulled out her cell.

"You have him in your cell?"

Asana winked. "I make it a point to keep all my contacts handy."

"Thank you." Taylor glanced toward the ivory plush rug that covered parquet wood floors in an old-fashioned herringbone pattern, having the sudden urge to lie down on tufts and curl against their softness. She wasn't used to feeling vulnerable.

It was a feeling she never wanted to experience again. Ever.

"Friends, sisters, help each other, Taylor. You don't have to thank me. I know one day you'll help me when I need it."

"I only hope I can—and also that I never have to."

Asana made the appointment for the afternoon after an offer of double payment in cash.

"What do your parents think you're doing here?" she asked.

Taylor shrugged. "Funny you think they know where I am. However, I did tell my father's secretary I was enjoying the city with a friend."

"Well, when you're recovered, we'll do that."

"I hope it's quick." A rush of nervousness made her suddenly nauseous.

Asana's face shuttered, and she looked away.

Taylor gripped her arm, forcing her to turn back. "Tell me."

"You're going to be uncomfortable physically for a few days. And, well, mentally, that can take longer."

Taylor shook her head. "I've never been more sure of anything in my life. I won't be sad about this."

Asana shrugged. "Maybe not, but if you are, it's totally normal. I didn't think I would be sad. But I was. Nothing a little anti-depressant can't help."

Taylor grinned and patted her purse. "Got those taken care of already."

"I'm glad you reached out." Asana took her hand. "You shouldn't have to go through this alone."

"You're the only one I trusted enough to help." And that was the truth.

"I'm making it my business to fix problems." Asana smiled and pulled her in for a hug, and Taylor melted, her head falling onto her shoulder.

Taylor grinned, and while it didn't completely reach her eyes, for the first time in the last forty-eight hours, no, the last three months, she finally felt like maybe she was going to be okay.

CHAPTER FORTY-FIVE

There's a part of me that wants to get mean. To get loud. To really fuck this place up. But there's another part of me that knows if I do that, the entire persona of who I think I am and who I want others to see me as will shatter. For the first time in forever, I don't know what the fuck to do with myself.

Kisses,
Taylor

Asana

Now

In Asana's world, what they had going on right now would be considered a serious clusterfuck. And it was in the real world too. The web of lies and secrets woven between all of them and around them was a tangled mess that if not solved ASAP was going to lead to major fuckage.

"I appreciate all you guys are saying, but I have to tell them." Annabelle was shaking her head. "I hurt my sisters."

Taylor shrugged. "Hey, you stole from me and I knew about it. Read about it in the Spill Book. I could have asked for my stuff back. Could have told all the sisters you were taking from them, but I didn't." She grinned mischievously. "Don't you remember how I'd always be wherever you were when you snuck off?"

Annabelle frowned. "Yeah."

"I wanted to see what you were taking."

"None of that matters. Listen," Asana interrupted, clapping her hands sharply to bring them back to attention. "If you confess and someone presses charges it brings bad press not only to Alpha Delta Lambda but to Panhellenic life as a whole. And the university. You can't."

"I *need* to apologize." Annabelle shared that she had a stack of letters already written. After every theft, she took a pen to paper. Signed confessions. Hundreds of them. Admitting to every single thing she'd stolen. Stamped. Addressed. All she had to do was open the safe where she kept them in her yoga room and put them in the mail. "And Greg . . . I need to do something about him too. He can't just keep swinging his dick around and hurting people."

"You aren't responsible for Greg," Taylor said softly. "What he's done is completely his fault, not yours."

"I know, but . . ."

Brooklyn handed Annabelle a tissue. "No buts. Karma will bite him where it hurts."

"In the balls." Taylor nodded.

"My name might be Karma," Annabelle muttered.

"Please," Asana groaned. "Do not put your mouth anywhere near that predator's balls."

A small smile twitched on Annabelle's face. "I promise I won't. And I promise he will pay for everything." Annabelle blew her nose, then let out a big breath. "I need to pay too."

Asana drew in a breath through her nose. She didn't know what Annabelle had up her sleeve, but she felt the need to help with some damage control.

Dealing with this, with Annabelle, wasn't half as hard as some of the dumbasses she had on Duke Corp's board. "You're not paying anything. You can apologize in person, but nothing in writing or you're just asking for this same blackmail thing to happen all over again. *And* I'm going with you."

Annabelle started to shake her head, but Asana put up a hand to stop her.

"Please don't disrespect me by ignoring my advice and offer of assistance. I'm really fucking good at my job, and I've gotten worse people out of worse public gaffes than stealing a fucking elephant and a few trinkets from college girls."

"Well . . ." Annabelle bit her lip. "It's a little deeper than that."

"How deep?" Asana started to mentally assemble a list of what she needed to do. The people she needed to contact.

"Have you seen *Ocean's 8*?" Annabelle asked.

Asana cringed. "Yes." *What the fuck.*

"Yeah . . . so . . ." Annabelle cleared her throat, her head falling back as she stared up at the ceiling. "I'm sort of like the character Tammy, only less high-tech and connected. I'm a fence, mostly for desperate housewives."

Asana pursed her lips and drew in a deep breath. Normally she wasn't the praying type, but Lord help her now. "Okay," she drawled. "So, it's a bit deeper."

"A lot fucking deeper." Taylor looked shocked. "Is your garage full of shit that's 'fallen off a truck'?"

Annabelle laughed. "No." She bit her lip. "But I may or may not have a lot of diamonds . . ."

"No. Stop." Asana's tone wasn't as sharp as she wanted but still held a sting. "We can go into details later. And we can discuss your apology campaign later too. Right now we need to get something else under control. In case you guys have forgotten, we have someone who blackmailed us to come to Rush Week, and stole our actual confessions. Someone who wants money from me and for Annabelle to go to jail. I think maybe instead of apologies, we need to confess what we're being blackmailed for."

Taylor gritted her teeth. "I'm so tired of this. Who the fuck is it already?"

"We need to draw them out," Asana said. "Knowing everyone's secrets will help."

"Like what? Bait?" Brooklyn asked.

"Something that they won't be able to resist." Asana's mind started to calculate all the ways in which they could draw someone out into the open. "What do they want?"

"To punish us." Taylor rolled her eyes.

"Exactly, and we need to know why."

"Isn't it obvious—rejection?" Taylor shrugged. "Think about how many girls were rejected by us, how many wanted to be us. Chances are it's a pledge or PNM that was dropped."

"But you don't just ruin people's lives five years later because you were dropped from a sorority."

"Hey, you never know what someone is going to do when rejected by society. Maybe it was a lifelong dream? Maybe she had a mother like Lily Walker." Annabelle grimaced.

"I don't know. I think it's a lot worse." Asana paced the room. "And I think it's probably more than one person."

"Hey, while I love to play amateur sleuth with you guys and sit around like we're going to start making a string board and map out all the motives, blah blah blah, we're just wasting time." Taylor ran a hand through her hair, smoothing where it was already smooth. Where Asana had threaded her fingers through it last night. "We've already been here a few days. There's only a few days until Bid Day, when they claimed they will take us down completely."

"She's right, we need to figure this out faster than we are."

Brooklyn gulped down the rest of her coffee. "And we need more caffeine. Let's get the sisters back together to confess."

"We can try that. If they're willing to share in a group. Might be better one-on-one. Also, I think it might be time for me to access my network." Asana sighed. "I thought this was going to be a simple, stupid fix. I shouldn't have waited this long." She'd tried to do this on her own, but really, the longer they attempted to figure this out on their own, the longer it was going to take, and they were not getting results.

And if there was one thing Asana couldn't abide, it was not getting the results she wanted. As if to prove that point, her eyes met with Taylor's.

CHAPTER FORTY-SIX

All it takes is one brick out of place for a building's foundation to crack. I'm gonna be that brick.

Kisses,
Asana

Brooklyn

Then

Brooklyn stood nervously in the library stacks. This was a bad idea. A *really* bad idea.

Meeting Greg alone to confront him was probably the dumbest thing she'd done this year—and she'd done a lot of dumb shit.

But he needed to face the consequences, and so far, he'd done no repenting. And given his friends, his power on campus, "consequences" wasn't in his vocabulary.

She'd hidden her camera up between a few books and was just waiting.

Footsteps sounded in the otherwise quiet stacks, and her skin prickled. Every instinct told her to bolt. That she was tiny compared to him, and though she regularly worked out, and she'd put up one hell of a fight if necessary, it would do little if Greg was determined with his intent.

She counted the seconds, holding her breath until he rounded the corner, hands shoved in his pockets and eyebrows raised.

"This a date?" he asked with a smirk.

Brooklyn resisted the urge to smack that look off his face. "No. The opposite of a date."

"Okay," he drawled out, his eyes scanning rudely over her breasts, and then settling into his bored expression. "What's with the clandestine meeting, then?"

"I know what you did."

He didn't even flinch. "And what's that, shorty?"

The *audacity* of him to act like nothing had happened or that he didn't even care. "You roofied my friends. You raped Taylor."

Greg chuckled, rolled his eyes. "That's rich."

"It's the truth and you know it. How many more?"

Greg stopped laughing, his hands coming out of his pockets. For a split second she thought he might make a move toward her, but he stayed put, hands clenched. "Prove it." The coolness of his voice belied how tense his body was.

"I can actually. I was filming a TikTok when you carried her unconscious body up the stairs. Go on, look."

This time Greg did flinch. His skin went a shade lighter. But he didn't pull out his phone.

"You're lying," he said through clenched teeth.

"I'm not."

But the anger slipped away as quickly as it had come and he chuckled a slow laugh that wasn't really a laugh at all, just more like noise. An eerie *ha-ha-ha*. "No one is going to believe that she didn't want it."

"Really? Why?" Brooklyn cocked her head, actually interested to see what kind of an excuse his sorry ass was going to come up with.

"Because, all your sorority chicks want my dick. Hop on pop, hop on top."

"You're wrong, and disgusting." Brooklyn crossed her arms

over her chest, partly because she was cold and her nipples were poking out and a guy like him was likely to see that as an invitation, and partly because she felt the need to hold herself there, to keep from running.

"Whatever, you know if you got the chance you'd fuck it too." He made a motion toward his crotch.

Brooklyn tried not to gag. "No thank you."

"What do you want from me, then?" The way he said it told her he thought she was just wasting his time.

"I want you to own up to what you did."

Greg shook his head, looking at her like she was a naive little twat who didn't understand how the world worked. "Not a chance."

The asshole clearly didn't know who she was. Or who she'd been. Or the her that she hid from everyone at school. Because if there was one thing Brooklyn was not, it was naive. "Not a chance you'll admit it?"

"Hell no. She asked for it. Bitch was rubbing on my dick all night. I only gave her a little push."

"Little hard for an unconscious woman to ask for it."

Greg rolled his eyes. "It's called body language."

"So, comatose equals 'come get me'?"

He chuckled harshly. "Again, what do you want? Money?"

"Hush money?"

"Call it what you will. But you're wasting your time, and I just want you to go away."

"So, you admit to raping her?"

"Yeah, whatever. What happens at swap stays at swap."

Brooklyn pressed her lips together. She had a confession. On tape. All she had to do was upload it, and Greg's life would be ruined. But so would Taylor's. And she couldn't do that to her.

"You know I can go to the Panhellenic and Interfraternity

Council boards. Have you tossed out. Have your whole fraternity shut down."

This time Greg bristled, took a threatening step forward. Every bone in her body begged her to back up. Not to become his next victim. But the loyal part of her, the part that wanted him to pay for what he'd done to her friend, stayed rooted in place.

"You wouldn't dare," he said through gritted teeth.

"I would. Especially if it keeps my sisters from being hurt."

Greg cursed under his breath, hands running through his hair, and he stared through the stacks as if he might be counting how long it would take for someone to come to her assistance.

Brooklyn suppressed a shudder.

"Again. How. Much." He slowly turned his gaze back toward her, anger and hate in his eyes.

Brooklyn wanted to scratch those angry eyes out. How dare he act like he was a victim in this, or had any right to his anger. He had zero.

But the fact of the matter was, he had asked her if she wanted money. Which to be honest, she definitely did. Her daddy was starting to make her do things she didn't like—the choking for one, but at least it was him on the receiving end and not her—and living like that was making life harder and harder.

If she had money free and clear, well . . . She only had two years left to pay for school.

"How much are you willing to pay?" she asked.

Greg grunted, and in that one sound she felt the respect she had for herself take flight.

"How much do you want?" he asked.

Brooklyn mulled over the costs of her living and going to school for the next two years and threw out a number. A very large number.

Greg's eyes didn't even bulge. "Give me your payment app."

"What?" He had that much money on tap? People weren't even supposed to be able to send that much money at once. Payment app rules. God, it made her sick, but she pulled up the QR code for him to scan and watched her account balance increase by five zeros.

Greg smirked again. "You know you could have asked for more."

"Maybe I will." She shrugged.

"This isn't going to become a thing," he said, and from the sound of it, she knew he meant it. And Brooklyn wasn't interested in being drugged and dumped into the William Bacon Oliver Lake and found miles away bloated and blue. Dead.

"It won't become a thing. We're done."

Greg nodded, shoved his hands back in his pockets, and walked away whistling, like this hadn't just been her accusing him of raping her friend, and him admitting it and paying her off to keep her quiet. Like she hadn't just accepted money to not get him in trouble for hurting her friend.

She didn't know who to be more disgusted with. Herself. Or him.

Brooklyn rushed from the library, across campus to the track. The only way she was going to feel any better was to sweat, and practice wasn't for hours. She changed into her running clothes, not bothering to warm up as her feet pounded the rubber and polyurethane.

Sweat poured as she rounded the finish for the seventh time.

"Brooklyn?"

Her name came through the breeze, the voice familiar, and she turned when she shouldn't, tripping over her own feet and falling flat.

Pain ricocheted up over her knees, and she rolled over to see them both bloody.

"Motherfucker."

"Ohmygod, I am a motherfucker. I'm so sorry." Drew, as in

turkey-costume-frat-boy Drew, hovered over her. Without hesitation he ripped off his shirt and pressed it to her bloody knees, and
Brooklyn's heart melted.

"Not your fault." Was it bad she thought about how this was
going to fuck with her OnlyFans? "Never fallen for a guy before."
Even she winced at the corniness of that joke.

"If you wanted me to take my shirt off, all you had to do was
ask." He winked, then pulled the fabric away. "Does it hurt?"

"Stings a little."

"Can I get you some Band-Aids?"

Brooklyn held out her hand. "Help me up?"

"Of course. Want me to carry you to the PT room?"

"I can walk."

"But you remember, I'm really good at carrying?"

She chuckled. "I remember."

"If you won't let me carry you, will you let me take you out to
dinner at least?"

Brooklyn glanced at his sweaty, muscled torso. Real passion
stirred in her belly—something she never felt with her zaddies.
"Are you going to wear a shirt?"

"Not this one. Unless you prefer me topless."

"I was kinda hoping for the turkey costume."

Drew grinned. "I'd dress up however you wanted, Brooklyn."

"Pick me up at eight?"

"Absolutely."

For those few blessed moments, she forgot about Greg and what
a fucking traitor she was. Because she could never show Taylor this
tape. Taylor would know she'd taken money from Greg. And that
made her just as bad as him.

CHAPTER FORTY-SEVEN

I think I know what I'm going to take. And it's going to really mess with a lot of people's heads. That's power.

Kisses,
Annabelle

Taylor

Now

Taylor had never wanted to watch the world burn more than she did in the last week. More specifically, whoever had the nerve to steal *her* Spill Book. Her idea. Her application. Her decision to put it into the time capsule that shouldn't have been resurrected for another ninety-five years.

For the last two hours they'd been talking with the other sisters, and she'd listened to their confessions, bored to tears with what they thought was juicy.

I screwed my English professor so he'd change my grade.

I spread a rumor that so-and-so had chlamydia.

I stole my roommate's ID card so I could get lunch every day while she was in the shower and she never knew I was using her swipes.

I told everyone some girl had broken a rule when she hadn't because I didn't like her.

I stuffed extra ballots into an SGA box because they paid me a hundred dollars.

I cheated on my finals.

I slept with every guy in Sigma Chi.

Blah blah blah, and as it turned out all of them had been invited to the alumna Rush Week events, but none of them were being blackmailed. That special attention had been saved for Taylor, Asana, Brooklyn, and Annabelle alone.

None of these sisters were guilty, that was obvious. From what Taylor was deducing, the blackmail might be coming off as revenge, but it was feeling a lot more like the thief wanted power over them. This was about control.

"Ohmygod," Taylor said with a groan when the last sister had left an idea looming. She covered her hand with her mouth, afraid her thoughts would come spilling out in a tumble of verbal diarrhea.

She stared at Annabelle, who looked up at her bleary-eyed from where she'd sunk into one of the hotel chairs.

"I think I know who stole the Spill Book," Taylor said. "There is only one person who has wanted to keep control of ADL. Of us."

"Who?" Brooklyn asked, wrinkling her brow.

"Please, Brooklyn, for the love of God, *stop* wrinkling your brow. Wrinkles!" Taylor knew she sounded shrill, and probably insane, but she couldn't help it. Smooth surfaces were very important to her. "And you know exactly who."

But Annabelle's eyes widened in the same moment that Asana said, "Sonofabitch."

"More like uppity bitch," Taylor said.

"Who?" Brooklyn said a little louder, looking between the three of them.

"I can't believe her," Annabelle said, seething, and leaped out of her chair to stalk the room. "Nothing is ever enough for her."

"We need to draw her out," Asana said, "and then nail her to the fucking Greek letters that hang off our house."

"Seriously, who the fuck are you talking about?" Brooklyn stomped her foot.

"The one and only, the bestest president to have ever ruled ADL, the one who can't seem to let it go. She's always saying that she'll do anything to make sure the reputation of her sorority was intact— and yet in a weird reversal she seems to be completely sabotaging us." Taylor stared pointedly at Annabelle. "Lily Walker."

"No way," Brooklyn said, shaking her head. "Why would your mom do that?"

Annabelle offered a bitter smile. "Why does Lily Walker do any of the things she does?"

"Because she's a bitch," Asana offered.

Annabelle laughed. "That is true, but it's more than that. My mother isn't just a former president of ADL; she lives for Greek Life, she bleeds for ADL. And we're threatening the balance of her control and the reputation she's built. Maybe she doesn't want to actually spread our secrets. Maybe she just wants us to pay?"

"Damn, that's fucked-up." Brooklyn nodded. "But also, why would she care now? We're not even actives anymore."

"*If* it's her," Asana said, tossing doubt back in the ring. "There's still a question of motivation. Like why would she do that, if it was only going to throw shade on her as being a part of the sorority?"

Taylor had had more confrontations with Lily Walker over the years than any other. And thank God, her own mother wasn't like that. Why hadn't she thought of Lily from the get-go? It was all making so much sense. Lily never planned to expose them. Just fuck with them, Taylor was certain.

They had a day full of sorority activities, but as soon as she could get Lily alone . . .

"Guess we'll need to find out." Taylor was ready to nail the bitch to the wall once and for all.

CHAPTER FORTY-EIGHT

I offered to call my cousins. I'm not afraid to admit to my good friends where I come from. And sometimes arrogant pricks need to be taken down a notch. She said no. So, I need to find another way to fuck him up. Money talks, and it's a language I fully understand.

Kisses,
Brooklyn

Annabelle

Then

Annabelle adjusted the pink headband on her head, hair curled softly around her shoulders. She'd just gotten it re-highlighted to hide the brown of her roots so she could look blonder, hotter, sexier. Or really, just so she could look like everyone else.

She also wore a foundation a shade lighter than her olive skin. If she had to hear one more person comment on her skin tone . . . She was Italian, for goodness' sakes. Get off her about it. What they should be asking was how she abstained from eating pizza and pasta the way she wanted to. Though that too would be clichéd.

"Oh, I love that headband." Brooklyn finished making her bed in the mirror reflection. "Who are you getting pretty for?"

"Greg."

Brooklyn stiffened, her taut and sculpted frame rigid in the reflection. "Oh."

"Why are you all so against him?" Annabelle whirled around. "What's he done to you?"

Asana, who she was currently not speaking to, had gone so far as to accuse Greg of roofying Annabelle last year at a frat party. Ridiculous. Why would her boyfriend roofie her? That made no sense. He told her he was totally fine just kissing and messing around. Understood her need to wait until marriage for the rest.

And she had emphatically told him the back door was off-limits, though some girls thought it wasn't. Her mouth on the other hand had done some very sinful things. Not that he ever returned the favor, but he was plenty generous with his fingers.

"Nothing." Brooklyn frowned. "I just don't want you to get hurt. Greg is a player."

Annabelle pursed her lips. Her hands flew to her hips. "Really? And what would you know about it?"

Brooklyn didn't say anything. Annabelle kept her face hard, but inside, she wished Brooklyn would say something. Share with her what everyone kept dancing around. Give her the confirmation she needed to walk away.

"We've been dating for a year now, Brooklyn. Our families vacationed together last summer on my daddy's yacht. He was a perfect gentleman and my parents love him." Well, he was mostly a gentleman . . . except for that one time . . . "Tell me why you think that about him."

"I want you to be happy, Anna."

"You don't get to call me Anna when you're talking smack about my boyfriend." *Tell me something real.*

Brooklyn sighed deeply, as if she were the most tired person in the world. Annabelle wasn't sure why, but that sigh made her angrier than any question about Greg's character.

A flash of Greg on the yacht swirled in her memory. The night she'd had too much champagne. The morning after, when she'd thrown up for hours and her mom told her it was bad shrimp.

Annabelle saw Greg kissing her, as if she weren't actually there, but a ghost floating above the sparkling lights of the yacht that shone like diamonds on a nighttime ocean.

Annabelle frowned. The vision wasn't a memory. She and Greg had kissed, sure, but not like that with her pressed up against a wall, his hands yanking at her dress.

"I'm sorry." Brooklyn looked sad, almost pitying, as she said it, but the expression was quickly gone as she left their shared room at the ADL house, leaving Annabelle to wonder about the night she was sick on the yacht.

And how many other nights she'd drank too much around Greg.

Woken up sore and chalked it up to whatever workout she'd done the day before. A girl didn't stay in perfect shape without two hours a day on the treadmill and Pilates three times a week.

What did her friends know that they weren't telling her? Where did Greg go when he snuck off in the middle of the night, his location turned off on his Snap?

With a huff Annabelle left her room, locking the door behind her. The hallway was empty. Staring at her from across the five-foot expanse was Taylor and Asana's room.

The door was decorated with glitter and their names cut out in pretty flower paper. Behind the bubbly door was the lockbox that Taylor kept the Spill Book in. No doubt whatever secrets everyone was holding would be in there.

Secrets about Greg.

Everyone seemed to be tiptoeing around her when it came to him. Even herself.

She took two steps. Contemplated knocking to see if anyone was inside. Reached forward.

Pulled back.

The urge to slip inside, to pick the lock that held the deepest, darkest secrets of everyone in their sorority for the past few years, held such strength inside her that she barely felt like she had control over her own limbs. As though, if she didn't answer this call, her body would do it for her.

Annabelle swallowed, knowing she'd already spent entirely too much time in the hallway staring at her friends' door. Knowing that if she didn't move now, either inside or away from it, she was going to be stuck here forever in limbo.

Taking the Spill Book would teach Taylor a lesson about trying to control everyone. Taking revenge on people she didn't like or who didn't follow the rules—it wasn't right. A pledge just last week had broken the five Bs rule, asking Taylor about her ex-boyfriend Brad. Everyone knew that breakup had been rough for Taylor, and the dumb pledge was probably just trying to make sure she was okay. But the pledge had ended up getting reviewed by the honor board when Taylor let it slip that she'd confessed to cheating on a test.

Annabelle wasn't even sure the girl was still in school here. Messing with Taylor meant bad things happened. Staying on her good side meant you were safe.

Annabelle needed to be safe.

Taylor knew her secrets.

Just once, Annabelle wished she knew Taylor's too.

Resisting the strong urge to take, take, take, Annabelle forced her body toward the stairs.

Away from temptation.

Away from punishment.

Away from the truth.

CHAPTER FORTY-NINE

*I saw Brad with another girl. I didn't think I
was the jealous type. Especially since I broke up
with him. But as it turns out, I don't want Brad,
and I don't want anyone else to have him either.*

*Kisses,
Taylor*

Brooklyn

Now

In the bright white of the ring light, the slight puffiness beneath
Brooklyn's eyes was a lot more noticeable than she would have
liked. Twenty-four hours since she'd woken with a hangover, and
she still held on to the damage. She had twenty minutes until
she had to meet the rest of BATA in the lobby to confront Lily
Walker, who'd been MIA the day before.

"Morning, y'all," she said, smiling into the camera and re-
adjusting the headband keeping her hair off her face as she applied
her morning routine of lotions, potions, and makeup. A woman's
skin care routine was sacred. "It's been a minute since I did a get-
ready-with-me video, hashtag GRWM! And I thought I'd take
this morning to share with you some of the things people don't
always talk about with sororities."

She held up her toner, pouring a bit onto a cotton round and wiping it onto her face. "This is one of my favorite new toners. I feel like it's really diminished my pores." And since they were a sponsor, she tapped the table before setting it aside and pulling out a lotion next, holding it up for the camera and squirting it into her palm for a little ASMR. As she rubbed lotion in circular motions on her face, she continued her little pep talk. "Before I was even out of high school, I knew I was going to rush and I knew I was going to do whatever it took to get into Bama. I had my tops picked out, ADL at Bama being my fave."

She showed off the primer, her nails clicking on the label of another sponsor, and then sprayed it onto her face, rubbing that onto her skin as well.

"Mostly people just like to talk about all the partying, the mean girl stuff they think happens, the 'hazing,' or how they were kicked out of a sorority, and of course scandal always gets views, right?" She laughed softly, ignoring the fact that she was currently embodied in a massive scandal the public didn't know about.

Sifting through her facial bag, she pulled out her concealer and started to tap it onto the slight discoloration and puffiness beneath her eyes, annoyed the under-eye masks she used earlier today didn't do the job. Though she supposed she was asking for a miracle with a hangover and too much stress. By Bid Day she was definitely going to have dark circles that showed the stress of this process.

"So, why did I join a sorority and stay a part of it? Well, I wanted the sisterhood. A core group of friends that I could do fun things with, share secrets with. People who had similar values. Belonging to a sisterhood was very important to me. We worked hard on our philanthropy when I was at Bama, and even now as an alumnus, I continue to donate to the causes that are important to us."

She pumped foundation onto her finger, tapping it in tiny dots around her face before dabbing it in with her makeup pad.

"And I'm still friends with my sisters. I'm here this week with all the actives and PNMs who want to be actives. Tomorrow is Pref Day, and I can't wait to see what happens in two days on Bid Day. That run from the stadium down Panhellenic row to the ADL house is still one of the most amazing moments of my life. And y'all know I married the sweetest man ever and have two adorable kiddies. Just sayin', Greek Life is a good life. If you make it so."

Using her contour stick she made lines on all the right angles of her face and started to blot them in with a foam egg.

"But there are some people who ruin it for the rest of us. Sour people. People who feel they've been slighted or offended somehow. And there are plenty of wrongdoings too, trust. I was once made to sit on a washer on spin cycle while my sisters circled all the parts that jiggled. It can be nasty."

Brooklyn blinked into the camera. A flash of paisley scarf jiggling around the neck of the sister who'd been in line behind her. An image of Taylor trying to pull off the scarf. The sister desperately holding on to it. Then the dark bruising of a hickey exposed. The shaming, pointing fingers.

The hickey giver had been Brad—Taylor's ex-boyfriend.

What was her name?

Brooklyn lined her eyes next, turning to the left and right to see if they were even. "But it doesn't have to be that way, is I guess what I'm saying. Maybe to get all these people off our backs, to stop talking about how toxic Greek Life is, we should stop being so mean to each other. Stop forcing each other to do things that aren't comfortable."

She pulled out her eyeshadow palette and picked a shade of light gold. Whatever happened to that sister? She'd dropped out, Brooklyn knew that. "Stop making people drink until they're sick. Go out with boys they don't want to. What does that prove?

What does harming another person prove about sisterhood or brotherhood?"

Brooklyn shook her head. Hadn't that sister with the scarf been forced as a hazing exercise to kiss Brad?

"Nothing, except that the person in charge is an asshole, pardon my French, but sometimes it needs to be said. It's real vile what happens when people take things to an unacceptable and unhealthy level. And that's not what being a part of a sorority or fraternity is all about."

Mascara wand in hand, she squinted into the camera as she applied. "It's supposed to be a chosen family. Friends for life."

Lana. That was her name.

Brooklyn put a light pink blush on, and a little highlighter on the tip of her nose, before lining her lips with a bright magenta liner. "I'm not trying to get all preachy here with you." She smiled sweetly into the camera. "That's not really what I'm about, y'all know that. But it was just something I felt needed to be said. I'm just sad for those who can't have fun, and feel the need to put their sour grapes into everyone else's cups. Be kinder to one another."

She pressed her lips together and stared directly into the camera. "And you know what, we've all done bad things in our lives, right? Things we're not proud of." She laughed to lighten the tension. "I know I have, and I don't mean that shade of green I painted my bathroom that turned out real bad. You know the one I'm talking about. The paint choice that shall not be discussed!"

It'd been a project she and Drew did, letting their kids pick the color, and it had ended up looking more like booger than sage.

"Anyways." She pulled off the headband and started to curl her hair. "Be kind, y'all, to each other, to yourselves. And, one last thing, karma's a bitch, so if you've done something lately you feel bad about, or maybe you took something from someone, or you were spreading rumors about someone, you should probably make it right before it bites you in the bum."

Lana. Lana. Lana. What happened to Lana?

Brooklyn fluffed her hair and blew a kiss into the camera.

Time to face the music. She ended her reel and held her breath as she pressed send on a video call to her husband.

Drew's handsome smiling face came on-screen. "Hey, babe, you're looking gorgeous as usual. Miss me?"

"So much." Brooklyn bit her lip. She'd been contemplating exactly how to tell him what happened in college. And she probably should have done it in person, years ago, but if everything went to shit, she didn't want Drew to find out through the media frenzy that would certainly follow. "I have something I need to tell you."

"I'm all ears, baby girl."

Why was he so nice? Drew moved through the house to their patio, the Florida sun shining on his hair.

"It's about me, in college."

Drew grinned, the look the same one he gave her when he guessed what she was about to say. A look she'd grown familiar with over the years because they'd been such a power couple. But this was not something he would know, not something that a power couple normally had to contend with. Drew was about to get the shock of his life.

Brooklyn blew out a breath. "I had another name besides Brooklyn in Bama when we were in college."

"Ah, Sporty Spyce?" He raised a brow, the crooked grin still in place.

Brooklyn's mouth fell open, and then closed as she tried to process him saying her sugar baby name, her OnlyFans handle. "Wait, you knew?"

Drew chuckled and shifted on his chair, the sunlight covering the screen like rays for a moment, making him and their surrounding backyard appear ethereal. If she were at home, she'd pose in that perfect sunlight with whatever product she was sponsoring.

"I wondered when you were going to tell me," he said.

"How did you know?"

"Remember when you asked me if I'd been on OnlyFans and I said no?" Drew gave a sheepish smile.

"Yeah." Her stomach started to have a funny little flutter. "Don't tell me you . . ."

"No, no," he hurried to say. "That part was true. But after you asked, curiosity got the better of me, and I had to look."

He'd looked. Had likely seen all her photos of her feet, the shower scene in the girls' locker room. And still he'd kept on dating her. Treating her like she was someone special to him. "And you never said anything?"

"I thought you'd tell me in time. Besides, I figured you had your reasons for doing it. Who was I to judge? I dressed up like a turkey every Friday night." He knew. He knew and he didn't care.

Brooklyn laughed. "You were my turkey." But OnlyFans wasn't the only thing she needed to tell him. He had to know she'd been a sugar baby. "There's more."

"I know about that too. Google knows everything."

"And you still . . . wanted me?"

Drew grew serious, the jovial smile gone, his eyes intense as he stared at her through the camera. How she wished she could sit in his lap and feel his arms around her. "Of course, why wouldn't I? Parts of you might be Brooklyn in Bama, Sporty Spyce, Ginger Mommy, but what I like best of all is you're mine. Together we're Brew. I love you for you, and all the pieces that make you into who you are. I don't care what you did to put yourself through college, just like I'm sure you didn't care I was shoveling shit on a farm every summer."

Her mouth was dry, her throat tight with emotion. "How did I get so lucky?"

"Luck doesn't have anything to do with it, baby girl. We chose to be where we were, when we were there. It wasn't luck that convinced me to ask you out, and it wasn't luck that you said yes."

"Then, I am on purpose the luckiest girl alive," she teased. "I miss you."

Drew winked. "I miss you too."

There was just one more thing she wanted to share with Drew, something she'd been thinking about since arriving back at Bama and all the secrets of their pasts coming to the surface. "I'm going to start a scholarship fund for young women who were in my position—sugar babies trying to put themselves through college." She explained about the money that Greg had given her, and how she needed to give it back to the world, to girls like her who'd needed to make money fast.

At the time, she'd used it to pay for school, but she'd made more than enough now being an influencer to give it all back.

"I love that idea—let me know how I can help."

"I don't know what I'd do without you, hon," she said, "but I do know this is one thing I need to make right without Mr. FixIt."

"I believe in you, and you know I'm here if and when you need me."

"I know. I'll be home soon."

"I'll be waiting."

Brooklyn ended the call, feeling lighter than she had since before she'd ever found herself on Greek Row.

CHAPTER FIFTY

I got a C on my essay. The prof thinks I didn't sufficiently supply Robin Hood with enough motivation for robbing the wealthy to feed the poor. Well, I think I did. In fact, I know I did, because I gave him my motivation. Good luck finding your phone, Prof, it's now being used by old George out on McFarland Blvd. I usually bring him a sandwich on Sundays.

Kisses,
Annabelle

Asana

Then
Last summer

Music pumped through Club X in NYC at a decibel level that made Asana's body vibrate. The sensation was euphoric. The sway hypnotic.

Taylor's "procedure" had been a week ago, and today was the first day she'd climbed out of bed looking ready to take on the world. Asana wasn't about to let that go to waste.

Taylor needed the club scene. A chance to let go and be someone else, if only for a night. To see what it was like to live in Asana's world.

This was a club they shouldn't be allowed in. Neither of them was twenty-one. But Asana didn't need to be of age to get in. They knew her by name.

And it wasn't like she was going to be drinking anyway. No. Mostly when she went to clubs, she danced until she collapsed in exhaustion or collapsed into bed with someone new.

But not tonight. Tonight, she and Taylor were dancing with each other. Eyes for no one else.

"Thank you," Taylor mouthed, her words lost in the music, arms above her head as she gyrated.

Asana grinned. No thanks was required. They weren't just friends but sisters for life.

As they danced, the high of the music, the atmosphere zinging through their veins, two dudes humped their way between them—interrupting what was supposed to be just the two of them.

"Hi," shouted one, his breath a mix of stale beer and horny dog.

"Hey," Asana shouted back.

"Dance with me."

Nothing turned her off more than being told what to do— even worse was when the offender was trying to separate her from her friends. Asana danced sideways to look at Taylor, to see if she was okay with their unwanted guests. Taylor rolled her eyes and shifted so they were next to each other, but she didn't say no. Asana slipped her hand into Taylor's, their fingers threading, needing the connection. She half expected Taylor to pull away, to put her hands on her dance partner's chest or shoulders, but she didn't. She squeezed instead.

For some reason, in the clubs, man-boys thought they could do whatever they wanted. That a girl dancing in a short skirt meant her ass was for the taking. And these two didn't seem to be any different.

Asana's dance partner started to sing, breaking out into an off-key babbling with the rhythm of the song, as if he thought he were the next Justin Bieber, when he really was a grade-F beaver. She raised her brows in Taylor's direction and watched as her friend's dance partner swiveled her around and started to smack her ass rapid-fire, as if his hand were a machine gun and her booty a target.

"What the fuck." Taylor's shout was loud enough to be heard over the music, but it didn't stop her partner, who was now slamming his crotch against her rear as he smacked her.

Asana's partner decided it was also a good idea to do that, but she wasn't having it. She shoved him off, grabbed Taylor's hand, and said, "Sorry, boys, she's taken."

Then she pulled Taylor close, wrapped her arms around her, and danced forehead to forehead, bodies swaying in actual rhythm with the song.

"What the fuck was that?" Taylor asked.

"Crazy fuckers."

They laughed, and danced some more, and before Asana could figure out what was happening, Taylor was kissing her. A clash of liquor and cinnamon gum. Sweet, spicy, and warm. Then they were running out of the club, climbing into the waiting car, the partition up as their lips locked. By the time they made it back to Asana's house, she could barely breathe, her body on fire for Taylor.

Hand in hand they hurried up to her bedroom. And the door had just barely shut before Asana's spine was pinned to the wood panels. Taylor pressed her body to hers, kissing her again, long and languid. Hands in her hair. Hands on her hips. She gripped Taylor's ass, pulling her tighter, closer. Wanting, and needing this more than anyone she'd ever touched.

Taylor started to walk backward, tugging Asana with her until they hit the bed, falling down beside each other in a tangle of limbs and heated breath.

"We're really doing this?" Asana whispered, stroking a finger over Taylor's face, her lower lip. "No regrets?"

"No regrets." Taylor sat up on her knees and tugged her dress over her head.

"EARTH TO ASANA." Jared snapped his fingers in her face, bringing Asana out of her memories and into the present meeting, which she really should have been paying attention to if she was going to follow through with her revenge plans.

"Did you hear me?"

Asana blinked, focusing on Jared's dumb face and waving fingers. The rest of the Machine gathering was staring at her as if she'd lost her mind. Maybe she had. What was she actually doing here?

"I'm sorry, what?"

Jared groaned and exaggerated a near fall backward before snapping upright and clapping in her face. If she had a weapon, a pencil even, she would stab him in the forehead. The only reason she'd even stayed in this secret society was so she could have insider knowledge on what they were doing.

"Asana, you will tell Alabama sisters to vote *yes* on question B. That's your job."

Question B in the local election was about the rights of members of the LGBTQ+ community. They didn't want people to talk about sexual or gender identity or even carry pride flags. Why the hell would she tell people to vote yes and eliminate people's rights?

Coming from New York City, and being who she was, she couldn't fathom ever telling anyone to vote against the rights of people's preferences. Just another reason why she needed to carry out her ultimate reprisal.

"Why do you care so much?" she asked, her voice flat. "Who someone loves or desires isn't any of your business."

"It's a sin, Asana." This came from Greg as he moved to stand behind Jared.

The audacity of the word "sin" coming from Greg Hamm was so stunning Asana blinked rapidly, forcing down a shocked laugh.

Asana stared hard at the devil, wishing she could stand up and tear his hair out, punch him so savagely in the throat that she destroyed his trachea, and he slowly suffocated to death.

Enough was enough.

For show, Asana nodded like a good little Machine lackey. She smiled tightly and scribbled *Say yes to question B* in her notebook while they watched. Later, she was going to burn this, along with everyone sitting in this meeting.

CHAPTER FIFTY-ONE

*I think being a sugar baby has messed me up for
normal dating. Drew keeps wanting to take me out,
and not expecting anything in return. No blowies or
even a hand job. Or maybe he's not really into girls.*

*Kisses,
Brooklyn*

Annabelle

Now

For half a decade Annabelle had been hiding behind her fear.
Keeping secrets. Protecting a predator.

To be fair, she'd thought Greg was just an asshole cheater.

But all the warning signs were there. The way her friends had
warned her off him when she was in college. The fact that none of
them came to her wedding—and why would they after the massive
blowup right at graduation. How Taylor even now seemed to have
a hard time making eye contact with her.

There were two people in her life that needed to go down.
Two people she kept close because they were her own symbols of
protection. Because maybe she was a little afraid of who she was
without them.

Lily Walker and Greg Hamm.

Outside the Tuscaloosa FBI office, she slid her hands reverently over the gold Louis Vuitton box in her lap. She brought it with her whenever she went out of town in case Greg took it upon himself to snoop. The light was dim here, and in her sunglasses, she was practically in the dark. She took them off. Being in the dark had gotten her to this place to begin with. There was a reason she was here. And this box had it all.

Greg wasn't exactly a saint himself, beyond his inability to take no for an answer. Took a criminal to know one, she guessed.

She touched the trophy diamond at her throat. What she was about to do was going to not only put Greg behind bars but also destroy the life she knew. The life her son hadn't even begun to understand. He was only in preschool. However, she wasn't just doing it for herself, for her friends, she was doing it for Liam too. Because the last thing she needed was for her son to grow up molded in the image of his father.

With a deep breath, she pushed open her car door and carried the box to the office, where an agent met her at the door. Making the phone call had been one of the hardest things she'd ever done.

"Annabelle Walker," he said.

Finally, someone had gotten her name right, and not assumed she was Mrs. Hamm.

Her grip was tight on the box as she held it close to her. But to turn around now would only invite suspicion onto herself.

Yet she couldn't help thinking this was insane.

This was . . . the right thing to do.

"You said you had something for me?" he urged. "Would you come inside? We'd like to take an anonymous statement, as promised."

Annabelle handed him the box and nodded.

She closed her eyes, taking in a deep breath as she followed him farther into the office. Every step took her closer to an uncertain fate. But she had to remind herself that she and Liam would be all right. For now. She had plenty of money stashed to lay low while the Feds crept around. Needless to say, her own little fun side hustle would need to be put on hold.

As she entered an interrogation room, an excited electricity whirred through her veins. Taking Greg's freedom might just be the greatest heist of her life.

The agent tapped the box, sitting across from her at a table that no doubt countless criminals had sat at before. "What's in the box, ma'am?"

"Evidence." Annabelle sat up straighter, and though her mouth felt dry, she exuded the confidence of a woman on a mission, a woman in the right.

Time for Karma to do her job. Annabelle explained about her husband's financial activities, and how she'd grown suspicious a few years ago and started to collect what she thought might be evidence. Turned out that Greg was into a whole lot more than embezzlement. But bribery and extortion too. She left out the fact that she'd collected said evidence to blackmail him should he turn on her.

Thank God she'd cleaned up her safe room before going to Rush Week just in case things went sideways with the Spill Book. A girl could never be too careful. And thank goodness she'd been good enough to make sure she never left a trail. If Greg found out it was her who turned him in, he could try to take her down, but it would all be heresy without proof, which she knew he didn't have.

The agent shook her hand at the end of the interview, walking her outside. "Thank you for your help, ma'am. We'll be in touch."

She hoped that by the time Greg was taken down, Bid Day would have passed and she'd be safe at home with her son.

Annabelle climbed into her car, the thrill of turning in her husband evaporating and leaving her legs as cold and brittle as thin icicles. Not exactly the relief she'd been hoping for. Had she done the right thing?

Part of the reason she'd stayed with Greg so long was because he was an excellent criminal lawyer. But that was probably a dumb excuse. It wasn't as if she loved him or even respected him. And she felt guilty for bringing a child into the world, but that hadn't been the plan. At least not part of her plan. Liam was a blessed surprise and had changed her outlook on life.

If she was lucky, the Feds would let her keep the house, but probably not. All of Greg's assets would be frozen for years, the money taken, the house taken, to pay back what he'd "stolen."

But Annabelle would be all right. She had her own account in her own name that wasn't associated with Greg at all, and the agent had promised her money wouldn't be touched. And given she was the heiress to a billion-dollar real estate mogul, no one would ask questions about how she had gotten her own money.

So maybe she'd just build a new house, with an even bigger and better "yoga" studio.

Maybe a part of her had always known that she was going to need to take Greg down. To safeguard herself. Her child.

To save future victims from Greg.

She just wished she'd done it sooner.

Maybe when she'd been back in college and realized what kind of a person he really was. How Greg had caught her red-handed, threatened her, and she hadn't wanted to face the consequences. When she kept waking up after dates with him dazed and confused. When her parents had basically arranged a marriage between them when she'd ended up pregnant without even consenting to sex.

Greg had taken away her choices. And now she was taking his.

CHAPTER FIFTY-TWO

Is it normal to play Among Us for six hours straight? It also feels a little like practicing for real life. There are so many sus people around here.

Kisses,
Asana

Taylor

Then

Taylor scanned the room, deciding that at today's tea party, they were going to do something different.

"No blindfolds," she said. "I want us to all look each other in the eye today."

Beside her Annabelle shifted on her feet, and she could feel Brooklyn's and Asana's stares.

Yes, it was unlike her, but Taylor liked to be unpredictable. People thought they knew her, but honestly, did anyone really ever know another person?

"Now turn to your sister on your right." Taylor turned, facing Asana. "Take their hands in yours."

Everyone followed. Asana gave a tiny, intrigued smile.

"Tell the sister in front of you why you love them." Taylor met Asana's eyes. "You're a loyal friend."

Asana smiled. "You're Elle Woods masked as Regina George." And then she leaned in, whispering against her ear, "And one hell of a lay."

Taylor laughed, her heart quickening. How was she going to get through the rest of today when she just wanted to take Asana and drag her upstairs? But of course, she couldn't do that. Not now, not ever. She'd be crucified if people learned she was bisexual. A good Christian girl, sleeping with girls? That was a sin. She couldn't let anything get in the way of her political aspirations, even herself.

Beside them, Annabelle told Brooklyn she always knew how to make someone smile. And Brooklyn told Annabelle that she brought out the sweet side of everyone.

"Switch," Taylor said, taking Annabelle's hands, and the rest of the sisters doing the same. It was hard for her to look at Annabelle and not see Greg, but one of the reasons that Taylor wanted to do this was to remind herself why she'd liked Annabelle so much in the first place. "You're unapologetically daring."

Annabelle's eyes widened, and she sucked in a breath, the relief at Taylor finally doing something other than glaring at her evident. No doubt she'd been afraid of being frozen out of the BATA foursome. But Taylor hadn't taken it that far. Part of her was maybe just waiting for Annabelle to get rid of Greg so they could go back to being the fab four.

"You're confident," Annabelle said through a wobbly smile.

They stared at each other, not really speaking, both of them studying the other. There was so much Taylor wanted to say. All of it tucked up in the knot in her throat, held tight there by some unforeseen force. Holding her hand, complimenting her, this had to be enough. Taylor nodded.

Then it was time to switch, but before she could move away,

Annabelle had thrown her arms around her and was hugging her tight enough that her necklace dug into her chest. At first Taylor couldn't hug her back, and the longer the seconds ticked by, the more awkward the hug became, until she finally too hugged her back.

"Switch." Brooklyn laughed, tugging Taylor away from Annabelle. "Are you guys all right?" she whispered.

"Yeah. Fine. Now pay me a compliment." Taylor straightened her shoulders, pulling the hardness back in place.

"You're good at bringing us together."

Taylor smiled. "You always know how to catch the perfect angle and make a girl look good on camera."

They went around the room, telling everyone how they felt, the positivity vibing. This was one of the reasons that Taylor had wanted to belong to a sorority. The friendships, the hopefulness. To have a bunch of other women standing beside her and behind her.

No, she couldn't tell them what happened in the spring semester. Or what happened over the summer. Or what was still happening right now.

In person, she liked the positivity and knowing that her sisters would stick up for her, but that didn't mean she was ready to trust them with her darkest secrets.

Those would have to remain locked in the box, spilled on the pages of a sequined notebook.

Afterward, it was a cupcake decorating contest. They made a mess in the kitchen, had a few flour fights and plenty of icing taste tests. It was a hard choice between a pussy cupcake, dick cupcake, and shit emoji cupcake, but in the end, Taylor's pink kiss cupcake won.

She met Asana's eyes over the large island counter covered in the detritus of the baking contest, wondering if she knew she was the inspiration.

At the end of the sisterhood event, Taylor clapped for the attention of her high-on-sugar ADL sisters.

"You all chose Alpha Delta Lambda for the sisterhood, and we chose you for the same reason. I'll choose all of you every day from here on out. If you get mad or sad or whatever, remember today, the nice things you said to each other, and brush off the bitter, because we need each other."

Everyone was still upset about the loss of a few members recently during one of their friendly challenges—which some antiquated idiots considered to be hazing rituals. The dryer jiggle. But seriously, good riddance to bitches who broke girl code.

Taylor glanced at Annabelle in particular, completely aware of the double standard she'd set where her close friend was concerned. Forgiveness wasn't one of Taylor's strong suits, but Annabelle couldn't help being duped by Greg. He was a predator. In the Brad and Lana sitch, it was Lana who was the predator.

Taylor just hoped one day, Annabelle would wake up long enough to see Greg for who he truly was.

CHAPTER FIFTY-THREE

Coach Cunt, that's her new name by the way, almost made me ineligible to play. I don't know how she would have done it, but she legit told me she was going to. I personally hold the record for most goals in a game of any female soccer player since soccer was a thing at Bama. Bitch better give me my award.

Kisses,
Brooklyn

Asana

Now

Lily Walker strolled into the coffee shop the same way she walked into any Panhellenic building, as if she owned the place. Forgoing the line, she approached the counter, ignoring the "excuse mes" from the other customers. Clearly recognizing her, a barista pulled out a mug and poured Lily a cup, then said, "On the house."

Asana would've been impressed if she wasn't so disgusted by the woman right now. In opposite corners, her friends sat, hidden, to watch. The clandestineness of it was a bit silly, but necessary so as not to spook the bitch.

"Asana." Lily smiled and leaned down to kiss her on her cheek. "This was a nice surprise."

Asana found it hard to smile, and decided against it. This was business.

Lily sat down, rearranging herself until she was perched so perfectly in the chair, she might have been a doll placed there.

"To what do I owe the honor?" Lily's smile was so practiced, so full of fake cheer, it was hard not to gag.

"Ironic you should put it that way." Now Asana did smile, unfolding her crossed legs and leaning closer. "Give me the book."

Lily's smile didn't even crack. "What book?"

From the corner of her eye, Asana watched Annabelle turn around from where her back had been to the door. She was wearing a ball cap—very un-Annabelle-like of her. Instead of remaining where she was supposed to, she stood and took the chair right behind Lily.

Unapologetically daring.

"You know which one," Asana continued. "I assure you, if you give it to me now, we won't have to drag this out, and your name won't be paraded through the papers, social media, television channels." Asana waved her hand, letting the list of places she was willing to expose Lily play out in the other woman's mind. If it came down to it, she'd use the ultimate trump card—a certain Mr. Walker was a Matinee member. The only reason she hadn't so far was because she cared about Annabelle.

"Asana, dear." Lily lifted the cup of coffee to her lips and sipped thoughtfully. "I think you have me confused with someone else."

"I don't. And the longer you waste my time, and yours, the closer your daughter gets to exposing you."

Now Lily's face did the slightest twitch. "What does Annabelle have to do with this?" Her laugh was supposed to sound nonchalant, but there was an underlying hint of worry to it. Asana knew she had her.

"As much as all of us. Why did you do it?"

"Pardon me?"

Asana blew out a long breath. "Since you read the Spill Book, I think you'll understand something about me. I'm like a dog chasing a toy, only worse, Lily. When I want something, I don't just go after it. I tear it apart."

Lily sat back in her chair for the first time since arriving, appearing worried, her knuckles white as she gripped her free coffee.

"Give me the book, Lily. Walk away from this nonsense."

Lily's lips pulled back over her teeth, vicious and precious all at once. Her voice was a low hiss as she spoke, stabbing the table with her finger to punctuate every word. "I read your dirty little book. Your entire class was a poster child for the seven cardinal sins: lust, gluttony, greed, sloth, wrath, envy, pride. Eight if you include"—Lily looked around as if someone might jump out of thin air to accuse her of something, then leaned forward and whispered—"lesbians. You all destroyed the sanctity of sisterhood. You're an embarrassment and need to be wiped from the ADL records."

Asana didn't let her relief show that they'd guessed correctly about Lily's vendetta, but on the inside, she started to relax. She wasn't at all surprised that Lily had pulled out the seven— make that eight—deadly sins, and it was hard not to wiggle her fingers in front of her face and make ghostly sounds as if she were terrified of God's wrath. Despite Lily's judgment, Asana still believed her friends, her sisters, were good people. Yes, they'd made a few mistakes, but people made mistakes all the time.

Asana shook her head, giving Lily a pitying look. "Actually, quite the contrary. And that's why I'm here. Because what you're doing, what you're threatening to do, is what is going to tear apart not only the sisterhood, the bonds already formed, but the future of Panhellenic life. You want to expose the secrets of hundreds of ADL sisters? Then you're willing to risk exposing your own family."

Lily Walker's lips pinched. "You don't have any idea what you're talking about. I'm the one on the Panhellenic board. You're going down."

"If we go down, so does ADL, your pride and joy." Asana leaned forward. "Trust me when I say, you might want to check your own house before you start casting stones."

"Lies." Lily abandoned her coffee, sitting back hard against the chair, folding her arms. Having read the book, she knew her daughter was a thief. And if she had any brains at all, she'd know her husband was a cheat.

"Maybe that's what we say the book is?" Asana spoke low, controlled. "That you made it up. A jealous mother, a has-been who has spent her whole life trying to get back into the house."

"What?" Lily blanched.

"I won't just stop there. I'll go after your husband, tear apart his chain of hotels, your income streams. I'll expose him. All of his sins. Try me."

"You would hurt Annabelle." Lily shook her head, completely ignoring the fact that she was doing that very thing.

"What do you think she'll find more horrifying: Her own mother trying to destroy her or a friend she hasn't seen in five years?" Asana glanced at the Dooney and Bourke purse cradled on the back of Lily's chair. She'd worked hard to not react to Annabelle expertly unzipping it during the conversation. "Is it in there?"

Lily grabbed the purse, clutched it to her as if it were a lifeline. "No."

Asana worked as hard as the parent of a toddler enduring a tantrum not to roll her eyes. "Just give it to me so we can both get to the sorority meeting."

"No."

"I didn't want to have to do this, but really, if you're not willing to save yourself, someone has to save you." Asana lifted a brow at Annabelle.

Behind Lily's shoulder Annabelle frowned, holding up a stack of papers clipped together.

Lily whirled in her chair to see her daughter.

"Anna, what are you doing here? With that?" Lily ripped open her purse to see that the papers were gone.

"Photocopies, Mom? What is this?"

"Give it back," Lily said, her voice mom-in-a-grocery-store soft and full of warning.

"Where is the book, Lily? Why do you have copies of it?" Asana demanded, her voice just as low.

This time, Lily smiled, an evil look in her eyes. "How does it feel to be wrong, Asana Duke?"

"Not as bad as you're going to feel if you don't tell me where it is." Asana wasn't about to play games with this plastic bitch.

"I don't have it. I wasn't lying. Someone gave me the copy."

"Mom? Who?"

But Lily only sat back in her chair and sipped her coffee as if the world wasn't about to implode. Though Lily's mouth didn't move, and she made no sound, Asana could have sworn she heard Lily laughing like a fucking lunatic.

A photocopy? Really?

"Fuck."

CHAPTER FIFTY-FOUR

I'm going to hell. Greg and I had sex and I barely even remember it. Is there a thing as double hell?

Kisses,
Annabelle

Brooklyn

Then

Maybe she was naive, or maybe she was lucky, but for the last several years, Brooklyn had four amazing sugar daddies that paid her way. Number five, however? The last time she'd seen him, they'd finally consummated their arrangement and he'd made her wear a ball gag.

The experience had been unpleasant, and that was putting it mildly.

Brooklyn wasn't into bondage, though she didn't knock anyone else if they liked it.

He'd paid several months in advance, which at the time, she'd thought of as great security. Now that money felt like being locked in.

Even nasty Greg's money sitting hot in her bank account didn't make a lick of difference considering she still had three weeks left to fulfill her end of the contract. Breaking the contract would give her a bad reputation among the sugar world. Then again, she didn't need to do it anymore with the G.H. fund.

Brooklyn bit her lip and opened her purse, shoving in the stack of bills that she'd just withdrawn from her account. The fat load was more money than she'd ever held in her life—and exactly what she owed her daddy for breaking the contract. The sugar world was cash only.

And the scared little girl, the one who remembered being hungry and cold, staring at the hole in the side of the trailer she lived in, listening to her parents argue, that little girl who'd made a promise to herself that she would change her life—that she'd never end up poor or hungry or wanting again—wanted to hand those bills back to the bank teller, say that she'd changed her mind.

The other side of her, that never dreamed her exploits on OnlyFans and TikTok would lead to her taking money for companionship, and from men who were less than stellar (except for Daddy #3), demanded she zip the purse closed and leave the bank. She could just add to her sugar baby site what her hard noes were and move on. But . . . for some reason this felt like a turning point for her.

"Is everything all right, miss?" The teller eyed her as if Brooklyn might have been robbing the bank rather than pulling out the money for the rest of this month to pay back her . . . was he technically her boss? God, Title IX would have a field day with that considering he was on the board of the university, and she'd lied to him about not being a student.

This wasn't done. Returning the money. Breaking up.

She was going to lose her reputation.

But she was also all right with that.

The money Greg had given her was enough to get her through graduation. She could play soccer and be an active board member for ADL, and not have to worry about what strange things a lonely old man might make her do. And besides the three must-dos for the sorority, she could go a day without shaving her legs. Maybe even not get a full Brazilian.

"Sorry." Brooklyn flashed her best smile. "Just tired."

And she was. Tired of so much bullshit. Tired of feeling like she wasn't good enough. Tired of feeling like she had to prove herself over and over and over again.

She marched out of the bank, and practically ran right into Drew. All the blood in her body shot straight to her face. They'd gone on four dates before she ghosted him. He was just too damned . . . *nice*.

"Whoa, did you just rob the place?" Drew's hands were shoved in his pockets and he rocked a little on his heels as he studied her.

Brooklyn didn't laugh, his joke falling flat considering she had several thousand dollars in her purse and her nerves were already on high alert.

The last thing she could take right now was too-nice Drew asking questions. He seemed like he actually cared. What was wrong with him?

"No." Brooklyn scooted around him and climbed onto the bus, prepared to take it downtown, and then she'd order an Uber to take her . . .

Where?

She couldn't just show up at *his* house. And she couldn't show up at his office on campus. This entire exercise felt like one in futility.

She sat down on a hard seat as the bus rolled off, jostling her with it. Ignoring the hiss of brakes and the door opening, as the bus stopped for someone. She pulled out her phone and sent a private message to her sugar saying they needed to talk.

"You look entirely too serious."

Brooklyn glanced up to see Drew sitting across from her. Hadn't she run into him getting *off* the bus?

"Did you just stop the bus to get back on?" she asked, incredulous.

"Yeah." He grinned, his arms going back to rest on the empty chair backs on either side of him. "Truth is I'm stalking you."

Her mouth fell open. "Okay, Joe," she said, in reference to the famous stalker in *You*.

"Kidding." He held up his hands. The smile faltered on his face, replaced by a look of concern. "Are you okay?"

"Totally." She lied right through her teeth, flashing a fake smile.

"Never seen you look this . . . tense, even on the field."

"You've seen me play?" That got her attention.

He grinned. "Stalking you, remember?"

Brooklyn would have laughed if she didn't have more pressing things to worry about. Drew was entirely too wholesome to actually be a stalker.

"You still a member of Sigma Chi?" she asked, crossing her legs and trying to ignore the silence from her phone.

"Actually no." Drew ran a hand through his hair. "Wasn't really into that scene. Plus, the drinking was messing with my game."

She cocked her head. "What scene?"

"The get-drunk-and-take-advantage-of-girls scene. Not my style. I thought it would be a lot more fun, I guess. It wasn't."

She nodded. "I can understand that, especially with a guy like Greg Hamm running the frat."

"He's a total douche."

"Couldn't agree more."

"Coffee?"

She glanced down at her phone, where the request to meet went unanswered. She could always ghost him. Give the money to charity. Because there was one thing she was sure of and that was that she didn't want this kind of money anymore. And she definitely didn't want to be gagged ever again.

"A date?" She wrinkled her nose.

"Oh no, I hate dates." He shook his head so hard his hair fell over his forehead. "I would never suggest a date. Not after last time. Ew."

This time Brooklyn did laugh. "I didn't mean it like that."

"Like what?"

"Like ew."

Drew grinned. "Me either."

"I'm sorry I, uh, kinda ghosted you."

"You did? I guess I kind of was wondering when you'd text me back. But I know how busy you are . . ." He trailed off, looking embarrassed.

Ohmygod, he didn't even notice I ghosted him?

Brooklyn sucked in a breath. "I'm a bitch."

"Nah," he said. "I've met some bitches. You're not one of them."

"Well, then, I'm a mess."

"Aren't we all?"

Brooklyn didn't think she deserved a guy like Drew. He genuinely *liked* her. When had that ever happened? "I might ghost you again."

"I'll just have to come find you and bring you back to life." He stood up and offered his hand. For the first time since she'd been in college, Brooklyn actually took the hand of a guy that was into her and not looking for something.

At least, that's what she thought. What if this actually was some sort of sick fantasy game?

"Wait." She tugged her hand back.

He raised a brow, his hand stilling in the air before he could pull the cord to stop.

"This is going to sound random and strange," she said.

"I've probably heard randomer and stranger."

"Are you on OnlyFans?"

He chuckled. "No. Too afraid I'll see someone I know. Why? Last boyfriend have an account?"

"Yeah." It was only a partial lie. Not a boyfriend. Technically.

"Never had one. Heard my sisters talking too much about selling feet pics. I was worried I'd see one and I've experienced their dogs enough."

Brooklyn laughed, though it sounded forced to her ears.

"One more question?" she asked, to change the subject, and took his hand back in hers.

"Lay it on me."

"How do you take your coffee?"

"Is this a trick question?"

"No."

"All right, then I take it any time of day."

Brooklyn laughed again. "Let's get off here. I see Cozy Cups and they have great couches to sit on."

They exited the bus and she didn't know whether to be excited or disappointed in herself that she'd waited three years after starting at Bama to think about a real relationship. After talking for hours over coffee, Drew walked Brooklyn back to the ADL house.

She thought that like on their other dates, he would hug her and walk away, but this time he pulled her in and pressed his lips to hers.

Unlike with any other kiss she'd ever had, every inch of her skin tingled, even her toes curled in her sneakers. She wrapped her arms around his neck, sinking into him as his tongue brushed lightly over her lips. A tentative question, and she opened her mouth, a confident *yes*.

Drew's body was all hard lines, honed from hours on the field and in the gym. And hot damn, did he know how to kiss.

The light outside the house flickered. A warning. Stupid rules.

They pulled away, his lips wet and his mouth beckoning her for more.

"Wow, that was . . ." he started, but Brooklyn cut him off, throwing herself back into his arms. Fine for public displays of vulgarity on house property be damned. She wanted more.

"Brooklyn!" the president's screech was enough to wake the sisters who'd founded the house a hundred years ago. "One-hundred-dollar fine."

Brooklyn didn't stop kissing him.

"Two hundred!"

She wrapped her arms tighter around Drew, not letting him go.

"Don't make me go to two-fifty."

"Okay, I can't let you go broke for a kiss," Drew said with a laugh, pulling away.

Brooklyn laughed at the irony—she'd never had to pay for a kiss before. She reached into her purse, grabbing a couple of bennies from her withdrawal earlier. "I can't think of a better way to spend my money." She handed it over to the president, who glowered at her and then slammed the door.

"Still know how to climb into a window?" Brooklyn asked.

Drew looked at her, serious. "Shouldn't we wait?"

Brooklyn shrugged. "For what? I want you, Drew."

He blew out a shuddering sigh. "I want you too."

"Climb up to my window."

Fifteen minutes later, she had Drew naked in her bed, with the door locked and assurances that Annabelle wouldn't be home anytime soon.

In the dark of her room, they stared at each other, lying side by side. Why the hell did she feel like a virgin?

Maybe because this was the first time she was about to have sex with a guy who didn't expect anything in return?

"You're gorgeous," Drew whispered, brushing her hair away from her face. He leaned in to kiss her. "Are you sure you're okay with this?"

Brooklyn laughed softly. "I am, and thank you for asking. You're entirely too sweet."

"I'm not always sweet."

"How so?" She slid her fingers over his toned arms. Her thighs were pressed to his muscular legs, and she itched to squeeze them.

"Sometimes . . ." His hand skimmed over her hip, and he grabbed her ass, tugging her forward until his rock-hard cock was pressed to her lower belly. "Sometimes, I'm shameless."

"No shame here," she whispered.

"Sinful," he murmured, licking a path from her neck down to her breast. He sucked her nipple into his mouth, and she arched her back, letting out a moan.

"I like sin." Brooklyn ran her fingers through his hair, silently begging for more.

"Naughty." His fingers slid over her belly to the slick folds between her thighs, where he took no time to find her clit, applying the perfect amount of pressure.

Brooklyn gasped. "I like this side of you."

"I'm about to make you like me a whole lot more."

Thirty minutes after that—she'd already come three times and dubbed herself a pillow princess. The best fucking sex of her life.

CHAPTER FIFTY-FIVE

I'm going to host an anonymous party. I miss those from NYC. Masks, but not the stupid kind where people can see half your face and know who you are. Full-coverage face, and naked everything else. Fucking permitted. Prudes not welcome.

Kisses,
Asana

Taylor

Now

The last of the PNMs had left the second Pref Day party, and Taylor let out a long sigh of relief. She'd always hated Pref. The PNMs were so high-strung by the eighth day, afraid they weren't going to get chosen, that they tried way too hard. And some of the actives made it even harder for them, by acting off or touchy, or testing them in ways that made them falter.

Taylor for sure had been known to be a bitch, but she was also hyperaware of how difficult it was to act normal when you were trying so hard to prove yourself.

She wandered around the house, finding herself standing in front of their old house mom's bedroom. The door was open. All sense of Mama Jenny had been washed away and replaced by what could only be explained as the Lily Walker special.

"You thinking about Mama Jenny? She was really nice," Larissa said from behind, her tone sad.

Taylor smiled at the current president of the sorority, still wearing that tacky scarf in her hair. "She was."

"We're really lucky that Lily Walker has agreed to take her place."

Taylor didn't make a comment, because she didn't think anyone was lucky to have Lily Walker in their life. She used to think Annabelle was lucky, as they'd sat in the audience that very first Convocation Day and stared up at her on the stage, but since then she'd not only gotten to know Lily Walker; she'd seen how very ugly she was on the inside.

Yesterday's incident in the coffee shop was no exception. They were nowhere close to figuring out who had stolen and made a copy—possibly *copies*—of the Spill Book, and Lily was as tight-lipped as a politician caught with his pants down.

"What do you know about how we used to do things when I was president?" Taylor asked.

Larissa cocked her head, staring at Taylor with doe eyes that were hard to decipher. She was either a liar or she was truly an innocent. Hard to say.

"I don't know what you mean?" Larissa smiled so sweetly it made Taylor ill.

"Doesn't seem like much has changed."

"I think it has." She shrugged. "We don't do the tea parties anymore."

So, she did know about those. "Probably a good thing."

"Why? Because your notes were stolen?"

"You know about that?"

She shrugged again, a little too nonchalant. "Lily told me."

"Did Mrs. Walker happen to tell you who gave her the copy?"

Now the president smiled, a secret knowing smile. "No."

She was *lying*. Taylor cocked her head. "But you know."

"I do."

"Who was it?"

"A sister doesn't kiss and tell. Remember what I said? No more tea parties." Larissa laughed, and straightened her stupid scarf headband.

"Even when it puts her sisters and her house in jeopardy?"

"Why would we be in jeopardy?" Larissa cocked her head, pursing her lips in confusion. There was something familiar about her face, and something about it that made Taylor want to slap her.

"There are things in that notebook that shouldn't be shared."

"Like what?" The way she asked, so innocent as if she had no idea, put Taylor on edge.

"A sister doesn't kiss and tell."

"Hmm. Touché."

"Seriously, this could be a PR nightmare." Why wasn't Larissa taking this seriously? Taylor was losing what little patience she possessed.

"Maybe or maybe not. Maybe people need to know the way you and your pledge class were." Larissa dropped the pretense of sweetness.

"But it's not just going to be the way we were. They are going to think it's the way *you* are too. Think about all the attention Greek Life is getting right now, the universities that are banning Panhellenic groups and activities. The Spill Book, the secrets, the hazing, that's not a good look for ADL."

Larissa laughed again, but the sound of it was hella creepy. "I hate to say 'it's your funeral,' because that is super cliché and of course I don't wish your death"—she looked off in the distance as if she was in fact actually contemplating Taylor's death—"but I'm as silent as the grave you stuck your stupid Spill Book in."

"I didn't put it in a grave. I put it in a time capsule."

"Same thing, really. The grave of your reputation. Eventually the truth was going to come out. I just sped up your timeline."

Taylor clenched her fists at her sides, already full of regrets for having stuffed the fucking book in there instead of burning it when she had the chance. "I'm telling you that it's bad to protect whoever it is you're protecting, and that this will not end well for you or for ADL. For the sake of the house, please, just give it back."

Larissa just stared, her entire demeanor suddenly vacuous.

"Is it money?" Taylor asked. "I've got plenty of it."

"Maybe that's the problem."

"What problem?"

"Spoiled rich girls getting away with murder."

"We didn't kill anyone."

"It's a figure of speech." Larissa rolled her eyes. "Besides, you murdered plenty of girls' self-esteem. We don't want you associated with us. We invited you here to kick you out of ADL."

"Who is *we*?"

"Me, the board, Lily."

Taylor stuttered a laugh. "Lily Walker?"

"She and the Panhellenic board are disgusted with you."

Taylor doubted it. If the Panhellenic board had gotten involved, this entire situation would be out of Larissa's hands. Taylor cocked a brow, challenging. "The Panhellenic board has seen our Spill Book?"

She shrugged, and this time rather than just playing coy, Taylor could tell, she didn't really have an answer for that. There was no way Lily was going to show her copy to the board. Of that, she was certain.

"Not agreeing with how one board handled things or not is no reason to ruin people's lives. But fucking with me, Larissa, now that's a reason."

Larissa actually looked momentarily wary. Was it too much to hope that she wasn't completely on board?

"We did great things for ADL. We built up the philanthropic endeavors to double what they were, bringing us to the number one house to raise money for animals not just in Alabama but in the country."

"That was good. But you hurt a lot of people. More than you helped."

"And you can't tell me you haven't ever done anything that someone might consider 'bad'?" Taylor made air quotes as she locked eyes with Larissa.

"No one is innocent. Especially not you."

"Why are you punishing us?"

"I'm not." Now she crossed her arms over her chest, completely backpedaling, or at least finally admitting she had no idea what she was talking about.

"I'm going to ask you one more time. Who took the book? You were there when the capsule was opened to give the ring back to Mama Jenny's family. Who took it out?" Taylor took a step closer, towering several inches over the twat, and let all the anger she felt show right on her face. If Larissa wanted to play games, then she was going to get the full Taylor Collins. "As president of ADL you took an oath to protect this sisterhood, this house. You're going against that oath by keeping your mouth closed. And do you know what happens to bitches who fuck with me?"

Larissa swallowed, her arms falling to her sides, all the blood draining from her face.

Taylor put her face only an inch from Larissa's and said through gritted teeth, "Keep your mouth closed and find out."

Tears gathered in Larissa's eyes as she battled with whether to cave or not. Taylor snapped her teeth.

"Fine. I'll tell you. But you have to promise me something first." Larissa took a step backward.

Taylor straightened, looking down her nose. "You have my word. But I'm not listening alone."

"Fine. One other."

"Agreed. Let's go."

Taylor texted Asana to meet her in Larissa's room. Once they were assembled together, the door shut and locked, Taylor didn't hesitate to ask, "What do you want?"

"I want you to apologize."

It was on the tip of her tongue to say, *That's it?* because she could have asked for more. But clearly Larissa wasn't really one to negotiate well—a huge clue she wasn't the one blackmailing them either. "Yeah, sure. Who am I apologizing to?"

"My sister."

"Okay." Taylor drew out the word, unable to help the annoyance that leaked into her voice.

"Who's your sister?" Asana asked before Taylor could.

"Lana."

"Lana and Larissa, how cute," Asana mocked.

"And who the fuck is Lana?" Taylor skimmed through her mental Rolodex trying to remember.

"You remember Lana, the girl you forced into a closet with your ex-boyfriend," Larissa accused. "Well, they are getting married now. So the joke's on you."

"*That* Lana." Taylor laughed. Hard. This was absolutely ridiculous. Her eyes went to the scarf in Larissa's hair that she was always fiddling with, the same one Lana used to wear. "So, you stole the book for Lana? Some sort of revenge?"

Apologizing to the woman who broke the don't-date-Taylor's-ex girl code was going to be so annoying.

"I didn't steal it for *her*. I stole it to protect ADL, the sisters whose names you tarnished."

"They tarnished their own names," Asana pointed out. "Where's the book?"

But Taylor keyed in on Larissa's tone. She didn't steal it for *her*. Then who?

Asana held out her hand, impatiently tapping her foot on the floor. "Hand over the book before I call the police to report you've stolen property."

"Who did you steal it for?" Taylor asked.

Larissa ignored her, started to argue with Asana about the police, but Asana held up her hand. "Shush. You have no standing here. And if there's one thing you should have learned by reading all of that Spill Book you couldn't wait to get your greedy hands on, it's that you don't—"

"Fuck with Taylor." Taylor started to yank open Larissa's drawers, tossing shirts and skirts behind her.

"Stop!" Larissa's voice was shrill enough to crack glass. "I'll get it."

"Now." Asana clapped her hands.

Larissa pulled a lockbox from under her bed, plugged in the combination, and opened it.

Seeing the bedazzled Spill Book presented in all its glory had Taylor's chest seizing with regret, joy, and nostalgia all at once. Before Larissa could take it out, Taylor snatched it from the box.

"Mine, thank you," Taylor snapped when Larissa made a half-hearted attempt to snatch it back. "Now, if you please, who exactly did you take it for if not Lana?"

Larissa's face grew tense and pinched. "And you'll keep your promise to apologize?"

Taylor gritted her teeth. What was with the apology? So stupid! "Out with it."

"It's a long story." Larissa shoved the lockbox back under her bed and stood.

"Then give us the CliffsNotes version," Asana said impatiently.

Larissa sat down on her bed with an overly dramatic sigh. "Lana told me about the book. I told Lily about it when we opened the capsule to find your old house mother's ring and I found the book. She asked me to take it out of the time capsule and give it to her. But I didn't want to give her the original because, as president, it's also my duty to protect. So I just made her a copy."

Asana laughed out loud, the sound sharp. "Give me a break. Why would you take it out anyway, unless you were curious to read it yourself?"

Larissa's face colored. "Lily is . . . she's a special friend to my father."

"Ohmygod, she's having an affair?" Taylor pressed a shocked hand to her mouth, wondering if Annabelle had a clue.

Larissa rolled her eyes. "As if that's really shocking. She's not even with her husband anymore. It's not cheating."

"It kind of is," Asana said sarcastically. "They are still technically married."

Taylor studied Larissa, trying to figure out if she was lying, but from all appearances, she was telling the truth. What the fuck? There must have been trouble in the Walker household, and Lily was such an uptight bitch she hadn't even confessed that to her own daughter. It explained why Lily was willing to take up residence at the ADL house as their house mother. And it explained why when Asana had grilled her at the coffee shop, threatened Lily's husband, she'd only said "You'd hurt Annabelle." Not that destroying her husband would hurt Lily. Because Lily didn't care about her husband, she'd already moved on. For all they knew she could have filed for divorce, though she suspected that wouldn't have stayed out of the papers.

"Don't tell her I told you," Larissa said. "But she seemed like . . . I don't know, kind of crazy when she read it."

"Are there any other copies like the one you gave Lily Walker?" Asana asked, keeping her face neutral.

"Yes." Larissa bit her lip, as if she were trying to keep the name of the other person inside.

Taylor took a menacing step forward. "Stop with the games. Give us the names."

"Just one. Maggie. She's a journalist. She said Lily contacted her and told her I'd give her a copy."

That could be true. She wouldn't put it past Lily reading through the Spill Book and figuring out that Maggie might want revenge. But that left the blackmail letters, and just who had sent them.

"And you just gave it to her, like it was no big deal." Taylor was seething. This little idiot had no idea the damage she could have done.

Larissa shrugged. "You all should suffer for what you did to my sister."

"You know, Lana was an adult, just like you, when she was in college. And she made her own choices."

Larissa clenched her fists at her sides. "Sometimes even adults don't get to make their own choices, Taylor. Sometimes other adults take those choices from them. You of all people would know that."

Taylor opened her mouth to respond, but no words came out. She closed her mouth, breathed in through her nose, and then said quietly, "Don't compare me to your sister. I didn't drug her and force her into that closet with Brad. She could have said no at any time."

"And suffer the consequences."

Taylor laughed. "If you think the consequences she would have suffered for a hazing exercise at all compare to the prices I've paid, then you might want to be your own first patient, 'Doctor' Larissa."

Larissa stared at her hard, her lips white around the edges. "I'm not the bad guy, Taylor."

"We're done here," Asana said, threading her arm through Taylor's and leading her out of the ADL house. "We need to have another conversation with Lily."

CHAPTER FIFTY-SIX

*I had a threesome last night. A dude and a chick.
It was pretty hot, not gonna lie. Would do it again.*

*Kisses,
Taylor*

Annabelle

Then

In all of her life, in all of her little escapades, Annabelle had never planned anything quite like this.

The idea came to her last night at the football game. All the frat boys cheering on their number one star—Greg Bleeping Hamm.

Finding out that Greg's parents and her parents had donated all the money to the team to buy the elephant trophy that signified their big win at the Sugar Bowl had set off a firestorm.

Since she'd forced herself not to take the Spill Book, the itch to *take* something big had never been so strong, like a physical ache deep in her bones.

When she saw Greg, arms up on the brick wall of the stadium, caging in a freshman girl from TriDelt and whispering something that made her nervous laugh, she made up her mind. Um, they were exclusive, what the Prada was he doing?

It wasn't the first time she'd seen him flirt with others, but she'd always brushed it off. Greg was flirty.

Greg wouldn't cheat on her.

Greg's parents and her parents loved each other so much.

Her mom had told her that she needed to hold on to Greg. That he was the one. That they approved of her marrying him.

Greg wouldn't hurt anyone.

And then she'd found photos of herself on his phone. Naked. Unconscious. Splayed out like a freaking Thanksgiving feast.

She'd confronted him.

He threatened to let the photos out. She'd been shocked, devastated, sick for a week until Brooklyn had scooped her up off the bathroom floor and demanded to know what was wrong. When Annabelle told her about the photos, she expected a backlash from her friend, but all she'd gotten was a huge hug and a confession. Brooklyn had photos like that out there. And she'd brought up the OnlyFans page, showing her pictures of her feet and other things.

"He can only hold it over your head if you let him," Brooklyn had said. "And no man should have that power over you."

After that, Annabelle hadn't felt so alone, so ashamed—well, until she tried to talk to her mother about it. Lily Walker had blamed Annabelle for letting herself get into a situation like that. And then told her she better not get herself into "trouble" and humiliate their entire family.

So, yeah, the idea had come to her last night at the football game. To steal the prized diamond elephant that they all thought was so important. She was going to break the thing apart, and it was going to feel so good.

The most important thing she'd ever taken.

The most important thing to the people who didn't protect her—money. Reputation. She was going to ruin it for them.

Getting the keys to enter the stadium and locker rooms hadn't been hard. After all, she was really good at taking things.

The biggest problem for Annabelle was the security guards and cameras.

As for the guards, that's where sisters came in handy. She dared a few of the pledges to make a distraction under the pretense of winning this week's challenge. She also warned them off from talking to anyone about it. That was against the rules. And she may or may not have alluded to having access to the Spill Book and their secrets.

So right about now on the north side of the stadium, four of her pledges were having a mid-afternoon wet T-shirt contest—surrounded by students who came to watch, of course—and the security guards wouldn't be able to look away. They wouldn't even notice her, especially when she snuck in wearing a janitor's uniform—another thing she'd easily swiped. And when they eventually reviewed the tape, they'd see a janitor with a Greg Hamm face mask.

In broad daylight, she snuck right into the men's locker room. Rubbed Paul "Bear" Bryant's iron nose on the plaque like the players did for good luck, and then walked up to the elephant's glass case. Nearly a foot tall and a foot wide, the elephant stood on all four legs. The entire body was made from platinum and diamonds. His trunk was curled upward as he trumpeted. On the side, a ruby-encrusted *A*. Annabelle swallowed around her dry throat. She was really doing this.

Protected only by shatterproof glass, and a key lock—how stupid were they?—inside the men's locker room. No camera in here.

The lock was easy to pick, and she lifted the glass. Because she'd tricked Greg into letting her give him a BJ inside the locker room when she was scoping it out, she knew there was no alarm. Which was so stupid. This elephant was worth at least twenty-five mil.

Her pulse raced, lips tingling. This was a bigger thrill than even Bid Day.

Reverently, she slid her hands over what had to be more than six thousand diamonds. But there wasn't time to admire the craftsmanship, or the sheer opulence of it. Then she slipped the diamond elephant into the trash can she was pushing around, making sure to hide it with garbage.

In its place, she left an elephant made out of towels, just the way they left them on the beds of the hotels her family owned. *How's that for an F-U, Mommy?*

Annabelle wheeled the trash can to the back door, keeping her head down as a coach walked past and mumbled a hello on his way out. Nobody ever looked the help in the eyes. Proved easily just now as she stood there, millions of dollars in the trash in front of her. Part of her wanted to get caught. To see the look on her mother's face when she saw what she'd done.

But what would feel better was to flaunt it in her mother's face every time she saw her. To know what happened and her mother be clueless. For once, Annabelle wanted to hold all the power.

Annabelle slipped into the stairwell where she'd left her backpack. If she was lucky, no one would be the wiser of what she'd done for hours. She'd been tracking the comings and goings, the maintenance schedules. She shucked off the janitor's coveralls, wrapping the elephant with the grungy material, and then stuffed them both in her bag and hauled its heavy weight onto her shoulders.

Down the stairs she went to the emergency exit where her girls were. Before she opened the door, she dumped a bottle of water on her own white T-shirt. Then busted out the door pretending like she was part of the whole thing.

Thirty seconds later, she gave the signal, and they took off running, the heist of Bama history, the trick of her life, almost complete.

She'd never felt better.

Annabelle hopped onto an electric bike and took off down the street toward her sorority house. Brooklyn was at a soccer team event, and wouldn't be home until the morning, because after the game she had plans to go to her boyfriend's place—and Annabelle had watched her pack a bag. They'd been humping like bunnies, and if he snuck through the window one more time, Annabelle was going to lose it.

She locked her bedroom door, hands shaking, and took out the tools she'd been collecting from a bin beneath her bed.

Pliers—*check*.

Magnifying visor—*check*.

Wire cutters—*check*.

Her entire body vibrated as adrenaline pumped through, and she had to take a moment to just breathe in normally. When she didn't calm, she lay down on the ground, staring at the ceiling.

"Get it together. You didn't just steal twenty-five million dollars' worth of diamonds to muck it up at the end." The pep talk didn't really help. The only thing that was going to push her past this adrenaline high was to get to work.

Annabelle laid a soft velvet mat down on her desk and sat the glittering elephant in the center, where she swore it winked at her. She blinked. *Get it the fudge together, Annabelle!*

With a deep breath, she pulled on her visor, the diamonds magnifying. No doubt each diamond and ruby on the elephant had been registered, an identification number laser cut into each. And if she were selling them to a normal jewelry store, they would absolutely be able to identify each one if they looked.

Annabelle may be new to this particular task, but she wasn't an amateur. She'd done her homework. A black-market professional could remove the etchings, and honestly, it was up to those who'd bid on the diamonds to ensure for themselves that they couldn't be traced.

The pliers shook in her left hand; the wire cutters trembled in her right. As she brought them closer to the elephant, the shaking subsided, as if the work itself was what calmed her. Being ambidextrous was going to help her with speed. Using the pliers, she pulled each prong apart, cutting when she needed to, and set aside the loosened diamonds.

Every second that ticked by was a test of her endurance. Every second bringing her closer to either jail or freedom.

"Sugar cookies."

Footsteps outside the door had her slamming her visor up, dropping her tools, and rushing to the door. Though the footsteps passed, the racing of her heart did not ease. So far, she'd cleared only the trunk of diamonds. At this pace it was going to take her a week to finish the job.

Annabelle turned her back on the door, but voices on the other side pushed her into a panic. The lock wasn't enough. Anyone with a key could burst in here at any moment.

Her hip bounced into Brooklyn's chair as she whirled in a circle trying to figure out how to secure the door. Perfect. A chair under the door handle for good measure. And she stopped herself from pushing a dresser in front of the door, the noise of which would only bring curious people to her room.

Feeling safer, she sat back at her desk, put her visor back in place, and picked up the pliers. The sense of calm she'd felt before her momentary panic returned, and she again started to pry apart the prongs, setting the ten-carat marquise-shaped diamond eyes aside. They were worth nearly half a mil each, and the biggest diamonds on the elephant. The trunk and ears were much smaller, hundreds of quarter carats. The toenails on the elephant's feet were made of four rounded carats each. As she plucked apart the masterpiece, she couldn't help but admire the craftmanship that went into such a magnificent trophy.

A few hours into her project, with only the head an empty carcass, she covered it up, locked her door, and took a break to show her face downstairs, swiping a salad and an energy drink. Taylor eyed her oddly but didn't follow her as she made her way back upstairs to finish the job.

And thank God too, because this was going to take all night. Visor on, energy drink drained, she settled in for the hours it would take to complete.

Finally, at nearly five in the morning, the elephant was a mangled mess of platinum with a pile of sparkling jewels next to it. She dropped the pliers and wire cutters, her hands cramping from hours of use.

Despite her discomfort, Annabelle grinned at the mess. Her first major heist. The rush of adrenaline coursing through her was better than any high—not that she did drugs often, but she'd taken Taylor up a few times on a bumblebee.

She wrapped the mangled metal in a towel and put it in a trash bag to be deposited in a random dumpster on campus later. As it was worth several thousands of dollars alone, she'd considered having it melted down, but decided it wasn't worth the risk.

The larger jewels she wrapped up to be sold on the underground page she'd started a few weeks ago in anticipation. Others were clustered in carat count and bagged. Though she'd heard her parents say that the elephant had cost twenty-five million, Annabelle was hoping to bag just half that amount. Still worth it.

Maybe she could become a fence—easier than being a thief, that was for sure. She could buy stolen jewelry and break up then resell it.

Just as she was lying down to get at least a couple hours of a nap before class, her phone blew up as the warning bells announced there'd been a robbery on campus. At first everyone thought it was an armed robbery of a student. But Annabelle knew the truth. She slid back the false wall in her closet that she'd put in when Brooklyn was at practice a few weeks ago, storing the broken pieces of Greg's and her parents' legacy.

Less than a week later, with an account brimming with cash, she stepped into a small jewelry shop a few towns over.

She found exactly what she was looking for. A platinum chain with an amethyst at its center. "This one please."

She paid cash. And by the next morning, she'd replaced the amethyst with the single diamond she'd kept from her heist. The amethyst she had made into a ring, and presented it to their house mother for her birthday a week later.

The elephant had seemingly vanished without a trace. A mystery to never be solved.

"Why do you keep smiling?" Taylor asked her, eyes narrowed as they finished a sisterhood meeting.

"Is a girl not allowed to be happy?"

Taylor focused on the diamond Annabelle had a habit of touching quite a lot—she should probably calm down with that.

"Where'd you get the necklace?"

Annabelle sighed, and smiled. "My parents."

Part V

BID DAY
Sisters for Life

CHAPTER FIFTY-SEVEN

Drew is the first guy my own age I've ever kissed . . . and you know . . . slept with. He's also the best I've ever had. I can't decide if that's lame or not.

Kisses,
Brooklyn

Taylor

Now

"You're getting a divorce?" Annabelle's hands were flat on the table in Brooklyn's hotel suite, her knuckles white as she stared at her mother. "And you didn't think to tell me?"

Lily Walker sat stoically straight, her face full of righteousness.

Guilt at Annabelle's hurt made Taylor's stomach clench. The news had been a shock to Annabelle, and really, from the revelations they'd had this week, Annabelle could use a break.

Confronting Lily about her marriage wasn't the reason they'd invited her here, and to be honest Taylor was surprised she'd even shown up. But the bait had been too good to resist—a meeting of the sisters that Lily would preside over. Almost too easy, really. She marched into the room as if she owned it, some of the bravado dwindling as she took in the scene and sank into a chair.

"Divorce happens, Anna, don't be such a Pollyanna." Lily flicked her bleach-blond hair over one shoulder. Then glanced toward

Brooklyn, disgust in her eyes. "Where is everyone? I thought I was coming for an alumni event, not an inquisition."

"They aren't coming," Asana informed her in that cool, badass way of hers that Taylor admired.

Lily started to stand.

"Mom, why would you do this to me? To us?" Annabelle had tears brimming in her eyes.

"I already explained my reasons." Lily's gaze slid again toward Brooklyn as if the answer lay there with Ginger Mommy.

"Why do you keep looking at her like that?" Taylor wasn't one to beat around the bush, and it was obvious Lily had something she wanted to say to Brooklyn, or about her at least.

Lily's lip curled, transforming her face into something ugly, vindictive. "You, you little slut, sleeping with older, married men. You ought to be ashamed of yourself."

"I assume you're referring to my sugar baby days, since I'm not currently sleeping with anyone but my husband." Brooklyn smiled, shaking her head as if Lily were one of her toddlers throwing a tantrum. "I'm not ashamed of my past. It was all consensual. And from what I hear, you aren't any better."

Annabelle shifted her gaze toward Lily. "Is *he* why you're getting a divorce?"

Lily's gaze found Asana's. "No. He came after. Turns out my husband had a thing for matinees."

Asana's chin notched up. "I told you I could make his life hell. When did you find out?"

"Find out what?" Taylor asked. This conversation had taken a decided turn down Cryptic Lane, and Taylor hated being left out of the loop.

"Maggie told me." Lily smoothed a hand down her cream-colored slacks. "She knows a lot about you, Asana."

"Yes, please enlighten us." Annabelle's normal plucky voice had an edge to it that bordered on hysteria.

"Matinee?" Brooklyn whispered, her eyes scanning the room as if she'd heard of something like this before.

"Like a show?" Annabelle's exasperation was clearly growing. "Who cares about a bleeping show!"

Asana let out a sigh, sliding a patient gaze toward Annabelle. "It's a website for people who want to have an affair. My website."

Taylor wasn't sure if she should laugh or rail against Asana, who'd always joked in college that marriage was an institution people needed to be freed from. Never in a million years would she have guessed Asana would create a space to do just that.

"You're a homewrecker," Lily said. "And so are you." She turned her gaze on Brooklyn. "My Mark was happily wed before you were in the picture."

"Mark?" Brooklyn frowned, then her eyes lit up. "Oh wow. You're having an affair with one of my daddies?" She started to laugh. "And he's Larissa's real daddy too?"

"Just how many of our sisters' daddies did you sleep with?" Taylor asked. "That's two in one week from what we've found out."

Brooklyn smirked. "Enough of them."

"And you have no remorse." Lily was growing more agitated by the second.

"A girl had to do what a girl had to do." She shrugged. "I can't change my past. If my circumstances had been different, would I have done something different? Maybe. But you, Lily, I would suggest a different type of man altogether. Your tastes seem to be for lovers with a roving eye."

"How dare you?" Lily stomped her foot like an angry child, her knee bouncing against the table, causing her to cry out.

Annabelle stood, reached for her mother, touching her arm. "Mom, we didn't invite you here to insult you or place judgment; we just need to know why you would go so far with the Spill Book? Risk so much?"

"I could ask you the same thing, Anna." Lily's eyes dipped to the diamond at Annabelle's throat—the one the little thief had taken from the elephant trophy.

Taylor smiled, proud of Annabelle for wearing her trophy like a mocking F-U to her mother.

"Did you tell Maggie to blackmail us?" Taylor asked, pulling the conversation away from personal hurts and back to the subject at hand.

"Blackmail?" Lily shook her head slightly, appearing genuinely surprised. "Of course not. I only contacted her as a journalist to see if she was interested in doing a piece."

"A piece on our Spill Book—that could expose all of us?" Taylor asked.

"No." Lily licked her lips, nervous. "I told her to keep your names out of it. That it should be a piece exposing the dark sides of sororities in the past and how in current times, we are eradicating all that bad behavior to preserve the sanctity of sisterhood."

"But don't you see," Taylor said, smiling sadly, "you did the opposite. You gave matches to the woman with a stick of dynamite."

THERE WAS SOMETHING primal about flames. The heat drawing a human closer. The dancing orange and blue licking at the air mesmerizing, entrancing.

Fires could be good.

Fires could be bad.

For Taylor, in this particular moment, it felt a little bit like both. It was nearly one in the morning of Bid Day. In eight hours, the PNMs would open their envelopes and find out which sorority had picked them. They would scream, hug, cry, and then they'd start running.

Taylor clicked the lighter, holding the tiny orange flame to the bottom corner of the Spill Book.

The book that had started it all, and nearly ended it all too.

The flames caught, greedy as they ate their way up the cover. She was outside the hotel, in the back by the dumpster, not wanting to set off the alarms inside by doing it in her tub. As the heat encased the book, nearly reaching her fingers where she held it at the top, she dropped it to the ground, watching it burn. She should have her friends here with her. Let them be a part of this, but the urgency to get it done had been too overwhelming.

Maybe she should have let it burn five years ago.

Maybe she should have never even opened its pages and demanded the secrets of her sisters.

Taylor wasn't really one to think about should have, would have, could have. She was a woman of action. A woman who'd always walked to the beat of her own drum, and decided what that beat was. Not following the music. She *was* the music.

She glanced behind her at a noise, hoping at this hour she wasn't asking for attention or trouble. The only people that stood behind hotels by dumpsters in the middle of the night were the cleaning crew, the homeless, and the ones up to no good.

A cat ran by, giving a little warning mewl in her direction.

Taylor considered herself to be the cleaning crew for the Spill Book mess.

There'd be a whole different mess to clean up when she got home. As soon as Elijah realized she couldn't have children, he'd ask for a divorce. Or maybe an annulment. She'd be like one of Henry VIII's wives, scorned for not giving him a son, and the people would applaud him for discarding her—even the women. That was perhaps the saddest part of all, that even women who experienced her own plight would side with her husband. Because among Elijah's conservative set, a woman's place was on the delivery table.

For the longest time, she'd thought that's where she wanted to be, or at least where she should want to be. But this week, the reminders of who she was, who she'd thought she'd become, had been overwhelming in pointing out the wrong turns she'd made.

The Spill Book tremored as the flames grew, turning the pages to black. It popped, as if the flames themselves belched in their greedy hunger to consume.

For a split second, she almost stamped out the fire. There was more than a small part of herself that wanted to preserve those secrets. That was part of the reason she'd put them in the time capsule. It wasn't all scandal in there; some of the secrets spilled spoke of strength, of perseverance, of sticking it to whoever the oppressor was. All the women in her lives, the ones who'd documented their college years, their past confessions, in that sparkly pile of scorched memory, were incredible, no matter what.

Taylor took a step back from the burning book, realizing that if she didn't put enough distance, she'd likely stamp it out. Out of preservation.

Out of respect for their pasts, and the need to share what they'd overcome, what they'd done.

Some memories were worth keeping.

But these weren't her memories. Not all of them anyway.

And if someone had already been willing to exploit them, chances were someone would do it again. And again.

There was a click of heels on the pavement, and this time Taylor knew it wasn't a cat. She whirled around, reaching for the mace she kept in her purse, only to see Asana standing there. She was stunning as always. Sharp and hard and beautiful.

"What are you doing?" Asana's eyes cast down to the tiny pile of ash and the slowly dying fire. "You didn't wait for me."

"Putting the past to rest couldn't wait."

Asana cocked her head, glancing up. "You know burning the Spill Book isn't going to change the past."

Taylor shrugged.

"Burning that book won't erase our memories," Asana said. "It only makes it so people can't read them in the future."

"These aren't my memories to share."

Asana stared at her, nodding slowly. "But some of them were."

Taylor swallowed around the lump in her throat. Every time she looked at Asana, she felt everything. Every hard memory she had, Asana had been there for. And every beautiful one too. "Do you still hate me?"

Asana's heels clicked as she moved closer. "I never hated you."

Taylor shifted her eyes to the burning book. "I'm going to leave Elijah." Before now, she hadn't realized that was what she was going to do. Before now, her fate had been tied to Elijah's decision. Before now, the loss of her husband had not been her choice.

"Why?"

"He doesn't want *me*. He wants the woman he wanted me to be." Saying it aloud lifted some of the weight, the pressure, of what she'd forced herself into the last few years. "I lose who I am when I'm with him."

"Elijah's an idiot," Asana said. "He knew who you were when he married you."

"Maybe he thought he could change me." She shrugged. "And I let him."

"And he won't accept you for who you really are?"

Taylor shook her head, flicking her gaze toward Asana. "No. And I can't be the one he wants. I don't want to be the one he wants." Why would she keep pretending? Keep burying herself behind him when what she wanted was to be the one on top?

"Do you love him?"

"I used to. When we met, he was incredible, kind, generous, intelligent . . . but he wants a wholesome wife, not one with ambition. One who will give him kids. Support his dreams, but have none of her own."

Asana sighed. "Then you're making the right decision. What do you think he will say?"

Taylor laughed. "Everything he says is written out in a speech he practices over and over. One-liners he just gives out at the drop of a hat. Do you think he'll have one for me saying I'm leaving him?"

"Maybe he'll surprise you. Say he wants you to be yourself."

Taylor shook her head. "Elijah hates surprises."

Asana's fingers drummed on her arms where she'd crossed them. "Then I think you have your answer. The Taylor I used to know dominates, not the other way around."

"And I'm ready to be myself again."

Taylor nodded, watching as the last of the flames died down. She pulled the tiny broom and dustpan from her large over-the-shoulder bag, sweeping the remnants up, and then depositing them into a ziplock.

"What are you doing with those? Looks like you're about to scatter ashes."

Taylor flashed a conspiratorial smile. "I am."

"Really? Where?"

"I haven't decided yet. But it feels like these memories deserve to be laid to rest properly."

Asana uncrossed her arms and gave Taylor's shoulders a little squeeze. "I agree. Want some help?"

"I'd love for you to come with me."

"Your car or mine?" Asana asked.

"Yours includes two guards."

"It does."

"Let's take mine. As hot as Guard One and Guard Two are, this feels like it needs to be just an us moment." Taylor glanced up at the hotel. "Or maybe we should get Brooklyn and Annabelle too. Bury it all for good, together."

CHAPTER FIFTY-EIGHT

I stole the Spill Book. I made a copy of it and put it back. Just kidding. Wanted to see if you were reading, Tay.

Kisses,
Annabelle

Asana

Then

"Fake it until you make it" was a motto Asana had heard often. But it wasn't something she'd ever had to ascribe to.

She was rich.

She was beautiful.

She was smart.

She was savvy.

But today, those attributes didn't mean jack, when it came to trying to convince Taylor their being together wasn't a cataclysmic event to their social lives. Or when she was about to take down the Machine. The coup of the century.

Well, not really the century. There'd been the time in the early 1990s when the SGA had been essentially shut down after allegations of harassment, assault. One person running for president even burned a cross in an opponent's yard—literally, what the fuck is up with that? Taking away their power helped.

Asana hated that this small subset of white, male assholes was able to just rule the school, rule the city, the county, the state, and eventually planned to rule the nation and the world. The Mach board worked closely with the alumnus members, taking instruction on what to do and when to do it. Even a Duke couldn't do that. Though she'd had plenty of people in her ancestry line that had tried. And to be honest, Asana was bent on domination herself.

And not just in the bedroom or at clubs, though she loved to give a guy on all fours a good spanking.

Despite the warmth of the evening, a chill swept over her skin as she reached for the door knocker to the Greek house on campus where the Machine had started taking their meetings secretly, and a few elite members were allowed to live. But tonight's clandestine assembly wasn't typical. Tonight was hedonism at its finest.

Just past midnight, she was draped in a black cloak with nothing underneath. Covering her face was a masquerade mask. Rather than the pink she used for an ADL swap, she opted for light blue covered in rhinestones and feathers.

Bang. Bang. Bang.

The door knocker echoed in the night, and she blew out a breath to try and calm her nerves.

On her way here, passing through the quad she'd caught sight of two figures chatting, the way their hands moved familiar. She'd squinted into the dark, second-guessing what her gut said—that was Brooklyn and Taylor. And then had freaked out that maybe they were coming to this party. That her friends were going to get caught up in the mess she was about to create.

The door opened. A man dressed like a butler with a black plague mask covering his face greeted her. "Password."

"I.D.G.A.F." Asana rolled her eyes at the stupid password Greg had chosen. But also, how ironic.

The butler took her cloak and stepped aside, and she entered the house fully naked, the lights dimmed low, soft, heart-pulsing music playing. Every inch of sparsely covered furniture was covered in writhing bodies, naked except for their masks. Mattresses and pillows littered the floors along with more bodies.

This was a sex party. A celebration at the end of exams. But it wasn't just Mach members present. No. Asana had made sure there were more guests on the list than expected. Powerful men were here. Powerful women too.

Growing up a Duke, working for Duke Corp, and listening in on Duke Corp conversations had trained her for exactly how to handle matters, and how to exploit people and situations. And how to take down an enemy.

No one knew what she'd done. How she'd found out about a local massage shop that was rumored to have women working there that were human trafficked. How she'd hired them to give "massages" to the Machine's actives and alumni at this party. Why not kill two birds with one stone? And to add a little icing on her annihilation cake, she'd asked Taylor for enough anti-roofies and bumblebees to make sure someone was arrested.

In a few minutes she was going to call in a tip anonymously from the landline that still existed in this house. Afterward, she'd get the hell out. But in the meantime, she had to be known. Despite the masks, their voices could be recognized, and she needed people to know she'd been here to take the heat off her when the Feds arrived.

Masks were good at covering faces—and made it hard to remember people, if you didn't know them. Strangers would always remain strangers. But Asana had made a life, and would have a future career, in recognizing people. Their mannerisms, their eyes, their body language, their shape.

She easily found Greg, fucking a woman bent over the pool

table. By the moans, she could tell that at least this one was conscious and willing. Rare for Greg. She passed him by, looking for Jared, who was never too far from his leader—and she was right. Jared lounged on a leather chair a few feet away. Watching.

Asana sauntered close, his eyes turning toward her. She indicated where Greg was pounding away. "Like what you see?" She straddled Jared, his erection hard against her.

Even harder was her ability not to shudder.

"Yeah," he groaned, hands slipping over her hips.

"Want to bend me over?" she asked.

"Yes," he croaked.

"Or maybe this instead? So, you can watch?" She gripped his thin cock, running her fingers up and down, disappointed because if she was going to fuck a guy for revenge, he could at least make it worth her while. Oh well. She plucked a condom from the bowl beside him, her breasts pushing against his face.

He ran his dry tongue over her skin, and she grimaced behind her mask. Gross.

"Put it on," she said, and he listened, surprisingly, taking the condom and tearing the foil wrapper.

Asana lifted her hips, taking him inside—which took serious concentration to determine if he was, in fact, inside, given the lack of girth—and rode him as he watched Greg. She whispered in his ear, "Do you recognize my voice?"

Jared shook his head and she laughed. "Yes, you do."

"Asa—"

"Shh, don't say it. This is an anonymous party." But now that he knew who she was, Asana stopped talking and rode him hard, grinding her hips against his, bouncing, gripping his shoulders like it was the ride of her life. And to at least get something out of it, she slid her fingers between their bodies, circling her clit until she got off.

Jared, clearly obsessed with Greg, watched him the entire time until he grunted as he came nearly in unison with his friend.

What an asshole.

Asana slid off Jared's lap, leaving him with the soggy condom, and walked away, disgusted with him and what this whole place represented.

Time to make a phone call.

Asana slipped through the house, passing the gyrating bodies, noting the servers, the few giving massages, glad she was going to be helping them out as she took down this mess.

But as she rounded the corner to enter the office where the phone was, she practically ran into another naked woman. Instantly, she recognized her as Maggie. But Maggie didn't seem to recognize her, as she smiled beneath the half mask and pushed Asana against the wall.

"Where are you going?" Maggie pressed her body to Asana's.

Maggie pressed her well-built, soft body to Asana's. Her nipples brushed over Asana's breasts, and she shivered. The last girl she'd slept with was Taylor—who had firmly put distance between them lately. Maybe the phone call could wait a few minutes.

"Right here," Asana said, technically not a lie.

"Good answer." Maggie dropped to her knees in front of Asana, pressing her lips to her navel, and then lower, her tongue sliding into the right spot.

Asana cried out, and Maggie stopped. "Is this okay?"

Was it okay? Maggie wasn't Taylor. Just thinking about her made the ice around her heart crack in a painful fracture. But Taylor didn't want her. And this was just sex. Pleasure to ease away the pain.

"Yes," she breathed. "Yes."

Maggie gripped the back of Asana's thigh with one hand, the other caressing between her legs, a finger, then two, sliding inside her as she licked. This was not a side of Maggie Asana would have ever guessed existed.

But wearing masks provided an anonymity that allowed people to do things they might not have ordinarily. Asana threaded her fingers into Maggie's hair, crying out as she came, back pressed against the wall. And then she returned the favor, Maggie's leg over her shoulder.

When she was done, she stood up, meeting Maggie's eyes. "Go home."

"What?" Maggie shook her head. "I know who you are."

Asana ground her teeth. "You need to go home. Now." And then she walked toward the office to make the call.

The dean of the university was going to freak out.

She wasn't just exposing the Machine's bad behavior and pointing fingers.

Oh, no, she'd gone deeper. Found out dirt on every single person and used it against them when planning her attack. There were perks to being friends with Taylor and having access to the Spill Book.

Greg Hamm and the entire arrogant group was going down.

Like clockwork, the next morning, actually less time than she thought, Asana heard the first mumblings of chaos. Then Dean Hooper made an announcement. Then came the secret invitation to the Machine meeting.

Asana grinned with glee when she got there, and Greg Hamm was nowhere to be seen.

Jared cleared his throat. "I assume you all heard about what happened last night. I was one of the fortunate few to escape arrest." He glanced at Maggie, who had clearly warned him. "But it appears our distinguished president has been called to a meeting with the dean."

CHAPTER FIFTY-NINE

Have you ever seen a big baby cry? I have. Greg Hamm caught crying in front of a judge. And I'll take a bow for that act, because I'm the one who put him there.

*Kisses,
Asana*

Annabelle

Now

For more than a minute, Annabelle thought about having the diamond elephant remade. Reparations for what she'd stolen.

Needing a distraction from her constant internet searching of her husband's name—and coming up empty of anything having to do with the FBI—she scoured the black market for diamonds and rubies to create the elephant. But as she'd looked into having the metal frame created using a 3D printer, she'd changed her mind.

Why would she have that stupid elephant remade? For a moment, she'd let guilt muddle her brain. Any minute, their lives and their families' lives were going to be disrupted. Returning the elephant her parents and Greg's parents cared so much about seemed like a half-cookie way to make things better. That elephant represented everything that held her back. That elephant felt almost like it was ruling her life. Of course that was silly. It was just a pile of metal and gems.

But even objects held power over people. Statues, pyramids, the cross.

For her, it was the stupid elephant.

At nearly two in the morning, she closed her laptop, determined to forget about the elephant trophy, her husband, the FBI. To try to sleep even though her life was about to change. But maybe, just like it had nine years ago, Bid Day would free her from the metaphorical, and physical, prison she'd put herself in.

A pile of white-and-black confetti covered the bed beside her laptop—the result of the copied Spill Book and fun with scissors.

Her cell phone buzzed, and she half expected it to be Greg threatening and railing for turning him in. A tremble shook her hand as she reached for the cell.

A shudder of relief went through her at seeing Taylor's name flashed on the screen. For a split second she wished she'd allowed her phone to show a preview of her text messages, but she'd always been private, especially since some of her texts were not exactly sharing legal information.

Annabelle swiped on Taylor's name, her phone's facial recognition opening up the text.

> **TAYLOR:** You awake?

> **ANNABELLE:** Depends.

> **TAYLOR:** Want to attend a funeral?

> **ANNABELLE:** Who died?

> **TAYLOR:** Our secrets.

> **ANNABELLE:** Be down in five.

Stowing her laptop, she pulled on a jacket. The middle of the night was always a little chilly, even if it was summer. Had Taylor found out about Annabelle's trip to the FBI field office?

In the lobby, Brooklyn waited with Asana and Taylor, who was holding a bag of ashes.

"What's that?"

"The Spill Book."

Annabelle's eyes widened and she glanced up at Taylor. "Well, I'll be Prada'd. We really are attending a funeral."

Taylor grinned. "I think it's time we bury this bitch now and forever."

"She was fun while she lasted."

"So many memories."

Annabelle bit her lip. "Guys . . . I'm so sorry about my mom."

"You aren't responsible for your mother's actions," Taylor said.

Annabelle nodded, still prepared to not speak with her mother for a long time—and to be honest, the prospect had been as freeing as laying her guilt aside about that shiny, stupid elephant.

"Let's go."

They climbed into Taylor's car in the hotel's garage and headed out onto the quiet, mostly empty Tuscaloosa streets.

"I still can't believe how many people wanted revenge for the Spill Book." Annabelle frowned.

Taylor met her eyes in the rearview mirror. "Same, but"—she grinned—"this entire week with you guys has brought us back together. And so I've decided to be grateful to crazy Larissa, your mom. And, well, Lana, I still think she broke girl code. Maggie, however, can go to hell."

"I'm not really inclined to judge Lana, considering we all broke codes," Brooklyn said.

"Well, you do you," Taylor sniped, but then she softened by saying, "I love you for it."

"I love you too. Maggie, however, what are we doing about her?" Brooklyn made an "ew" face.

"I've set up a time to chat with her tomorrow morning," Asana said matter-of-factly. "We won't have to deal with her for long."

"So, where are we burying her?" Annabelle asked.

"Maggie?" Taylor sucked in an ooh-are-we-going-there breath.

"No," Annabelle drawled out. "What's left of the Spill Book."

"I was thinking at the house. Where she was supposed to be buried for another ninety-five years."

Annabelle skimmed her fingers over the seat belt where it rested on her chest, tugging it where it felt tight, only to realize it was just tightness in her body in general. "Good idea."

Magnolia was lit only by streetlamps. All the houses were supposed to be fast asleep since the culmination of Rush Week was about to come to a glorious end today—Bid Day. Though to be fair most of the PNMs and actives wouldn't be sleeping. Too much excitement in their veins. Lives were going to change today.

The four of them had stayed late tonight at ADL, helping decorate for the parties—but apparently none of them had been able to sleep anyway.

Taylor turned off her lights as she drove. "I don't want to wake anyone up."

"Feels so clandestine," Brooklyn said with a laugh. "The perfect ending for this fucked-up week."

Taylor parked on the side of the road, and as Annabelle climbed out of the car, she recalled a night more than a decade ago when she'd seen a figure scrambling across campus, and had a very huge sense of déjà vu.

"I feel like we've done this before. Sneaking around campus in the middle of the night."

Brooklyn and Taylor stared at each other. "Maybe we have," Taylor said.

Asana laughed. "I definitely have."

A light went on in a house across the street, and sent them scrambling for the dark shadows along the side of the ADL house.

"They probably have a Ring camera or something," Taylor whispered.

"I'm sure they do. Let's hurry." Annabelle guided the way to the backyard of the property, past the garden terrace, and into the grassy pathway that led toward where they'd originally buried the capsule.

"Should I just sprinkle her like fairy dust?" Taylor asked, staring into the hole where the capsule would be put back later today when the sun had risen and the girls had made a run for their houses.

"Let's each dump some of it," Asana suggested. "This is a decision we're making together. To bury the truths, the lies, the hurts."

Taylor and Asana made eye contact, and Annabelle felt her face burn for what she'd seen in the dark just a few nights ago.

"What happens with an ADL sister stays with an ADL sister," Taylor said. "No more Spill Books."

"Just honesty between us."

"No matter what."

Taylor took out a handful of ash. A slight breeze blew the remnants from her open palm—and right at Asana, who sputtered.

"Ohmygod, it's in my mouth."

"At least it's just a notebook and not a person. When we spread my grandma, she got in my mouth. And now . . . I carry her with me always," Brooklyn said.

"That's disgusting," Annabelle said with a laugh.

They each in turn grabbed a handful, and were careful to let it sprinkle away from the others, until the bag was empty. In the illumination of the moon, and the security spotlights of the ADL house, the ashes shifted and swayed with the evening's gentle breeze, scattering until there was nothing left but a memory of their existence.

Annabelle felt scattered herself. Like she was the ashes, and what was happening behind the scenes in her "real life" was just as fleeting and dissolved.

"I feel better . . ." Taylor shook out her legs and arms, rolled her neck. "I don't know, somehow lighter."

"Me too," Asana said, mimicking the motions.

A light went on in the house, casting their bodies in long shadows on the lawn, and they froze, staring at one another. "Time to skedaddle."

"Wait." Brooklyn turned to stare at Taylor. "I have one last secret I need to share. The reason I didn't come to your wedding."

Taylor glanced back toward the house, where another light had just flashed on. "Okay."

"Elijah . . . He used to be . . ."

Taylor flicked her gaze back to Brooklyn, but there was something about her expression, a knowing that caught Annabelle's attention. *Oh, mother-of-pearl . . .*

"I know, Brookie." Taylor's voice was tight, sprinkled with guilt like one of her special cupcakes. "It's how I met him."

"What?" Brooklyn's stance faltered, as if Taylor's confession alone had knocked her back a step.

"Do tell." Asana's intrigue mirrored Annabelle's.

The lock on the back door unlatched loud enough to echo through the night, and the four of them ran back to the car. Safely inside, the engine purring to life, Taylor continued. "I followed you one night, saw you with him. I'd read your entries, remember?"

"Yeah."

"I'm not usually one for sloppy seconds, but after Brad and I broke up, and, well, you know what happened at the frat party. Well, I thought I'd try someone that could get me somewhere in my future. Elijah fit the bill." Taylor sighed heavily. "But I was wrong. So another confession, I'm going to ask for a divorce."

CHAPTER SIXTY

I can't decide if secretly dating an older man means I have daddy issues or that I'm just a really old soul who is done with college frat-heads.

Kisses,
Taylor

Brooklyn

Then

Bid Day never got old.

The anticipation of Brooklyn's first run four years ago was no different from now, in her senior year, when she volunteered to run with the new ADL pledges. She bounced on her toes, a smile splitting her face as Lily Walker held the bullhorn and did the countdown from five like she did every year.

The crinkle of envelope paper echoed in the stadium, as PNMs' hands shook with the anticipation and excitement of tearing into their Bid Day acceptance letters once Lily got to zero.

The screaming and cheering and stomping that was to follow as PNMs found out which sororities had chosen them was likely enough to set off a seismic event. Just like that Taylor Swift concert.

Brooklyn cheered just as loud, holding her ADL sign up in the air, ready to lead the run to the house on Magnolia. Fourth time around, and she still had goosebumps.

Lily told the girls through the bullhorn to find their active leader, and Brooklyn waved her arms, the sparkling sign catching the sun. Girls ran toward her, tears in their eyes, smiles so wide they showed all their teeth. Dressed in tank tops and shorts, their running shoes tied, with tanned skin, makeup on point, hair adorable. They were ready for the sisterhood.

"Alpha Delta Lambda!" Brooklyn chanted. "Sisters for life!"

The line of young women repeated her call, jumping up and down.

"Let's go home," Brooklyn shouted, turning her back on the line. She held the sign in the air and took off running. She'd broken records for speed on the soccer field, but this was no time for putting on the jets. Instead, she kept a leisurely pace, not wanting to leave a single sister behind. Not that a fast pace would have been possible given the crush.

Through the crammed stadium doors they went, and she turned around, jogging backward, holding the sign, and making sure her little ducklings followed in line.

They made their way down the road, taking the same turns she'd taken four years prior, until they crossed that invisible finish line in front of the ADL house on Magnolia. The actives who'd been waiting for them with balloons and confetti called out a chant of welcome.

"A-L-P-H-A, D-E-L-T-and-A, L-A-M-B-and-D-and-A! Boom, boom, we welcome you to boom, boom, ADL sisters for life. *Hey*—ADL sister! *You*—chose ADL—and we chose you! Alpha Delta Lambda! Alpha Delta Lambda! ADL for life!"

"Welcome home, sisters." Brooklyn dropped the sign in the yard and started to hug the new pledges around her.

Annabelle, Taylor, and Asana ran up to Brooklyn, high-fiving her, and then hugging the new pledges too. True to form, Annabelle handed out packets of tissues, and Taylor helped to fix lines of running mascara from happy tears.

"This never gets old." Brooklyn grinned, holding up her phone to make a short TikTok of all the excitement, the beautiful colors and celebration.

"Hey, y'all, Brooklyn in Bama here! It's Bid Day! One of my favorite days of the year. I'm here with all my ADL girls, and we're celebrating gaining a whole bunch of new sisters." She turned in a circle, the confetti sparkling in the sun. "Isn't this so fun? Well, I'm off to celebrate, but wanted to give you a little sneak peek. For all you alumni out there, once a sister, always a sister. For the rest of you, what happens at ADL stays at ADL. B in B out!" She made a kissy face and a peace sign, and then hit stop recording, because it was true. There were some things that just shouldn't be put online—and she would know.

"If only you'd use some of your videos for good."

Brooklyn whirled around to face Taylor, who was smirking at her, arms crossed.

She had a moment's panic thinking that Taylor knew about the video she'd shot in the library. Greg's confession. She'd never written that in the Spill Book on purpose. "What is that supposed to mean?"

"Nothing. Just . . ." Taylor flipped her hair. "Joking around."

But it didn't feel like a joke. And Taylor wasn't really one to be funny.

"Are you sure?" Brooklyn wasn't going to let this drop.

"Ohmygod, stop being such a pick-me." Taylor rolled her eyes.

"No, seriously, what is your deal? You've been tense for a week. This is the first time I've actually seen you look happy in forever. What's going on?"

"Oh, I don't know, maybe you never really know a person."

Taylor's glare burned into her, opening Brooklyn's soul up for examination.

How had she found out about the taped confession? Her cheeks flamed with heat, and judging by the mocking expression on Taylor's face, she'd seen it.

"I thought we were friends, B, and here you've had a dad you hated, a dad who *died*, and you didn't even tell us."

Brooklyn breathed a sigh of relief that Taylor hadn't seen the video. She was so relieved she couldn't even be mad about where Taylor had learned that information. "You read that in the Spill Book."

Taylor sighed. "Of course I did."

"Where I come from and who my father was isn't something I've ever wanted to talk about."

"Then why did you write it down?"

Good question. She'd always known Taylor was reading the Spill Book. Brooklyn shrugged.

"What, do you think I wouldn't keep your stupid secrets for you?"

"Not fair since we don't know all of your secrets. Maybe we should all get a chance to read the Spill Book?"

Taylor scoffed. "As if. You were there the night of my biggest secret. You have an idea of my darkest secret, I'm sure."

Brooklyn's hands shook and she shoved her phone in her pocket to hide it. "I do. I have his confession. On tape."

Fury was etched in the pinches of Taylor's face, crinkling her eyes and her mouth. She stepped forward and hissed, "Erase it."

"What?" Brooklyn frowned, confused at the way this was turning. Yes, she'd kept quiet about the video, but that was only because Taylor wasn't making a move to press charges. If she had . . . "Why don't you let me help you?"

"Be a good little sugar and fucking get rid of it. Do you know what a video like that could do to my future?" The menace in Taylor's tone, the way she seemed to want to hurt her. "Never ever stick your nose in my business again."

Brooklyn wanted to throw up, words getting lost somewhere in her throat with her breakfast protein bar.

Asana hurried over, looking behind her at the sisters on the lawn who were starting to stare. "Maybe keep it down a little here. What's going on?"

"I know all our secrets, and yet I don't share enough of myself for Brooklyn's standards. She'd like me to expose everything—on tape apparently."

Asana nodded, the concern she'd had a moment ago turning accusatory in her expression as she glanced at Brooklyn. "Okay, Taylor's not too keen on . . . sharing. As if we haven't been friends for the last few years. You know that, Brooklyn. Why would you insist she does it on video? Isn't the Spill Book enough?"

Taylor swung her gaze toward Asana, looking almost desperate at the same time she was full of fury. "I don't need you to defend me. I don't need you at all. Any of you."

Asana blanched. "Why are you being such a bitch?"

"Is this a BATA meeting I didn't know about?" Annabelle's carefree laugh stopped short when she saw all of them staring at her.

"Why don't you just go back to fraternizing with the enemy?" Taylor spat at Annabelle, and then marched off before anyone could respond.

Brooklyn swallowed, watching her go. Wanting to stop and pull her back but also too pissed off to follow through. Erase the evidence that would put Greg Hamm away? No way.

"What just happened?" Annabelle asked, staring after Taylor, who shoved a pledge out of her way in her haste to escape.

"That Spill Book is going to be the ruin of us all." Asana blew out a disgusted breath and marched off in the opposite direction of Taylor.

"We all hold too many dark secrets." Brooklyn shook her head. "And some of them bite."

CHAPTER SIXTY-ONE

My dad died. I didn't go to the funeral. And I didn't tell my friends. But the real confession is: I'm glad he's gone.

Kisses,
Brooklyn

Asana

Now

"We need to talk."

Maggie jerked, whirling around to face Asana as she closed her hotel door. "Stalker, much?"

Asana rolled her eyes. "I had a phone call this morning."

"Big whoop, so did I." If Maggie rolled her eyes any harder, they'd fall out of her head.

"You can play hard if you want." Asana kept her voice smooth, cool, unruffled. "But I know it was you digging around in my past. How much did you pay Larissa to give you a copy of the book? What kind of a costume did you wear to the club so I wouldn't see you take my picture?"

Maggie grinned in a self-satisfied sort of way. "I'm going to expose you."

Asana laughed, the kind that was meant to pull her down a peg. "And I thought we had something." Sarcasm dripped from her tone as she hinted at the Machine party where Maggie had been the one to come on to her. "What will they think when I say you're a jealous lover?"

Maggie shrugged. "Who cares? They'll be too busy reading a juicy exposé on a New York City princess who helps spouses cheat on each other, and that—gasp—she's been hosting sex parties since college, when she entrapped a bunch of her fellow club members in a sex scandal. 'The Real Asana Duke: Sex-Crazed Sorority Sister Turned Homewrecker.'"

She had to admit, the headline had a nice ring to it. "With a byline of: 'Written by one of her jealous and discarded fucks.'"

Maggie's face pinkened. "'Written by an anonymous member of the society she tried to take down.'"

"Anonymous? You won't even take the claim after all your hard work?"

Maggie scoffed. "People deserve to know who you are. I don't need to publicly declare myself. I'm going to get paid."

"Deserve?" Asana laughed. If only Maggie knew that Asana had also dismantled Matinee. No website. No records. As if the online cheating app had never existed. Taking a note from her secret society days: *little is known of Matinee and what is known will forever be a secret* . . . "You're kidding, right? You're placing entirely too much importance on my head. I think you have a crush on me."

Maggie straightened her shoulders, her chin jutting forward as she glared.

"About that payment." Asana's smiled widened. "You seem to forget who I am."

"I've never forgotten you." There was a hint of malice and something more in Maggie's tone—hurt.

"I'm a Duke, Maggie. If I say don't publish it, no one will." Asana was bluffing, of course, there were plenty of people who'd want to see Duke Corp crushed, but Maggie didn't know that.

"I'll publish it online."

"Then I will pay the website to trash it. You have no outlet." Also a lie. Because this type of exposé was the kind that would go viral in a breath, and even if it was up for only a minute or two, someone would copy it, and it would be all over TikTok before Asana could do a damn thing. "I have something to offer you."

"Is it three million to keep my mouth shut?"

"Better."

"The only thing better than three million is four."

Asana laughed. "That's true. But I have information you are not privy to yet. No one in the public is. But they *deserve* to know."

"What's that?"

"Greg Hamm." Annabelle had told Asana in confidence about her conversation with the FBI, but that whole thing was about to get blown open. Getting the scoop before anyone else would be extremely valuable to Maggie.

"No one cares about Greg Hamm."

"Oh, Maggie, I assure you, they do, and you'll be the first one to print it." Asana pulled a contract out of her purse. Thank God she had template NDAs for all occasions. "But before I tell you, you're going to have to sign this."

THEY WORE THEIR sunglasses, not only to keep their eyes safe from the UV rays of the powerful Alabama sun, but because they'd been up all night.

"We are so glad you all could come," President Larissa said, her hands clasped before her in sweet innocence, the way Annabelle had always done.

Except Larissa was no innocent. She was, however, a psychopath. Ironic considering she planned to apply to grad school to become a psychologist.

Lily Walker stood beside Larissa, looking more reserved than usual. Asana wasn't surprised to see her there, as she'd advised her to attend. At the end of the time capsule opening, Lily was supposed to resign from her positions as house mother and leader in the Panhellenic Conference. The alternative, if Lily chose to ignore Asana's directives, would be cataclysmic to her social position.

Asana glanced at her friends, who stood tall, each of them aware of their posture the way they always had been. Dancers, athletes, Miss Alabama, wherever it had started, it had ended with extreme confidence, and the women they were today. Glorious messes with great hair and pockets full of cash.

This past week had been so much more than just an alumni event, a Rush Week; it had been the opening and spilling of their guts. The burning of their secrets forever.

Larissa pretended to unlock and unscrew the capsule—as if it hadn't already been done at least two weeks before—to the oohs and aahs of the sisters present, to the news reporters who were excited to see secrets revealed.

But all that came out of the capsule were a scroll tied with a pink ribbon that listed the names of all the sisters, an ADL T-shirt with little pink hearts on it, a floofy pencil, a tattered copy of *Carrie* by Stephen King, a sweatshirt from one of their philanthropy events, pictures of them during their spirit-building events, a dried rose. As the items were released, people leaned closer, expecting something juicier, more exciting.

But they wouldn't find anything like that in there.

Not now.

Not ever.

As they left the overly hyped-up time capsule opening, current actives put in new items, before it was locked up tight and buried again. Asana listened to the reporters who were more than mildly disappointed at seeing a bunch of nothing. But the actives, the pledges, the alumni all kept up their excitement.

A good show, but also because being part of a sorority wasn't all juice and taboo. There was real fun, real sisterhood, a wholesomeness to it that was hard to come by elsewhere.

Best of all, Maggie was absent. Asana kind of missed her standing in the corner furtively taking notes. But she'd handed her a big payday not to come. And better yet, to keep her fucking mouth shut.

The Spill Book mess had been put to rest. Their friendships had been strengthened.

And Taylor . . . she glanced toward where Taylor was chatting with Larissa, completely unbothered by what had transpired over the last week. Bouncing back as only Taylor could.

Whether or not she left Elijah, whether or not she took Asana up on her invitation to join her on a trip to Fantasia, remained to be seen.

What was true was that after today, Asana was leaving Alabama, and finally going to take a real vacation. And there would be nothing hanging over her head to keep her from enjoying the hell out of it, coming so many fucking times, her body wouldn't remember how to work.

CHAPTER SIXTY-TWO

I'm putting this book in the time capsule, and no one knows. Though they probably wonder. We'll all be dead by the time they open it, and I can't wait for someone to look back and see if we all turned out as fucked-up as this book makes us seem, or if we lived our best lives.

Kisses,
Taylor

Annabelle

Then

Annabelle leaned back on the spa lounger, cucumbers on her eyes. She was between Brooklyn and Taylor, Asana on the other side of Taylor. The rest of the loungers were filled with her sisters.

After finals, they'd decided ADL needed a bonding event that was going to soothe all their nerves. Finals were always rough. Late nights, studying, bingeing, no sleep, endless amounts of stress.

But none of that compared to the way BATA had cooled over the last year since their argument on Bid Day. They had agreed to remain tight for the sake of the sorority. But the tension had not abated; instead it had only gotten worse. The secrets locked up tighter than the vault she envisioned having in her own house one day. If only there was a way for her to just shake them all out of it.

Her hand came to rest absently on her stomach. The one thing she couldn't shake—a baby.

"I wish every day could be as amazing as this," she said, more to convince herself than her friends.

"Same," came a chorus of answers.

Besides finals, she'd been under a tremendous amount of stress in her personal life—not including the foursome riff, which was tantamount to torture.

Greg had been brought before the honor board after a rumor had gotten out about him manipulating SGA votes and being involved in some sort of illegal party. Annabelle wasn't prepared to defend him, but that was before he'd demanded she help him. That she have her parents speak on his behalf. Because Annabelle's parents made enough donations to the school that their word was like gold around here.

Disappointing really. Because if Greg was doing the things he'd been accused of not only from the honor board but by her friends, then he deserved to go down.

Only, she couldn't be the one behind it. Because Greg had also told her that if he went down, so would she, and he touched the stone at her neck, the one she'd plucked off the neck of the elephant their parents had donated to the football team. No words had been uttered, but she could see in his eyes that he'd somehow figured out it had been her behind the missing trophy.

And now she was pregnant. Forever tied to Greg Hamm by the child growing inside her. None of her friends knew. How could she tell them? Bile rose up in her throat at the thought of confessing. She drew in a shaky breath to ease the building nausea.

Her parents had agreed to help him, on one condition—if she accepted his lame proposal.

There was also the promise from Greg's parents that they would be investing heavily in Walker Global, her father's international hotel chain, given their new connection.

It felt an awful lot like she'd just been bought and sold. Her choices ripped away.

Then again, Greg was planning to go into criminal law. He could get himself out of any mess, and her.

She felt locked between a rock and a hard place, and these cucumber eye patches weren't softening the blow of what her future held. Somehow, she needed to get some autonomy. To take control of a future ripped out from under her by everyone else. And she really needed her friends' support.

The ring Greg had given her sat in its pretty light blue box in the top drawer of her dresser. She'd accepted—if you could call it that—but hadn't put on the ring. That was one diamond she didn't want.

So, there it sat, and the fact that she was engaged to be married later this summer, just a few weeks away, and that a few months after that she'd have a baby, wasn't something she'd yet shared with her friends. They wouldn't be happy about it. Especially because they didn't like Greg.

Well, she didn't really like him that much either.

But being married to him might be the only way out of whatever mess she might bury herself in. Except she'd have to play it straight so he never guessed. She'd be the perfect wife. The perfect mother to their unborn child.

The perfect everything.

As long as she kept appearances up to snuff.

The attendant came in, the air misty with the scents of eucalyptus, and gave them each a crystal glass of champagne.

"This is the life," Brooklyn said.

"Amen," Asana muttered.

"This is a Tuesday," Taylor said in typical Taylor fashion.

"Tuesday might just be my favorite day." Annabelle smiled into her glass, careful not to let her cucumbers fall into the bubbles as she pretended to take a sip. Today was not the day to think about what her future held. But only to be in the present with her best friends, her sisters for life. Before she lost her nerve, she said, "You guys, I need to tell you something."

Annabelle leaned up on her elbows, letting the cucumbers fall, and watched as her three best friends lifted one cucumber each to eye her warily.

"I'm getting married." *And I'm having a baby.*

Taylor sat up all the way and threw her cucumbers, hitting the wall with a splat. "You would choose marriage over your sisters?"

Annabelle faltered. She'd wanted support, not censure.

"In the steam room," Asana said. "Now."

Annabelle wanted to say no, to stalk off and into the rest of her life without them. But more than wanting to run away, she wanted answers.

They crowded into the steam room, Asana jerking her head in indication for the lone woman sweating to get out. The heat was oppressive. Normally, Annabelle found the steam room soothing, but not today.

"I can't believe you're marrying that asshole," Taylor said.

"I was going to ask you to be my bridesmaid." Annabelle crossed her arms over her chest, sweat slicking down her spine.

Taylor scoffed. "Not in a million years would I bless that union."

"That's a bit harsh," Brooklyn started, but then bit her lip.

"You're just jealous, Taylor, because while the rest of us have been growing up and making adult decisions you've been too busy judging and slinging insults to get a real life." Annabelle sucked in a hot steamy breath that didn't seem to help expand her lungs at all. What she'd said was mean, and even if partially true, she was hiding her own pain behind insensitive words.

"Me? Jealous of you?" Taylor's laugh was bitter enough to curdle cream. "You have no idea what you're talking about. Little Miss Perfect with her Perfect Life and her Perfect Marriage to the Perfect Monster."

"That's not fair. Greg is no more a monster than Brad."

"False. And also, Brad, really? You're going to bring up my boyfriend from a million years ago?"

"Who else? It's not like you've dated anyone since," Annabelle shot back.

"Yeah, Taylor, have you dated anyone since?" Asana's tone was cold, harsh, and oddly enough filled with pain.

"No," Taylor said just as coldly. "I haven't."

"Okay, you guys, we're all in a touchy spot right now. Worried about finals and graduation, what we're going to do without Bama. Let's not let all that outside shit get in the way of our friendship."

Taylor started to laugh, laughing so hard she had to sit down. The heat of the steam room was probably going to give them all brain damage.

"Friendship? Why don't you tell our friends about your little side gig?" Taylor narrowed her eyes.

"My side gig?" Brooklyn took a step back, her features faltering.

Annabelle flashed Taylor a look. She knew about the OnlyFans page?

Asana stepped in front of Taylor. "Stop. We're not doing this here. We're not doing this now."

"You're right. We're not." Taylor stood up. "Let's just get through graduation. We'll act like nothing ever happened. That our lives weren't changed. And then we'll move the fuck on."

Annabelle's chest hurt. This was how they were going to end things? In an insult-slinging argument inside a mildewy-smelling steam room? She wasn't sure she could move on without them. Everything was happening so fast, and in a matter of months her entire world was going to be turned upside down. She needed her friends.

"You guys, wait, I just—"

"I'm not waiting," Taylor said. "And no one should wait for me."

CHAPTER SIXTY-THREE

Greg Hamm is back. What does a girl have to do to get rid of a douchebag?

Kisses,
Asana

Brooklyn

Now

Pictures and videos were all about the lighting. Movies that were filmed at night, with the best lighting, could look like the middle of a sunny day. But today, Brooklyn didn't need any lighting. No fake sunshine here.

The Alabama sun was cooking and had beamed bright and scorching down on them as the pledge sisters had rounded the corner from their run, and as they'd opened the capsule—not for the first time—since they'd packed it up five years ago.

The sadness she'd thought she'd feel today at this being the end didn't come. Maybe that was because the four of them had already booked a retreat in Florida for a week in October, and between that they planned to do a Zoom happy hour every two weeks together.

"All right, y'all ready?" Brooklyn shouted to the entire ADL sisterhood behind her. Pledges, actives, alumni. They lined the front of the house and the second-floor balcony. A sea of optimistic and gleaming smiles.

"Yes!" The resounding shout was loud enough to rattle Brooklyn's eardrums, and she loved the enthusiasm of it.

Not only because of how happy everyone was, but because they'd finally settled down the bullshit about the Spill Book.

Gawd, what a pain in the ass.

And thank God for Drew. She couldn't believe that she hadn't trusted him sooner. When they'd met in college she'd thought him a blessing then, and now she knew for sure he was. Having his support, his unconditional love and acceptance, was the cherry on top of her sundae of a life.

Sporty Spyce was going to come out. The scholarship almost guaranteed it, but to help other young women who were in her situation was worth it—especially with Greg's money. Besides, if her viewers weren't willing to accept all of her, then they weren't the right viewers for her. She needed to be transparent, and authentic. Letting herself be free of the burden of her secrets was already changing her for the better.

"Get ready!" Brooklyn held her selfie stick up in the air and pressed record. "Heyyy, y'all! Ginger Mommy coming at ya from Bama Rush Bid Day! Right behind me I've got all my ADL sisters, both new and old. Say hi, y'all!"

The Alpha Delta Lambda sisters waved and cheered for the camera.

And Brooklyn maneuvered her stick to record every one of them.

"One of the things I always loved about being an active member of ADL was our chants and dances. So here we go, friends!"

Brooklyn nodded, and one of Asana's guards took over the handling of the stick to film their dance.

Brooklyn, Asana, Taylor, and Annabelle started it off with their old "Crazy in Love" choreography, then bopped out of view of the camera for the actives to do their thing, followed by the new pledges' dance. Afterward all of them came together to do an ADL chant, hundreds of sister voices raised with good spirits and confidence.

After they finished, she grabbed the selfie stick back from Guard One, taking note of how he eyed Asana like a hungry tiger. Interesting.

"Thanks for joining us for this fun week at Bama Rush, y'all! Now it's time for me to say goodbye. We've got a fun party to have, and all I'm gonna tell you about that is: what happens at Bama stays at Bama! Kisses."

Brooklyn blew a kiss and then turned off the recording button.

As she rejoined her friends, Annabelle stared at her phone, face paling.

"What's wrong?" Brooklyn asked.

Despite the harrowing look in her eyes, a tremulous smile curled Annabelle's lips as she turned the screen to face them.

"Greg's been arrested."

Brooklyn took the phone to see an article written by Maggie Rosenthal. She scrolled through the photos of Greg Hamm in handcuffs outside the Tuscaloosa mansion he'd shared with Annabelle. How had Maggie gotten the scoop so quickly?

"I can't believe it worked." Annabelle slapped her hands over her mouth, as if she hadn't meant to say that.

"What worked?" Asana looked intrigued, taking the phone from Brooklyn. "Well, God damn."

"Let me see." Taylor looked next, giving an slow whistle. "You did that?"

Annabelle glanced around as if she expected to be pounced on. "Yes."

"I'm impressed," Asana said, a hint of something in her eyes. Had she known about this already? "I think I might need to offer you a job."

"I think I'm going to lay off . . . working for a little while."

"What happened, Anna?" Brooklyn asked.

"It was time for Greg to face karma."

"Karma's a bitch," Brooklyn said.

"And so am I." Annabelle grinned.

Taylor slung her arm around Annabelle's shoulders. "You still can't say it, can you?"

"What?"

"Bitch."

"I can say it."

"Let's hear it."

"Oh, stop." Annabelle playfully batted Taylor's arms away.

"Just somehow managed to take down her husband for embezzlement, but can't cuss. Like a true Southern lady, she annihilates her enemies with style and panache."

"Think it will stick this time?"

"This time?" Taylor asked, giving Asana a skeptical look, which Brooklyn mirrored. How many people had tried to take Greg down?

"Yes," Annabelle said confidently.

"You guys." Brooklyn held out her arms, urging her friends in for another hug. "I'm so glad this happened. I mean, not all the mental torment, but that it brought us back together. I missed you all so much."

"Sisters for life," Annabelle said.

"Forever."

CHAPTER SIXTY-FOUR

I stole one of the Greek letters from TriDelt. No one even saw me. Hail Mary, full of grace . . .

Kisses,
Annabelle

Taylor

Then

Taylor had always wanted to be a legend. And what better way to immortalize herself and her friends than to leave behind the legacy of their lives in a nice shiny time capsule?

ADL had been formed one hundred years ago, and she'd been racking her brain as president to figure out what to do for the centennial celebration. She'd have asked her friends, but ever since the spa, they weren't exactly on friendly speaking terms.

The idea of the time capsule just popped into her head one day. Well, *maybe* she'd been bingeing episodes of *Criminal Minds* in order to make herself feel better, and someone had put the head of a dead guy into a time capsule.

But she wasn't putting in the head of a dead guy. Just all the deep, dark secrets of her sisters that she'd collected over the last four years. And theoretically, those secrets might as well be hundreds, thousands of dead heads. To lay to rest the secrets that seemed to have broken them apart.

She grinned as she scrolled online looking for a time capsule to purchase, then one-clicked it with an overnight rush. Too bad they didn't have same-day delivery.

Downstairs in their massive chapter room, the sisters waited eagerly for the centennial planning meeting.

"We're going to make a time capsule," Taylor announced. "Each of us is going to put something into the capsule that represents our time here at ADL, and in one hundred years, and the bicentennial Founder's Day, they will open it and see what ADL was like a hundred years in the past."

"That's awesome," Brooklyn said, though her usual chipper tone was somewhat subdued. "I wish we had one now we could have opened to see what it was like a hundred years ago."

"Right?" Taylor said without looking at her. "Me too, so let's make it really special."

As everyone started to work on their list of what they'd want to put into the time capsule, Taylor kept it to herself that she was putting in their Spill Book. No doubt if she mentioned it, they would all freak out about someone stealing it and exposing their secrets.

But who would do that?

She rolled her eyes just thinking about it. Their secrets were safe for a hundred years, and then by the time it was opened, they'd all be dead, and the sisters a hundred years from now could get a good read out of the raunchy and scandalous book. Taylor sure had.

"The capsule will be here tomorrow, so meet here and we'll fill it up."

On the way out of the meeting, Mama Jenny stopped her with a soft hand on her sleeve. A little older than Taylor's mother, Mama Jenny was a staple of the house the last four years. Lending an ear, keeping the place running, and always willing to give a hug to a homesick sister.

"How are you doing, honey?" she asked.

"I'm fine." What in the world was this woman trying to do right now?

Mama Jenny offered a soft smile. "You know, staying mad is only going to eat away at you. But it doesn't have to. Forgiveness isn't just a way of healing hearts, but of souls."

Taylor narrowed her eyes.

"And friends, well, a woman cannot survive without them."

Taylor gritted her teeth.

"BATA was a thing around here, honey, and I know it's not my place to interfere, but the four of you, well, you've been a joy to mother."

Taylor wanted to retort something nasty. To say she already had a mother. But there was no point in being mean to the woman who'd also held their secrets, watching them come and go, and took care of them without judgment.

"Thank you," Taylor said.

Mama Jenny held out her hand, the fluorescent light shining on her ring finger. "Can I put this ring in?"

"Isn't that the one Annabelle gave you?" Taylor suspected that the stone in the ring had been stolen just like a lot of Annabelle's "gifts." There was a large amethyst in the center and it was surrounded by diamonds.

"Yes. I want to leave a cute note for the new house mother. Working with you ladies has been the honor of my life." She leaned close. "And my daughter-in-law keeps eyeing the ring like she's waiting for me to die."

Taylor shook her head, incredulous. "That's rude, Mama Jenny. I'd tell her to her face she gets nothing. And it wouldn't be a sin to do it either. We all know you're going to heaven."

Mama Jenny smiled and squeezed Taylor's arm. "You're such a sweetheart."

"Only to you. Don't tell anyone. We can def put it in there, and then your daughter-in-law can't get her hands on it unless she lives another hundred years."

Mama Jenny smiled conspiratorially. "Exactly."

"Our time capsule, we can do what we want with it."

Mama Jenny nodded emphatically as she hurried into the chapter room to tidy up and make sure all the girls had left.

Asana was waiting for her at the top of the stairs. "Time capsule?" Her eyebrow was raised in that conspiratorial way she always had about her.

"Yeah."

"You really think that's a good idea?"

From the way Asana was looking at her, Taylor was pretty sure she'd concluded what the fate of the Spill Book would be. Taylor wished she could say something that would make Asana trust her. That would make Asana hate her less.

But she wouldn't. Because Taylor had pushed her away. Taylor had broken her heart. When Asana asked them to be exclusive, to tell their friends they were together, Taylor had freaked out. She wasn't ready to share their relationship with the world, and what it meant for her—that she was bisexual. That people would look at her differently. That her parents would make her confess to their priest and force her into some sort of intervention. That any chance she had of being in politics, her relationship with Asana would be used against her. It was bullshit is what it was, but she was too afraid to take the chance.

Too afraid to take the chance that people wouldn't like her anymore. She was a coward. Of that, she was fully aware. But it didn't make her say yes. To protect herself, she'd ended things. Not her finest moment. And she was full of regret.

"I do." She lifted her chin.

Asana nodded but didn't speak, her cool expression saying she was pretty sure she was going to have to clean up this mess, just like she'd cleaned up a lot of Taylor's messes.

When Taylor thought she'd never hear Asana's voice again, she finally spoke.

"Sisters for life," Asana said, but there wasn't so much inflection in her tone as there was bitterness.

"Asana—" It was on the tip of her tongue to apologize. But Taylor didn't do that, not with anyone. Not even with herself.

Asana turned around, arms crossed over her chest, pink nails drumming impatiently against her sculpted biceps. "Yeah?"

"Sisters for life."

"Right." And then Asana walked away, and she didn't turn back. Taylor had to work pretty damned hard not to chase after her.

All she could hope for was that one day in the future, they'd have a reason to come back together. To put all the bitterness and squabbles behind them. To be as carefree and excited as they were freshman year.

Until then, the time capsule would hold their secrets, their hopes, their existence in the cold cavern of its metal casing.

"There you are." Brooklyn smiled tentatively as Taylor reached the top floor, where her single bedroom was.

"What's up?"

"I, um, wanted to do a video of all of us. We're about to graduate, and I think we need one last TikTok before we all head off to our futures."

Taylor was keenly aware of Brooklyn's hesitation, especially since her blowup earlier in the year about videos.

"Do you think we'll never see each other again?" Taylor had been planning on ghosting them all. She'd been done with the BS. But there was something about what Mama Jenny said about needing friends.

Brooklyn keyed in on her emotions, and smiled.

"Nah, it's all for show. We're BATA, and BATA has to stick together." Brooklyn winked, and tugged Taylor into her bedroom, where Annabelle and Asana waited.

As they made one last video, Brooklyn's enthusiasm seeped into her, and Taylor smiled for real into the camera. She'd been working hard to let go of her resentment, her anger, and she wasn't proud of how she'd acted toward her friends. How she'd pushed them away. But some things were hard to come back from.

A few days later, the centennial celebration was in full swing, the capsule set up on its pedestal, the top open, as each of the sisters came by and plopped a trinket inside.

Taylor's package was the biggest of all, the Spill Book. Several eyes followed the brown wrapped paper she'd tied with a bright pink bow. How many of them wondered what was inside? How many suspected?

She stood and watched with an inner glee as their deepest, darkest secrets were buried forever.

Never to be seen by a single one of them again. Unless of course some asshole dug up the capsule early. But what were the odds of that happening?

ACKNOWLEDGMENTS

No book is created alone, and this one is no exception.

Without my incredible agent, Kevan Lyon, who persistently supports me and guides me in my career, this book would never have been possible. Thank you so much to my amazing editor, Tessa Woodward at HarperCollins, for trusting in me to write this juicy, fun book! To all of the amazing people at HarperCollins, thank you for your support and hard work to make this book stand out!

I owe my endless gratitude to my daughters, who helped me stay true to Gen Z culture and language, and not to sound like the Gen X that I am. Thank you for indulging me in daily OOTDs and FitChecks and answering random questions. And to my oldest, you are a rockstar for reading and re-reading the drafts of this book! I love you all so much! Thank you for believing in me.

Thank you to my beta readers, Christi Barth, Evie Hawtrey, and Heather Webb, for your guidance and support. And thank you to all of my writing buddies and agency sisters who listened to me talk about this book nonstop over glasses of wine—and hey, you learned a few new words, didn't you?

Last, but never least, thank you, dear reader, for picking up this book and reading all the way to the acknowledgments. You all make a writer's world go round.

Kisses,
Michelle

ABOUT THE AUTHOR

Michelle Brandon is a pseudonym for Eliza Knight, an award-winning and *USA Today* bestselling author. A travel junkie and fan of wine, when she's not writing, she can be found lounging on the beach with a delicious book or taking a long restorative walk. Surrounded by palm trees and wild animals, she lives on the Suncoast with her husband, daughters, two slobbery doggies, and a turtle named Fish.